Enter The Night:

Book One

of the

Morgan Crowe

Trilogy

Maggie Berkley

ISBN: 0615669883

ISBN-13: 978-0615669885

Maggie Berkley at http://maggieberkley.jigsy.com/

cover art by Kristy McPherson at http://kristymcpherson.jigsy.com/

Praise for Maggie Berkley's Morgan Crowe Trilogy!

Enter The Night

"Ms. Berkley crafts a masterpiece that will have you begging for more (and wondering when Book Two will be out)." ~ **Angelique, Happily Ever After Reviews, 5 Stars and a Recommended Read**

"A truly interesting story that keeps the reader wanting more and wondering what is going to happen next. Be prepared to meet a lot of characters from the fantasy realm." ~ **Danielle Friedl, Got Erotic Romance, 4 Stars**

"**Enter the Night** is a riveting tale of suspense, betrayal and the tangled web of love. **Maggie Berkley** has left me wanting more and to see what's next for Morgan Crowe." ~ **Samhain Queene, Dark Diva Reviews, 5 Stars and a Recommended Read**

"**Enter The Night** is an intriguing read. Combining various elements of mystery, suspense, and romance, author Maggie Berkley has crafted a winding tale of action and adventure set against the backdrop of a mystical fantasy land. With a host of plot-bending twists and turns, **Enter The Night** is sure to keep readers guessing as to the ultimate outcome of Morgan's fate, and they will no doubt find themselves cheering her on through each new obstacle threatening to destroy her despite her valiant efforts to survive. A surprisingly compelling read." ~ **Chelsea Perry, Apex Reviews, 4 Stars**

"This debut novel by Maggie Berkley is amazing! A twist of Laurell K. Hamilton's Meredith Gentry series and some awesome characters brings new light to the Fae realm. The plot is intriguing and quick paced. The combination of myth and an overarching quality of new material makes the novel an original in its own right. There is no doubt that Maggie Berkley was out to impress with this novel. I didn't want to stop reading until I got to the very end and now I want the next book in the series **Behind The Throne**." ~ **Sarah Dizon, Night Owl Reviews, 4 Stars**

"Maggie Berkley begins the Morgan Crowe Trilogy by introducing the reader to the colorful characters that populate the ShadowLands of the Sidhe. Morgan knows that no one can be trusted. She knows that even the man she loves will betray her in the end. Assassins are sent to kill her in the human. She fights for her life and the lives of her unborn children. The few Sidhe she can trust are in danger themselves. Can Morgan keep one step ahead of Queen Moirethe? Will Morgan live long enough to give birth to her children?" ~ **Candy, Sensual Reads.com, 4 Stars**

Behind The Throne

"In **Behind The Throne**, you will find everything from a love flame coming back, new alliance being made to protect the ones you love, kidnapping, vengeance and so much more that you must read this book to better understand the life of Morgan." ~ **Monica, Happily Ever After Reviews, 5 Stars**

"Sometimes sequels don't live up to the wait but I can honestly say Maggie Berkley did not disappoint with **Behind The Throne**. Ms. Berkley has continued to build the characters who inhabit her world and make them stronger. Even as things become more and more tangled, you have to follow Morgan on her journey. I have a feeling there's a big surprise in store for not only Morgan but the reader as well. **Behind The Throne** is not to be missed. I can't wait to see how Ms. Berkley ties up all the loose ends in book three." ~ **Samhaim Queen, Dark Diva Reviews, 5 Stars and a Recommended Read**

"The sequel to **Enter The Night** by Maggie Berkley is just as action packed and sexy as the first but taken to a whole different level. Anxiously, anticipating the conclusion to this trilogy!" ~ **Sarah Dizon, Night Owl Reviews, 4.5 Stars and a Top Pick**

"In the second book of the Morgan Crowe Trilogy, Maggie Berkley reveals more mysteries from Morgan's past. She uncovers secret allies who work behind the throne to help keep Morgan safe, and vicious enemies who will stop at nothing to see her dead. Khelvan and Morgan are forced to re-evaluate their opinions of each other so they can work together to save a Vivienne. Morgan's children are born into a violent world. They have their own parts to play in Morgan's story. Can Morgan rescue Vivienne, the one person who went out of her way to help her, or will her association with Morgan cost Vivienne her life?"

~ Candy, Sensual Reads.Com, 4 Stars

Maggie Berkley

To my husband and son. Thanks for giving me some time out from being a wife and mom to finish this book. I love you.

To Shannon Skipper. Thanks for standing by me when the world seemed dark and bleak. You're my hero.

Special thanks to Kristy McPherson, for creating such an awesome cover!

Maggie Berkley

Enter The Night:

Book One

of the

Morgan Crowe

Trilogy

Prologue

Long ago in the ShadowedLands:

Hurrying down the corridor, Adolis barely avoided colliding with two nobles in the midst of deep conversation. As he scurried passed, one of the nobles turned a glacial glare his way while snarling a snide comment under his breath about the hunchback's parentage. That didn't matter much to Adolis for he was used to being looked down upon. He knew his parents weren't Sidhe, that his father was one of the NightKin, creatures of shadow and night, and his mother a Were, a mortal able to change into a specific animal form. A rough beginning to a rough life, that was until he was rescued from the Court kitchen's by the dark Lord of Tech nDuinn. In appearance the hunchback took after neither parent but looked like something altogether else, a creature dark and twisted, his body useless except for running messages and spying for his Master.

Muttering his apology, Adolis hurried around the corridor before slowing his pace as he neared the open Court doors. Stepping closer to the walls, he prayed none would notice him as he blended into the shadows to avoid any further "accidents" for it would not do to belay his Master's orders. As he neared the Courts of the High King and Queen of the Mor'sin'dar, the voices within the chamber grew louder as whispering of rumors rose in volume like the buzzing of bees. He winced and almost covered his sensitive ears at the noise but instead forced himself to concentrate on the words being said.

"She hath returned."

"How dare she show her face here."

"I thought she was banished."

"I thought she was dead."

Edging closer to the open doorway of the grand throne room, Adolis peered around the corner and looked around. Flashes of color, bright as gemstones and dark as blood, filled the room as the Lords and Ladies of the Mor'sin'dar lingered around in small groups, waiting to see if the rumors spoken were true. The great thrones themselves, glorious in their untold wealth, sat vacant on a towering dais as they waited in regal silence for their rightful owners to claim them.

Soon a hush overtook the great chamber as the stone walls on the far side of the throne room melded open to reveal the unearthly beauty of the High King and Queen who ruled the Mor'sin'dar Sidhe. Ethereal in appearance, the graceful couple emerged with a confidence only the aristocracy contain. With his right fist upraised and the Queen's delicate left hand lying nonchalantly across it, the High King led his wife up the steps of the dais as his eyes swept the vast room.

King Silvas's face revealed nothing of his thoughts as violet eyes glittering in the hollow lights like shinning stones in a stream. Full lips drawn in a straight line, his jaw set, he was a handsome man and he knew it. Thick black hair fell over his broad shoulders and down his back like a silken cloak, decorated in gemstones and loose roped braids fancied among those in the Courts. Dressed in a deep wine-colored robe that clung like a second skin to his body, it left very little to the imagination where it split in the front in a deep V down his muscled chest. The darkness of the material brought out the stark contrast of his skin tone which shimmered in an iridescent light of its own, drawing more than a few appreciative looks from those around.

Several of the Court women tilted their heads down, their lips lifted in subtle smiles, and sighed in delight. To the eyes of the observant it was obvious that there was more there than a passing fancy for the King was a lustful man who had been known to enjoy female company on an occasion or two.

Beside him his wife, Queen Moirethe, walked; her beauty pale compared to his of darkness. With hair the color of golden honey, those who viewed it couldn't help but think of the rich, sweet delicacy as it caught and reflected the light in the grand room. Caught up in various braids and curls, the style was reminiscent of a wren's nest with small glittering birds chirping merrily in song to announce her arrival. Arrogant jeweled green eyes looked out over those gathered around as her chin tilted up a fraction, stretching her slender neck to accentuate the elegant curve of it and draw the eye of the observer.

Many of the women of the Court tried to imitate Queen Moirethe's own natural coloring though most failed miserably, becoming only a pale imitation of their glorious ruler. The material of the dress she wore was made of a matching wine to that of her beloved, decorated in seedling pearls and gold to compliment her King's own robes. Perfect, pristine and beautiful, the Queen reminded Adolis of a statue carved of the most expensive marble; cold and empty as the hard stone that came from the ground.

Pressing himself tighter against the wall as several nobles passed by, Adolis watched the rest of the procession enter with the King and Queen. Following a few feet behind were three young men, each gloriously handsome and dressed as majestic as their parents. The eldest son, a tall slender blonde with the same cool aloofness as the Queen that sired him, was Prince Ansil. As he glanced around the throne room with bored haughtiness, his gaze caught many a female eye and in return they smiled invitingly at the chosen heir, the next King of the Mor'sin'dar.

Beside him stood Prince Khelvan—tall, dark, and devastatingly handsome. Glowering at his brother's back the Prince's expression showed irritation, as if he were not happy to be there. Every once in a while his gaze would move across the large chambers toward the hall doors as if searching for something or someone not there, then return to stare forward in solemn stubbornness. For a moment Queen Moirethe caught her middle child's attention and hissed a quiet demand at him, only to be rewarded with a sullen glare. A slight movement caught Adolis's eyes and he watched as Khelvan slowly drew out then shoved back his dagger into its sheath. *Dangerous, that one.*

The youngest of the Princes, Heurodis, was distracted by his reflection in the polished mirrors decorating the Court walls. He smoothed back his hair with the palm of his hand then stumbled with his next step. He quickly caught himself from falling with the help of one of the Royal guards that stood at attention along the walk then shook off the guard's hand with a disgusted look. Snapping out an insult, the young Prince marched up the dais his family had ascended and straightened his clothing before tossing his honeyed hair back over his shoulder. The soft sound of crystal beads tinkling followed his movement as he took his seat on the vacant throne one step below his parents. After a smug glance at his siblings he settled back into his chair and turned his attention to the crowd below.

Spoiled, haughty, and beautiful, the Royal family drew the eyes of everyone, noble and servant alike. Watching in awe as they took their thrones Adolis almost missed the shadow that breezed by him. Barely feeling the subtle tickle of feathers against his cheek, he turned his head to watch the young woman wrapped in a black feathered cloak stride by. Startled, he stared into the face of one perhaps more cold and beautiful than the Queen herself. Where the Queen was golden and light, this one drew the shadows to her and a chill set in the air. Standing tall and slender, the woman's wild dark hair reached her thighs, with a snowy white lock framing her face. Eyes as black as a starless night stood out in a face pale and illuminant. Around her the shadows moved, flowing around the ceiling as if ghostly birds circled overhead. The soft sounds of fluttering wings and caws echoed through the room. From the corner of his eyes he swore one of the bird shadows land upon the stranger's shoulder and turned its head to stare at him with a beady eye.

Adolis's breath came out in a light steam, wafting before his view as the woman paused before entering the great throne room of the Mor'sin'dar. No one in the Court seemed to have noticed her yet as all eyes remained drawn to the magnificence of the King and Queen and their children but quickly that changed. Suddenly King Silvas's violet eyes snapped to the open doors, his jewel-like gaze meeting the inky blackness of the woman standing beside the Lord of Tech nDuinn's servant. Nodding to the dark woman, the King gave her admittance to the throne room and leaned back in his throne with a knowing smile. Whispering quickly filled the room as the rest in attendance turned to watch the newcomer.

As she entered to take a stance before the thrones, Adolis studied the bird woman, unbelieving that this delicate creature was the famed assassin who so long ago was banished from the Sidhe Courts. Many rumors swirled around the Morrigu's removal, though the truth was never fully revealed, having been hushed and brushed under the carpet. The most popular rumor was that she killed Lady Gilthantrious and her House as an insult to Queen Moriethe and that the Lady's death caused much disruption between the Royal couple.

The golden Queen looked toward the woman who had caught her husband's interest, eyes first widening in recognition, and then narrowed with irritation. Her chin rose as her lips twisted in disgust. Sitting straighter on her throne, Moriethe motioned with a sweep of her hand to the Morrigu.

"So, the Battle Crow hath returned. On what ground doth thou dare to enter the ShadowedLands and the presence of this Court?" Her voice, though smooth as silk, brought the sting of steel to it.

Remaining silent, the Morrigu locked eyes with the King's before lowering her gaze to the ground. With a graceful move she knelt on bended knee and leaned forward, one dark clothed arm stretched out to touch the stone floor before her as if to steady herself. Ebon glass hair fell across her shoulders, shrouding her face in a curtain of silk and a gasp filled the Court as voices erupted, making the room a whispering beehive again. Faces turned to study the dark-haired woman as Adolis did and now bets to how long she would be permitted to remain in their sight circulated around the chamber.

"Didst thou not hear my words, Lady Death?" The Queen's voice cut through the chatter. "I do not recall..."

Holding up a hand, King Silvas interrupted the finishing comment as a smile curved up the ends of his lips. "Morriganna, daughter of the Thulath, why hast thou returned to this Court?" His deep voice wrapped around the room like warm velvet, caressing with words and sending a shiver through all who heard. A noble woman next to Adolis gave a breathless sigh and licked her lips as if in anticipation of more to come. The King leaned forward in his throne and beckoned the Morrigu forward, ignoring the glare his Queen shot him.

Rising with the grace of a predatory cat, the assassin moved the few feet to the base of the dais. Guards rushed forward, circling the steps with lowered weapons but with a slight flick of his hands King Silvas dismissed them to return to their positions. With a warning look they returned, keeping careful watch over the Morrigu and their King as the assassin climbed the stairs. Stopping one level below his throne she once again took her place on a knee, head lowered in respect.

"Thou may speak, unless thou hath lost that ability in thy banishment."

Lifting her eyes to his, the Morrigu's face was as void of emotion as a statue. "I came asking a boon, my King."

Chatter erupted again.

"How dare thee come here seeking a boon, old crow..." Queen Moirethe found herself interrupted again as her husband lifted his hand in a sharp motion. Pursing her lips tight, she shot him a venomous look that spoke volumes before leaning back in her throne, lowering her arms on the armrests. Her hands grasped the ends, fingers tightening until her knuckles whitened.

"Thou hast not been given permission to return to the Courts or our presence, Morriganna. Why doth thou risk my wrath upon returning now, especially asking for a boon?" Once more, the richness of his voice draped over the room.

"My King, I hath always been loyal to thee though I hath been banished from the Courts these many years. Is that not time enough for my punishment?" the Morrigu asked, her voice barely above a whisper. While the people of the Court strained to listen, her words were directed to the King's ears alone and Adolis leaned forward to catch more. The shadow crow perched upon her shoulder caught a strand of her dark hair in its beak before tilting its head to eye the King with a scarlet gleam.

"As long as my Queen lives, thou shall not return." The King reached down to run the tips of his fingers along her cheek, caressing her skin as if it were of the finest silk. His smile gentled, turning almost wistful as memories flowed behind his eyes.

With a sly glance at the regal woman sitting in the throne beside the Mor'sin'dar monarch, the Morrigu answered back with a twisted smile tugging her lips. "As long as she lives…"

Returning the look with an icy glare of her own, hatred twisted Queen Moirethe lovely face but before she could respond verbally King Silvas replied to the assassin's implied threat.

With a deep sigh he shook his head in disappointment. "Do not think such thoughts or I will hath thee punished further, my hungry one. I see the years of thy banishment have not softened thy wicked tongue."

"I wouldst not be me if it did." Returning her attention back to the man before her, Morriganna managed a brief smile, though it did not reach her eyes.

"Thou should…" the Queen spoke again, only to be cut off by her husband once more.

"No, my Queen," King Silvas words grew soft and faraway as he studied the assassin's beautiful face. "She is punished enough not being in my presence." Leaning back in his throne, hands folded across his abdomen, he watched for the Morrigu's reaction to his next question. "What boon dost thou ask?" The corners of his lips rose in an arrogant smile.

The room became still as if all within strained to hear her answer.

Morriganna paused for the span of five heartbeats before she spoke. "Allow me leave to enter the Courts of the Sin'din'dar. Rumors rise that King Tibault seeks an assassin and well..." She shrugged. "As thou knows I am in need of employment and if I cannot be at thy side again, then I ask thee to give me leave in order to join the other Court."

Prince Khelvan looked up at her request, his eyes growing sharp at the mention of the King of the Sin'din'dar before he narrowed his gaze on the woman kneeling before his father. Then, as if catching himself, he looked away again, though his attention remained focused on the scene before him. Prince Ansil watched with open interest, his eyes moving from his father to the strange woman before moving back again. Prince Herodius ignored the whole thing, seeming blissfully oblivious to the ramifications taking place and continued to flirt with several of the Queen's ladies-in-waiting.

A deep chuckle rose from the King. "Thou seeks to work for King Tibault, my rival?" He watched her under lowered lids, his lips pursed slightly as he pondered her words. "Doth thou truly believe that thou wouldst be welcome there, my beauty? One who spills so much blood and revels in warfare? Doth thou seek to be my enemy?"

"Never, my King. I could never betray thee, but I hath too long been amongst the humans. They wear on me and I need the sounds of my kindred's voices."

"And ifin he would not accept thee? What will thou do then? Join the Ssri'tel'quessir Court?" he joked.

Laughter rose around the room, careful enough not to displease the King, but loud enough to make a point to the Morrigu. The Ssri'tel'quessir were Sidhe who no longer kept their glamorous form. Their bodies grew twisted and darkened, matching the ugliness that embedded their souls by creating new physical shapes to present to the world. More than one of the nobles joked aloud that the Lady Morriganna should join the Ssri'tel'quessir Court for she was not a favorite among the Mor'sin'dar and their memory was long and unforgiving.

With a smug smile on her lips Queen Moirethe leaned back in her throne, her fingers tracing patterns on the bejeweled armrests as a shark-like smile lifted her lips. The dark look she threw the assassin's way promised pain and much more. *Later, bitch*, it seemed the jade depths spoke.

Ignoring the Queen's heated gaze, Morriganna drew in a soft sigh. "I highly doubt I would be welcomed there, my King," she answered.

"Too beautiful," he mused, watching her then he raised his voice to continue his comment. "Though thy temper and perchance for causing death and chaos in thy wake should please them. Mayhap I should send thee to the Ssri'tel'quessir Court."

Encouraged by her husband's response Queen Moriethe relaxed back in her seat, while the smile on her lips turned vicious. "Or better yet to the Goblins, my King. They wouldst enjoy someone of her...qualifications."

Laughter rose again but this time stilted.

"Perhaps..." Pursing his lips together in a thoughtful expression, King Silvas glanced around the nobles of his Court before returning his gaze back to the calm, beautiful face of his assassin. "Go. Thou hath my permission to go to the Sin'din'dar for as long as thou wishes."

Startled by her husband's reply, the Queen sputtered, "I think not! She was sent to the human lands, not to take holiday in the Shinning Court! Deny her boon and send her away!"

Sitting up straight, King Silvas's voice rose in a commanding boom, loud enough to shake the walls and courtiers alike. "Enough! I hath made my decision. Is there any who would seek to challenge me?"

He looked around the room, meeting each Sidhe's gaze with his own cold jewel-like eyes. As one the two older Princes glanced around, their eyes meeting several in the Court as if seeking any who would defy the decree, but none protested the King's decision. Queen Morithe turned her head away, her face etched with fury and dug her fingernails into the armrests of her throne. Once order was back in the throne room and his Queen was silenced enough not to give outburst again, King Silvas continued.

"Go now, my Battle Crow. Go to King Tibault's Court and do not return to my sight unless I call for thee. To do so again will be much more painful than thy banishment. I will see that thou art accepted into the Shinning Court."

With her face void of emotion, the Morrigu nodded her dark head and rose to her feet, leaving the throne room without a backward glance to her King.

The chamber was suddenly a flutter with movement as voices erupted into questions. Several of the courtiers left in a hurry, racing to pass around new rumors to those who could not make Court this day. Following suit, Adolis quickly scurried back down the hall toward his Master's quarters to deliver the news. Why his Master wanted the information was none of his business for his task was only to deliver it; fast and accurate.

1

San Francisco, California (now):

After a toss of her hair back over her shoulder, Morgan Crowe squinted her eyes to gaze down the sight of her Sharps 2200 sniper rifle at her intended victim. As she adjusted the scope for better definition she watched while her target move through the throng of people crowding around him. With a smile plastered on his face, he wove between supporters like a butterfly floating from one flower to another, barely pausing on his journey as he shook one hand then another.

Shifting her body on the blanket she lay on as she stretched, Morgan settled herself in for the wait and flipped back down the cover of the scope to prevent light from reflecting off the lens. She already knew where the guards were positioned as they watched for trouble and the ear bud wedged in the opening in her ear kept her informed if they spotted trouble, namely her. After a quick glance at the cloudless, pale blue sky, Morgan glanced at her watch then lifted a small hand scope hidden in her palm and peered through the viewer. At twelve-fifteen in the afternoon her target was scheduled to make a speech for the next two hours as he applied for his chance to become the next President of the United States.

Tall, handsome, in his mid-forties, Daniel Whitlocke seemed to be a shoo-in for the Democratic choice for President. His charisma and intelligence made him a nationally recognized icon and after writing a book that became a New York times bestseller, a following appeared that started a craze for enlightenment because of his 'words of wisdom in self-help and recognition'. Later came the endorsements from political, entertainment, and sports figures, as could be seen by the number of celebrities that stood forefront around the podium. Self important drones who thought because they made more than six figures a year on nothing more than luck and that they had their faces plastered on the big screen and televisions that they knew what was best for the world. Good luck to that, she snorted.

The candidate Morgan watched through the scope wasn't a good man, not even close. Hell, he wasn't even human. Instead this supposed leader was a creature known to her kind as a Bollag, one of the darker Fae in Ssri'tel'quessir society who thrived on destruction. How he escaped from the ShadowedLands and what he was doing in the mortal realm, she could only guess but if truth be told she didn't really care anyway. Her job was to eliminate the garbage and the fact that it was a Ssri'tel'quessir brightened the deal. It had been a while since she had anything worthwhile to hunt but old loyalties and questions quickly scrambled to fill her mind as she took a second look at the crowd gathered.

Why was he here and were there more than just her intended victim? The Veil that shielded the human world from those of the Fae were sealed shut from within, guarded by the High Kings' own guard and nothing but a direct order would open them. To do so and to allow creatures such as the Bollages to cross over would be a violation of the treaty the Faekind had with the humans, a treaty created over a thousand years ago. With a mental shake, Morgan shrugged the unsettling thought back out of her mind as she fixed the candidate in her crosshairs. Those politics she was long out of. *None of my business*, she reminded herself as she eyed the Bollag.

Several supporters stepped up to the podium and as one lifted his hands, the crowd around began to quiet down to listen while news reporters and camera crews readied themselves for a series of Q and A's to take place after the speech. Morgan sighed as the throng roared after the announcer introduced their "next President." *Stupid-ass humans. Following blindly like cattle to the slaughter. Peace and wisdom, my ass.* The first thing the Bollag would likely do as

President would be to start a war. Hell, he might even stage something here in the good ol' U.S. of A. Once again disturbing thoughts crept to the forefront of her mind. What he was doing out of the Faeiry Realm, the ShadowedLands, confused her. Did a war breakout between the Light and Dark Courts? Is this a way to prevent the humans from taking sides with one or the other? Give them something to occupy themselves with so no one will notice anything amuck in case the Sidhe war spills over into the human world?

Oh well. It'll give me something to do during my banishment.

Slipping the hand viewer back into her pocket, Morgan flipped open the lens cap and peered through the scope again to zero in on the candidate. A charming smile filled with warmth split the handsome face the Bollag wore in disguise. Hazel eyes sparkled as he gazed around the field of listeners, and then stepping up to the microphone, he cleared his throat before he began his speech. With rapt attention the humans gathered closer, focused on their hope for the future.

Instead of the handsome shell of a human male dressed in Armanti, the creature Morgan watched through the view finder was tall and gangly, built in a skeletal nature with unhealthy yellow skin stretched taunt over sinewy muscle. The illusion of a charismatic smile was replaced instead by a rotten toothy grin. It spread wider as he looked over his intended victims and pawns with coal black eyes that were filled with diabolical glee.

I should leave them with what they deserve.

For several minutes she mulled the idea around in her brain until she rejected it with a touch of regret. Danu knew she enjoyed a good war for fighting was her bag of tea, but a wholesale slaughter, even of mortals, was not something she wished. After all, this was now her home and it was best to make do with what she had. To sit back and leave it in the hands of this glory seeking Bollag would not do. The sound of Whitlocke's rich, honey-warm voice shook her from her reverie.

"My friends and fellow Americans: Fourteen months ago, when I proudly announced my candidacy for the Presidency of the United States, I declared that this campaign would be a marathon, one that would need strength, endurance, and support to run. Today, with the wind at our backs and the sun blazing down on us, with friends by our side and courage in our hearts, we are nearing the finish line. And I tell you this with all honesty, we're going to win this race.

"We're going to win because we believe in the American dream. A dream so powerful that no distance of ground, no expanse of ocean, no barrier of language, no distinction of race or creed or color can weaken its hold on the human heart. And I know this because, my friends, I'm a product of that dream and I'm proud of it."

Blah, blah, blah. Morgan's forefinger caressed the trigger as it itched to squeeze and end the annoying prattle the Bollag gave.

Under normal circumstances Fae were immune to most human weapons. Being able to regenerate any wound within a matter of a few moments made them hard to kill, but a bullet to the brain could ruin anyone's day, especially if the bullet was made of cold iron, the one human material that could kill any of the immortal Faeiry.

Overhead a black shape flew, slowly circling lower and lower until it settled on a tree branch not far from the stage the Bollag stood on. Whitlocke's gaze turned from the crowd and settled on the crow as the large black bird flexed its wings before settling in. Although his expression remained intense and unconcerned the Bollag's words stumbled for a second and Morgan could see the his eyes sharpen as he turned his gaze back to the crowd around him, searching the sea of faces for any hidden danger. A bead of sweat appeared on his forehead and slowly trailed down his cheek to disappear under the collar of his starched white shirt.

A small smile tugged at the corners of her lips. *He knows I'm near.* Chuckling, Morgan relaxed her lower body as she flexed her fingers, getting ready for the shot. No need to hurry for this was an important speech, one he would not leave just because a crow flew in to listen. That was why she chose today to kill him. Why today he would die.

Putting the tip of her finger on the trigger, Morgan wet her lips and settled her weight enough not to detract from the shot itself. As the Bollag looked up, she could tell by the slight widening of his eyes the moment that he spotted her. With a grin she squeezed the trigger.

Good bye, shit-bag.

The force of the bullet snapped Whitlocke's head back, the rear of his skull exploding in a colorful crimson fountain as bits of blood, bone, and brain splattered those people unfortunate enough to be standing directly behind him. As one the crowd around scattered like insects while screams and calls of help filled the air. The airwaves crackled to life as the Bollag's bodyguards sprang to action and called out for a search grid, intent on finding the Presidential candidate's murderer. *Good luck at that.*

Before Whitlocke's body hit the floor, Morgan jumped up and stretched her neck and shoulders then with a thought vanished the blanket, rifle, tripod, and any other traces she might have left of being on the roof. Ignoring the scene below, she turned and disappeared, teleporting away as the door to the roof was thrown open and a multitude of men emerged, guns in hand, to search for the killer.

~~~

After a long soak in a bubble bath Morgan toweled off then walked over to the closet in her bedroom. Standing in the doorway of her walk-in, she rubbed her chin as she pondered the selection before her before finally settling on a front-laced black leather halter and a pair of extremely low-rise blue jeans.

Dressing, she cast a quick glance at the clock; nine-sixteen p.m. More than enough time to finish dressing, eat a late dinner and arrive at the club before eleven. The girls never expected her anywhere until midnight so a little surprise might be nice for a change. Humming, she slipped on a pair of Balenciaga black leather boots with four-inch heels before turning on the TV to listen to the late night news. Pursuing her selection of daggers she picked one, checked the sharpness of its blade then slipped it into the top of her boot.

Returning to her dresser, she brushed out her dark hair while watching the news show reflected in the mirror. A pretty Asian woman reported the news.

"A small fire was just put out over on Prescott. No one was hurt, though there was major damage to the apartment complex."

Setting the brush down she picked up a small crystal decanter and dabbed a few drops of perfume at her pulse points and between her breasts. Turning away from the mirror Morgan leaned her butt against the dresser and crossed her arms under breasts to watch the television screen.

"Headlining news was the assassination of presidential candidate Daniel Whitlocke earlier that afternoon in San Francisco. No word yet as to the identity of the assassin nor had any organizations stepped forward to take claim of the action. The funeral and memorial service is planned for Monday morning. The other candidates will be attending to pay respect."

Moving back to the bathroom, Morgan admired her reflection in the full-length mirror and smiled at the sight that greeted her. Full breasts thrust out from the soft leather, the soft tops exposed where they pushed up. Under thick, black hair silver hoop earrings dangled from her ears. Nude colored lips curled up in a wicked grin and smoky eyes glittered in delight.

Damn. She turned and looked at her ass. *Even I'd fuck myself.*

Grabbing her wallet and keys she headed out.

~~~

The Inferno was a very popular, busy two-story club located between Sixth and Vine in downtown Portland. Catering to all walks of life it boasted a wide selection of music and alcohol. Morgan watched as a young couple walked through the club's iron front doors, briefly hearing the loud music within before they closed behind them to once more surround her in the sounds of the city. Pulling her driver's license from her wallet, she headed toward the bouncer before pausing as a young transvestite hurried in before her, sweeping long blond hair back over his/her shoulder. With a chuckle she followed behind, entering the club to find it jumping. The pulsing of music, gyrating bodies on the dance floor and the smell of smoke, sweat, and sex lingering in the air filled her senses.

With a smile on her face and heat in her eyes, Morgan moved through the crowd as the rhythm of the deep bass caused her hips to sway to and fro. Her smiled brightened as she entered the main room; a large warehouse floor with a huge main stage. People of various styles, races, and "genders" danced on the stage, banging on metal drums as neon paint splattered the surrounding area, hitting their faces, bodies and anything else nearby. The dance floor itself was filled with people. Their sweating forms undulated and thrashed as each dancer tried to upstage the other. Couples pressed tightly together, pulsating with lust while others tossed their heads left and right, their hair flying around them in a frenzy. The bar itself sat on heavy black grating, high above the main floor. Low tables littered the area where people sat and drank, watching others in their strange rituals of self expression.

Weaving her way through the crowd, Morgan headed up the metallic stairs to grab a drink before looking for a vacant table. The smell of smoke, alcohol, sweat, and lust filled the air, assaulting her senses in waves as men and women paused in their talks to smile, nod or frown as she passed by. Behind the polished wooden counter the bartender glanced up from pouring a beer and caught her eye. As she sidled up to the bar his handsome face split into a smile. Setting the frosty glass on the bar before him, he wiped his hands on a bleached white towel and moved over to her.

"Hey, gorgeous."

"Hey, yourself, Tony. A scotch, please." Morgan smiled back.

With a nod he grabbed a glass and turned to the shelves of gaily colored bottles filled with alcohol. Leaning back against the counter, Morgan studied the surrounding area and quickly spotted one of the women she came here to meet seated on the balcony.

"Here to find Prince Charming, Morgan?" Tony slid her a drink before holding up a hand to decline payment, a roguish grinned plaster on his face.

"Oh, baby." Morgan batted her eyes at him with a sweet smile. "You're my Prince Charming. If only you didn't bat for the other team, I'd knock boots with you in a heartbeat."

They both laughed at the joke before he was pulled away to fill another drink order, for Tony was gay. His lover, a high-powered lawyer who worked at Pierce, Smith and Hansen, sat two stools down the bar from her and he winked, mouthing, *'Too bad'*.

Feigning disappointment Morgan stuck out her bottom lip then turned to head up the grated stairs to the third. Claiming a low-backed chair near the railing she sat down and gazed out over the balcony to watch the crowd below jump and sway in time to the erotic tempo that shook the floor. With a grin on her face the other woman at the table turned to Morgan, wiggling in her seat while her hips swayed back and forth. A naughty smile tugged at her lips as she glanced around the room to scope out the men. Married or single, it didn't matter for as long as they breathed and had a dick between their legs, they were fair game as far as Terri O'Quinn was concerned.

"Hey, girl. About time you got here." Terri stuck her tongue between her lips and grinned.

"Yeah, yeah. Quit bitching." Sipping on her scotch Morgan leaned back in her chair to watch as a gorgeous blonde woman bound up the metal stairs only to drop into the seat next to her. With her hair wild around her shoulders, the blonde brushed it back from her face to reveal eyes wide with exhilaration. Little beads of sweat lined her upper lip and dotted her forehead, showing a beautiful face flushed by exertion. The guy she just finished dancing with gave a short two-finger salute to her from the floor below before walking over to the crowded bar to join his friends.

Laughing, Terri's dark brown eyes lit in mischief. "So, Lisa, is he the one?"

"Huh?" Turning to face her friend, Lisa Montgomery lifted a glass of Coke and rum for a sip. "Him?" she asked, nodding toward the bar and the guy now talking to Tony. "Hell no. He has no real rhythm. Probably be lousy in bed." Giving a short laugh, she looked around before draining the rest of her drink. "You find anyone yet?"

"Nah." Terri shook her head, sending strands of glossy dark hair to fall into her eyes. With a casual brush of her hand she swept it back out of the way then lifted her tequila glass and took the shot. With a quick shake of her head she made a face at the sharp sting of the alcohol and then quickly bit down on a lemon slice. "Damn that's good." She grinned. "And no way. I'm not sleeping with any of these losers."

Feeling watched, Morgan glanced at the blonde from the corner of her eyes. Though she hadn't said a word, Morgan could feel Lisa's unspoken question.

"Don't even ask," she said before turning to face the two ladies sharing the table with her. "You look like you were having fun."

With a mischievous grin on her face Lisa picked up her drink again and lifted it to her lips. "You know, looking for Mr. Right and having fun with all the Mr. Wrongs."

A snicker escaped from Terri and shifting in her chair, she raised a hand to call for another round of drinks. "I'm planning on getting good and drunk tonight."

A low whistle came from Lisa as her eyes lit on someone behind Morgan. "Whoa...who is that?"

The other two women turned around to spy a tall, handsome male in a dark gray shirt and slacks heading over toward them. Short sable hair was brushed back from his face to reveal a strong, clean-shaven jaw, high cheek bones, a generous mouth and eyes as blue as the Mediterranean Sea. When his gaze met Morgan's his lips parted into a knowing smile.

Dimples was the first thought that popped into her mind. *What the hell?* was the second. Turning abruptly around Morgan finished her glass of scotch as her mind whirled into action. That man was definitely not human for she recognized the aura of glamour encircling him. He was Sidhe but of which Court? Anxious, she lowered her hand under the table to hide it from his view and gathered a ball of eldrick magick within it. Feeling the summoned energy crackle around her fingers she silently for his first move. *How's they find me?*

"Hell-lo, gorgeous," Lisa smiled, flashing white teeth as the predator in her came to the surface. A man would have to be blind to miss the invitation that lit up her baby blues.

Instead of taking the blonde up on the silent offer he gave her a short nod before returning his gaze back to Morgan. Noticing his interest in their friend, Terri turned to Lisa and cleared her throat, raising her eyebrows in question. Knowing the man's attention lay elsewhere, the blonde nodded in answer to the silent question then the two of them stood up.

"I need to go to the ladies room," she said as Terri mouthed *'Have fun'* before both women disappeared into the crowd of people.

Bitches.

Morgan knew a setup when she saw one. For the four years she had known them, one or the other had tried to set her up on dates, thinking for some reason a man in her life was what she needed to lighten her attitude. Pfft, a good screw was more like it. Men were nothing but trouble and as the wonderful Madeline Khan once said in the movie *Clue*, men should be like Kleenexes—soft, strong, and disposable. Turning her attention back to the man behind her, Morgan raised an eyebrow as her expression grew colder.

"What do you want?"

With a chuckle, he moved to take the chair that Lisa had vacated moments before. "I am Lorne."

Studying his face through narrowed eyes, Morgan mentally worked her way through his glamour, moving past the illusion he wore to make himself appear human to the outside world. His true appearance changed very little to her sight, only growing leaner and revealing the soft upturn eyes and gently pointed ears of the Sidhe under longer hair that glistened like ebon glass. "And that means what to me?"

Resting his arm on the table, Lorne leaned forward and lowered his voice, as if not wanting to be overheard. It was not like anyone could over the thunderous music of the club. "Dost thou know why I have come?"

"Answering a question with a question, how so like our people." Morgan raised her scotch glass and took a sip before continuing the conversation in her native tongue, feeling her unease sharpen. "Mani ume lle quena?" (*What dost thou want?*)

31

Staying this side of caution, Morgan set her senses to heighten for in her line of business one could never be too careful. Someone was always out to get you. The hand she kept hidden under the table flexed and curled as she prepared herself to hurl the eldrick bolt at him before making her escape. Since her banishment from the Mor'sin'dar and her inconvenient removal from King Tibault's Shinning Court, Morgan had been living incognito as a human for the last several hundred or so years. Just when she was starting to have fun, this comes along. Oh well, it had been awhile since she shed a little blood and Sidhe bled just as easily for her as humans did.

"Fifteen-fifty, please."

A waitress stopped at the table to bring the drinks Terri had ordered minutes earlier. She gave a polite smile, placing several glasses of various concoctions on the low table top, then straightened back up.

Without hesitation, Lorne tossed a fifty on the table then smiled at the waitress, his eyes caressing her face before returning back to the woman beside him. "Keep the change."

The waitress, a short Asian woman with too big hair and too much makeup, stared at him for a second, her eyes lighting up at the tip as a smile split her ruby lips. She looked him over with an expert eye, tossed her hair over her shoulder with a flourish and then wiggled off in her high heels to her next customer.

"I need to speak with thee." He eyes turned serious as he lifted Terri's tequila to his lips and drain the glass. "But this is not the place. May we meet elsewhere?"

Mor'sin'dar. Morgan slowly blinked her eyes then stared at him as if a second head just sprouted from his neck. Did he know who she was? "Are you serious? Why would I do that?"

"Say yes."

Staring at him with a stony expression for a few moments, she pondered her luck in this whole thing and shook her head. He could be an assassin sent by her enemies to try and be rid of her once and for all. But on the other hand he could have been sent by King Silvas, maybe to call her back to Court. Flip a coin, heads or tails? Spying Terri and Lisa watching her from the bar, Morgan sighed and nodded, closing her eyes to the beginnings of a headache coming on. Just for curiosity she was willing to risk it but on her terms.

"Ahh...hell sure, why not? It's been awhile since I've spoken to anyone Sidhe but I expect to be caught up on everything going on in the Courts, understood?" *This should be interesting.* A vague memory niggled in the back of her mind, trying to catch her attention. Mentally she brushed it aside like an annoying fly then opened her eyes as he stood, leaning toward her.

Flashing a breathtaking smile, Lorne reached out a hand, flicking his wrist as if to present her with something when a single purplish black Cala lily suddenly appeared between his fingers. Morgan blinked, staring dumbly at it when suspicion reared inside her. *Whoa, what's going on here?*

"Thy favorite, correct?" His voice lowered to a seductive level as he handed it to her.

"Yes," she murmured. No one had ever given her flowers before and his response to her was a bit confusing. Most Sidhe tended to run when they saw her but he gave her a flower. What was his game?

Starting to feel paranoid, Morgan took the stem between two fingers and set it down on the table before her but not before the tips of his fingers caressed hers. The touch was soft; barely a brush of skin but it left a slight tingling that shot through her body. It had been a long time since she had touched another of her kind and the feeling left her startled at her body's response. Apparently he felt the same from the startled reaction that briefly crossed his face.

He blinked then cleared his expression before putting on the charm once more. "Cormamin niuve tenna' tae lea lle au'." *(My heart shall weep until it sees thee again.)*

Watching as he disappeared into the crowd Morgan frowned. Releasing the power coiled within her hand she moved her eyes back to the lily lying on the table, troubled by the gift. Gifts had ties and all Sidhe gifts had consequences for accepting them. There was a reason why grandmothers warned small children never to accept gifts from the Fae Folk, but the thought vanished as Lisa and Terri rushed back to the table and sat down, curiosity written all over their faces.

"Ok, what happened? That was quick."

Ignoring them Morgan turned her gaze back out to the crowd down below, finding the soft glow of Lorne's glamour and watched the mysterious Sidhe as he left the club. Rubbing her knuckles where his fingers had brushed them, her thoughts turned back to old memories, memories of the magick that flared when Sidhes made love. What the hell did she just get herself into? The only reply to her silent inquiry was Terri lifting her empty shot glass and frowning.

"Damn. He drank my tequila!"

2

"Morriganna."

Cracking her eyes open to slits, Morgan kept her breathing soft and steady as she glanced around the shadows of her bedroom, trying to discover what had disturbed her sleep. Other than the soft thrum of her fish tank on the far wall and the light purring of her little gray kitten, Sonji, nothing else touched her sharp senses. All was as it should be; quiet and peaceful.

She waited a few moments longer, hoping whatever it was would reveal itself then when nothing further happened, sat up. Scanning the dark room for a sign of something out of place Morgan slipped out the gun she kept under her pillow and thumbed the safety off. Someone had called her name; she knew that, but there was no sign of anyone or anything that stood out to her senses. Other than a dim light emulating from the fish tank the room stood in total darkness, clouded in a blanket of night. Glancing over to the small window that sat high on the wall to the left of her bed, she stared at the blackness beyond. Eyes narrowing, Morgan strained her hearing to find some sign of the noise that had awoken her.

At a slight movement by her side, the dark haired woman's eyes snapped down to find Sonji opening tired yellow eyes. After a wide yawned that revealed wickedly sharp teeth, the little kitten watched her mistress warily. Slowly the feline reached out one tiny paw and touched Morgan's thigh as if reassuring herself that everything was all right, that it was too early to get up and she needed to go back to sleep.

"Morriganna."

Morgan tensed, her body stiffening at the hollow voice that sounded both near and far. Cocking her head, she concentrated her hearing then shivered as a sudden cooling breeze brushed across her bare flesh, causing her nipples to harden and the muscles in her abdomen to clench tight. The hair on her arms stood on end as wintry chills from the lowering temperature ran down her spine and under her skin.

Gradually a presence filled the room, as a hazy fog rose and surrounded the bed. Sonji arch her back in fear until the soft gray fur stood on end and bared her teeth in a hiss as if sensing something not quite there. Retreating toward the edge of the mattress, the kitten jumped off and raced under the bed to hide, abandoning her owner to fend for herself. While the fog grew and thickened the mirrors and windows in the room frosted, starting first at the corners and then spreading quickly toward the center.

Morgan shivered at the unnatural coldness, pulling her bedspread over her nude body to cut out the chill as her breath appeared before her in small puffs of wraithlike clouds. With a sigh, she settled back to wait, watching the fog hang on the air, and replaced her gun under the pillow.

"Morriganna." The voice echoed around her, growing stronger as the force of power it took to transmute through time and space grew.

Recognizing the voice that had woken her from her sleep, Morgan wrapped her arms around herself for warmth and shook her head, surprised. The voice was one she hadn't heard in years and couldn't help but feel a twinge of relief to know she was not forgotten after all. *Maybe my luck is getting better. Two visits by Court Sidhe in one night. Maybe Silvas is bringing me home but couldn't it have waited for the morning? What a crappy time to be calling.*

Glancing at the clock face on her nightstand, she yawned and rubbed her eyes with the palms of her hands. Four-thirty in the morning. It was too freaking early. As seconds clicked by then minutes, irritation grew, driving out any want for communication of one of her kind. He sure seemed to be taking his own sweet time and she really didn't have much patience for it. Not to mention that scrying by water made the room an icebox and she preferred sleeping in the buff.

With a growl, Morgan tugged her blankets up over her shoulders, swearing under her breath as she tried to stave off the chill. Usually the cold didn't bother her as her body adapted to any of the elements, but this was no natural frost forming. After several long minutes of silence, the caller decided to speak again. *About time*, she snarled, trying to keep her teeth from clacking together.

"Good evening, Morriganna, I hath need to speak with thee."

"Well hurry up, Eryn and do it quick. You're freezing my ass off."

The feeling of pulsating power filled the room, giving it an illusion of walls coming alive and breathing while a brief moment of vertigo swept over the seated woman. Breathing deeply to still her equilibrium, she leaned her head back against the wall and drew her knees up to her chest as she closed her eyes. It was always disorientating talking to someone who wasn't there, but considering this was the first "call" from any of the Mor'sin'dar since her banishment, who was she to complain? It was nice hearing a voice from her past.

Until the day her High King lifts her banishment from the Mor'sin'dar Court she would have to make do with the company of humans. Though inventive and chatty, often irritating and somewhat amusing, Morgan desperately missed the company of her own people. One reason why she accepted the unknown Lorne's offer and overlooked the inconvenient time for this scry. Feeling a soft breeze caress her cheek and neck she opened her eyes, drawn back to the moment at hand.

"Morriganna, thou needs to be careful. I hath come to warn thee, though I cannot reveal more except that trouble stirs within the Courts. An assassin has

been sent to find thee."

The rich warm voice of Eryn Sye, an informant of hers from her more active days, filled the room. He was always reliable for information if not more, but it had been years since they last spoke. With a frown Morgan blinked away the last remnants of sleep from her mind and pulled herself up to lean against the backboard of her bed. "What are you talking about, Eryn? I'm not part of anything anymore."

"Something is happening in the ShadowedLands, Lady Death. Rumors are spreading and thy name hast been brought up several times."

"Brought up? Brought up about what? By whom?" Morgan's mind raced as she tried gathering her thoughts. Assassins were being sent after her? But why? She had the protection of the High King during her banishment. Something was wrong. She suddenly sat up straight. Rumors are spreading through Court and now a Mor'sin'dar unknown to her sought her out. "Why would people be talking about me? About what? Coming back? I can't until the High King bids me free passage to return." Her breath caught as a flitter of hope filled her chest. "Is that it? Am I going to be allowed back to Court? Is King Silvas lifting the ban? Who sending the assassin?"

The room chilled a little more in response while from under the bed Sonji voiced her displeasure with a pitiful meow. Morgan ignored her cry and concentrated on what her friend was saying. "Talk to me, Eryn. What's going on?"

"Just be careful, Morrigu, for thou hath enemies that are hidden. I know not more except things are not as they seem and the High Lords are leaving Court. Thou needs to be wary of all that thou meet and do not let thy guard down. Things are not right here. I cannot say more. They are coming." Eryn paused. *"I wish thee well, Crow."*

"But is King Silvas going to lift the ban? Will I be allowed home?"

Morgan asked, her heart beating at a quick pace at the thought of seeing her homeland once more. She waited for him to continue, but bit by bit the unearthly cold created by the water spell left the room as Eryn's presence faded, the scry ending.

"Damnit."

Frustrated and irritated with him for leaving without answering her questions, Morgan reached over and turned on the reading lamp on her nightstand. Assassins she could handle and enemies...those were few for she dealt with them swiftly. The question was who was stirring up problems and why...why were the High Lords leaving? Those sedentary old fools rarely roused themselves for anything beyond a good game of dice anymore and she was surprised King Silvas would allow such power-bases to leave. With a snap of her wrist, she pulled back the covers and slid her legs out of bed, placing them on the carpeted floor to stand. The bed covers rustled as she moved, drawing her back into the normalcy of everyday life rather than the unnaturalness of her reality. Rubbing the bridge of her nose, she breathed in deep then glanced down as a soft meow reached her ears. Slowly Sonji crept out from under the bed, her eyes wide as she searched for the thing that had sent her skittering away earlier.

"Shit," Morgan muttered, rolling her shoulders to stretch away the crick that threatened to knot up a muscle between them. "I'm awake now. No use trying to go back to sleep."

With her thoughts moving in a chaotic whirl through her mind at Eryn's cryptic message, she padded barefoot and naked out to her living room. Maybe it wasn't a wise move accepting this Lorne's invitation but if anything it could be a good way of getting information, information Eryn was sorely lacking with. After grabbing the remote off the coffee table, Morgan flopped down on her couch and curl up, pulling a blanket kept folded on the arm over her. Turning on the TV she quickly flicked through channel, passing all the infomercials before finally settling on a soap opera from Mexico. With a brief yawn she settled in for a long morning.

3

The drizzly rain poured down around commuters in the early morning, beating a rhythm on the plastic roof of the bus stop that sheltered the group of people huddled underneath the dome. Cars zoomed by, splashing unwary bystanders with water, drenching them and setting off the mood of the day.

Cupping her palm over the end of a cigarette, Morgan moved to light the end. With a sideways glance at the humans not far from her she snapped her fingers, producing a small flame then quickly drew in a breath as the paper and dried tobacco lit up. Letting the gauzy smoke slip between her lips, she turned her eyes toward the building across the street from the bus shelter she stood in, trying to ignore the chatting from two teenage boys that shared it with her. All she wanted at this point was to get home for a nice relaxing bath. She hated Oregon rain; cold, heavy drops that refused to let up. With a sigh, she leaned back against the wall of the shelter and let her mind wander.

The past three days had quickly passed since Lorne's introduction and Morgan dismissed any notion of speaking to him or one of her kin again. Rather than mope about the loss of contact, she continued life as normal and, as she took another puff of the cigarette, filling her mouth with the steamy smoke before letting it out in a ring, she decided working was the best thing to keep her mind busy. Sooner or later she'd find out the news, about whether or not King Silvas would bring her home.

"Yeah, ya should have seen him; the guy was scared shitless when he saw me."

A gaffing chuckle came from the hunkering teen beside the speaker. The boy took a step forward to search for the bus, and then moved back under the cover, keeping his shoulders bent forward under his leather jacket and scratched the side of his jaw. This one resembled a delinquent, his eyes slightly feral as they scanned over Morgan's pea green military jacket to the side of her face. She ignored him, though well aware he was trying to see what she looked like, but a thick grey wool scarf and a black knit cap pulled low over her head hid her appearance well enough in the gloom that she wasn't concerned he could identify her. Not that she was worried; more than likely he was studying her in order to decide if she was worthy for him to hit upon.

"It was the Red Bull," the other guy said as he postured to his friend, pushing his glasses back in place with a finger. "Red Bull and coffee. My eyes were wild. I love Red Bull."

From the way the speaker was hopping back and forth from one foot to another, there was no doubt he loved Red Bull. His veins were probably filled with the caffeinated stuff and from the jumpy nervousness that emitted from him she'd be surprised if he didn't love something else. Feeling annoyed at having to suffer the conversation, Morgan filled the time as she waited thinking up ways to disembowel the annoying human when movement from across the street caught her attention. About time.

From the building across the busy road, three men exited, pausing for a brief moment as one turned to lock the door. Two of them stood well over six feet, shoulders like bulldogs and hair cut short in a buzz. Water dripped off their heavy black raincoats as they waited for the shorter man, their eyes scanning the sidewalk along the building front. Keeping her eyes on the target, Morgan stepped off the curb, aware of the look the two boys in the shelter gave her. Down the street the long-awaited bus suddenly appeared, bright lights glaring in the drizzly rain and as one they turned their attention from her to the vehicle.

With long strides Morgan hurried across the street, holding her coat close to her as if she was racing to get out of the rain. She eyed the three men, quickly taking in their appearance and sizing them up. Shorty was obviously the one in control; the great boss, her target. Though shorter than the other two, he took some minor effort to keep himself in shape. His designer coat hung tailored over broad shoulders and was tied sharply around his narrow waist. From what Morgan remembered from his dossier he liked to work out in a private gym in the four point two million dollar condo he lived in. Money's nice, but it does squat when your time to go sneaks up and bites you in the ass.

Her target, Victor Crawley, seemed absorbed in his conversation as he chatted on a cell phone, his hands animated as he spoke. One of the bodyguards stood by him, holding a umbrella over his boss's head to keep the rain from him but every good deed goes unnoticed for Crawley ignored the heavy droplets soaking into the man next to him. Instead he turned his back as if annoyed by the image.

Morgan snorted. Of course he didn't care because he was a Bollag and Bollags cared about nothing that didn't cause destruction. To her eyes, Victor's appearance faded, showing the thin skeletal form of his kindred, except he had a small curved horn growing out of his forehead. His papery thin skin was stained scarlet and stretched tightly over the wiriness of what little muscle was wrapped around his structure. His eyes flickered upward toward the roof of the building, narrowing as if he sought something. A caw echoed in the dismal sky as a large black bird stared down at him atop the structure, eyeing him with one beady onyx orb.

Hurrying across the street, Morgan stepped past oncoming cars and narrowly avoided getting splashed as the vehicles zoomed by. Behind her the bus pulled up to the curb with a loud mechanical squeal of the breaks, unloading and loading passengers before continuing along its drudging way down the road. The two punks were now gone, replaced by a mother struggling to keep a rowdy child from plunging head first into traffic.

Stepping onto the sidewalk, Morgan's eyes briefly met the dark blue ones of one of the bodyguards. Flashing him the briefest of smiles, she shivered as if cold and pulled at the scarf to keep her face warm. In return, his gaze roved over her appreciatively before he turned his head to whisper something to the tall man beside him. As she walked past them, the first guard took a step back to give her room. Before he could finish his movements, Morgan clipped him with her left hand, the heel of her palm striking the edge of his jaw as a nasty crunching sound filled the air. With a gasp of pain and surprise, he stepped back past the other guard, holding his jaw with both hands before falling to his knees.

As the second guard stepped in her way, Morgan brought the edge of her boot down on the instep of his leg, while pressing down hard against his knee. With a snap, his kneecap broke like a twig. A sharp cry escaped him as he went down, clutching his leg with both hands, to land hard on the water-soaked ground.

"What the fuck?"

The words barely escaped the target's mouth before Morgan whirled on him, a thin blade revealed in her hand. With an upward punch, she rammed the stiletto through the bottom of his jaw, shoving hard as it moved through flesh and bone until it entered brain matter. Eyes wide with shock, he stared at her, his mouth slowly moving as the synapses in his brain went off, declaring death to every portion of his body. His limbs convulsed as she lowered him to the ground. Victor blinked, the rain pelting him in the face as his life slowly drained from his body.

~~~

Rubbing her forehead from an oncoming headache, Morgan watched as a waitress set her salad down in front of her, then stared out the window of the small café, watching the rain outside slow down to a light drizzle.

"Will there be anything else?" the waitress asked, her hand raised to the small green apron wrapped around her narrow hips and the ordering pad she kept in the pocket. After receiving a no, the waitress gave a polite smile and then headed to another table.

Picking up her fork to spear a tomato, Morgan pondered her last assignment. What in the Nine Hells was going on? Two Bollags in a week? Were they pouring out of the woodwork now? With a sigh, she munched on the juicy red fruit, chewing thoughtfully before being interrupted by a sharp beeping. Reaching into her pocket, she pulled out a cell phone, pressed *On,* and lifted the phone to her ear.

"Whatcha need?"

"Hey, Morgan, it's me." Lisa's cheerful voice erupted from the little phone with the force of a cheerleader on speed. "Just calling to let you know I got the contract. I fly out to New York on Monday to go shop and I'll be gone for…hmmm…at least a week. Is this not the coolest job in the world?"

"Oh, yes, very cool." Morgan stabbed her salad with a fork and brought it to her mouth. While she chewed and swallowed it, Lisa spoke again, her voice growing more and more hyper in speed and tone.

"Who gets to spend thousands of dollars on clothes and not get into debt? I love this. And the best thing is, next week I fly down to L.A. for Fashion Week and make orders. Need to start working on my tan. Oh my God, I don't even have a decent bikini."

"Make sure you bring me back something then. I favor Dolce." With a chuckle, Morgan absentmindedly searched her salad for another tomato before spearing a cucumber slice instead and taking a bite. Swallowing, she set her fork down. "And don't forget to wax."

A loud squeal echoed from the phone. Wincing, Morgan held it away as she reached for her wine. "Oh, you're just evil," the voice on the other end cried out.

Lisa had just recently gotten a job as a fashion coordinator and personal shopper at Mario's and several of her clients were high-powered business women, spoiled wives of basketball players and the Nuevo rich. Many of them, pleased with her clothing selections for them, were quite generous and showed their pleasure by tipping her a good forty-percent above her normal commission. Whoo hoo, money to spend.

"I'll find you something special."

"Okay, babe. I'll be waiting with bated breath."

"Do I hear 'bitch' in your voice?"

Morgan chuckled at the question. How quickly Lisa was learning to understand her. "Well, no, sweets. Of course not."

"Yeah, right." Laughter sprung out of the receiver, flowing like a bubbling spring. "So is Terri giving you a workout today?"

With a snort, Morgan rolled her eyes. "As if. I got more chasing after a mugger."

"What? You got mugged?"

Once more Morgan snorted. "I don't get mugged. Some idiot tried to pickpocket me and I wound up chasing him over six blocks in my heels. Pissed me off so much I beat the crap out of him when I caught up, then broke his leg for good measure. Shit, Lisa, he's damn lucky I didn't break a heel."

"Oh, I believe that." She laughed.

With a quiet smile, Morgan drained her wine as her friend continued talking. She knew Lisa thought she was joking. After all, no one knew about her "business" and it was of course best. She'd have to kill them and move on if they ever found out, and since she was stuck in the mortal realm it was better to adjust and pretend to be something mundane than have to move and make new acquaintances.

After speaking for a few more moments, Morgan slid her cell phone back in her pocket before picking up her fork again when her thoughts returned back to the Bollags. *I need to talk to someone.* She wondered who from the Courts was in the area. Eryn was out; she had tried contacting him after his surprise call, but no answer. Either he was trying to keep his contact with her quiet or he was in hiding.

Options growing limited, Morgan curled her lip in irritation. Finished with her lunch, she stood up, pulling a twenty from her wallet, and left the bistro. Trying to make sense of the sudden flux of Bollags, she decided to take a walk down to the park near the river, hoping to come up with some kind of answer.

~~~

By the time she made it to the Waterfront Park, the sun was out again, shining bright in the pale blue sky. The light from the brilliant orb danced over the Willamette, the pale colors in the sky reflecting off the sharp little waves in the water, creating an almost glittering, jewel-like effect.

Slipping off her jacket, Morgan stepped over to the metal link fence along the walkway and rested her forearms on the railing, leaning forward. Sounds of commuters traveling across the busy bridges intersecting downtown to Northeast Portland filled her ears as she watched seagulls dive into the dark water. Brushing back several stray tendrils of hair that the wind blew into her face, she watched as the silly scavengers circled and dove in search for food, their squawks of complaint rising as only one of the flock managed to score a fish. Soon an all out brawl took place as the birds fought to capture the squirming meal from the talons of the one who caught it first.

Foul creatures. Morgan scrunched her shoulders together as the wind tugged another length of dark hair loose and waved it around.

"Lirimaer, thy beauty has sorely been missed."

Turning around at the sound of a masculine voice dripping with sex, Morgan spotted the Sidhe from the club. Feeling slightly irritated by the fact that she hadn't sensed him walking up behind her, she pushed her erratic hair from her face, then shoved her hands in her jeans' pockets.

"Lorne."

Grudgingly, she silently admitted she was pleased to see him again after dismissing the idea of him keeping his word. Further yet, surprise came when he reached out and took her hand in his large one, raising it up to kiss her knuckles. The feel of his warm lips pressed against the sensitive skin bought feelings of longing to rise to the surface.

"My lady. How hast thou been?"

"Alive." Morgan turned her eyes back over the water, ignoring the tingles his touch sent as they shot straight down to her groin. Shifting her body, she removed her hand from his. "And you? Been busy?"

Reluctantly, he let go of her, his touch leaving behind a ghost trail before nodding. "I have." He shrugged and looked away, watching as some children ran past.

Growling, Morgan bit her tongue to keep from saying something spiteful. Avoidance was not a quality she liked, especially from a guy. Refraining from smacking some answers out of him, she wrapped her fingers around the railing and squeezed tight, until her knuckles turned white, and took a deep breath.

"So, what have you been up to?" she asked as soon as she pulled her temper back into control, then glanced up at him, watching his face as he watched the children play.

Once again he shrugged a broad shoulder. Morgan felt her temper spike.

Great; moody and secretive. What was it with guys, she wondered, shaking her head in irritation. Danu, how she hated the games that men played. Why do things have to be so complicated?

At her silence, Lorne's gaze returned to hers, his eyes filled with hunger. *Well, two can play at this game.* With a yawn, Morgan turned around to rest her back against the railing and watched a couple walking quickly across the street to a parked car. The man pulled out a set of keys from his pocket before unlocking his door, then got in and leaned over to unlock the other door so the woman could get in. With a snort, Morgan crossed her arms over her chest. Chivalry was definitely dead.

"So, how hast thou been?" Lorne asked, moving closer to her. Sensing her irritation, he lifted a hand toward her then lowered it as she stepped out of his reach, yawning again.

"I've been okay, just bored." This time Morgan turned away before looking back at him with sharp eyes. "Why?"

"We still need to speak." He watched as her shoulders visible tensed.

Raising an eyebrow, Morgan cocked her head and narrowed her eyes. A shadow of a smile curved the edges of his lips.

Morgan's gaze dropped to his mouth, taking in the lushness. Damn, it had been so long since she had been near one of her own. Closing her eyes, she bit her bottom lip and turned away. "Okay," she said and cleared her throat, feeling a chill wrap around her body from his nearness. "I guess it would be good to talk."

"So where wouldst thou wish to go?"

Shrugging a slender shoulder, Morgan opened her eyes to find him leaning against a light pole, thick arms crossed over his chest as he studied her. She glanced around, spying a few people in the distance walking their way. "Some place a bit more private. Follow me."

Taking the lead, she headed across the manicured lawn of the park toward Skidmore Fountain in order to hop the MAX train back to her place. Crossing Naito Parkway, they headed across a cobblestone plaza, past the fountain where Skidmore got its name and to the slightly raised platform under the Burnside Bridge to wait for the train. On the opposite side of the street from the platform, several disheveled men leaned against the brick of the building. The words *Mission* in faded yellow print stood out above a closed door as several of the men talked or played cards while waiting for the doors to open for the night.

Behind Morgan, the echoes of teenagers skateboarding in the open side enclosure filled the air, sounds of boards flipping and young men joking as another couple entered the platform to wait. With a brief glance toward the homeless men, the woman wrapped her arms around her waist and leaned toward her date, whispering something to him. The man looked around, his eyes stopping on Morgan, and then nodded in agreement. Lorne stood by in silence, observing all as they waited.

Soon the MAX train pulled up and the doors opened. They entered, taking the first seats they saw. The door slid shut and the train lurched forward as the buildings outside began rushing past. With a glance at the man beside her, Morgan straightened her back and slowly relaxed her posture.

She caught the small knowing smile that lifted the corners of Lorne's lips as he settled back in his seat and it irked her. From the amused look in his eyes she knew he was aware of her interest in him and the threat of the unknown, which was usually enough to cause her to proceed with more caution, was superseded by her need of Sidhe companionship. She was curious, she admitted and wondered what his lips would feel like under her own before reason set in. *Why was he here? What did he want?* Irritated, she looked away from him, her lips pulled into a tight line.

Drawing in a deep breath, Lorne turned toward her when the dramatic sounds from the theme for Darth Vader filled the train car. Morgan tossed him a dark look before moving her gaze to stare out the window to watch the scenes from the city quickly pass by.

Lorne pulled his cell phone from out of his pocket and winced as he pressed the a button before lifting it to his ear. after listening for a moment he mumbled under his breath. "The meeting tis not until tomorrow, my Lord." Then he paused to listen as he glanced at her. Irritated, Morgan clenched her jaw and tugged her pea jacket closer around her body. After a quick, "Yes, my Lord." Lorne closed the phone and replaced it in his pocket.

Curiosity, annoyance and a want for Sidhe sex warred within Morgan. The assassin in her warned her to be careful, to get rid of him as quick as possible, but the woman in her wanted a bit of Sidhe companionship. Biting the inside of her bottom lip, she pondered her options, deciding to question him before anything else. It would be easy enough to get rid of a body if the answers weren't to her liking.

As the train pulled up to her stop, she stood up with Lorne following and walked off the MAX before heading down several blocks passed the Memorial Coliseum and finally stopping at a large warehouse not far from the north of the Willamette. As she stepped up to a metal door to the side of a large docking door Morgan flipped open a small covered box and pressed several buttons in rapid secession. After a small click reached her ears she pushed open the front door, inviting Lorne to enter first with the wave of her hand.

4

As Lorne passed by her into the darkness of her home, Morgan reached up inside to a ledge over the door and grabbed a handgun she kept stored there. Since light wasn't necessary for her to see, she closed the door behind them with a loud thud then stepped forward, placing the barrel of her SIG Sauer to the back of his skull. Lorne froze, slowly raising his hands then paused when the soft click of the hammer being drawn back reached his ear.

"I'd think carefully about what you do at this point," she whispered in his ear.

He hesitated then spread his arms slightly, showing his hands were empty. "What art thou doing?" he asked, standing still in the dark.

With her free hand Morgan quickly ran it over him, searching for weapons. Finding nothing, she removed his cell phone from his pocket and circled in front of him.

Lorne's nostrils flared as she passed close by though he kept his eyes straight ahead and kept still. After setting his phone down on a small table behind her, Morgan turned on the lights, watching him blink as his eyes adjusted to the sudden light. Taking several steps back, she kept her gun steady on him and waited till his gaze settled once more on her face. From his expression he didn't seem surprised by her actions. Instead he seemed calm as if he waited to see what she would do next.

"Now, who are you and what do you want with me?" Morgan asked, thoughts of the Bollags she killed within the past few days swirling in her head. The fact that a Sidhe shows up in the midst of it, plus the early morning warning from Eryn…she was too paranoid to ignore the coincidences.

"Thou cannot stay here for it tis not safe."

Morgan stared at him with an icy expression, her mind whirling with unspoken thoughts. "What are you talking about?" she asked as he slowly lowered his hands, watching her warily.

When she didn't pull the trigger right away, Lorne turned his head to glance around. She followed his eyes as they darted around the open bay of the warehouse, taking in the dark furniture made of steel and glass before settling on the mural that graced the wall. For several long minutes he stared at it as if mesmerized the woodland scene. Tired of his silence, Morgan demanded, "What's up?"

"Thou art the Morrigu, favored of King Silvas, correct?"

Inside Morgan struggled to maintain her cool while declining to answer the question, instead asking him one herself. "You already know I am. What do you want?"

Turning his attention away from the mural, he locked eyes with her. "Not everything is as it seems, Lady Morriganna. Please understand I am not here to harm thee. I am only here to help."

"Help me? Who sent you?" Curious, she eyed him, but when he tried to take a step toward her she gave a quick head shake. "Just stay put unless you want to be ventilated."

Lorne looked at her intently, and then shrugged. "Fine."

Giving a low growl, Morgan shrugged off her jacket, leaving it on the floor where it had fallen, then walked over to the glass bar to pour a scotch one handed. "So whose hit list am I on?" She lifted the lid from a crystal decanter half filled with an amber liquid, then picked it up to pour a whiskey glass with the stuff. After setting the decanter back in its place, she replaced the lid and grabbed the squat glass before making her way over to the couch. Sitting down, Morgan crossed her legs and leaned back with her gun lying on her thigh, keeping the barrel pointed at Lorne as she sipped her drink.

A deep, nervous laugh rose from Lorne as he ran his fingers through his hair, eyeing her. "Thou art a headstrong woman."

"So I'm told." Morgan sipped her drink, tasting the smooth alcohol with the faintest hint of pear. "Now what do we do?" She rotated her wrist, sending the liquid to twirl in a gentle wave inside the glass.

The corner of his mouth twisted, lifting his lips in a teasing smile. "What wouldst thou like?"

"My question answered." Morgan sipped at her drink again. "I must say I'm intrigued. It's not every day I have a man under gunpoint in my place. So, you're not here to kill me or so you claim. Then what do you want?"

She watched as Lorne took a step closer to her and shifted her gun in her lap to level it at him. He ignored the threat and reached down to uncross her legs, lowering himself to his knees before spreading her thighs to slid between them. At the touch she hissed softly, feeling heat radiate off his palms as he moved his hands over the fabric on her legs. Though her body flared to life she kept the barrow of her gun on him and studied his face.

"Tis more like what I want to do to thee," he spoke, his voice lowered in a husky whisper as hunger filled his gray eyes.

Morgan tensed as her stomach tightened and went all a-flutter at the heated look. He offered her sex. Not that she was celibate, but sex with a Sidhe, one of her own kind, was a thing she desired. After all the last time she had been with one of her own was the night before she left her cheating ex-husband forty years prior. Mouth suddenly parched, she licked her lips and raised her glass to drain the rest of the scotch before dropping it on the floor. As it clinked on the hardwood, her breath caught, feeling Lorne's hand slowly creeping up along her inner thigh.

Flaring her nostrils as she breathed in his rich scent, Morgan's voice lowered to a husky whisper. "You really need to back off. I can only think of one thing around you and I really shouldn't. Not until I figure out what to do about you."

Instead of doing as she asked, Lorne moved a little closer, bending his head so his mouth was a scant inch from hers. Cupping her face as his lips brushed over her slightly parted ones, he drew in the soft sigh that escaped from Morgan before his mouth locked onto hers. Closing her eyes, she enjoyed the feel of his tongue caressing her own. His hand lowered down to cup her breast, his thumb brushing her nipple. With a groan she felt her breasts grow heavy with want, the taunt buds tightening with ache as the need to rip off her T-shirt and feel his touch on her bare flesh warred within. Putting a hand up she pushed him away from her, trying to get space between them.

Breathing heavily, Morgan leaned back in the couch. "You don't play fair, Lorne. That's dangerous."

He reached out a hand to lift a stray hair from cheek, caressing the side of her face with the tips of his fingers. "And thy teasing of me is not? Thou knows that thou wants me to touch thee. I felt the call when we first met."

Clearing her dry throat, Morgan shook her head to gain some sort of clarity. "You're wrong." Her voice sounded husky even to herself.

A wicked grin passed over Lorne's mouth as he leaned in, running his tongue gently over her lips. Leaning back out of his arms, Morgan watched him as a smile blossomed on her lips. *Well, he's definitely a good kisser. I'll give him that.*

"Am I, my Lady?" He leaned his head down to place a soft kiss at the bend of her neck. The tip of his tongue teased her throat, and then he scraped his teeth lightly against her pulse. She knew he was trying to distract her and doing a damn good job. Deciding to put her curiosity on hold, Morgan let her hormones take charge. After she'd been satisfied, then she'd deal with the problem of what the truth was.

Sliding the safety on her gun, Morgan lowered it to the floor then sunk farther into the cushions as Lorne began to place slow kisses up her throat to her ear, his breath warm over the sensitive spot behind it. Reaching up, she wrapped her arms around his shoulders and pulled him closer. He nibbled at her earlobe, sending a current of lust shooting through her body then wrapped kisses down along her jaw to her chin before finishing up at her lips.

"Sweet Danu, thou doth taste sweet," he muttered as he nipped her bottom lip, his hand cupping the back of her head to hold her still for his invading mouth.

Sighing deep, Morgan moved her hips as she pressed the apex between her legs against his waist. "If you don't stop I won't be able to control myself."

"Dost thou really wish me to?" His question was redundant she knew, a stupid thing to ask when both of them were willing to go all the way. *Hot monkey sex here I come.*

"Hell no," she moaned as Lorne cupped her breast again, his hand gently squeezing and kneading the soft flesh.

Lowering his face to hers again, Lorne's kisses grew heated as his lips hardened against hers. Morgan returned it eagerly, leaning her slender body into his muscled one while his arms slowly wrapped around her in a heated embrace. As she opened lips in offering, he slipped his tongue inside her mouth to dance, eliciting a sigh from deep inside her.

Lorne groaned deep, moving his hips as he pressed against her to create a heated friction. The pressure between them grew until it was almost unbearable. Wrapping her fingers in his hair, she pulled him down to kiss him deeper, the hunger between them getting stronger. She relished the hard feel of his body next to hers and the taste of him in her mouth. Breaking off the kiss, Morgan stared up into his heady eyes and licked her lips.

In a burst of urgency, Lorne scooted her body over until she lay back against the cushions, then tugged at Morgan's shirt until he could raise it up and over her head. Lifting the cups of her bra up to bare her breasts, he captured one hard bud with the flat of his tongue.

Sliding a hand down between them, Morgan yanked at the waist of his pants, trying to undo his belt with a fever she now felt rising within her. Shuddering from the sensation, she hurried her hands and reached into the front of his pants, grasping him with a firm grip to feel the hard length. With a smile she managed to get the belt loose then pulled at his pants to undo them.

Pushing him back against the arm of the couch, Morgan quickly shimmied out of her jeans and panties, sliding them down her thighs before kicking them behind her. Settling herself over him, legs on either side of his hips, she reached between them and guided him into her entrance before lowering herself down. With a deep groan, he closed his eyes and moved his hands on her hips, gripping them tightly before setting a rhythm.

"Thou art most beautiful," he whispered as he moved in her.

For several long moments, heavy breathing filled the air, soft moans of pleasure escaped between kisses as she moved her mouth over his. Gripping the arm of the couch, she rode him hard, enjoying the feeling of being full, of being one with another of her kind. Electricity lit her nerves, shooting through her body in a low rush and her skin felt alive. Oh, the joy of Sidhe, how she missed it. Lowering her head forward until her forehead rested on his lips, she closed her eyes and bit her bottom lip to keep back her cry. Chills of pleasure rippled throughout Morgan as she finally broke and cried out.

"Oh, yessss." She hissed.

Placing her hands on either side of his head, she quickly moved her hips, feeling the buildup come swift and powerful. A quickie, it was, but she didn't care. It was just great to feel another Sidhe again, the touch of their flesh, the melding of their auras.

Harder and faster they moved, sweat beading on their skin and their breathing grew harsher. Morgan dug her nails deep into his shoulders, urging him on, uncaring that she tore his skin. The coppery scent of blood filled her nose, as a soft hiss of pain filled her ears but she refused to release her hold. Keeping her eyes closed, she threw back her head and smiled.

Morgan licked her lips and she watched him through slit eyes. Sweat glistened on her skin from the strenuous exercise of their passion. She could feel a drop of perspiration slowly rolling down from her neck, down along her breast before continuing down her side.

"Do you like?" She purred.

"Oh yes." Lorne leaned up, licking away a droplet before rubbing his cheek against her skin. Sitting up he cradled her body to him, resting her back against his bent legs so he could enter her at a sharper angle.

A sudden scream tore from Morgan's throat as the orgasm hit hard. Her toes curled as wave after wave ripped through her body, causing muscles to clamp down tightly around him again and his cry suddenly mingling with her own. Together their bodies shuddered at the intensity as Morgan threw herself forward, wrapping her arms around his neck, and then drew him closer as they rode out their glorious orgasm.

After several shuddering moments, their breathing slowly calmed as their bodies stopped their trembling. Tilting her face down to his, Morgan brushed a kiss over his lips and breathed in, enjoyed the intoxicating scent of their lovemaking. *Shit, that was good.*

"Where is thy chambers?" Lorne whispered into her ear, his breath warm and tickling on her skin.

At her nod toward a set of stairs past the kitchen area, he carried her upstairs to the loft and the large bed. He laid them down with her body still cradled up to his chest, framing her with his muscled thighs while his large hands roamed over her back. Their mouths met again, his lips brushing hers as if to claim her as his.

Sighing, Morgan let her tongue lick his in soft delicate strokes. *Let him have his illusions.* Pulling away from him, she stretched out on her front and grinned to herself. *I had my orgasm.* Now was the time for answers. Sliding her hand beneath the headboard, she turned her face toward him while watching him out of the corner of her eyes. His hand roamed down the curve of her back to caress the firm mound of her ass as a dreamy smile curled up the corners of his lips.

Rolling over to her side, Morgan draped her arm over her waist as her fingers caught a strand of dark hair and played with it, drawing his attention to her lush breasts. As he licked his lips and reached for one of those soft mounds, he found himself suddenly cross-eyed, staring into the dark metal barrel of a Glock.

"Now…where were we? Oh yes, I remember. Who are you really and why are you here?"

~~~

Uncomfortable, Lorne removed his hand from her breast and cleared his throat, feeling the erection that was starting to spring back to life suddenly go limp. The look on Morgan's face was all business and no means of seduction was going to dissuade her from the answers she wanted this time.

Brushing his fingers through the front of his hair, he looked thoughtful as if trying to make up his mind at what to say. Finally he met her gaze. "As I said, my name is Lorne and I was sent here to look after thee."

"Who sent you?"

Lorne hesitated then answered. "The Lord of Tech nDuinn."

"Lord Requiem?" Morgan spoke softly in confusion, then her eyes flashed back to his. "So you are Mor'sin'dar."

"Yes."

"I don't recall ever seeing you before." Morgan studied him with narrowed eyes. "So why would you help me? Why the dread Lord? It's not like I'm liked much there. In fact since my banishment I'm not much liked anywhere. So once again I ask, WHY are you here? I expect the full truth this time or I have no problem scattering your brains on my back wall. I've needed a reason to redecorate anyway."

Watching her eyes go from a light jade green to an icy obsidian black, Lorne felt the hair on the back of his neck rise in warning. She wasn't bluffing. One minute she was a lover, the next his executioner. She would kill him without hesitation. Letting out a heavy breath, he raised himself to an elbow, watching as she adjusted the gun to his height.

"King Silvas is dead and the Queen hath decided to reinstate the bounty on thy head."

"Silvas?" Morgan's voice grew soft and unbelieving. Her eyes glimmered with unshed tears and her jaw ticked as she clenched her teeth together. All within the Court knew of the bond between the Morrigu and her King but witnessing her grief he couldn't wonder if there had been more to their relationship. Closing her eyes, she held her breath, as if trying to control the emotions rolling around inside her. A slight shift on the bed and she cracked an eye open, steadying the barrel against Lorne's forehead. "I *will* kill you."

"Queen Moirethe still wants thy head, but tis not all." Lorne licked his lips nervously. "She is willing to forgo that for thy humiliation, to prove that thou were not fit for the position thou hath held, but what that plan is tis unknown. What didst thou do to cause her to hate thee for so long?"

Long minutes of silence stretched between them before Morgan answered his question. "I gained the love of a King." Lowering her gun, she laid flat on her back, placing the weapon on the nightstand beside the bed before she rubbed the bridge of her nose. "Danu, I've got a headache."

Watching her struggle to control her emotions over the news Lorne sat up, shifting his body until his back rested against the headboard and bent a knee. Stretching his neck side to side, he felt the bones pop and moved his eyes back to her nude form. She was definitely beautiful, too beautiful. Moving his gaze back up to her face, he realized she was watching him dispassionately.

"You're staring at me."

Frustrated, he shook his head and looked away. "Sorry..."

"No skin off my ass."

With a sigh, Lorne rubbed his jaw. "Listen to me. Lord Requiem thought thou needed to know. He warns for thee not to trust anyone, especially anyone from the Courts."

"I know better, Lorne. Trusting is not in my nature." Sitting up, she pushed herself to the edge of the bed. This was the second warning given to her in less than a week. Abruptly she stood and walked to the chair where her robe was draped over the back. Picking it up, she wrapped herself in the warm material, then turned back to him. "I need to think. Show yourself out."

Lorne stared at her unbelieving for a moment before he climbed out of bed. She was throwing him out, out of her bed, out of her house, after a great bout of sex. With a deep sigh, he got up and headed out of the bedroom, back down the metal staircase, and walked through her open living room to where his discarded clothes were sprawled about. Taking his time while he dressed, Lorne turned his attention to the great mural on the far wall, the painting of a woodland landscape. He was positive that the scenery was from somewhere within the ShadowedLands, the Ancient Ones' place of origin.

Slight movement from the corner of his eye caught his attention. He stared at the right of the painting, of a scene of a small pond nestled between a small grove of trees. Stepping closer to the mural, his eyes narrowed as he concentrated on the landscape, wondering what it was about the picture that caught his attention. Then he saw it. The water rippled. Stepping back in surprise, he blinked and narrowed his eyes again in wonder. Raising his hand, he carefully ran his fingertips over canvas and paint. Paintings like this were rare in the Courts, magickal artifacts that could transport their owner to another realm. Only those keyed to the magick could use it, otherwise it just remained a painting, though a rare and beautiful one.

Glancing back up to the open door at the top of the metal staircase, Lorne shrugged on his jacket, biting his bottom lip in thought. When Lord Requiem asked him to seek out the Morrigu in the mortal world, he never thought to get this close to her. He meant to find her, relay the message, and then get the hell out of there, for there were too many spies everywhere. The moment he set his eyes on her at the club, he couldn't resist doing more than warning her. Shaking his head at the situation, Lorne headed out, wondering what was going to happen next.

5

The next night Morgan sat at a table at the Inferno downing her usual scotch as she mulled over the information Lorne had given her during their more than interesting interlude. Why was the mysterious Dark Lord of Tech nDuinn interested in her welfare, she wondered. It had been hundreds of years since she had heard that name, much less thought of him. Ash blond hair, dark eyes, coldly handsome. Beyond appearance, she couldn't remember much more about him than that he worked at times for her Sire for the High Lord had always been a figure surrounded by myths.

After calling a waitress over to order another drink, she turned to watch her companion dance. The table Terri had found was prime, allowing them an excellent view of the interior of the room and from this area she could see who entered and exited, keeping an eye on everyone. The club itself was packed this night with the smell of bodies, smoke, and sex to an almost stifling degree. *Oh* by Ciara played overhead, her sultry voice steaming up the room as couples around the dance floor gyrated their bodies to the erotic rhythm.

Terri danced by herself, her hips bumping and grinding with a seductive ease in time with the beat as all around her horny men stared in the vain hope that she would, just by chance, give them the go ahead to claim her for a dance. She ignored them, of course, turning away instead to watch herself in the mirror as she smiled secretly at crushing their pitiful dreams. Gathering her long, dark hair in her hands, she caressed the sides of her neck and face, and then slowly ran a hand down her abdomen to her groin as if enticing an invisible lover to do the same. Lips in a seductive pout, eyes closed, Terri was a wildcat on the prowl.

Several of the men on the balcony near Morgan watched the dark-haired dancer, their eyes never leaving her sensuous body as it writhed in dancing ecstasy. Shaking her head in disgust Morgan looked away, gazing back out over the dance floor when her attention was caught by a man stalking out of the men's restroom. What caught her eye wasn't the fact he was strikingly handsome and built like the Rock, but because of the glamour of invisibility he wove around himself to keep from being detected by mortal eyes.

Hmmm.

She watched his eyes narrow as they swept over the crowded room, taking in all around him. The light from the strobes reflected off his eyes as he glanced around, the greenish tinge flashing from them reminding her of a feline stalking its prey in the setting sun. When he turned his head to watch a gorgeous blonde sashay by, she noticed a small tattoo on the side of his neck peeking out from under his dark hair. Leaning forward, she squinted her eyes, recognizing the mark as a slave brand from the Courts.

"What the hell?" Morgan muttered under her breath as she kept her eyes peeled on him. The man was a Were. In the Sidhe Court Weres were mortals that could change their shapes to those of a specific animal. Their kind usually bred wild, though were captured and taken as younglings to serve as pets and servants to the Court nobles. A majority of them were treated bad; those who caused trouble and could not conform to their new roles were sent to the pens to be later used as game for the Hunt of the Wild Ride during the harvest time. Apparently this one was owned by someone in the Courts, though which Court and by whom she wasn't sure. He was too far away for her to recognize the brand.

Her eyes quickly surveyed the surrounding area, searching for sign of the Were's master, but found nothing. Either he was under magickal restraints to keep him from running or he was highly trusted, in a position of standing with his owner. Leaning back in her seat again, Morgan studied him. He stood tall with dark hair that brushed over broad shoulders and wore a close-cut moustache and goatee. Black leather pants covered his thighs like a second skin as a thin black tee shirt stretched tightly across his muscled chest and abs.

Even from this distance, she could see he was impressive. The magnetism that radiated off of him was incredible, forcing her attention to stay rooted on him as her eyes followed his every move. The air surrounding him shimmered with a dark menacing aura that caused the crowd of dancers he walked through to part for his passage though they were unaware of his approach. The Were was a killer, of that she was sure. She'd recognize his ilk anyplace.

Lifting her glass to her lips for another drink, Morgan was curious as to why he was here. It was for no good, she was certain, remembering Lorne's warning of High Queen Moirethe's bounty on her head. Not that she really cared, but hey, this was her favorite club and she didn't want anything coming between her and her fun.

The stranger continued to stalk through the crowd as a leopard through the jungle, pulling his upper lip up in a snarl as a young man dressed in loose-fitting trousers and a silky blue shirt knocked into him. The young man turned to apologize then stumbled to a stop, looking confused when he saw no one. Ignoring the human, the Were's gaze raked the room in arrogance as if looking for his next prey. Muttering under his breath, he narrowed his eyes as he looked back out across the sea of people until his gaze met Morgan's.

The Were's eyes widened in surprise, his nostrils flaring as if he were seeking her scent above those in the club. Quickly his face went dark, erasing whatever emotion had just passed over it, before heading in a purposeful stride in her direction. When he reached the table, he stared boldly into her eyes.

"I hath been looking for thee, Morrigu," he stated, his voice low and strained with a bitterness that was surprising. He seemed familiar as something inside her tugged at a hidden memory, triggering…what she didn't know and it bothered her. She hated mysteries.

Keeping her silence as she shifted in her chair in case she needed to rise suddenly, Morgan lowered her hand to slide down to her boot and removed the knife she had hidden there before tucking it up behind her wrist. Better to be safe than sorry. The menace she sensed rolling off him from before now clashed against her own aura, causing the small hairs on the back of her neck to stand in warning.

The Were's golden eyes raked over her face as if memorizing every nuance, then narrowed as a dark grin tugged at his lips. Pulling out a chair, he turned it around, straddled it then sat down, resting his forearms on the back before leaning toward her. They stared at each other, ignoring the whirl of activity going on around them before he spoke again.

"Thou really dost not remember me." His statement came out in a rough whisper meant mostly for himself before deepening into a more aggressive tone. "How low the great and mighty Lady Death hath fallen." Deep laughter broke out from him, sounding as dark as the stormy sea.

Morgan's eyes flicked over his face, taking in the smug look that lazily crossed it. In an instant she knew this was a man that she intensely disliked, yet still found intriguing. It didn't help that his rich masculine scent wrapped around her like a fur stole. Morgan took another drink as she fought her body's reaction to him and kept her face blank. Was this the assassin the Queen sent after her? A Were to seduce her into letting her guard down? If so it wasn't going to work.

"Should I?"

The Were studied her for a few moments, then shook his head in disgust. "I wouldst hath never thought..." He cut off his comment, leaving his deep voice to echo in her ears. Chuckling, he wiped a hand over his face before looking back at Morgan as if she were a puzzle to be figured out. "Then allow me reintroduce myself. I am Malachi," he said as his eyes raked over her body, lingering on her breasts, "and so far I am not impressed with that which I see."

Definitely not. Irritation at the unwarranted insult flared within Morgan, sparking off her anger. "Fuck off, asswipe," she growled, glaring at him. What was this creature's problem? He acted like they knew each other, though she was certain they'd never met before. If he came here wanting to get his ass kicked, she'd be more than happy to oblige him.

"Maybe thou hath not lost it after all." He chuckled again. "All the pomp and glamour. What happened to the woman whose very presence demanded fear and respect?"

Tightening her grip on the knife, Morgan glared as the Were flashed a smile at her. She was sure that he knew what lay in her hand and didn't care. *Well, I'm not easily impressed either.*

Leaning his chair forward on two legs, Malachi grinned; his smirk cold and slightly evil as he studied her face. "What a pity…"

Before she could react to what she sensed from him, Malachi dived for her, knocking them both to the floor as he wrested the knife from her grasp. Finding herself trapped between the carpet and his hard body, Morgan glared up at him as he lay over her, her eyes narrowing into dangerous slits as he lowered his head till their lips almost met. She could feel his breath brush across her lips as he whispered in a husky tone, "Soft."

Morgan stared up into his eyes, surprised at his strength and speed, and felt herself drawn into the golden orbs while unconsciously her mouth opened as if inviting him to taste her. Something wove in the air around them, entwining and drawing her in until she had the strangest urge to kiss him, to feel those lips on hers, but a gasp of pain escaped her instead as he tightened his grasp, twisting the knife from her hand to drop it on the floor with a clatter. Though he was strong she was stronger but rather than put up a fight she decided to give him his way to see what he was about. So far it was all pomp and grandeur with no serious threat of harm and if he thought because she was weaponless that she was helpless then he had much to learn. A quirky grin lifted the corner of her mouth as she stared up at him and she relaxed her body. She watched as Malachi's eyes wandered down between them, zeroing in on her breasts pressed against his chest and felt the heat from his gaze grow stronger. The hold on her wrists tightened as he slowly lowered his body further on to hers, the pressure forcing the air out of her lungs to leave her breathless.

By the feel of his growing erection pressed hard against her thigh, Morgan could tell his body reacted as strongly to her as she did to him. Pressing his hips hard against her, he moved his face in lazy figure eights over hers, his nostrils flaring as if he was scenting something delicious. His eyes closed for a moment and smiled at what almost seemed like pleasure softened his face for a fraction of a second.

From him Morgan caught the lingering scent of alcohol underlined by a faint trace of blood. Under that a spicy musk and masculine aroma emanated, one that he wore like a badge and she found herself more than a little aroused in spite of her dislike of him. Her nipples hardened into tight little nubs, the sensation sending a shock of electrical currents to her groin, setting a small fire to ignite. Some Sidhe had been known to bed their pet Were though she had never been interested before. Now she could almost understand their weakness. Opening his eyes to glittering slits, Malachi drew in a deep breath through his nose, smelling her arousal.

"Feeling the heat, baby?" he asked with a wicked knowing grin, digging his hardness into her before letting go and standing up. Adjusting the tight bulge in front of his leather pants, he stared Morgan with a calculating look, then turned away.

Danu, Morgan swore as she stared up at him, remembering the feel of his size and the animalistic way he moved over her, betting he'd be great in bed. Knew he would be. She looked away, irritated at the way her thoughts were heading. This was not something she was interested in. To bed an animal…her lip curled in disgust as she sat up, rubbing her wrists. Damn creature, something was not right here.

Slowly getting to her feet, Morgan dusted her ass off with her hands before bending over to pick up her knife and sliding it back into the sheath in her boot. Feeling wary she studied Malachi as they sized each other up in the way gunslingers did in the old westerns. Still feeling the effects of his presence, Morgan's eyes narrowed with a dangerous glint as she regained her chair. Turning it around, she sat down, her whole body on edge and still excited from his nearness. Glancing around, she noticed the scene drew unwanted attention from several people close by. Ignoring the looks they gave her, she turned her eyes back to the Were. Fighting an invisible being in a crowded club was not a good idea.

From down below a scream erupted, drawing everyone's attention toward the far area in the vicinity of the restrooms.

"Oh my God, there's a dead man in here!"

Bouncers quickly wound their way through the crowd to check out the problem as several of the dancers stalled in their movements, turning to linger with morbid curiosity at the commotion. Before long the music cut, leaving the room in an odd silence compared to the blaring sounds that had filled it just moments before. Crowds gathered around as the houselights went up, causing more than a few people to swear at the sudden sharpness the light caused to their eyes. As a bouncer stepped back out of the restroom, he motioned to a waitress who frantically ran to the bar and called 911. Three other bouncers began ushering customers away from the area as sounds of grumbling and "What's going on?" filled the room.

Keeping her eyes glued to Malachi's face, Morgan watched him smile broadly, flashing her even white teeth with a hint of wicked-looking fangs in place of incisors.

"Tis a little late for that," he joked, though his eyes were void of any sense of humor. Licking his lips, he watched her reaction as if interested to see what his actions would produce. Instead of giving him what he wanted, Morgan looked toward the chaotic scene impassively.

Suddenly, as if from impulse, the Were reached out a hand toward her. From the corner of her eyes she watched, tense, until Terri's voice stopped his actions. Irritation flashed across Malachi's face as he lowered his arm.

"Oh my God, Morgan, did you see it? Someone died in the men's room. They think he was knifed, a drug deal gone bad." Terri grabbed her friend's shoulder, moving breathless beside Morgan as she peered over the crowd that was forming near the men's restroom. A few police officers stood around the door questioning people as others took up guard by the front entrance. It seemed this was going to be a long night. "The dumb ass is probably gonna get the club shut down for the night. Where the hell is my drink?"

Terri hadn't even noticed Malachi, her excited gaze directed toward the gathered people, but even if it wasn't she would have missed him anyway. He still wore his glamour of invisibility, hiding him from the eyes of everyone in the club but Morgan.

"Tis time for me to go, Morrigu." His eyes raked over Morgan's body once more, stopping when they reached her eyes. She thought she detected a longing there, but looking closer knew she must have been mistaken. All she saw in those golden orbs was contempt and irritation.

"What happened in there?" Morgan had asked, nodding to the men's room, noticing the crowd had dispersed to the sides of the club as more officers arrived. By this time the overhead lights where on, the music killed by the DJ and the noise level noticeably lowered. Terri answered her with an "I already told you, they think a drug deal gone bad," as she was drinking her tequila, but it was to Malachi the Sidhe was asking.

"A death." His words were matter-of-fact, explanation withheld. He stared directly into her eyes as if challenging her to make another comment. She wasn't about to get drawn in to a verbal fight with someone who wasn't 'there' in front of a mortal, friend or not.

"Huh," Morgan grunted, glancing sideways at Terri before glaring at a couple of guys who decided now was the time to come hit on the women. They caught the look and turned tail, which was good because at that moment she was more interested in doing violence than being asked her sign. With a heavy sigh, Morgan glanced away toward the restroom, finding the door was now propped open as an emergency team wheeled a stretcher into the room. From the angle they stood at Morgan could see two of the coroners squatting down beside a body, the thick soled booted feet pointed toward the door. Moving with expedience they worked in tandem, slipping the corpse into a large black plastic body bag.

Great, I could be here for hours, Morgan glanced back to Malachi. He was without a doubt someone to be wary of, irritatingly annoying and attractive in a highly erotic way. He was a killer and proud of it. That didn't bother Morgan; after all she lived around death her whole life and was an assassin by trade. Whatever it was that attracted her to him also repelled her. As if he had read her thoughts the Were met her eyes and smiled. Exasperated by the knowing look he gave her, she turned away and decided it was time to go. She needed to get home and check her thoughts, but in order to do so she needed to be able to leave without gathering the attention of the human law keepers.

First Lorne, now this guy. What the hell was going on? She wanted answers and her best bet was to find someone who could give them to her. Without a second thought Morgan muttered something under her breath to Terri about having a headache and needing a drink. Moving toward a throng of club goers hovering near the top of the stairs she wove her way through them, leaving

Malachi watching after her. With one last glance back, Morgan's eyes narrowed, meeting his with distrust before teleporting out of the midst of the humans she was gathered in.

6

The list of contacts for Morgan was limited. The few Court Sidhe that lived among the mortals, whether banished by the Kings or by their own will, was few and far between, and those that she got along with were even smaller. Eryn Sye, the thief that warned her in the first place, was unavailable or just not answering her summons, same as Lorne. As for Lord Requiem, she didn't know him well enough to risk revealing anything to. That left only two others—Sorrien, her ex-husband, or Lord Aeron, the last Mor'sin'dar banished from Court. That was like asking a prisoner how he wished to die. Boiling oil or the rack?

Unwilling to owe a favor to the man who was the cause of her banishment, Morgan decided Lord Aeron was the better choice of the two. Though the Mor'sin'dar Lord was a darkly handsome man, he was pure arrogance and bitterness, still angry that he had been banished to the mortal realm by King Silvas. Of course it didn't help that she was the one who removed him from the Courts—her and her sisters.

Normally she stayed far away from him, an uneasy truce they quietly agreed upon, but today she needed to breach it. She knew from his attitude when she called him that he was not happy, actually he was downright pissed at having to see her again, but tough shit. She needed to get information and he was the only one she knew with connections still in the Shadow Court; so as much as she disliked him, now was not the time to voice her opinions.

The next morning Morgan pulled her car into a parking spot, turned off the engine, and took a peek into the rearview mirror to verify her lipstick was still on her lips, and not on her teeth. After she was satisfied with her appearance, she climbed out of her Mustang before shutting the door firmly behind her.

With a quick tap, she locked her car door and headed into the gray stone high-rise located deep in downtown Portland. A bronze plaque outside hanging by the door informed all that entered that A & M Marketing and Research owned the building. Marketing and Research, huh? It seemed the High Lord of War made a career change.

After giving a quick check in with the security guard at the front desk, she moved to the steel door elevator and pushed the up button, then stood back to wait. A few people in the lobby glanced her way; several of them, mostly men, watched in appreciation.

At a ding, the elevator doors opened and several people stepped out, all in business casual. As the elevator vacated, Morgan entered, followed by two other people; a man appearing to be in his early to mid-thirties with dark well-groomed hair and a woman, slender and tall, in her late twenties. The woman's blond hair was well coiffed, placed over her head in a tight bun, giving her a strained appearance. One moved on either side of Morgan and as the elevator doors slid shut, they turned and faced the front.

Leaning back against the railing, she smirked and studied their reflections in the mirrored doors. Guards, was she that easy to spot these days? Ms. Pinched Face looked in pain, her blue eyes narrowed as she tried to appear nonchalant about being in the elevator, her tweed skirt tight around her thighs, making the Sidhe wonder if she recently had a weight gain. *Gotta lay off the Ho-Ho's,* Morgan chuckled to herself, meeting the anal-looking woman's eyes in the mirrored surface. Blowing her a small kiss, the assassin turned her attention to the elevator's other occupant.

The man beside her was less formal, instead watching Morgan watch him. He nodded at her, a shadow of a smile touching his lips as he looked appreciatory over her shapely form and he clasped his hands behind himself, standing at ease. He probably was ex-military from his looks. Tall, broad-shouldered, lean-waisted. As he shifted, the telltale sign of a gun bulged against the fabric of his coat. *Oh boy, guess I need to be good*, she chuckled. It seemed Lord Aeron was still careful, even living among the humans in the mortal world. She wondered if the bullets the guns held were made of cold iron.

Turning her eyes to her own reflection, Morgan studied herself. She was taller than the other woman by a good three inches. Her own dark hair gleamed in the elevator light, cascading over her shoulders to her slender waist, pulled back from her face by a set of Ray Bans sitting on top of her head and set off by several small gold hoop earrings that dangled from her ears. She wore a sleeveless embroidered vest, a deep burgundy with green and gold threading which gave her tanned skin a nice healthy glow. The vest pressed her breasts tightly together, giving her an over abundance of "blessings", which the man next to her used his height to take advantage of.

When Morgan shifted her footing, the crow-shaped charm on her belly ring caught the light and glittered against a smooth flat abdomen, accenting her heart-shaped hips. A tattoo of a scorpion with a beautiful purplish flower held in its claw rode the area before her right hipbone, and from as low as her low rider jeans clung to her, anyone with half a brain knew she was a waxing kind of gal. A male's diver watch and soft black leather stiletto heeled boots set off the outfit. Catching the guy's eye, Morgan winked at him, and then walked off the elevator as it beeped to announce they had arrived at their destination, her hips in full sway.

Stepping out into the foyer, she looked around, her "escorts" following her out but staying near the elevator as she moved to the reception desk. Running her tongue over her bottom lip to wet it, she leaned over the desk and flashed a smile.

"Morgan Crowe. I don't have an appointment."

The lady behind the desk, coldly blonde and polished, set a bland look on Morgan, reaching up to press a well-manicured nail on the headset she was wearing. "Mr. Warman is not available. You will need an appointment, Ms..."

"Crowe, and I don't need one." Flashing her teeth in a tight smile, Morgan headed down the richly decorated hall as the two guards from the elevator moved to apprehend her. With a thought, she set up a ward in the hall, preventing them from stepping forward and chuckled under her breath when she heard curses erupt behind her as they hit the invisible wall in force. In the distance she heard the receptionist speak soft and fast, warning Mr. Warman and calling for more security.

Let them try and drag my ass off. Morgan flashed a dark smiled as she pushed open the heavy iron doors that blocked off Lord Aeron's office from the reception area and then closed them firmly behind her with a loud clank. Walking across the dark marbled floor as if she had all the time in the world she glanced around the room, impressed by the décor. Though the room was kept dim and shadowed she knew it was done mostly out of effect on visitors than for anything else. A thick burgundy carpet sat on the cold floor; strange-looping sigils she recognized as a curse to the unwary in her native language dotted the lush fabric. A glossy onyx leather couch sat to one side, two chairs opposite it with a small low table between them. On one side was a stoned fireplace, a low blaze burning inside. Toward the end of the room, a heavy rosewood desk with two leather chairs sat in front. Lining the walls on the left of the room were bookcases and display shelves. On the left, a hazy mirror that may or may not have been enchanted by Sidhe magick. Behind the desk was a thickly-curtained floor to ceiling window. The curtains currently were pulled tight together. Much better than the stupid archaic stone and moat throne room of his keep in the ShadowedLands.

Reaching the giant rosewood desk with its heavy glass top, she stood before him, legs apart, hands on hips and stared at the dark Sidhe intently while she waited, impatient for him to acknowledge her. Slowly, he turned his attention from the secretary before his desk to her and with a brief gesture he dismissed the woman. After gathering up her notes the beautiful redhead left, closing the door behind her.

Morgan studied the man she had not seen since his removal and crooked a hip as she crossed her arms under her breasts. Other than wearing designer suits and having cut his hair to the latest style, Lord Aeron looked just the same as he did in Court, infuriatingly arrogant.

He sat reclined; his long legs crossed at the knee while using the same hand that dismissed his secretary with to brush back his thick black hair from a broad forehead. His dark eyes roamed over her body in a lazy caress, stopping only to linger on her prominently displayed breasts then continued up until they reached her eyes as a tight smile curved his lips.

"Well, well, well. What brings the beautiful Morrigu to my humble Hall?"

Shifting in his seat, Aeron leaned farther back into its shadowy recesses as he watched her under hooded eyes. Shadows hid half his handsome face from her view, leaving to sight only a pair of sensuous lips and a cleft chin. Two small golden embers glowed from the darkness, giving an adequate idea of where his eyes were. They disappeared for a brief moment and then reappeared as he blinked.

Drawing in a deep breath, Morgan worked on trying to keep calm. It seemed that anytime she'd been in his presence all she wanted to do was break something. Apparently time had not changed those feelings. "I want you to do something for me." At another blink of his eyes, she continued. "Do you still have contact with the Hounds Master?"

Berith the Hounds Master, bred and raised the hunting mastiffs the Mor'sin'dar used in their Wild Hunts. The enormous green-furred hounds known as the Cusith were relentless hunters, feared for their veracity and viciousness when it came to their prey. They never gave up the hunt nor could those they chased escape them.

"Why would you come here to ask me about the Hounds Master?" He shifted in his seat, raising a large hand to cradle his chin. "You really shouldn't get involved with Court mess again. It's just a bit of free advice I'm giving."

"I'm not asking. The Court mess came to me. I was happy in my life but Queen Moirethe couldn't leave well enough alone. And now I find out King Silvas is dead. How come no one told me? I had to find out the hard way." She bit the inside of her lip, trying to keep from flinging insults when he abruptly stood up to move around the desk and into her personal space.

Morgan was nearly six-foot but Aeron stood a few inches taller, leaning his face toward hers as he watched her expressions. She could tell he was trying to intimidate her, expecting her to step back but hell, she never did what was expected. Instead she stared up at him, daring him to do something more. She wasn't intimidated by some spoiled pussy boy, not when he drew her into the fighting circle, not when she removed his hand with his own blade. From all appearances, he re-grew a new one. That or he had the old one reattached.

"Back the fuck off me, asshole or I'll take you down." She lowered her voice to a soft whisper. Most who have heard that knew better than to tempt fate, but some idiots never learn. Personally she thought the warning was clear. But then again, perhaps it wasn't.

"You still think you're better than the rest of us, don't you? Silvas's favorite." He circled around Morgan, keeping close enough that she could feel his hot breath on the back of her neck. "So beautiful, so soft, yet underneath lays as much rot as the rest of us. Just because you're the Battle Crow doesn't mean you're immune to life's simple lessons."

The cocky look on Aeron's face set Morgan's blood to boiling. No one looked at her like shit and walked away without limping. He purposefully drew this response out of her as he did the day so long ago of the challenge. Still riding on the emotions from her encounter with the Were Malachi, she refused to heed her own warning and reached out to grab his shoulder, intending to stop him, but in a swift move he caught her wrist, turned, and spun her around to pull her close to his hard body.

"Never forget, little girl, I am a High Lord and you stand within my Hall." His voice sounded harsh in her ear as he brushed his lips against the sensitive place behind it. "The essence of death as granted by your father may run deep in your blood, but you have not yet stepped into your full power. So, until you do…" Morgan felt his tongue, warm and sensual, run from behind her ear to trace her jaw before a crack echoed through the chamber and a sharp pain radiated from her wrist. "Remember this lesson. You are not all powerful."

Morgan cried out in pain and shock before returning the blow with one of her own. Balling up her fist, she pulled her arm back and slammed it hard into his jaw. The blow knocked his head back, the force enough to snap any normal man's neck, but a Sidhe is not normal. Instead she dislocated his jaw, driving it out to an angle. Aeron let out a harsh breath of air, stumbling back, though the hold on her wrist was still strong.

At that moment the doors to the chamber blew off the hinges, shattering the heavy five-inch thick iron into pieces as they flew across the room. They turned in unison, surprised at the interruption and watched as the Were from the other night strode in, his eyes narrowed in fury before he turned golden orbs to Morgan. She stared at him in surprise as he nailed the High Lord with a black glare that spoke volumes.

"Leave her alone, Lord Aeron. The deal was made, so walk away now."

Deal? Morgan's eyes shot to the tall Sidhe beside her as she jerked her broken wrist out of the High Lord's grip. *What in Danu's name was going on? Why was Malachi here and what deal was he talking about?*

"I did not summon you, animal," Aeron spit out before popping his jaw back into alignment, rubbing at the bruise quickly growing there. He shot a venomous sideways glace at Morgan before turning his attention back to the furious Were.

Holding her arm close to her body, Morgan glared back at Aeron before turning. "I take it you two know each other?" she growled between gritted teeth as the bones in her wrist began moving under skin, connecting together to right themselves. Looking between the two men, she backed away from the Mor'sin'dar High Lord, feeling her senses come to full alert. Rubbing her wrist, she wiggled her fingers to make sure her hand worked properly before moving it behind her to grasp the familiar butt of her SIG Sauer.

Rather than listening, Malachi stepped in front of her, his eyes flickering over her face before narrowing menacingly on the handsome dark-haired Sidhe. "What happened to her?"

Aeron rubbed his hand over his jaw, sneering. "Don't use such a disrespectful tone with me, anima..."

A deep inhuman growl rose from Malachi, cutting off anything further the Sidhe was about to say. "I asked what happened to her!"

Aeron's eyes narrowed, his expression thoughtful as if debating whether or not to further push the furious man before him. Something in his eyes sharpened at some thought, and then he tightened his lips in a blunt line. Morgan's eyes narrowed as she watched, prepared to pull her weapon when needed. What was said next surprised her. The haughty Sidhe cleared his throat. "We had a minor misunderstanding, that's all."

His tone was polite, almost respectful. What the hell was that? A Sidhe Lord much less a High Lord back down to a Were? Something was definitely not kosher was going on.

With a quick motion of his hand, Malachi once again cut him off. "If thou doth touch her again, no one can save thy sorry ass from a slow and painful death. Remember, even the immortals are mortal after a certain point."

"Yes," the Mor'sin'dar Lord repeated, "mortal after a certain point. Words you would do well to remember."

Ignoring the Were's implied threat, Aeron walked casually behind Morgan before moving toward a small iron wrought table. She moved aside to keep both men in view as she watched the scene before her play out. There was no way Aeron would tow down to a Were unless the assassin's master had something over him or was someone of importance. She was liking this lesser and lesser by the second. A soft *clink* reached her ears as the High Lord lifted a crystal carafe from the table top. He swirled the ruby liquid within the decanter then lifted the stopper, a brief smile dancing across his lips.

"The Morrigu came to me, saurar." *(disgusting one).*

Malachi took this time to turn his head to look at her. "Go home, Lady Morriganna," he growled between his teeth. "Thou should not have come here. Tis dangerous for thee."

A dark eyebrow rose as Morgan stared at the handsome Were in disbelief. "Dangerous...for me? Who in the Nine Hells do you think you're talking to?" With a jerk of her head toward Aeron she continued. "This pussy boy doesn't have the balls to carry on any of his threats."

A snorting sound reached her ears as she watched Aeron from the corner of her eyes. The Sidhe ignored her, instead pouring a small glass of the elixir, setting the bottle back down and picking up the glass. With a shake of his dark head he moved over to sit back behind his desk to watch. *Yeah, hope you get some enjoyment out of it, buster. I'm not done with you yet.*

"Go home, Lady Morriganna," Malachi ordered her, his posture stiff and tone sharp.

With a cold stare as her answer, Morgan felt her temper rise at his insistence. Who the hell did he think he was? She had questions that needed to be answered, needed to find out how King Silvas died, who were these enemies she was supposed to be on guard for, and what Queen Moirethe was up to. No woman has ever ruled the Mor'sin'dar and the fact that not a single High Lord objected to Queen Moirethe's ascension to supreme ruler was baffling. She knew the Queen would send assassins after her and that didn't bother her, but this?

"You need to leave here, Were. No one asked you to come and this meeting is private." She stared him down, a silent war of wills until finally Malachi flexed his jaw and looked away angrily.

"Crow," Aeron spoke, catching her attention. She flicked her gaze sideways at him, peering through narrowed eyes to watch his lips as he spoke in an almost hissing manner. "What is your dealing with Queen Moirethe's assassin? I didn't realize you were now in league with her."

Morgan's eyes snapped back to the lone Were. He belonged to Queen Moirethe? That answered why he was looking for her, but why was he here now? Why so insistent she leave? Obviously there was something going down between him and the High Lord and it had to do with her but what? Letting out a slow cleansing breath, she tried gathering her thoughts to answer. Aeron was no friend of Queen Moirethe's but neither was he a friend of hers. For years before her banishment, she and the High Lord fought, battling in words and weapons but his own hatred of the Queen was well known. Why, no one knew, but rumors had spread that he rejected Queen Moirethe's advances and whatever she said to King Silvas was enough to get Aeron banished from the Courts. Her eyes flickered back to Malachi.

The Were's face was furious, restraint holding back his tongue as he fought for control of his volatile nature. "If thou break the bargain, I shall hunt down thy family and I shall send them back to thee in tiny fucking pieces."

The High Lord's body stiffened from the threat. "I'm not an idiot, saurar. I know they are already dead." Casually strolling around the desk, he moved back behind Morgan, glancing calming at the gun gripped in her hand before leaning his head down until his lips reached her ear. His voice lowered to a whisper, bitter and harsh. "Be careful who you trust, Lady Death, but know there are still some in Court who believe the Morrigu will one day return and save them and so they watch out after you."

Morgan's jaw clenched at Aeron's warning, at the words she had heard so many times before. Malachi's eyes narrowed even more, glinting like a sharp, deadly knife as his pupils narrowed to slits. His entire body went still as he watched them, knowing the Sidhe whispered something to her that he couldn't hear. Feeling the Mor'sin'dar Lord smile as he pressed his lips to her shoulder, she wondered what games were being played in that room, for she could feel his attention was fully on the Were before them.

Sliding his body around her, Lord Aeron walked back to his desk and sat back down in the deeply cushioned leather chair. Bringing his drink to his lips, he nodded his head slightly, eyes studying her emotionless face.

"I believe this meeting is over. You can see yourself out."

With a sharp nod to him, Morgan tucked her gun back in its holster and then turned on her heel. Ignoring the questioning look on Malachi's face, she headed out of the office, pausing only when the High Lord called out to her.

"I'll ask if he wants to speak to you."

Keeping her back to them, she nodded and stiffened as she left the room, leaving Malachi and Aeron behind.

7

The stone walls around Lord Requiem rumbled with anger as he stalked down the dark corridors of the Mor'sin'dar Court with purpose. Reigning in his mood,knowing it affected his surroundings, the High Lord of Tech nDuinn walked with purpose, his thoughts focused on one thing and one thing only; the summons from Queen Moirthe. Irritation washed through him at the memory of the command delivered to him after breaking his morning fast. The scroll's wording, so tightly clipped, requested, no demanded his presence immediately. Jaw clenched tight, the Dark Lord breathed deeply, transforming his exterior once more into the icy aloofness he was well known for.

Toward the end of the hall a door opened as a small group from Queen Moirethe's elite Hunters appeared, causing those traveling in the closed-kept corridor to quickly change course or risk running into them. Ignoring the smug and haughty looks on the men's faces, Requiem continued along his way, determined to make his meeting on time without interference from those obnoxious Hunters. Weaving his magick around his body like a cloak, he muttered under his breath while he became incorporeal and continued his pace. As if he were a ghost the High Lord ignored them along with the other citizens and creatures of Fae that shared the dark passage, and moved through their bodies as if they didn't exist except as a soft whisper in their minds. The icy touch of his presence caused the Hunters to pause in their step and shiver, feeling the Lord of the Dead travel through their very souls before they resumed their conversation and headed to their own destination with a disturbed look on their faces.

Along the ebon walls dark gargoyles clung, their skin glistening with an oily substance. They turned their heads to follow the High Lord's passage as light flickered off them from torches held captive in thick iron brackets set high above the heads of those that passed by below them. Heavy woven wall hangings decorated the dark halls, muting the harshness of the place and dulling the murmuring of those that spoke. Deep in his thought, Requiem just barely missed stepping a tiny winged being as he lowered a heavy shod foot. The tiny creature raised its harpy like face to swear and waved a fist up in the air, before looking up at who it offended. With a deep gulp, its mottled complexion blanched when it saw whom it cursed. Quickly, it scampered off into the shadows and chattered blessing to the High Lord for paying it no mind.

Twin iron doors stood at the end of the great hall, opening of their own accord as Requiem neared them. Fae and Were servants scattered out of his way as he slowed his approach and sauntered toward a large ebon throne that took up most of the back wall. The beautiful woman reclining on it glanced at him, waved a hand to excuse a frightened servant, and then lifted a glass goblet filled with blood red wine to her lush, ruby lips. Narrowing his eyes, the High Lord watched the Queen take her time to drain the glass then dab at the corner of her mouth with a dainty silk napkin before giving him her attention.

"Dost thou need something, Lord Requiem?" Queen Moirethe's soft voice filled the great chamber. She motioned with her empty glass around the room and the retainers within, a droll look on her beautiful face. "Canst thou not see I am busy?"

The High Lord raised a dark eyebrow. "Thou wert the one requesting my presence. I shall try not to take up much of thy valuable time." Stepping forward he lifted a hand, holding out a rolled parchment which was tied with a black silk ribbon.

Queen Moirethe glanced at the offered paper then motioned to a servant. The Were, an older looking male with graying hair, quickly scrambled forward to take it from Requiem and rushed back to his Mistress's side.

Clasping his hands behind his back, Requiem waited, keeping his face clear of any emotions that might betray his true thoughts about the woman. *Bitch, play thy games with someone else. I do not have time for thy pathetic posturing.* As one of the elders in the Mor'sin'dar Court, he was deeply disturbed by the trouble this woman was creating. Already the other High Lords were in deep discussion about whether to confront the Queen about her unwillingness to step down and allow one of her son's to claim the throne. Such a thing should have been done the moment the body of King Silvas had been discovered in the tunnels below.

"I went to the Isle of Bone today." Moirethe unrolled the parchment, glancing over the fine script, then re-rolled it and handed it back to her servant to put away.

"I know."

The Queen cast him a sharp look at his admittance.

"The Cauldron Witch *is* my sister." Requiem's smile was tight.

"Did she mention why I wanted her?"

"Should she have?"

Queen Moirethe narrowed her green eyes and frowned as the High Lord stood like an Arctic statue in front of the throne. He met her gaze with a challenge, daring her to question him further on the subject. It amused him, her anger. The high tilt of her chin, the tightening of her mouth and the fact that he knew she feared him. Gathering the shadows of the dim room closer about him, Requiem stood in silence as the Queen struggled to keep dominance in the meeting. Her back stiffened, nostrils flaring as she looked down upon him. The Death Lord waited in patience, his hands loose at his sides and watched the marid of expressions cross the beautiful blonde's face, then her eyes narrowed, jaw setting in a stubborn angle.

The two Sidhe stared at each other, silently facing off as neither was willing to concede to the other. Suddenly Queen Moirethe sat up in her throne, swinging her legs in front of her as she grasped the arms of the hard chair with clenched fingers.

"Dost thou not hath something else to do now?"

"Why did thou summon me?"

"Because I could." Moirthe smirked.

"Perhaps thou should be more wise on who thou dost summon in the future. Not all High Lords are as patient as I." A slight smile lit Requiem's lips, revealing a dimple in his cheek. He inclined his head, took a step back, before abruptly turning on his heel. As the smug look on the Queen's face fell, a knowing chuckle erupted from the Dark Lord. He strode out of the throne room to leave the Queen fuming but the heavy doors of the throne room closed behind him, cutting off her curses.

Martinet, Requiem's twin brother, stood waiting outside the throne room. Both were tall and well built but where Requiem wore his ash blond hair shoulder-length, Martinet wore it close-cropped. Where the first was clean-shaven, the second wore a well-trimmed beard. Where the Lord of Death favored black, the Sleeping Lord dressed in rich colors.

"Thou art a hard man to find." Martinet fell into step with his brother as he walked down the corridor.

"I hath been busy. My work is never ending."

"As thou say. I go hunting for the weekend with a few of the Lords and thought to ask the High Lord of the Mnishai to join us." He looked at his twin. "Dost thou wish to join us?"

"Busy. I shall be in and out of Court. There tis something I am looking into. Go ask Prince Khelvan, for he is a good falconer."

Martinet choked at the suggestion. "Thy humor is amusing. The Royal son is a pampered prick. To ride with him would be to play to his ego and we hath no time for a spoiled son of Queen Moirethe." Shaking his blond head in disgust, he continued. "Already he races to seek allies for his bid for the throne. King Silvas left his Court a mess by dying with no pronounced heir."

"I am fairly sure the King looks out from Mag Mall and curses the inconvenience his death has caused for everyone involved. Now, brother, I really am in a hurry. Can we talk later?"

Nodding his head, Martinet slowed his step. "Tis no problem."

With a heavy sigh Requiem stopped and turned back to his twin, recognizing the irritation in his voice. Putting his stormy mood aside, he placed a hand on his brother's shoulder. "Forgive my harsh words, Martinet, for I do not mean to make light of thee. Truly, tis just…I need to be elsewhere and I need to make arrangements in order to be there."

Spotting movement farther down the dark hall, the High Lord kept the area in the corner of his eye as he looked at his brother. "Thou canst reach me anytime, but what I am wanting to do…tis very important, to me and for the Court."

"As thou say, brother."

Martinet nodded and stepped aside as Requiem passed by him. As the Death Lord continued down the hall his mind whirled with the rumors that spread through the Court. Many whispered about the break in tradition the Queen had taken after her husband's death and about the nature of the King's demise, rumors of her participation. It also spread about the Princes and how they were plotting to take the throne for themselves, as they should, but the Queen had many friends, allies that throughout the years she had managed to buy, seduce, or threaten to gather their cooperation.

Rumors also spread of strangers within the Halls, strangers connected to a guest of Queen Moirethe who appeared not long after King Silvas's unpredicted death. Chaos reigned now that the King was dead, the Court all in a shambles but a few spoke of recalling the Morrigu to discover how the King had died and to see if any had a particular hand in it. Just the thought of the assassin who was beloved of the King caused Requiem to pause his thoughts and contemplate his own fixation with her. After the Lady Morriganna's banishment the Thulath charged him with watching over his only child, a task he did with misgivings, but over the years misgivings became intrigue for he saw a side that no other had seen of the stubborn woman. Because of the magical bond her father had set between them, unknowingly for the Morrigu, Requiem experienced the varied stages of anger, loss and loneliness she went through from banishment. He found a kindred spirit and one who drew his interest beyond mere guardianship. An interest that the lady's father would not approve.

He pondered the message Lorne had left him about finding the Lady Morriganna, her wariness of strangers and they way she interrogated him about why he was there. There was more that his servant had not revealed about the meeting and that disturbed him. Lorne was brought back from Annwn for one reason and one only, to warn the Morrigu of the brewing trouble that was circling her, not to become involved romantically. Soon the Sidhe would have to return to the place he was brought from for his time was borrowed only. A flicker of jealousy rose, causing the Dark Lord's jaw to clench as he pushed those thoughts aside. The Lady Morriganna was a woman grown and the choices she made were her own. Glancing back at the closed doors to the throne room, the Lord of the Mnishi mentally winced at the continuous ranting of Queen Moirethe that permeated through the stone halls.

The shadow down the hall moved again, peering from around a stone gargoyle. Beckoning the small figure forward, Requiem sent forth a spark of magick and forced it closer against its will. It struggled then gave up, gliding across the floor by the High Lord's power. Recognizing the figure from earlier and realizing it was one of Queen Moirethe's little spies, he didn't bother to ask who sent it or why. Instead without a thought, Requiem snuffed out its life force and caused the smoky essence of its soul to flow into a small glass globe he produced from thin air to be later questioned, before slipping it into his shirt pocket.

With a final nod to Martinet, Requiem stood, grim-lipped, and disappeared leaving his brother alone in the dark halls of the Mor'sin'dar.

~~~

From a heavily-draped corner of the Queen's chambers, a sultry figure moved out of the shadows. With a brief smile turning up the corners of her lips as she leisurely moved toward Moirethe, the woman reached for a crystal goblet of dark wine that was offered to her by one of the Were slaves.

"Do you think he suspects?" She asked, her voice low and husky, almost a purr.

Moirethe turned her head to glance at the redhead before looking back at the closed doors. "Lord Requiem is full of himself if he believes his opinions hold much value." With a swish of her rich velvet skirts, the Queen of the Mor'sin'dar moved to the fireplace, rested her hand on the mantel, and stared into the flickering flames dancing within. "I do not care what he suspects. There is nothing he can do in the first place. Let the fool think what he will. I am the Queen and my word is law."

"And thy children?" Taking a sip of the wine, the redhead watched the Queen under lowered lids, giving her the appearance of being bored and nonchalant.

"What of them? They will do as I demand; after all, I am their mother besides being their Queen."

"Thy youngest will follow thee blindly, but the two oldest, not so I think."

Tilting her head to glance at her visitor, Moirethe narrowed her eyes dangerously. "Viraska, thou came here to offer thy services to rid me of the Morrigu, not to interfere in family business. Limit thy thoughts and opinions."

A soft smile caught Viraska's lips. "I beg pardon, thy Highness. Thou art correct, business at hand. But..." She trailed off as she set her goblet down on a tabletop before settling in a nearby chair. "There is a favor I must ask thee, about payment for our arrangement."

"Yes," the Queen said, watching the Bone Hag with caution, "payment. What is it that thou requests?"

With a smile, Viraska steepled her fingers and smiled, leaning back in the plush brocade of the chair.

8

Malachi's heavy black boots echoed resounding thuds through the corridor as he walked through the Lower Hall of the Shadows, his mind storming over events of the past few days. His surprise at how quick he found the woman he was sent to locate relieved him from what to report to his Queen. She had sent him out to find the Morrigu only a few weeks earlier and worried at what to tell the temperamental Queen if he should fail, but imagine his surprise at finding her at the very location his informant had insisted on meeting him at.

Too bad the human was past his usefulness. Instead of supplying Malachi with anything useful, all he did was try to coerce him into shelling out more money for information that was old and misinformed. A quick dagger to the gut stopped that problem, and instead of returning to the Courts empty-handed he was able to report he located the woman his Queen sought.

The only problem now was the knowledge that the Morrigu had visited Lord Aeron. Why she sought out that prick was beyond him. Rumor had it that she was the one that dispelled the haughty Lord from the Courts by King Silvas's command and that he was not fond of the assassin. In fact, he was supposed to despise her. Finding the Battle Crow in the Sidhe Lord's office, Malachi did the only thing he could think of—barge in and disrupt the private meeting. *Queen Moirethe will not be pleased.* He ground his teeth together as he mulled over what Lord Aeron told him after Morriganna left the Sidhe's office.

Slowing his steps, Malachi became aware of a tension set in the Halls as he passed the other Weres. A few leaned against the walls and spoke quietly among themselves, but quieted to watch when he passed by. Thrusting all thoughts of Lady Morriganna and the Sidhe Lord from his mind, Malachi concentrated on what was going on around him. As loud footsteps caught behind him, he turned around, seeing Claude, a fellow assassin in Queen Moirethe's service.

"Malachi, I hath been looking for thee. The High Queen hath summoned thee and she wants thee in her chambers immediately."

Malachi narrowed his amber eyes and flared his nostrils. "What does that bitch want now?"

"I am not sure, but it may have to do with thy disappearance." The young Were stepped back from his leader as Malachi turned sharp on his heel and grabbed the assassin's shirt in his fist, pulling the young man's face closer to his own.

"My disappearance?" he growled out. "What rumors are being spread?" He could barely contain his growing fury. Only gone for a few weeks and already he was sure rumors spread through the Halls like wildfire as others sought to take his place.

"Na...na...nothing, sir. The High Queen tis just anxious to have her favorite back in Court and she called for thee as soon as it was known that thou hath returned." He paused at the fierce look in Malachi's eyes, then swallowed and continued. "Not long before now the High Queen called for High Lord Requiem. They spoke in her chambers for a bit, then the High Lord left the Court. The High Queen is furious. Tis then she demanded thy presence before her. I came as quick as I could locate thee."

The young Were stumbled back as Malachi let him go with a rough shake. Turning on his heel, he headed to the High Queen's chambers with a purposeful stride.

After announcing himself and waiting for admittance, Malachi entered Queen Moirethe's chambers and looked around. Several servants were patching a few tiles on the walls and a floor to ceiling mirror was shattered. The High

Queen was screaming at an underling, who was in turn cowering on the floor before his Mistress's feet.

With a quick glance around the chamber, Malachi quenched his anger before making his way to Queen Moirethe and lowered himself to one knee, head bowed in supplication. As he waited in silence to be noticed, his thoughts grew chaotic as he became more unsure about how this meeting would go. The High Queen's temper was blazing, the troublesome Lord Requiem's visit obviously ending bad. Holding his silence, he watched the servant before him quake in fear then flinch as the icy beauty struck the male with an open hand. The resounding sound of the slap rang through the chamber.

"Out of my sight or I shall hath thee executed."

"Yes, thy Highness," the servant stammered, skittering away from the raging woman. He hurried from her chambers, keeping his head bowed and shoulders hunched as he left.

Taking a deep breath, Queen Moirethe closed her eyes and stood still. Malachi watched her beautiful face calm, the anger fade to be replaced by a peaceful façade. After several heartbeats, she opened her eyes and turned her dark green gaze upon the supplicant Were.

"Malachi, I hath been waiting for thee."

"Highness, I came as soon as I was given word." Malachi's eyes followed the beautiful woman as she moved gracefully to a comfortable looking chair, padded in deep wine velvet. It sat before a fire enclosed by a gorgeous filigreed metal screen, the dancing flames behind it creating abstract shadows along the wall. She sat, leaning back as she tilted her head to the side, a sly smile crossing lush lips.

"I hath missed thee, my pet." Stretching out her long legs before her, she motioned to a servant with a wave of her finger. Hurrying forward the female

Were offered a crystal goblet filled with a pale rose liquid. Raising it to her lips, Queen Moirethe took a sip, and then rested the cup on the arm of her chair, her fingers playing along the stem. "So report. Tell me what hath transpired since thou wert last in my presence?"

Swallowing a lump in the back of his throat, Malachi pushed his personal thoughts aside and kept his tone even and respectful. "I found her, thy Highness, and made contact, but she is very wary of all strange to her. She knows that I am thine."

"Of course she does." Queen Moirethe sipped at her wine again, teasing Malachi by licking the edge of the goblet with the tip of her tongue. She smiled as he watched every movement of her mouth. "But now thou must show thy true mettle and get her to invite thee into her home and bed. Twill be interesting to see how good an actor thou canst be. In order for what I have planned, thou must be in her bed." She turned sharp eyes to her assassin. "Is that not correct, my pet?"

"That is correct, thy Highness."

Holding out her glass for the servant to gather, she stood up and walked over to her personal assassin. Watching as she reached out her hand to brush her fingers through his thick, black hair, Malachi remained perfectly still, holding his breath as he tried to judge his Queen's mood. One never knew what action she might take—one minute icy calm, the next striking as a coiled viper. So far she seemed mellow, almost pleased with his responses.

A dark smile gathered up the corners of her mouth as a chuckle escaped her throat. Curling her fingers, she continued to play with the silky strands of his hair before the gentle touch turned violent. Her fingers twisted, gathering the strands in a tight hold as she jerked his head back so his golden eyes met her cold green ones. "Who are those still allied with her, my pet?"

"A minor Lord by the name of Eryn Sye."

"And has he contacted her yet?"

"That I know not, thy Highness." He resisted gritting his teeth from the pain, carefully keeping his handsome face neutral.

"Find out." Releasing him, she walked over to the stone fireplace to stand before the dancing flames. The glowing waves illuminated the pale dress she wore, giving a gently shaded outline of her slender figure to all behind her. "Is there anything else thou needs to tell me?"

Warning bells went off in Malachi's head. "Only that she had also visited High Lord Aeron. What they spoke of I have not knowledge, for when I had arrived they wert in the midst of an argument." *What all does she know?* Queen Moirethe had spies everywhere, but still…

A niggling feeling entered the back of his brain as he thought of the Morrigu. The woman was attractive as all Sidhe were, beauty to rival the Queen herself. To admit anything he might think or feel about the Queen's enemy was a weakness he could never show. Shoving his wayward thoughts away, he moved his attention quickly back to his Queen.

"Thou art not doing thy job very well, Malachi. I sent thee and thee only for one reason, because thou dost get the job done, no matter what." Turning to face him, her icy beauty was breathtaking. With a regal lift of her chin she held her head aloft as she leveled her eyes on his face. "I want her preoccupied. I want her so enamored of thee that nothing else matters. Others seek to bring her back and that must not happen."

"She is resilient, thy Highness." A flash of anger crossed the Were's face for a split second. "But she showed a slight curiosity in me."

"Curiosity?" Delight filled Queen Moirethe as clear crystal laughter echoed in the chamber. "Thou meanest attraction." Watching him carefully, her eyes narrowed before she walked to a large golden desk. Opening a small lacquered box on the top, she pulled out a vial, holding it up between her finger and thumb to show him the softly glowing bluish liquid. "Take this." She held it out for him.

Standing, the Were made his way to the regal Queen and took the vial from her. Studying it, he raised an eyebrow in question.

"The first chance thou hath, slip this into her food or drink." A dark smile split her lips, showing even white teeth. "It will cause her little attraction to grow and make her more...docile ." Reaching into the box again she pulled out another small vial, this time one filled with a thin white powder. Handing it to the Were she raised her eyes to his, a sly look crossing her face. "And this one will insure a pregnancy."

Malachi stilled. Catching himself, he slowly slipped the vials into a pocket, his mind racing. A pregnancy? Why would...? Malachi swallowed and nodded. A child of his? Never had he thought he would be allowed to mate and have a child, but why with the Morrigu? What game was his Queen intending on playing? "Is there anything else, thy Highness?"

"No, thou art dismissed. Do not fail me, Malachi."

"Never, thy Highness." With a bow, the Were headed out of the chamber only to be stopped as she spoke again.

"Oh, by the way. I have decided to loan thy services to another for the duration of this task. From now on, thou will report to her until I have notified thee otherwise. Is that understood?"

Squaring his shoulders, Malachi's lip curled in anger. With a sharp nod of his head, he left the room and headed down the hall, ignoring the looks from servants who scattered at his approach.

Loaning his services? To someone else? Rage filled him as he headed down to the Weres lair and the alchemist that resided there. While he walked, he pulled the vial of powder from his pocket and looked at it. If a Sidhe female became pregnant from a non-Sidhe lover, she was humiliated and banished until the child was born. What happened to it was up to the mother. Sometimes the infant was either abandoned, left to the elements, or taken by another. Very rarely was the baby raised by the mother herself. If the Sidhe was the father, interest was never shown, for unless it was full-blooded Sidhe, it wasn't worth another thought. Lady Morriganna was already banished. What would impregnating her do to her but make her pregnant for several months? The thought of his child being abandoned…

Replacing the vial back in his pocket, Malachi growled. He knew that the High Queen's ultimate goal was to see her enemy humiliated and destroyed. Though banished, the Morrigu still had a few allies, and having her pregnant by a Were, Queen Moirethe believed the prejudiced Sidhe would turn on the assassin like rabid dogs. Even those she could count on as friends would reproach her about giving birth to such abominations. Once Lady Morriganna lost the few allies she had, there would be no one to object to her imprisonment and eventual death.

As he entered the alchemist lair, Malachi shoved aside his disturbed thoughts and ordered a cologne he could use to accentuate his natural pheromones. If he was ordered to seduce the Morrigu it was best to go in fully armed. After that he headed off to his personal chambers to bathe and rest before searching for his new Mistress.

9

Leaning over the paint-faded railing around the lion's den, Morgan stretched her neck to get a better view of the fierce cats eating their midday meal. The large golden beasts sunk their teeth into the carcass, ripping off large chunks of bloodied meat before lazily chewing the pieces, ignoring the crowd above watching them with morbid fascination. She liked watching the lions, liked watching the easy strength of their muscles stretch and flex under their hide with each subtle move they made.

"Thou wished to speak with me?" A deep male voice reached her ears, rich with honey and a soft Courtly accent.

Shifting her eyes, the first thing that caught Morgan's attention was a tightly-wrapped scroll in his large hand. The second was a cowboy hat that tilted down over his brow, shielding his eyes from the overhead sun. The Sidhe's lips tightened in a grim line as his dark gaze fixed upon her face and settled his forearms to rest on the iron railing, shoulders hunched.

Her eyes traveled down his body, taking in his lean frame under tight faded blue jeans, dark brown cowboy boots, and a black tee shirt that stretched over his chest and broad shoulders. Silvery hair brushed his shoulders, looking soft enough to want to run your hands through. The silver was not from age, though the Lord of Beasts was ancient in years, but the sort of metallic silver that brought thoughts of wealth from men and women alike, inviting all who viewed it to covet. But the expression on his face was not inviting, far from it. In fact, he looked mean enough to jump down in the lair below and join the lions for a bite to eat.

"Thanks for agreeing to meet with me, Lord Berith."

The Hounds Master growled low in his throat, his eyes never leaving the scene below as he slid the rolled paper along the railing. "Even gone thou still cause mischief with the Courts, Lady Death."

Reaching down for the scroll, Morgan took it before looking over the information held within. "Not my problem. I held my end of the punishment."

With a slight shrug, Berith rubbed his jaw, a thoughtful expression on his handsome face. "Since King Silvas's demise the Queen placed in her bid of power. She refuses to give up the throne and let one of her sons step up. Instead she sits back in her chair and watches the rivalry and politics. A war is brewing in the Court as the Queen and her supporters fight to keep her position." Eyes shifting until they lit on the woman next to him, the Hounds Master's voice lowered as if they were conspirators. "There are those in the Courts wondering if thou will be returning and whose side thy sword will swing for."

Ignoring the implied question, Morgan re-rolled the scroll before tucking it down the top of her boot. With a shrug, she scanned the small crowd around them. "I'm not to return to the Court as long as Queen Moirethe lives. I swore that to Silvas. Wouldn't do to break my word, now would it?"

With a chuckle, the tall man stretched his neck, rolling his broad shoulders forward, before returning his attention back to the lions. The magnificent beasts had finished their meal, two of the females standing to wander back to the shade for a rest as the third, a large male with a thick mane, roared, baring his sharp teeth for the world to see. With a lazy turn of his head the lion seemed to view those humans above as if choosing who among them would make for a nice tasty meal. Suddenly bored of the game he rolled over, presenting his belly to the warm autumn sun and kicked his feet into the air as he scratched his back on the hard rock before turning to rest on his side. With a yawn he closed his eyes, ignoring the bloody bones and skin from his lunch.

"Prince Ansil would accept thee back into the Courts ifin thou wouldst join with him."

"What about his other brothers? Surely they want a piece of the throne." Brushing her hair back from her face with her fingers, Morgan gathered the dark locks behind her head before tying it up with a rubber band she kept around her wrist.

"Prince Khelvan seems preoccupied outside the Court and his relations with the Queen are strained at best, reasons unknown. But there are those who would support him among the High Lords."

Morgan's mind went back hundreds of years before, remembering the haughty young Prince and felt her ire rise. The fool was no better than his mother—power hungry and ever searching to turn anything or anyone to his advantage, including the innocent daughter of their rival Court. With a soft snort, she tossed Berith a disgusted look.

He gave a facial shrug, raising his eyebrows as if knowing her thoughts. "Much has changed since thou had left, Morrigu. People changed, alliances shifted."

"I didn't leave, I was banished. Big difference, Lord Berith."

Touching the rim of his hat in concurrence, he continued as if never disrupted. "Prince Herodious is an idiot. A puppet of his mother and those she aligns herself with. It is said when she decides to step down, it would be to him she sets her allegiance to."

"I don't care about the politics. What happened to King Silvas?"

"He was found deep in the bowels of the Underarch below Tir nag Goll. Why he was there none know or at least are not revealing. My thoughts are that he was going the back route to see the Cauldron Witch."

Mulling this bit of information around in her thoughts, Morgan's eyes glittered dangerously in the sunlight. The only reason the King would seek out the Witch in secret was for something important that he didn't wish the Queen or anyone from the Courts to know. Something bothered him, bothered him enough to seek out the Seer.

"Was he calling me back?"

Grim-lipped, Lord Berith turned to face her, silence his only answer. Understanding the Hounds Master knew nothing of the High King's private musings, Morgan closed her mouth and rubbed it thoughtfully.

"Who's releasing the Bollags into the world? Who gave them permission to pass beyond the Veil?"

Berith's eyes sharpened at the mention of the foul creatures of destruction. "None have. The High King would never…" His mouth snapped shut as anger washed over his face like a tidal wave. Muttering under his breath, he faced the lions once more as fury made his golden eyes glow slightly. "The bitch…what games does she play? To release the Bollags would only lead to…"

"The Goblin kingdom would demand equal entrance. To ignore the treaties now…" Shifting her eyes, Morgan took in the Hounds Master's expression. "She's creating a distraction, to keep eyes off her claim. Has the Sin'din'dar Court said anything yet about what's been happening?"

Berith shook his head, turning to put his back toward a couple with their children, and lowered his voice so only Morgan could hear him. "Rumors abound, of course, but none validated. King Tibault waits and watches but thou knows he will seek an opportunity to strike if the Mor'sin'dar leave Queen Moreithe on the throne. He will see it as a weakness."

Morgan nodded to herself. "Yes, and the High Lords?"

"All but left. They gather themselves beyond the Veil, pulling their support from the Court and waiting for some kind of outcome." He eyed her. "Art thou returning now?"

Clenching her jaw Morgan stood silent for several moments.

"She broke conditions of thy banishment by sending her assassin searching for thee. None of the High Lords would blame thee for returning. Thou could investigate the High King's death without fear of further retribution."

Ignoring the question, Morgan gripped the railing, her knuckles turning white from the strain. "Thanks for meeting with me. I'll talk to you later."

Lord Berith nodded and turned back to the lions in time to watch the great beasts settle down for their afternoon nap. After looking him over one last time Morgan walked away, her mood grim as she disappeared into the crowd of strolling families enjoying the sunshine.

10

After removing several bags of groceries from her car, Morgan enter her home and set them on the kitchen counter. As she put them away she pondered the information Lord Berith had given her that afternoon. So deep in her thoughts she was that she didn't hear the man walking up behind her until his smoldering voice caught her off guard and strong, warm arms wrapped around her waist.

"Hello, melamine."

Acting on instinct Morgan rammed an elbow into his gut as she reached around with her other hand to capture his thumb, twisting it back with enough force to break the bone. As his hold on her loosened she twirled around, ready to strike upward with an open palm to the nose only to hold back the blow once she saw who it was. Releasing his thumb Morgan stepped back, ignoring the look of pain crossing Lorne's face as she returned to her groceries.

"I don't remember giving you keys to my place."

Rubbing the throbbing digit Lorne leaned his hip against the counter and watched the icy look that crossed her face. Taking a deep breath, he slowly let it out before trying again. "I did not think thou would mind if I visited."

Glancing back at him from over her shoulder, Morgan grunted as she reached for another box. Stifling her irritation she placed it in the cabinet, closing the cupboard door with a slap of her hand. "So, what have you been up to, *sweets*?" She stretched the term of endearment sarcastically.

"Not too much." Uncomfortable, Lorne shifted his stance, keeping a wary eye on her, unsure how she would take his next statement. "Just trying to find more information about what troubles are heading thy way. Lord Req..."

"I am more than capable of taking care of myself, sweets," she bit out, "and by the way, do you know someone named Malachi?"

Lorne suddenly froze, his eyes darkening to a stormy gray as he stared at her. "Yes, I know of him." His voice lowered. "Why?"

"Because he seems to be showing up at the most inopportune moments. I met him the other night at a club." She looked at Lorne, watching his face for any answers that he might accidentally reveal. "It seems he is Queen Moirethe's assassin."

Silence filled the room as Lorne stared off into the distance, his eyes growing hard as stone as his mouth tightened in a grim line. After a few moments, Morgan reached up and rapped his forehead. "Hello, are you in there, Lorne? Talk to me and it better be good."

When he spoke again, his voice was barely above a whisper as if memories filled his mind. "Yes, I know of him." He gave a resigned sigh, looking away from her hard stare. "He..." Turning his gaze back on her, he captured her eyes with a steady eye and held them. "Thou must promise me, Lady Morriganna, stay away from him. He is very dangerous."

"So am I, Lorne." Morgan pursed her lips, watching the agitation in his body language. Something was up and she had an idea what it was. Giving up on her groceries, she stalked over to her living area and sat down, draping an arm over the back of the couch before returning her attention to him. Time to test. "Talk."

Lorne's jaw clenched for a second, and then he seemed to suddenly find a picture on the wall fascinating. "Tis nothing to tell. He belongs to the High Queen. He was given as a pet when he was young and later trained as her personal assassin." He sucked in a breath between his teeth as he shifted to get more comfortable.

Morgan continued to level a stare at him, her eyes sharp as she searched his body language for what was unspoken. He cleared his throat uncomfortably, shifting his stance, then moved across the room to sit on a couch opposite her.

"Uh…"

"Uh?" Her voice lowered in irritation. "Tell me more, Lorne. Make me happy. You've been avoiding my questions since we met and I can guarantee you don't want to make me unhappy."

Lorne looked down before turning his eyes away, probing at his lip with the tip of his tongue. "I cannot."

Morgan sat there for a second, staring at him like he was a fool, then slammed a hand down on the low table between them, frowning when he groaned. "If you don't start being truthful I'll use a dagger. Believe me, I'll take great pleasure in it."

"What was between us is private. It happened years ago and cannot be changed."

"The King is dead, the Queen refuses to step down and has sent her assassin to find me." Morgan held a finger up in emphasis. "Find me, not kill me. Why? Lord Requiem, a High Lord I've had no business with, seeks to keep me safe and old friends of mine send warnings. Now the Bollags are running loose. What in the Nine Hells is going on?"

Lorne's gray eyes looked into hers, filled with anger, shame, and something like loss and regret. "Lord Requiem dost not tell me his thoughts as to why he sent me to watch thee. I was sent to see that thou wert still alive and warn thee but not interact further but once I saw thee I chose to disobey in order to know thee more. That tis all." Biting his bottom lip, he broke the skin, causing a thin trickle of blood to bead and trail down his chin. He looked away, a snarl on his lips. "The Courts are full of chaos now. Creatures of foul enter freely and the High Queen entertains them with impudence. The lesser Lords support her, the High Lords have either left or are being sent away, and now the Princes fight among each other. All is not well."

"And this has to do what with me?"

"Thou still holds fear in the Courts. And the anger the Queen held against thee is manifold now that the King is dead. Tis even rumored the Queen had a hand in his downfall." He closed his eyes, leaning his head against the back of the couch. "Tis all I know, bits and pieces."

Gritting her teeth, Morgan leaned back and swore. "Queen Moirethe has the deviousness but not the skill and power to kill Silvas. She would have to have had a partner, someone to do the dirty work for her." With a sharp look at him, she added, "Malachi?"

Lorne shook his head and winced, his color slightly fading as a small bead of sweat traced its way down the side of his face.

"You're right. A Were would have no chance against the high magick of a King. It would have to be someone with considerable skill." Looking up at the large mural on the wall, Morgan's thoughts drew inward as potential ideas wove themselves through her mind. A long list of enemies rolled out as she quickly checked off who could be the brawn behind the High Queen's brains. Too numerous, and she had no idea who remained in Court. A soft groan from the Sidhe pulled her back out of her thoughts. Raising an eyebrow in curiosity, she watched as Lorne's face contorted in pain.

"What's the matter? Are you hurt?"

Letting out a soft breath, he rolled his head to the side and looked at her. "Not hurt, but my time has come, my Lady. I had died long ago and the Lord of

Tech nDuinn brought me back for a task and I hath completed it." Drawing in a deep breath Lorne slowly closed his eyes, blocking his view of her, though a picture of her frowning remained etched deeply in his mind. "I was only given enough time to come back to find thee. It was not meant to go further than that. I apologize, but I…I could not resist once I saw thee, but it does not matter. I have failed. Queen Moriethe knows where thou art now…" Lorne broke off, rubbing his hands over his face.

"Aarrgghh!" Morgan growled, standing up to pace. "You're not making any sense. You're telling me you're a dead man sent to watch out for me?"

The look that crossed Lorne's face was one of exasperation. "I shall try to explain it to thee in simpler terms. Lord Requiem called me back from the Isle of Annwn to make sure that thou remained hidden from the Queen's assassin."

"I got that," she interrupted, her voice shifting softer to a dangerous warning.

"I know that thou knows that. Please allow me finish, yes?" He glared at Morgan. At her indifferent shrug, he continued. "As I was saying, I was given a limited amount of time here, just enough to…" He swallowed, and then closed his eyes. "My time is up now. Malachai has found thee and it is inevitable that…" He clenched his jaw again, opening his eyes to look toward the mural on the back wall.

Morgan stared at him for a long time before moving to sit on the edge of the coffee table. At her sharp intake of breath Lorne shifted uncomfortably on the couch, avoiding her eyes. "And you were to keep me occupied? That was your idea of protection?"

"It twas a chance to come back, to live again, but I never thought I would …" He turned his head to face her, his gaze locking with her own. "Lady Morriganna, stay away from the Were. He belongs to the High Queen and he rose in rank after thou had left the High Court. There is only one reason he would seek thee out and by sending him, an alpha male with his abilities, the Queen is certain that thou would take the bait. Thou wouldst not be able to resist him. No female can when he puts his mind to it."

Narrowing her eyes at the man before her, Morgan leaned toward him, threatening. "So inform me."

Lorne looked away again. "I know not. I cannot give thee an answer as to why he is here. I can only guess, but I do know he has his sights set on thee. Just remember, he is the High Queen's pet. The same High Queen who wishes thee humiliated and dead."

"I can take care of him if he tries to come for me. You forget who I am. I'm the Morrigu." An edge came to Morgan's voice. She gritted her teeth, feeling the need to hurt something or someone. It was when she turned to growl at him that she saw the pain written across his face. With a soft sigh, she leaned back.

"I should hath known better," speaking softly, the Sidhe looked down at his hands in his lap.

"Known what, Lorne?" she urged him. Getting him to answer her questions was like pulling teeth. Though Sidhe don't lie, they can do so by omission. He flinched at her words while staring at his hands before closing his eyes tight. She tried to see what was so interesting with his fingers but his thighs blocked her view.

"That it would not last. All I was supposed to do was warn the Morrigu, to try and keep her safe, away from the High Queen's assassin. Never in a million years would I hath thought that I would fall in love with thee."

"Fall in…" She was cut short as he held up his hands for her to see. His body began to disintegrate before Morgan's eyes, bits of skin and muscle flaking away like ash to fall to the floor beneath him in a gray pile.

"I am sorry I failed thee but the Dark Lord summons me back." His voice sounded haunted to her ears before his body suddenly burst into a dust cloud, falling in gentle waves to blanket the couch he sat on in ash.

11

"It's been a couple weeks since he disappeared. It's over, so go on." Terri raised her tequila shot glass to her mouth, tossing back the liquor before grimacing. "Damn, I love this stuff!"

Morgan looked over at the dance floor where couples writhed to the music, watching as the strobe lights pulsed, accentuating the dancers' sensuous movements. Manufactured fog poured over the floor, making its own seductive moves as it swirled around their ankles. The floor itself was a large pool of water covered by thick glass with colored lights reflecting off the liquid, a fantastical effect that lit everything in the room to create a mythical realm of lust and life.

She didn't feel much like partying, angry over Lorne's sudden death. His second actually, since he had only been here because Lord Requiem wormed some deal to bring him out of the Land of the Dead. That thought made her stomach twist and ache. How much did the Thulath know? It had been years since she had spoken to her father—even since before she was banished—and they had not parted on good terms.

Was the bastard part of this too? Was there another player, other than Queen Moirethe, in the game of her life? Putting two and two together, it now made sense that Lord Requiem had become involved; after all the High Lord was subject to Thulath, ruler of the Land of the Dead, and her father never could stay out of meddling with his only daughter's life. The time was coming to swallow her pride and contact him.

Sliding into the chair next to her, Lisa smiled, flashing even white teeth as she wiggled in her seat, her red silk clad body full of sensual energy. "Come dance with me, Morgan," she purred. "There are lots of gorgeous men out there." Motioning to the dance floor, she waved her hand toward the crowd gathered below.

"Not interested right now, Lisa," she mumbled, wanting to sit and drink to dwell in her moodiness.

Slamming down her second shot glass, Terri stood up. "Well, I'll go. I feel like shaking my ass."

With a grin, Lisa stood up and tossed her hair over her shoulder. Wrapping her arm around Terri's slender waist, the two swayed down the stairs and to the dance floor.

As she watched them leave, Morgan drained her scotch before setting the glass back down on the table top with a heavy thud. Misery was not an emotion she particularly enjoyed, remorse and guilt included. While raising a hand to motion over a waitress, Morgan's eyes glanced over the throng of people before stopping on one in particular.

"Shit."

Walking through the club's front door Malachi stalked in, looking like a man with a purpose. Dressed in a tight black tee shirt, low-slung leather pants, and heavy leather boots, he wore a black duster to finish the whole "bad ass" assembly. Morgan watched as the Were glanced around the room, ignoring the mass of people moving in rhythm before heading to a far wall to observe the crowd like a hungry caged panther. As if sensing her presence, he looked up and spotting her in the upstairs seating. The corners of his lips pulled up in a wicked grin as he mouthed *skank* before crossing his arms to lean against the dark smoky mirrored wall.

Rolling her eyes Morgan looked away, yet constantly found herself peering back at the cocky bastard. *What the hell does he want? Why was he here?* The way he appeared and stood it seemed as if he was waiting for someone or something. Immediately all her senses went to full alert as she scanned the crowded club. *What's he waiting for?*

The waitress returned, bringing the drinks and collecting the money before disappearing into the stream of talking couples on her level. Morgan grabbed her glass, then sipped at it while keeping one eye on the Were and one on the crowd down below. She watched as several people entered and left the club, until Terri and Lisa appeared back at her side. They grabbed their drinks, downing them with a breathless sigh before turning their attention on her.

"You're getting to be a drag, Morgan." Lisa gripped, setting her glass down hard enough that the ice chinked against each other. "Come on, I found a great guy for you."

Motioning down toward the dance floor she waved at a small group of men and flashed a breathtaking smile. A few waved back, matching her smile and more than one turned his gaze to settle on Morgan's face. She frowned and turned away, ignoring their obvious interest.

"Do I have the aroma of desperation about me now?" Morgan asked, tucking a strand of hair behind her ear as her eyes moved back to Malachi to find him leaning against the mirrored wall, strong arms firmly crossed over his chest. Whatever he was searching for was still missing for a dark look crossed his handsome face while his eyes scored the crowded floor.

"Come on, please. They're nice and really cute," Lisa continued, straining her neck to keep her chosen few in sight at the throng of people on the dance floor grew. "I even found a totally hottie for you."

"What?" Morgan blinked, realizing she hadn't heard a word her friend was saying. After a quick glance at Terri, who in turn rolled her eyes, Morgan let out an exasperated groan and nodded her head. "Okay, whatever, but only one dance and if he humps me know I'm going to put him down like a dog."

Giddy, Lisa bounced on her heels as Morgan stood before hooking her arm over hers. Tolerating the bimbo act that men seemed to like so well, Morgan silently followed along, dragging her feet as she went. Why Lisa kept the façade up was beyond her. After all, the blonde was a lot smarter than the Pam Anderson persona she seemed to enthusiastically exude. Well, to each their own and from the look on Terri's face she mirrored the same opinion.

Making it through the crowded club to the main floor Lisa led them diligently to the group of men, introducing each one quickly before motioning Morgan to one in particular. A tall blonde wearing a pair of the tightest jeans she had ever seen on anyone stepped forward to take her hand.

"Trent, Morgan. Morgan, Trent. Go dance." Lisa put her hands on Morgan's back and pushed her toward him, ignoring the dirty look the dark-haired woman shot her. Terri grinned at her reaction while she dragged a tall, dark-haired man out to the dance floor for some bump and grind before Lisa looked over the remaining two men. With a big grin on her face, she pointed at them.

"I'll take you both. Come." Beckoning with her finger, she headed to the middle of the floor with a sway of her hips.

Sliding an arm around the tall woman's waist, Trent pulled Morgan closer to him until their hips touched. Ignoring her first impulse to drive his nose bone into his brain, she allowed him to lead as their bodies moved to the beat. Heat from the club dotted her upper lip with perspiration and she watched with amusement as his eyes followed her tongue when she licked at it.

Oh great. Morgan winced as he lowered his face toward hers. *He's gonna try and kiss me.* She turned her face away as he hovered nearer, but he managed to recover without pause and instead brushed his lips against her ear.

"You are so fucking hot," he whispered, his breath stirring her hair while he ground his erection against her thigh in emphasis. She rolled her eyes as thoughts of disposing of his body whirled through her mind when her gaze met Malachi's. Eyes narrowing at the contact she stared, daring him to make the first move. She was more than ready to shed some blood, especially with this jerk humping her leg like a horny little lap dog.

He sneered in response and mouthed *ho*. Looking away, Morgan "accidentally" shoved her hipbone into her partner's groin, listening with satisfaction as he grunted at the impact, and pulled away from him while shaking off his hold.

"I'm getting a headache. Think I'll go sit this one out," she mumbled as she turned away while heading back toward the stairs leading up to the balcony. Stunned at being abandoned Trent stared after her speechless as she left him standing in the middle of the dance floor before muttering under his breath and heading toward the bar.

Her mood growing blacker, Morgan looked over at her friends as she considered taking off. She really didn't want company, much less crowds and everything irritated her. She needed to contact Lord Aeron again and see if he could set up a meeting with the reclusive Lord Requiem, plus try and contact her father. As she walked through the dancers she watched Terri dirty dancing with her partner, a large smile upon her lips, one arm raised overhead as her other arm draped behind her head. Terri's partner had a hand on her hip and followed her rhythm as they simulated a seriously erotic sexual act. Lisa on the other hand was sandwiched between her two dancing partners, each man moving with a predatory need as she swayed between them, a seductive grin on her beautiful face.

A sudden commotion stirred several dancing couples as a red-haired woman dressed in forest green and tanned hunting leathers appeared in the midst of them, dark power radiating off her in thick waves. Tall and slender, the woman's fiery hair was pulled back from her beautiful face in tiny elaborate braids to reveal delicately pointed ears and eyes tilted up at the ends, giving a strange cat-like impression as her irises glowed in a pale blue color. On her back she had strapped a large wicked-looking hunting bow and at her hip sat sheathed a falchion. To all in observance, it was obvious the woman was not human for her appearance was a primal etherealness that screamed otherworldly.

Turning with purpose she scanned the crowd until her eyes settled on Morgan. Then with a wave of her hand she sent out a wave of power that flung the dancing couples between them off toward the walls, knocking them into several of the other dancers along the way. Tumbling to the floor in a pile of tangled arms and legs, the humans scrambled to their feet in a hurry, drawing the attention of others in the immediate area. A few stared, though most continued dancing, having missed the woman's handiwork.

Morgan froze mid-step and stared, the small hairs on the back of her neck standing on end. *What the hell?* Without a second thought she kneeled, reaching under the leg of her jeans to withdraw the knife she kept hidden in her boot, and crouched in a fighting stance. The woman stepped forward and pointed at her, her voice silky and filled with power, reverberating around the room.

"I am sent to retrieve thee, Lady Death. Thy loyalties were thought to belong to the Mor'sin'dar and to the High King and now that he is dead thou art ordered to return to the High Court to face charges of treason."

Morgan opened her mouth to snarl out a reply when suddenly Malachi stood before her, shielding her from the woman's view. "Go away, Lady Arduin, for that tis not going to happen."

"Ah, so here is where thou hast runaway to, animal. I was ordered to retrieve thee if I found thee in my Hunt. Step away from the Morrigu and help me capture her. If thou doth I may tell the High Queen of thy assistance and she might forgive thy insolence and take thee back into her service."

"No," he growled, reaching inside his duster before pulling out two curved arm-length short swords. With a practice twirl he flicked his wrist, pointing the deadly tips of the blades at the Huntress of the Mor'sin'dar.

The crowd parted as bouncers making their way to the center, hurrying around Malachi and the strange redhead.

"Put your weapons away," one muscular ebon-skinned bouncer ordered as he worked his way closer to Malachi, who in turn ignored the command and continued watching the tall, graceful woman with hard eyes.

The music stopped as the house lights came on though the artificial fog still swirled about the floor in an eerie haze. Lady Arduin tilted her head, staring at a bald bouncer as he stepped toward her, his movements parting the light mist. She smiled coldly and with invisible fingers, sent him flying up to crash into the strobe light globe in the center of the ceiling. A nasty wet meaty sound echoed throughout the room as glass and sparks rained down on everyone, followed by a spray of bright crimson blood.

"Humans, stay out of Sidhe business and thou may yet live."

Screams filled the air as people rushed toward the exits in panic. Arduin laughed a chilling sound that echoed in the surrounding chaos. Two of the bouncers rushed Malachi at the same time the Huntress reached out for Morgan.

"Do not fight me, Lady Crow! Once I set my sights on a prey I never lose them."

"You forget who you speak to, Huntress. I've beaten you before in a fight. Do you really think you can defeat me this time?" Morgan spit back, readying herself for a fight. "Once we rode together in the Wild Ride. You know what I'm capable of."

Slowly the two women circled each other, each with eyes trained to spot the other's weakness. Lady Arduin drew her sword, a silvery blade that glowed like the moon, as Morgan's eyes grew darker until the whites were engulfed in ebon color. The dagger in her hand grew and stretched, becoming a slender sword that curved at the end and absorbed the light from the club until only the glow from the Huntress's blade lit the room. The temperature around them plummeted as the air turned frigid, ice crystals forming on glass and showing anyone's breath as a fine vapor.

"Thou cannot have her, bitch," Malachi growled. Then he swung his twin swords with blinding speeds, slicing the two bouncers across their abdomens, and stepped over their writhing forms after they fell to the ground, alive but bleeding. Knocking Morgan aside, he moved to face the Huntress, positioning himself between her and the Morrigu as he twirled his blades in warning.

Looking unconcerned at Malachi, Arduin cast him a pleasant smile. "Thou art a fool, animal, for thou will be slaughtered for thy defiance. Now step out of my way."

"No!" His face twisted in fury as his eyes blazed, changing from human to those of a hunting cat, showing the beast within fighting to get out. Stepping forward, he found himself trapped against an invisible wall. Furious at his predicament, he struck at it with his swords as Lady Arduin turned her attention back to Morgan.

"Fight me, Battle Crow."

"My pleasure." Morgan flashed her a dark smiled, dropping the glamour she wore to disguise herself as a human. Where before stood a tall, dark haired woman dressed in slinky black leather, in her place appeared a tall, slender woman of unearthly beauty. Her wild, dark hair reaching her thighs, with a lock of snowy white hair framing her face. Eyes that had once been a soft jade green were now as dark as a starless night, and tanned skin lightened to luminance paleness. The sounds of soft fluttering of wings and echoing caws filled the room as shadows moved, lengthening and swarming overhead to mimic birds circling the room.

All eyes left in the room stared at the transformation of Morgan, blinking in amazement and awe before one person stepped forward, determined not to let it affect her loyalty to her friend.

"You have to go through me first, bitch," Terri threatened as she stepped forward, her hands clenched into fists. Moving to Morgan's side, she narrowed her brown eyes.

Morgan let out an irritated breath at her friend's actions. Though Terri had training in martial arts for years, she was of no use against the magick of the Faeiry and the fury of the Huntress. It would be like pitting a toddler against a gladiator. No match at all.

"Stay out of it, Terri. This is not your fight." She swore under her breath as her friend rushed forward, intent on joining the fight.

With a flick of her hand, Arduin sent the petite brunette to fly backward against the far wall, the force of the blow hard enough to knock the woman out as an audible crack filled the air. With a groan she slid down the wall in a boneless heap.

"No!" Frantic, Lisa ran to her friend's side. Kneeling down beside her, she tried to revive Terri, and then decided it was best to pull the unconscious woman out of harm's way.

Circling around Arduin, Morgan looked for an opening to strike. She snarled, her nostrils flaring and eyes blazing in fury. "This is between you and I, Huntress. Leave the humans out of it."

Finding the opening she struck like a serpent and swung her sword, the blade cleanly slicing through the soft flesh of her opponent's throat, but Arduin managed to save herself by back stepping in time to keep from having her head severed. Wiping a hand over her wound, the redhead looked at her bloody fingers and frowned, then snapped her eyes back at the Morrigu.

"I am supposed to bring thee in alive, but I do not think the Queen would mind if I just bring back thy head." Lady Arduin swung her blade, wanting to return the favor of the wound, only to find Morgan's sword blocking hers. The two began fighting in earnest, their swords clanging against each other as they sought a weakness.

Side-stepping, Morgan blocked another blow from Arduin's weapon before turning and swinging her own blade. Ducking low her sword flew toward the Huntress's abdomen, slicing through the leather wrapped there and split it in two. Arduin screamed in fury as the dark-haired woman stepped back, her movements as graceful as a cat. With satisfaction, Morgan watched as bright crimson blood flowed from the wound.

"I will kill you, Arduin. Turn away and tell your Queen you couldn't find me."

"Never." The Huntress's sword swung overhead, swishing by Morgan to neatly cleave a lock of ebon hair from the Battle Crow's head.

Morgan raised an eyebrow as the clipped piece drifted to the ground, then lifted her sword to meet Arduin's. They clashed in a blaze of wills. Light against dark, they fought until a set of blades interrupted them. Malachi pushed the two women apart, though he kept his attention fully on the redhead. They stared at each other in silence for several long seconds, the Huntress's eyes blazing as bright as molten lava as she sized him up.

"Thy choice, Malachi. Bring her in or we will set the Wild Hunt on thee." With those final words, she disappeared.

Breathing heavily, Malachi waited a few minutes longer to see if she would return then turned to look at Morgan who stood in restrained anger. She could see the tenseness in his shoulders, the muscles bunched under the leather and cloth and glared at her would-be hero, waiting for him to speak first. When he didn't, she did.

"Why the hell did you do that?" she demanded, keeping her dark blade firm in her grasp. "I could have taken her."

He stood staring at her as if making some life-changing, all-important decision, then took a step forward to loom over her. Reaching out, he cupped the back of her head, holding her firmly in place, and pulled her in for a deep kiss. She stiffened, her arms going straight, too shocked to struggle. Then just as quick as it happened, he released her, stepping back. Without another look, Malachi turned abruptly on his heel and headed toward the nightclub door. Halfway there, he clutched a hand to his chest, falling down on one knee with a loud groan.

Frozen, Morgan watched as he stumbled to the ground. Too stunned by his impromptu kiss she didn't react as people ran around the room in panic while cries of fright and stifled sobbing filled the air. Instead, she blinked a couple of times to clear her confusion until a low moan from Terri pulled her out of her daze. Looking down, she watched her friend move her head.

"Did anyone get the number of the bus that hit me?" the petite brunette joked, then hissed in pain as her broken ribs shifted. Her eyes met Morgan's as a crooked grin crossed her face. "Interesting look. We're going to have to have a long talk later."

The Sidhe answered with a sharp nod, though her eyes slid back to the Were. The scent of blood hung heavy in the room, sending waves of distraction through her. Sensing Lisa kneeling down next to Terri again, she stepped back as the blonde put a hand on Terri's shoulder to keep her from moving.

"Lay still, Ter, or you'll hurt yourself more. The police and ambulance will be here soon."

Banishing her sword Morgan glanced around the room, ignoring the moaning of the bouncers and the frightened faces of the crowd to watch as Malachi got back to his feet. He managed to stagger out of the building without getting jostled by the crowd escaping from the chaos inside, leaving a trail of blood to follow behind him. Frowning, her eyebrows drew together as she wondered why he was bleeding. He had not been struck during the fight that she could remember.

"Stay with Terri, I'll be right back," Morgan ordered Lisa before following after Malachi, without waiting for an answer. As she walked, she drew her glamour back around her body, quickly changing her appearance to human once more.

The police and an ambulance were arriving by the time she caught up with the Were. Spying him ducking into an alley, she turned into it to find Malachi resting against the brick wall, leaning forward as he tried drawing in his breath. Coughing, he grasped his midsection as blood soaked his dark tee, dripping small splattering droplets around his feet.

"Go away, Lady Morriganna," he growled through clenched teeth, shutting his eyes tightly as pain ripped through him.

Ignoring his demand, Morgan moved closer. "What the hell is going on?" She lifted a hand to touch his shoulder, but jerked it away as he flinched. "What's happening to you? And why did you step between Arduin and me? I could kill you for interrupting a duel, Were. This is Sidhe business."

Opening his eyes Malachi glared at her through narrow slits, his pupils dilated from pain. "Duel my ass. She was here to drag thee back to the Courts to be executed," he bitterly spit out through clenched teeth before turning to head deeper into the alleyway. Taking a step away, he stumbled to a knee and swore under his breath at the pain it caused.

Moving up behind him, Morgan wrapped a hand under his bicep while leaning over to help him stand. "Why are you bleeding? You were never cut."

"Tis my Queen's handiwork." He kneeled back down, looked up at her with pain-filled amber eyes, and then jerked his arm out of her grasp. Leaning against a wall, he watched Morgan through wary eyes.

"Why would the High Queen damage her favorite pet?" she sneered, backing away while crossing her arms under her breasts. Irritation filled her to the core. She stayed away, did as she was ordered by King Silvas, and left everyone alone. It had been over four hundred years since she laid eyes on anyone from the Courts and this was seriously pissing her off, but rather than leave, she remained. Something about him drew her to him. Breathing in deeply the enticing scent of leather, wild musk, and something darker, more promising teased at her senses, making her almost lightheaded.

Ignoring her question, Malachi tried to straighten up, grunting as he moved a foot under him to stand. As he shifted his weight to push up, he cried out in pain, slumping forward instead while blood dripped down his pants to pool on the alleyway ground around him. In one swift movement, Morgan squatted down beside him and ripped his T-shirt open to reveal his chest.

Her eyes widened in a mixture of horror and sick fascination as she watched another wound slowly appear, opening across the top of his right pectoral muscle as if someone took a knife and began filleting his chest. Taut tan skin split, revealing red gleaming muscle underneath. Dark crimson blood spilled forth down his front as another spot—lower this time, on his abdomen— opened up in a gaping wound. He leaned his head back, closing his eyes tight while his breathing came quick and harsh.

"Shit," she whispered, reaching out a hand to the wounds.

Before her fingertips skimmed over them, his hand jerked up, grabbing her wrist and slowly bringing it to his lips. Brushing his lips across her fingertips, he breathed, "Do not."

Jerking his hand out of his grasp, she rocked back on her heels and studied his face. This was the man Lorne died a second painful death to warn her about.

He belonged to Queen Moirethe, or believing Arduin, had run away. She could either leave the jerk to bleed to death and never look back or she could heal his ass and find out things that were happening in the Court and the death of the High King. Decisions, decisions. What's a girl to do? Her curiosity outweighed her irritation at being left out in the cold. Cupping his chin, Morgan turned his face toward hers, forcing him to look her in the eye.

"I can heal you. Let me help." She wasn't squeamish about blood or wounds but anyone with this much damage to them was usually dead by now. There was something different about this Were, something that drew her attention. He was handsome to the extreme and she could feel the power of his body this close to him, but some niggling warned her deep in the back of her head. Of course, being her, she ignored it. He was the Queen's personal assassin and who knows, he might even have had a hand in the High King's death himself. Until she had her answers, he had to live.

Keeping her doubts about the situation to herself, she continued. "Why would Queen Moirethe do this to you?" *Besides for her normal sadistic pleasure.* She tampered down her own impulse to shove a nail into the wound to make sure he gave her the information she wanted.

Looking at Morgan, Malachi's golden eyes lost their hard edge, taking on a more soft appeal. "Because of thee. I lied about finding thee, refusing her order to hunt thee down and kill thee and this tis my punishment for disobedience."

Backing away, Morgan pulled her hand from him and shook her head, eyes narrowing. "I don't believe you."

What the hell was he talking about? Studying his face, she tried to picture if she had ever seen him before, though there was something familiar about him. What it was she couldn't put a finger on. Maybe she had come across a relative of his. After all, he was a Were and it was well known that the Morrigu used to ride in the Wild Hunt beside her King, but his eyes revealed the strangest thoughts she would never have thought would lurk in there for one of the Sidhe.

Taking a deep breath Morgan let it out slowly between her teeth, trying to relieve the stress she felt building. Pushing it aside, she focused on the problem at hand.

"Let me help you. I have a healing gift." Once more she raised her hand to touch him.

"No!" he barked, scooting out of her reach. "I do not want thee touching me." A wild, almost frightened look crossed his face. His eyes gleamed with a feverish glow within a pallid sweating face. His jaw flexed, nostrils flaring as he shook his head, trying to put distance between them, but he was going nowhere as hurt as he was.

"Why?" Morgan questioned him while moving a step closer. She kept her voice soft as she would with a skittish horse, feeling anxiety flood from him.

"Because, Lady Morriganna…" He grimaced as another wound opened on his chest, the mind-numbing pain driving him down to his knees. He curled up over himself, ducking his chin tight to his chest while sucking in deep fast breaths of air. His hands shook as another spasm hit him.

Dropping down to her knees next to him, Morgan grabbed his face, forcing him to look at her again. "Now damn it, Malachi. What the hell is going on? What game are you playing?"

A surge of anger filled her, followed by a touch of desperation at not knowing what he was talking about. Morgan's heart pounded hard against her ribs while her stomach twisted and rolled at the raw emotions exuding from his eyes, giving away his thoughts.

Malachi closed his eyes as if trying to block her face from his mind. "I am only a Were, just an animal to thee. I am beneath thy interest. But go now. I need to be alone." His breathing became hoarser and faster, sucking in shallow breaths. "Go," he whispered.

Morgan stared at the Were before her, at his sweaty, messy dark hair, his feral golden eyes, and his handsome pain-filled face. Even now, she felt her body drawn to his, the ancient attraction Sidhes felt for the Weres they owned and fought against. *Screw this.*

Shaking her head Morgan steeled herself to the pain, cursing what she was about to do and leaned forward, pulling his upper body into her lap. Holding him tight in her arms, she sent her senses into his torn body and let her healing touch flow to him.

Struggling in her grasp, Malachi cursed her in a halfhearted attempt for he was too weakened to break free. Drawing in a deep breath Morgan steadied her breathing, slowing down her heartbeat and concentrated on the task at hand but it seemed that as she healed one wound, another appeared on his body. The continuous warmth from her healing flared to an inferno, the heat of it becoming too much to bear as more and more slashes appeared on his chest, then transferred her hers.

Morgan screamed in pain as Malachi's wounds suddenly appeared on her body, her skin splitting as if an invisible hand sliced across her flesh with a wickedly sharp knife. Like the weapons she used, her healing was two-sided. Though she was created to kill, she had also been gifted to heal, but her healing came with a price. Each wound she repaired, she in turn took on, letting her natural regeneration mend her body.

Blood gushed quickly from the cuts that spread out over her chest, mingling with his and pooling on the ground around them. Feeling faint and lightheaded from the loss, Morgan's body began shaking from the pain. In her arms, Malachi fought, trying desperately to push her away, but she clung fast to him.

With a burst of strength, he managed to knock her off of him, leaving her to crumble into a pile by his side, sobbing at the terror of being skinned alive while watching the crimson puddle spread around her body.

"Never do that again, Morriganna! Never do that again!" Malachi hissed, crawling away from her to lie down a little farther in the alley.

Her vision dimming, Morgan watched as the shadows in the alley deepened. Swallowing hard, she rolled over onto her back, staring up in the dark sky, and felt her muscles cramp up. Feeling dizzy, she closed her eyes, wondering why on earth she cared enough to be in this mess in the first place. Oh yeah, answers. Feeling her natural regeneration take hold, she gave herself into the darkness as her flesh began to slowly mend back to smooth, unblemished skin.

12

Waking up with a start, Morgan gasped for air and sat up. With a quick glance around the room she realized she was sitting on her bed, in her room and froze. *How did I get here?* Rubbing her chest absentmindedly she tried to remember everything that happened that night. The club, Arduin, the fight, Malachi. *Fuck, I hurt.* Wincing from the heavy ache that bound her ribs with each breath she took, Morgan shifted her weight on the mattress and made a face as her leather bustier creaked and cracked like old wood. Looking down at her top she noticed the leather was no longer soft but stiff with dried blood and watched as the dark rust stain flaked off when her fingers brushed over it, drifting down like morbid snowflakes to sprinkle across the sheets.

Malachi. The last thing she remembered was his face, twisted in pain, before darkness washed over her eyes. Snatching the sheets off, Morgan stood up abruptly, only to feel a wave of dizziness wash over her and moved a hand back to the mattress to steady herself. Sitting back on the edge of the bed, she squeezed her eyes shut for a moment then opened them once the dizziness faded and glanced around the room once more.

With slow, languid movements, Morgan moved to the mirror above her black lacquered dresser then grimaced at the sight that met her eyes. *I looked like shit.* Dark circles shadowed under her eyes, smudged with make-up left over from last night. Streaks smeared down her cheeks, shadowy trails flecked with dried blood that ran down her face to her jaw. The tops of her breasts were streaked in dried blood as well as the black leather bustier and jeans she had worn to the club. Her skin seemed paler than normal, accentuated by her raven black hair that was half in and half out of pins.

Hell froze over and I crawled out. She ran a hand over her eyes before turning away, raising her glamour again to wrap her appearance in a spell to once more give the appearance of being human, and walked over to the bedroom door, sensing something was off.

Opening it, she glanced over the wide expanse of her warehouse. Nothing had changed. The walls were still painted a dark gray and the floor still covered in a short black carpet. A few weapons lined the wall as a form of art, along with death masks from the different countries she had visited throughout the centuries. On the far wall the painting she treasured, the only thing she took with her from the Courts, hung. The ShadowedLands. Her home. The land between life and death, dark and light, between Fae and human. The painting reflected the mood of the land and from its current appearance it seemed a bit irritated. The scene was eerie, shadows growing around twisted trees and limbs, a sliver of a moon hung high over the bows, half hidden behind muted clouds that promised rain. From the brush that dotted the forest floor golden eyes of predators reflected the faint light from above. Scattered across the ground like discarded garbage lay decaying leaves and bodies of small animals in various stages of rot. She could almost smell the sickly sweet stench of death.

Looking left and right, she found nothing of interest and pondered what to do next when the muted sound of water flowing caught her attention. Narrowing her eyes, she headed down the stairs and turned left, cautiously making her way toward the bathroom on the main floor.

Stopping in front of the door which was left cracked open, Morgan used her fingertips to push it in further as steam wafted out, confirming that someone was inside showering. She moved closer, pushing the door open to reveal black tile and fogged mirrors. Black tile counters and a sink lined a wall, and in a corner sat a black porcelain toilet. Dominating the right wall was a large glass shower. The glass was steamed up, but she could see the shadow of a person inside.

Standing in the doorway, Morgan stared at the shadowy movement, watching as it leaned into the steaming water, rinsing off the remains of soap. She knew who was in there, could tell by the size and the way he moved, but agitation set in again as she remembered their short talk and the warning about him.

The water turned off and the glass door opened as Malachi stepped out, reaching for his towel. Spying her, he stopped short, standing naked while water dripped off his muscular, tanned body. He paused, staring back at Morgan as if waiting to see her reaction.

Unconsciously she licked her lips, feeling parched. His dark shoulder-length hair was slicked back, water droplets rolling down the side of his tanned face and goatee to drip on his broad shoulders. His chest was smooth except for a light dusting of dark hair and not a mark marred his perfect skin, belying the damage that had been done to him last night in the alley. Moving her eyes farther down his abdomen, she watched his eight pack flex as he shifted slightly. His hips were narrowed, legs slightly apart, and, oh man, she sucked in breath. That was nice. Very nice.

Malachi watched her, one dark eyebrow rising in a silent question when Morgan suddenly felt nervous and licked her bottom lip before raising her eyes to his. Without a sound, he raised a hand out in offering, palm up, and waited. Her stomach clenched, and she hesitated for a moment before walking over to him. Her eyes never strayed from his, holding his gaze in a vise grip. She had never had sex with a Were before. Sidhe and regrettably humans, yes, but never a Were, though she had heard stories of their passion and aggression.

A fierce, possessive light gleamed in his feral amber eyes as he watched her reach for him. When she slid her hand into his he pulled her forward, before reaching out to run a hand behind her head, his fingers entwining in her tangled hair. Leaning his head down, he kissed her, parting her lips with his tongue, and dove in, plundering her mouth with his own. As his kiss became deeper, growing harder, his tongue entwined with hers, soliciting forth a moan of need. An inferno lit her body, flames of desire licking at her thighs as if she were about to explode into a ball of fire.

Abruptly Malachi pulled back to look down at her with hungry eyes. Morgan couldn't explain the myriad of thoughts that passed through his golden orbs as he reached up to untie the laces on her bustier, but at that moment she wasn't about to ask. All she could feel was his hot fingers as he peeled the leather off of her, dried blood flaking as the material left her flesh. He dropped the top to the floor, freeing her breasts to his view, and then knelt down in front of her to run his hands slowly down her abdomen. The touch tickled her skin, causing delicious heat to spread from her stomach down to the apex between her legs.

Slowly, his fingers drifted over the buttons of her pants, pushing each one through the small catches before sliding the tight denim off her hips. Removing her silk panties with them he smiled when a small patch of hair even met his eyes. With his help, she stepped out of them before he tossed them aside. Then looking up the length of her body, Malachi lifted his large hands to cup her breasts as he stood, brushing calloused thumb pads across her sensitive nipples.

Sighing, Morgan felt her legs tremble. His touch felt so good. As he slid back up her body, she felt his erection press against her stomach before he leaned in to kiss her again, capturing her mouth in a possessive move. Stepping back into the shower, Malachi pulled her in with him and turned the water on; letting it hit them with a strong force, the hotness of it almost scalded their flesh. Grabbing a bar of soap, he slowly lathered Morgan's shoulders, and then moved his hands over her full breasts, kneading the heavy flesh. His fingers played with her nipples, pinching and rubbing the hard buds, while drawing forth moans of pleasure from deep inside her.

Opening her mouth to receive his kiss, Morgan sucked hungrily on his tongue. With her right hand, she reached down to grasp his shaft, running her fingers along the length of it until she reached the head. Brushing her thumb over the tip, she caused him to jerk in her grasp. Chuckling, she smiled up at him as he lowered his mouth to her throat, licking and sucking at her flesh, tasting the slight saltiness of her skin and the blood dried there.

"I want to be in thee, Morriganna," he murmured against her neck, brushing his fangs against her tender skin. Lifting her up, he wrapped her legs around his hips and slowly slid himself deep inside her body. Crying out in pleasure, Morgan felt her insides stretch to accommodate his width and groaned at the intense feeling. Danu, he was delicious.

"Ah, yes, thou art so tight," he groaned, driving deep into her as he pressed her back against the glass wall. Drawing his head back he bared his teeth, revealing sharp incisors before he jerked forward to sink them into her skin. Blood quickly welled to the top, spilling forth in two thin streams over her shoulder and down her back as he marked her.

Digging her nails into his shoulders, Morgan leaned her head back, resting it against the shower wall as his thrusts pounded her against the fogged glass. The want she felt for him was so great that she was sure she would explode at any moment. Her legs tightened around his waist as he thrust up into her again, driving her body to new heights. Wave after wave of pleasure kept building as urgency quickly took hold. Closing his eyes, Malachi released his bite before leaning his head against her shoulder, holding her close to him as his hips moved up to meet her own.

"Oh, yes!" Morgan cried out. The tidal wave of an orgasm rocked her body as her inner walls tightened around him. "Oh, sweet Danu!"

Screaming, she threw her head back, hitting it against the wall. Glass cracked in a spider-web pattern behind her, but she ignored it, instead flowing with her orgasm. Her fingernails dug deep into his flesh as wave after wave crashed through her, causing her body to spasm for a moment before she opened her eyes to look deep into his own. Holding his gaze as she came, Morgan's grip on his shoulders magnified, not letting go as her nails tore past skin into muscle, releasing deep crimson rivulets to race down his back.

"That's it, baby. Come for me." She could feel his heated gaze through hooded lids, his face flushed with exertion. He thrust deeper, raising his mouth to hers to draw her tongue to entwine with his, while swallowing her cries of pleasure. His eyes closed, adding his own cry to the mix, while spilling his seed deep inside her body. With one last thrust, he tore his mouth away and roared out his release as his body spent itself.

For a few minutes, they stayed where they were, her legs still wrapped tightly around his waist, panting heavily. Leaning against the glass wall as scorching water sprayed over their skin, their bodies trembled together as they tried to regain control of their senses. As their heartbeats and breathing resumed to normal, Morgan lowered her head to his shoulders, feeling his skin, his heat, smelling the rich scent of him. She closed her eyes, breathing in deep his wet masculine scent.

Still sheathed deep within her body, Malachi pushed open the shower door and carried her out of the bathroom over to a connecting bedroom and bed, then sat with her straddling him. He wrapped his arms firmly around her body, cradling Morgan to his chest as he placed soft kisses along her bare shoulders. She snuggled closer into him, feeling warm and content, letting out a light sigh. *Danu, that was good.* For long several moments they sat like that until he broke the silence, taking her shoulders in his rough hands to push her back enough so he could gaze into her eyes.

"Queen Moirethe has it bad for thee, Morriganna. I do not believe she will leave off with Lady Arduin, but will send others."

Lifting a slender dark brow, Morgan looked at him with a dark smile. "Oh, I believe that too." Shaking her head, she closed her eyes for a brief moment, and then opened them again. "Besides, Moirethe doesn't scare me. I'm more than capable of taking care of myself."

His eyes narrowed, growing sharper at her tone. "Thou dost not trust me." The clipped tone in his words showed irritation.

Drawing back, she looked at him long and hard. "Of course not, Malachi. You can't honestly be naïve enough to believe that. We had sex, nothing more. Where do you get off thinking that all of a sudden I believe anything that comes out of your mouth?" Rubbing her forehead with her fingers, she frowned. *Shit, what is it with her and men?* The afterglow of sex was quickly wearing off with his words.

His face turned stony at her words, and then quickly grew softer, though she could still see a hint of his err in his golden eyes. "Believe what thou will, Morriganna, but unless thou listens to me, thou will be hurt. The Queen is not going to stop until she gets what she wants."

"Why would this concern you, what happens to me?"

She could feel Malachi's pulse quicken at her words. Clenching his jaw, he paused for a moment as if thinking of the right things to say. "I remembered thee from when I was a child. Not long after my family was captured and sold off. I remember when King Silvas bought me as a pet for his Queen and being made to crawl on my hands and knees to her throne for the entertainment of the Court." He gritted his teeth. Morgan could hear the pain and strain of memory in his deep voice.

"And I remember finally looking up at the faces of everyone, seeing them laughing and making sport of 'Queen Moirethe's new toy,' and I hated every one of you. But then I saw thee, standing behind King Silvas's throne in the shadows. Thou wert neither laughing nor making jest like the others. Instead thou seemed angry and later that day when I no longer entertained them, thou had taken me aside and sent me away with servants to a room with other

Weres."

He closed his eyes, resting his head back against the wall. "But before thou did, I remember thee petting my head as if…giving me comfort. That was when I fell in love with thee. I worshipped thee as a child and dreamed of the day that thou saw me, saw me as a man, not as a pet. Throughout the years I rarely saw thee, thou being the mighty Morrigu, and when I did, thou ignored me but after finding thee, seeing thee in that club, I…I knew I could not kill thee as Queen Moirethe ordered."

What he said had a ring of truth in it, but she closed her eyes at his admission, feeling wary. "I'm not easy to kill, Malachi. I've lived over ten thousand years and have killed some of the most powerful enemies of King Silvas. Why do you think you even had a chance?"

"Goddess curse thee, woman!" He grabbed her, kissing her hard until both of them were gasping for a proper breath. He pulled away first, leaning his forehead on hers, and looked deep into her eyes, his own feral amber ones narrowed. "Why dost thou have to be so fucking stubborn?"

"Because I am. Answer me, Malachi. Why should I believe you? Why is Moirethe so intent on her revenge? It's been over nine hundred years. It was one family and Lady Gilthantrious really wasn't as important to the Queen to make her seek vengeance."

"That I cannot say. I was not privy to her thoughts, not like others in her Court." He paused, running his fingers down along the length of her spine, tracing the bones in a lazy spiral pattern. "Rumors say though she was angry because thee and her King were lovers, that thou had his love, the love that should have been hers. So, did thee? Wert thou lovers?"

Setting a droll look on him, Morgan snorted. "No. Not lovers. I loved him, but as my King. It was the fact that I was loyal and only loyal to him. He was the only one I would listen to and Queen Moirethe, her greatness, could never get me to acknowledge her. If anything, it was because I refused to bow to her."

"Thou doth stretch her patience, Lady Morriganna. Tis dangerous. There are many who are loyal to the High Queen, many who used to be the High King's allies but are no longer." Lowering his voice, he confided in her. "But thou still hast friends."

Morgan's eyes narrowed at his statement. Was he saying this in hopes she would reveal who in the Court she still had contact with? Did he know about Lorne and Eryn? As the High Queen's assassin, he was privy to most of her secrets, no matter what he claimed.

"Friends? I've been gone too long to have anyone willing to hear me out or seek to align themselves with someone Queen Moirethe despises. No, there's something else up." Suddenly she sobered up. "Who killed King Silvas?"

Malachi made a facial shrug, keeping his eyes on hers. "No one is really sure. What tis known twas that a Barghest attacked him in the back halls."

"A Barghest? What would a Barghest be doing in the Courts? They roam the deep woods, not dwell in buildings."

"Well, apparently the High King had gone to the catacombs of Tir nag Goll. Why he was there no one knows, but at the time twas rumored that Cauldron Witch was living not too far from there."

"The Cauldron Witch." Drawing her eyebrows together, Morgan pursed her lips and watched him thoughtfully. "Why would he go to see her?"

"No one knows for sure, but twas not too long after his death that the High Queen placed the order for thine own. I was sent to hunt thee down and kill thee, but I could not. Twas when she placed the spell on me." He breathed in deep, rubbing his cheek against her hair. "Thou hast seen the effect of that last night."

Leaning her head into his neck, Morgan gave a soft sigh, enjoying the warmth of him as her body melted into his. "What is Queen Moirethe's plan?" she murmured, more to herself than out loud.

Shifting his head, Malachi kissed the bite mark he on her shoulder, smiling at the brand he left on her flesh as if marking the woman as his.

13

It was late the next evening when Morgan gathered her clothes and dressed. Glancing at Malachi as he slept in her bed, she left the room in silence, feeling uncomfortable with the whole situation. Taking one more look at him, she admired his firm, muscled back and the slight curve of his lower back that rounded in a tight ass. Her legs were still weak from the intensity of the sex, for several times during the night they had made love, stopping only long enough to eat and rest.

Her stomach growled as she headed down the staircase and to the kitchen to see if there was anything left in the refrigerator. Opening the door, she peered in, finding nothing of interest, and realized she wasn't in the mood to cook. Closing the refrigerator door, she straightened and headed out.

The sky was still dark as Morgan closed the front door behind her. She glanced briefly at her car, wondering if she should go for a drive, but rejected that idea. What she needed now was a walk, something to clear her mind. Taking a deep breath, she headed down the road in the direction of downtown, listening to the quiet sounds of the city and the sharp clicks of her boot heels on the concrete while giving her arms a brisk rub to rid herself of the chill in the air.

What the hell did she just do? Had sex with Malachi? Why the hell did she do that? She knew but didn't want to admit it to herself. It was because she was horny and he looked good enough to eat. She was angry over it but inside, deep in the pit of her stomach, butterflies fluttered at the thought of him. Closing her eyes, Morgan breathed in the air deeply to cleanse her mind and body. Danu, he had felt so good, his touch having sent sparks through her skin.

Shivering, she remembered the feel of his heated kisses on her lips, his tongue gliding across her skin. Five times they had sex that day. Four rough and heated, the last one slow and tender. She had to admit Malachi was a talented lover, very generous in bed, making sure her orgasms were greater and longer with each session. Hell, he had even gotten up and made her an omelet and juice to replenish her energy. Never had she had a lover do that for her before.

Opening her eyes again, Morgan continued walking, reflecting on everything that had happened last night. The attraction to him was instant, though she had fought it, but one night of lust gave way to passion. If they had still been at Court there would have been dire consequences for their joining, for the politics between Sidhe and Weres strictly forbade unions between them even though it was well known that behind closed doors some Sidhe masters dallied with their Were servants. But damn, he knew too many ways to please her, to bring her to orgasm without being shown. She shivered again at the thought, growing damp, before shaking off the memory and continued walking.

When she had asked why he had been such an ass to her when they met at the club, Malachi admitted shock at seeing her, and then jealousy at knowing she had a lover. When she asked how he knew, he just shrugged and said he smelled the Sidhe on her. And as to why he was at the nightclub last night? He knew since he refused to kill her himself that Moirethe would send another and would continue to until either the Queen herself was dead or the Morrigu.

Rubbing her forehead, Morgan followed the road. A car sped past her, disappearing after it followed the bend. There were too many discrepancies. Eryn warned her not to trust anyone, then Lorne showed up, and now Malachi, each claiming to have her safety in mind. The Were's admission of love (she shook her head at that) and Arduin's attack at the club were too many things happening at once. After walking twenty minutes, she found a small diner and decided to stop, her stomach growling again at the thought of food.

As she entered, Morgan noticed that only three people were in the diner other than a chubby waitress and the cook in the back. Sliding into a booth, she watched as the waitress hurried over, pad and pencil ready to take her order. After glancing over at the daily special listed on a chalkboard near the cooking station she ordered a club sandwich and fries for dinner along with a large diet Coke, then sat back and waited in silence, cradling her head in her hands.

"You okay, hun?"

Morgan looked up at the plump waitress to find a gentle smile on her face as the woman set the drink and meal down before her, before reaching in the pocket of her apron to pull out a bottle of ketchup.

"I'm fine. Just walked a long ways, that's all. My feet are tired and sore."

The waitress smiled and reached over to squeeze the dark-haired woman's shoulder. "We have some really good brownies made. I'll bring you a piece; all warm with a scoop of vanilla, on the house, dear. After all, nothing makes things better than chocolate."

With a tired smile, Morgan glanced up at her. "Thanks."

After the waitress left, she began to eat, feeling starved while glancing outside at the dark sky. She looked at her watch. 11:15 p.m. Late. Fuck. She wondered how her friends were doing. *Wonderful person I am, never even checked to see if Terri was okay.*

The front door of the diner opened as two men entered. Morgan glanced at them, momentarily distracted from her thoughts while she noted their disheveled appearance. One was tall and lanky with long greasy black hair, the other shorter and more defined in the chest with tattoos, his bleached hair spiked. Spotting her watching them, the shorter one leered before wiggling his tongue in a suggestive fashion. Letting out a snort, Morgan shook her head. Dumb ass. They looked like druggies, probably out to get some munchies before they scored a high for the night.

"Take a seat anywhere, boys, and I'll be right with you." The waitress motioned to the empty booths as she passed by, carrying a tray with the brownie ala mode and another soda.

"Not here for fucking food, bitch," the tall, lanky one growled as he pushed the waitress aside, pulling a gun from the interior of his jacket. She screamed as he grabbed her roughly by the arm and spun her around to use her as a hostage.

"Don't try anything stupid or I blow this bitch's head off!" he yelled, pressing the muzzle to the waitress's emple. The other customers froze or scrambled to the floor, covering their heads as sounds of whimpering and a lone cry filled the room.

Striding toward Morgan, the bleached blonde pulled a gun from his jeans and began waving it around with a smirk on his face. She glanced up at his approach, noting the intent look in his eyes, and dipped a French fry in her ketchup before popping it into her mouth. *Why can't I eat dinner in peace? It's not like life wasn't already exciting enough.* With a droll look on her face, she waited to see what his next move would be.

The blonde leaned against the table she was sitting at and waved the gun at her in a limp-wristed way. Leaning forward, he picked up a French fry from her plate, dipped it in the ketchup, and ate it, smiling.

"I know what I want to eat." He leered at her, eyeing her breasts.

Trying not to yawn, Morgan lifted her glass for a drink. "Walk away, little boy, while you still can," she muttered before taking a sip.

With a quick strike, he knocked the glass out of her hand, spilling the dark liquid over the tops of her breasts and bustier. Reaching out, he grabbed the back of her head, twisting her dark hair in his hands tight enough to make her draw in a sharp breath, and then jerked her head back to expose her throat. Leaning over, he then ran his tongue across the tops of her breasts, up along her neck, to her mouth, before kissing her hard. *Ah, so he wants to do it that way. Two can play this game.*

Opening her lips in invitation, Morgan tasted the sweet tomato base and potato plus alcohol, probably whiskey and not the good stuff either. He moaned, slipping his tongue into her mouth while he reached with his other hand to grope a breast, squeezing hard. Under lowered lids, she watched him, smiled, and then snapped her teeth together with enough force to sever his tongue. Quickly the flow of blood filled her mouth, the salty coppery taste filling her senses with a heady intoxication. A crimson tear rolled from the side of her mouth as her smile widened dangerously. The shock of the attack loosened the guy's hold on her hair and he stumbled back, grabbing his mouth.

Standing up, Morgan spit the tongue out on the floor before picking up a fork from the table and jammed it through the punk's left eye. Crimson liquid spurted as the orb burst like a grape, steaming over his face while he uttered a strangled screamed. With a shove, she knocked him out of the way, kicking the fallen gun under the table before continuing over to the other gunman.

"Shit!" the lanky man yelled, swinging the waitress around in front of him as a human shield. "Stop or I'll shoot her," he warned. Morgan, of course, ignored him.

"Go ahead, won't stop me from killing you." She continued forward with a shark's smile on her face. He pointed his gun away from the waitress to her, and then jumped as she reached out for it. Trying to jerk the weapon away, he squeezed the trigger, releasing the bullet to race out of the barrel and rip through her chest. With a grunt of pain, Morgan stumbled to her knees, blood pouring from the small hole, and swore under her breath.

The waitress screamed again, quaking in her skin as her eyes widened in horror at the chaotic events. The gunman shook, his eyes wild and kinetic from adrenaline while he spun the older woman around to face him before yelling orders to the rest of the diner's customers.

"Give us all the money in here!" he demanded in a shaky voice, waving his gun back and forth between the cook at the counter and the people curled up under the tables.

The bleached blonde Morgan forked let out a muffled groan, cupping his ruined eye as blood dripped between his fingers. He tried staggering to his knees, clutching the table for support, and pulled himself up.

"Tahf, the thsok mi oy. The bish stob mi oy."

"Asshole, you need to make sure someone is dead before turning your back on them."

At the sound of her voice, all eyes turned from the robbers as Morgan regained her feet. Scratching at the wound above her left breast, she ignored the wicked itch that spread from a healing wound while the hole in her chest closed itself from the inside out, pushing the bullet out from the opening to fall to the linoleum with a soft *plink*. Blood smeared wherever her fingers moved, creating an almost abstract picture on her skin to give her the appearance of a horror movie victim. Raising her fingers to her mouth, she licked the scarlet stain from the tip of one before giving her audience a wicked grin of amusement.

Staring intently at the lanky man, Morgan pointed her finger at him, and then rushed him like a linebacker, sending the three of them sprawling onto the linoleum floor. The waitress rolled away to cringe into a ball as Morgan rolled her intended target over and straddled the gunman. Reaching into her boot, she unclipped the switchblade hidden there then snapped open the knife. With a soft *shick* the slender blade appeared.

"I was having a pleasant meal here and you two fuckers ruined it. Thanks." With a sharp movement, she jerked the blade down and impaled his throat before pulling it out sideways at an angle. A hot spray splattered across her front and with a grimace Morgan slowly stood, grabbing a napkin from a table to wipe the blood from her face and knife before releasing the blade and clipping it back in her boot. Stepping away from the body, she looked down at the crying waitress.

"Sorry about that." Sighing, Morgan reached for her wallet, pulled out a couple of hundreds before tossing them on the floor next to her. "Keep the change."

Walking past the blonde leaning over the table that she had vacated a moment earlier, Morgan grabbed the back of his head and slammed it down hard on the linoleum top. The force of the blow rattling plate and cup as the fork submerged deep into his brain. For a moment his body stiffened, then his body jerked sporadically before falling limp to the floor. Pausing for a second at her table, Morgan grabbed the rest of her sandwich and left.

14

Slamming the door to the converted warehouse open, Morgan stalked in, tossing her keys on the small table to her right. The sandwich she ate left a stone in her belly and she regretted acting as violently as she did. *I should have handled this without killing*, she griped to herself. Keeping the lights off, she headed into the kitchen, looking for a drink and something to clean herself off with.

"Why didst thou leave?"

Spinning around, she spied Malachi sitting in her favorite plush forest green chair, watching her with his cat-slit eyes, his booted feet resting on her coffee table. Keeping his eyes firmly glued to her face, the were looked pale and worn, his hair damp and slicked back from his handsome face. He sat shirtless, with his muscular chest glistening from sweat and drying blood created by the criss crossing of slowly healing wounds. It seemed the Mor'sin'dar Queen once more inflicted her anger on him, showing that distance was no matter to her displeasure. Glancing at the wall clock behind him, she noted the time, and then lowered her gaze to him again.

"I needed to think about what you told me."

In one swift and violent movement, Malachi stood, storming across the room in broad strides as his boots echoed on the tile floor. Reaching Morgan, he grabbed her wrist, pulling her back toward him.

"Thou art hurt," he growled deep in the back of his throat as his eyes raked over her chest and the streaks of crimson over it. "Wert thou attacked? Did more assassins come for thee?"

Irritated at being manhandled, Morgan's eyes narrowed as her voice took on a dangerous edge. "Correction, Malachi. I was hurt, but now I'm fine. Now let go of me," she demanded.

He continued to stare down at her, taking in the blood smear across her chin and throat. "Who did this to thee?" he demanded, his eyes flashing in the dim of the room.

"Doesn't matter, they're dead." Pulling back, she tried to jerk her wrist out of his grasp, but his grip tightened, bruising her skin as his own knuckles whitened from his hold. Slender dark brows gathered together as she stared up at him, her demeanor turning icy.

"Let...go."

For several tense moments they held each other's gaze until reluctantly Malachi loosened his hold. Lowering his hand to take her own, he led her into the bathroom, turned on the shower, then began removing Morgan's leathers. With every touch he placed on her skin her body burned until it felt like a blazing inferno in need to be quenched.

As if sensing her need, Malachi grabbed Morgan's waist and spun her around to shove her hard against the shower wall, kissing her like a man possessed, touching her body everywhere he could reach.

Breathless, Morgan wrapped her arms around his shoulders, holding him to her as she raised a leg to wrap it around his waist. Quickly removing his own clothes to rid himself of all barriers between them, he slid deep into her. Across his chest, blood seeped from slow healing wounds his Queen's magick had made, covering her breasts in a crimson fluid that quickly washed away as the hot water from above pounded steadily down on them. Reaching down with his free hand, he grabbed her other leg and wrapped it around his waist with its twin before setting a pounding rhythm into her.

Adjusting herself so he slid in with ease, Morgan pressed her breasts into his chest, feeling her nipples grow hard and aching with need. Her mouth met his, devouring him with each kiss while she held his head steady to hers. Knocking back into the hard tiles of the shower, she moaned with his thrusts, feeling her own lust rise sharply.

Following with a groan of his own, Malachi bent his neck at an angle, lowering his mouth to her breasts to capture a hard nipple with his lips. Rolling the nub over his tongue, he tugged at it gently with his teeth before suckling. Placing his hands under her ass, he held her against the shower as he moved within, eliciting low moans of pleasure to escape her. The corners of Malachi's lips lifted as their eyes met, holding firm until sheer ecstasy flowed from the center of her core up through her body, causing her toes to curl and eyes to roll back in her head. She gasped, feeling a deep rumbling purr begin in the Were's chest at her reaction, and her breathing quickened as the soft vibrations he created worked their way throughout her. Closing her eyes, she leaned her head back against the wall and moaned.

For a moment Malachi stopped, pulling them away from the wall to carry her next door to the spare bedroom, and laid her down on the bed before climbing over her prone body. Cracking her eyes open to slits, Morgan watched as he placed himself back between her legs, sliding deep inside her before he began moving once more. Raising her hips to meet him thrust for thrust, she wrapped her legs tight around his waist as the rhythm of his pounding further heightened her senses.

Nipping at her neck, Malachi grazed the sensitive flesh with his teeth while he moved, drawing soft *ah-ah* sounds from her. Not being able to resist his animal nature, the Werepanther bit her shoulder as a growl ripped from deep within his throat.

"Thou art mine, Morriganna."

147

Lowering her hands down his back, Morgan felt his muscles ripple and stretch with each thrust as her fingers played along his smooth skin. Curling her fingers, her nails raked his back, bringing forth tiny ruby beads to wheel up to the surface before sliding her hands down to cup his ass. Hard, firm, and round, they clenched each time he slid into her and while holding him tight, she pushed him deeper, encouraging him to thrust harder. Spreading her legs wider to give him better access, she tossed her head back, closing her eyes tight as she prayed this would never stop.

Kissing up along the column of her throat, Malachi reached Morgan's lips before capturing them in a long, deep kiss, his tongue dancing over hers as he breathed in her heady scent. Leaning up slightly to catch her gaze, he watched her, his eyes possessive and proud. Nostrils flaring, he breathed in their sex as his smile turned dark.

Feeling uncomfortable with the intenseness of his gaze, Morgan lowered her eyes from his, looking instead at his throat and the furiously beating vein under the tanned skin.

"Look at me, Morriganna. I want to look into thy eyes when thou dost come." His voice was low and hoarse with passion, drawing her eyes back up to meet his. The color of them flared an intense amber, several shades darker than normal, yet glowing with a deep fire.

A wave of pleasure rose once again, building higher and higher and higher. Lowering one of her hands between them, she brushed her fingers along his abdomen, feeling the muscles bunch under her touch until she reached his manhood, slick with their combined juices. He groaned as she moved her fingers around the base of his shaft, feeling as he entered her, feeling the intensity of their becoming one in the most physical of ways.

Once again, Malachi dipped his head back to Morgan's shoulder and slowly licked at the bite he left on her, the mark he left claiming her to be his.

Raising his eyes, he watched as small moans of pleasure fell from her lips, the sounds spurring him on, making him drive harder and faster into her.

Keeping her eyes on his, Morgan's orgasm built, growing stronger until she could no longer contain it. A scream ripped from her throat, causing her to arch her back to trap her hand between their bodies.

"Oh, yeeesss!" she cried, the sound echoing throughout the room.

He lowered his head and bit down on her shoulder again, bringing forth another scream to tear from her as her body shook in contractions. His smile stretched as he watched the intense looks that passed over her face, and then sank his teeth deep into the fleshy base of her neck where it joined the shoulder, flooding her with orgasmic pain that shot right to her groin. His hands slid around her back as he lifted her off the bed, making his angle into her shift, but no less deep.

"Yes, Morriganna, let me hear thy scream."

Lost in the intense pleasure, Morgan was barely aware when Malachi joined her, shouting his own pleasure as her orgasm crashed down around her.

"Malachi!"

With one last cry Morgan's body jerked against him as his hands pressed flat against her back to hold her in place against him. She chanced one last look into his feral eyes before her head fell back, arms dropping down to her sides as darkness overtook her senses.

With a satisfied smile, the Were lowered her onto the bed, removing himself from her while laying her out on the sheets. When she began to stir, he ran a hand over her stomach as if imagining it distended with his child, knowing even if it was that he probably would have no voice in what would happen to the half-breed. With a frown, he sat up as Morgan's eyes fluttered for a moment before opening to spy the Were watching her intently.

"Wow. That was intense." She flashed a tired smile, wiping at the bead of perspiration running down her hairline.

Malachi answered in a crooked grin of his own as he moved his legs over the edge of the bed.

"Yes, it was." Leaning over to capture Morgan's lips with his own, he gave her a soft kiss, and then stood up. "Let me go get us something to quench our thirsts. I feel parched."

As she moved to sit up, he placed a hand on the side of her head, cupping her cheek before brushing his thumb over her soft skin.

"No, stay, I shall be back. I shall bring something for us to eat also." He wiggled his eyebrows suggestively as he turned to leave. Padding on bare feet from the bedroom back to the bathroom, his smile turned predatory as he grabbed his pants and redressed. With a brief glance back at the woman lying in bed, he headed out into the living room, sliding his hand into his pocket to brush his fingers against the small vials within.

15

"Morgan, where have you been? We've been worried." Lisa's concerned voice sounded tiny and annoying to Morgan as she cracked her eyes open to look at the clock on her nightstand. Making a face, she scooted up on her elbows and rubbed a hand over her eyes, trying to remove any sleep left in it. 2:18 in the afternoon. Damn, she slept in.

"Morgan...hello? Are you there?"

"Yeah, I'm here," Morgan mumbled, casting a quick glance beside her to find Malachi still out cold in the bed. His back faced her with a sheet draped haphazardly over his hips, bearing to view his muscled back that narrowed down to a lean waist and an absolutely gropeable ass. A smile teased the corner of her lips as she remembered the feel of his body over hers, the way his muscles bunched and flexed as he...

"Why haven't you called?" Lisa interrupted her friend's trail of thoughts, bringing an annoyed look to Morgan's face as she pulled back her sheets and shifted her legs off the bed. Standing up, she moved to the door of her open bedroom and walked out of the room, ignoring the way her kitten wove around her ankles, trying to get attention.

"I've been kinda busy."

"Oh yeah, I bet. It's that guy. Ain't it? The one from the club that you went chasing after." Lisa paused, as if gathering her thoughts. Then with a hesitant voice, she asked, "Morgan, are you going to tell us what happened? Who was that woman and why did you...?"

Padding down the stairs, Morgan made her way into the living room and flopped down on the couch, motioning to her kitten to join her. With ears alert and a mischievous look in her eyes, Sonji bound up from the floor, landing with a grace only a feline could have, and made her way over to her mistress. With a brief glance up toward her bedroom, Morgan scratched behind the kitten's ear, listening to the rumble of the tiny purr box, and sighed. She'd been living in this city for a while and really didn't want to move. She'd moved too much as it was and was tired of creating new histories for herself. It sucked meeting new people and frankly she kinda enjoyed the company she had but no human had ever known what she was, who she was, and it needed to stay that way.

"It's not something to be discussed over the phone, Lisa."

"That's fine," Lisa cut in. "Terri and I'll meet you some place, for lunch, you know. But we...we just need to know what's going on."

"You wouldn't believe me if I told you," muttered Morgan as she stretched her back, working on the kinks sleeping in left.

"Morgan, people died. I've never..."

"Not now, Lisa. I told you, not over the phone."

Morgan could picture her friend frowning, her bottom lip caught between her teeth and her normally smooth brow wrinkling in concern and confusion. Lisa was almost obsessed about not getting wrinkles and it was a standing joke how when worried Lisa's brow would furrow like a prune. But now was not the time for jokes.

"Then when?"

Running a hand over her face, Morgan debated on how to clean up this mess. For hundreds of years she spent painstaking time making sure no one knew who or what she was. Now, two people that knew suddenly *knew her*. It was time to fix this and move on. Glancing around the base of her warehouse, she shook her head with regret.

"Can you give me a couple hours and we'll meet, say, at four and we'll go get something to eat. Talk then."

"Okay, promise you won't try and flake out on us?" Lisa asked, her voice tinged with worry.

"You don't need to worry. I'll pick you guys up at Terri's. See you then."

Morgan hung her phone up at Lisa's goodbye and debated where to take them. Some place less public so she wouldn't be disturbed. Laying the phone on the couch next to her, she closed her eyes, leaning her head back as a touch of regret crossed her face. *Damn, I actually liked them.*

~~~

Morgan honked the horn of her Mustang, glancing through the passenger window as she waited for Terri and Lisa to emerge from the small house. Spying the front door opening, she leaned over to open the passenger side door, then sat back. The feeling the pommel of her SIG Sauer brush against her arm beneath her jacket gave the assassin small comfort and she sighed deeply, knowing what she needed to do. Tugging her coat closed in front of her, Morgan waited as her friends made their way over to her vehicle.

"Right on time," Terri said with a grin, leaning down to look at Morgan as she adjusted the passenger seat forward. She winced and rubbed her side, giving a half shrug at the questioning look Morgan tossed her. "Bruised ribs. I got a small hairline crack in one. That was some night."

Stepping back, she waited as Lisa slipped into the backseat, and then moved her seat back so she could get in. The pretty blonde gave a nervous smile, her eyes flicking between Morgan and Terri as she adjusted her seatbelt and clipped it into place.

"Yeah, sorry about that." Morgan studied Terri as she settled into the front seat. After the petite brunette closed the door, she shifted the car out of PARK and pulled onto the street. For several minutes, a terse silence filled the interior as Morgan drove, heading for the Interstate 84 before taking a right onto it. Settling in for a drive, she reached out and flicked on the radio, the sounds of Nickelback's *Photograph* creating a barrier for any intimate conversation, at least for a while.

~~~

Terri shifted in her seat, eyeing her moody friend as she drove. Seeing the stony look on the woman's gorgeous face did not make her feel good; in fact, her stomach twisted in places. She remembered the way Morgan fought with the strange woman; there was no mercy in her eyes and she seemed to actually enjoy the combat. Not to mention her appearance. Nothing good was coming out of this, she could feel it in her gut and the way Morgan kept facing the front, avoiding any conversation, reminded her of Adriana's fatal last scene on the Sopranos. Not good.

Thoughts flashed in Terri's head, memories of jokes Morgan made about breaking legs and it dawned on her that maybe Morgan's wise cracks weren't part of a sense of humor but in fact truth. Leaning back in her seat, she heard the leather upholstery creak under her weight and stared out the side window. The scenery flew by, interrupted every once in awhile by the side of a car or truck.

She remembered back to the first time she met the woman who had become her best friend. It was in June, during the Rose Parade and she had ducked into a small corner store to escape the rain and grab a pack of cigarettes. All she had wanted was a smoke but instead she wound up in the middle of a robbery. Some crack head was holding a gun on the clerk, demanding all the money out of the cash register and when she stepped in, a small bell ringing to announce her entrance he turned the gun on her.

She had froze, eyes wide and felt her heart thudding hard inside her chest and crept her way toward where he motioned. At that point, the old clerk, probably Korean or something started babbling in a language she didn't understand. The gunman turned on him, yelling and she could see him sweating profusely under his dark cap. Next thing she knew the gun went off and she screamed.

That's when Morgan stepped out of an aisle she'd been standing in, a rolled up magazine in her hand. The woman moved faster than lightning, and smacked the guy across the side of the head with enough force to snap it back. He grunted and stumbled against the counter but by then Morgan was on him, shoving him backward until he was almost lying on the top of it, her knee in his groin and the magazine shoved against the Adam's apple bobbing up and down in his throat. She grabbed his gun, twisted it out of his grip before placing the end of the barrel between his eyes.

Morgan glanced once her way then straightened, a smile curving her lips and moved back, but not before smacking him once more across the face.

"Care to call the cops?" She asked and Terri complied, pressing 911 into her cell phone.

Morgan's eyes flickered over to her for a moment before moving back to the road. Glancing over the seat back at Lisa, Terri could see the worry in the blonde's eyes. She didn't like this. Something was up. Morgan, though moody and secretive, was never like this. They'd been friends for several years now. Hell, Morgan had even gone to her family's Thanksgiving and spent Christmas with them. It was like a whole new woman sat next to her, someone she didn't know.

~~~

"Morgan…" Terri began, "I think we need to talk abou—"

"Later. Wait until we get there."

A perturbed look crossed Terri's face. "Morgan, its better if we…"

"I said later. After we get there, I'll answer all your…"

"No, now." Their eyes met, Morgan's cold green ones clashing with Terri's stubborn dark gaze. "You're not putting us off. This is important."

Looking out the windshield, Terri noticed a small sign for Blue Lake Park. "Here, turn off here," she insisted.

Morgan debated at following her friend's little order; after all, she was just a human and soon to be a removed problem but after a sideways glance at the short brunette, she complied, turning the car onto the off ramp and down into the shaded area. The road bumped as it became graveled and she passed several parked cars before pulling into a spot a little ways from the others for privacy. Keeping her face solemn, Morgan stared at the front window. A bullet to the back of the head, quick and painless, would solve this problem, but actually talking about it was almost too much to deal with. Cut and run, her instincts screamed, but for once she ignored that advice and listened to the leather squeak as Terri shifted around in her seat face her.

"Morgan, we've been friends for a fairly long time now. You understand that no matter what we will remain friends, no matter how bizarre the answers may be?" Leaning her shoulder into the back of the seat, Terri watched her friend, searching for some type of answer in her face. "We saw what happened, saw…something and that woman was trying to kill you. Talk, explain what exactly went down?"

Slipping the tip of her tongue between her lips to wet them, Morgan debated with herself, and then moved her eyes to look over at the woman in the front seat. With a passing glance to Lisa, she started. "I'm not from here."

"Kinda figured that," Lisa chirped in, only to be rewarded by a dirty look from Morgan. Scrunching back in her seat, she made a zipping motion over her mouth.

With a deep breath, Morgan continued. "As I said, I'm not from around here. Not Portland, not America, not even from your world. And though I've lived here for a very long time, my home is from beyond the Veil, a..." She made a slight motion with her fingers. "...gateway between Earth and the Lands of the Fae."

Watching the others' reactions, she returned to her tale. "I, as you figured out I'm sure, am not human. I'm Sidhe, one of the Fae folk from the ShadowedLands. I was sent here by my King—you could say banished—and I'm not allowed to return until my banishment has been lifted."

"Sidhe?" Terri asked. "You mean like an...elf?"

Morgan rolled her eyes at the comparison. So much easier it would have been to use a bullet. *Not too late.* She shoved it out of her mind. "We don't live in trees or go dancing through meadows. In fact, most of us aren't sweet or cute."

"I could see that," Lisa piped up, then hunkered back down after Morgan glared at her.

"So, when you went all...glowy and stuff, that's what you really look like?" Terri inquired. At a brief nod from Morgan, she added, "And the woman you fought, bad guy?"

Morgan shrugged as she looked away, searching the view outside her windshield. "It depends on who you ask. There are some who consider me the bad guy."

"Why did she attack you?" Terri asked.

With a shake of her head, Morgan remained silent, wondering what thoughts could be passing through her friend's head that moment. She could imagine it. A Fae, Sidhe, something not human. Maybe it was too much for a human of this day and age to take. She had never known Terri to show interest in anything fantasy or make believe, except if it had to do with playing naughty nurse with her current boy toy.

Her eyes flickered over to the petite brunette and watched her run a hand over her mouth, seeing the storm of questions in the other woman's eyes. For a moment Terri opened her mouth but it snapped shut as soon as she noticed Morgan watching her.

Lisa rustled uncomfortably in the backseat before speaking up, her voice soft and stilted. "So, ah, everything good then? Still friends?"

With a self-depreciating chuckle, Morgan looked down at her hands. "I've never done this before," she said.

"Done what?" Terri asked.

"Let someone who knew what I was live."

Lisa's eyes grew wide at the statement as Terri laughed. "Well, there's always a first." Patting Morgan's shoulder, she gave the woman a sweet smile. "Let's go get some dinner. You can always kill us later if you feel it's necessary."

16

Two weeks later found Morgan running down a dark street hard on the heels of three Bollags. Her surprise at finding the twisted Fae exiting her favorite nightclub floored her only long enough for them to get a head start down the road before she reacted. After muttering an excuse to Terri for bailing on her, Morgan slipped off her heels and took off after the human-enshrouded creatures. Damn, she hated running bare-footed in the city, especially on a dark, drizzling evening, so ignoring Danu knows what that littered the street she kept up the chase. She knew she owed Terri a night out, especially after abandoning her after the fight with Arduin, but it looked like tonight wouldn't be that night. Breathing hard with her arms pumping by her sides, Morgan's expression grew grim and narrowed her eyes in determination as she followed her prey.

I'm not going to lose them.

Lately she had been having trouble focusing whenever she had work, but tonight she was determined it was going to stop. Ever since Malachi appeared in her life, all she ever thought about was being around him. His body, his scent, the way he looked at her and kissed her. Swearing under her breath, Morgan tried pushing the Were from her thoughts and once more concentrated on the task at hand.

Following the Bollags as they turned left, she watched as they disappeared into a dilapidated four-story brownstone apartment building. Entering not far behind them, she ran up the stairs, taking two at a time, her long black hair fluttering in the wind behind her. Looking over his shoulder to check if they were still being followed, the last Bollag's eyes widened when he spotted his pursuer no more than ten feet behind him. With urgency, he pushed past his companions and sped up the stairs to jump over refuse and a bum passed out from too much liquor.

Gripping the worn wooden railing firmly in one hand, Morgan swung herself up and over it to land in a soundless crouch on the second floor, effectively blocking the Bollags as they turned to continue up. With a dark smile, she stood, moving toward them with deadly intent. Whatever game the Dark Queen played by giving free passage to these creatures into the world of humans, she was determined to remove the problem.

At the Sidhe's sudden appearance before them, two of the Bollags scattered. The leader growled, narrowing his blue eyes in a sneer before he charged her. Drawing her daggers from their catch on her forearms, Morgan swung up with a fist as if to punch him, instead allowing the blade to cleanly slice through his neck and the right side of his face. She followed through with a blow to his chest, sinking her second blade deep into his heart. The Bollag's eyes widened in disbelief as smoke exited the wound. With a thump, he fell to the ground. She stepped over his corpse, now alone in the hall. Her dark hair swirled about her shoulders as she turned her head to search for where the last two Bollags disappeared to.

At that moment a door to her right opened as a bedraggled young man stepped into the opening, tangled dark hair hanging over his eyes. They stared at each other for a second before he ran his fingers over his eyes as if to clear his vision. In an instant, she recognized his kind. Were. *What the fuck? Were they jumping out of the woodwork now?* The young man seemed confused, drug-addled, and from the way his hand gripped the doorknob, about to pass out. She wanted to question him—why was he here and where was he from?—but she didn't have the time. Morgan lifted a hand, her finger pointed at him, and she opened her mouth to speak when a blur from the side of her vision caught her attention. With wide steps, she moved toward the young Were, glancing at him as she passed him by.

"Stay here," she whispered, she positive he heard her command. Spotting the Bollags farther down the hall Morgan ran after them, picking up speed while she moved, her blades at ready as she gritted her teeth in concentration.

One Bollag turned to look back over his shoulder and stopped to stare in shock at the Morrigu as she ran toward him. Behind her, her black coat fluttered, resembling a pair of large black wings, the wings of the crows she so favored, and left him dumbstruck. Fear flowed through him and he began to quake. Finding no means to escape he turned, hissing, and ducked low as her blades swung at him with deadly intent.

They moved around each other like dancers—her slicing, him dodging— circling one another until with a flick of her wrist, she released one blade, sending it flying toward him. With a *thunk* it sank deep into his chest and as blood began to bubble from its wound smoke rose in reaction to the cold iron in her weapon. Screeching in agony, it grabbed its chest then erupted into flame until nothing was left but scattering ashes.

Pausing to pick up her blade, Morgan felt strong arms grab her from behind. One arm wrapped around her waist as a hand wrapped onto her long hair and jerked her head back to expose her neck.

In an instant, the young Were appeared, ripping the Bollag from her back. With one fluid motion, he twisted his hands and the creature's neck broke. The body slumped before he released it to the ground, and then he jumped back, not sure what he had done. Feeling the grip in her hair and around her waist suddenly go slack, Morgan turned to slash, pulling back her blade when she found no Bollag but the disheveled young Were watching her with shock on his wearied face. They stared at each other for what seemed forever before Morgan re-sheathed her weapons.

"Who are you, Were? What are you doing here?" She glanced around at her surroundings, taking note of the paint peeling from the walls, the cracked windows, and doors falling from the hinges.

The young man shrugged, looking nervous as he wiped a hand along his thigh. He seemed confused, almost not cognoscente of what was going on around him. Noticing his pallor and the dark circles under his eyes, besides the rank dirty threadbare clothes and his thin appearance, she approached him. Taking his chin in her hand, she turned his head left and right, looking over his face. A day's growth of beard pricked her fingers. He would be handsome cleaned up and with a little more meat on his bones.

She frowned, letting him go, and stepped back as she began breathing from her mouth. His body odor was strong from a long time without bathing but underneath was the musk and wildness his kind usually put out.

"Where is your pack?" she asked. Any Were this young very rarely was without an elder to teach and guide him. "Are you hungry? You have any place to stay?"

Peering up at her from under his stringy bangs, he shrugged again, unaware he scratched at his arm and the sores under the jacket sleeve. From the hazy look in his stormy grey eyes and his jittery nervousness Morgan figured he was coming down from his high and would need a fix soon. He was already starting to shake and his filth caked hand balled into a fist as he noticed her studying him.

"I'm always hungry," he muttered under his breath and looked away. "Look, I gotta go. Just thought you needed help and now..." His voice slipped away as he looked at the corpses on the floor.

"If you're hungry, I..."

"Not much of a nightclub, but still plenty of action." Those words interrupted Morgan's thoughts as she turned to find Malachi leaning against a wall, arms crossed loose over his chest. His eyes roved over the hall, lingering on her face before turning his gaze to the startled young man. A low growl filled the air as the two men stared at each other, the soft rumble coming from the young man beside her. Startled by his reaction, she turned to stare when Malachi took a threatening step forward.

The Werepanther's eyes flashed in the dim hall light before he spoke. "Run away, puppy."

Without being told twice, the young Were took off without a backward glance, his feet pounding on the stairs as he quickly made his way down then and out of the building. Disgusted by the way Malachi reacted to the man, Morgan turned away.

"Were you following me?"

"The Wolf was interested in thee, checking thy scent. He should have left when he scented thou were mated."

Ignoring his comment, Morgan nudged the dead Bollag with her toe before squatting to rummage through his pockets. Not finding anything of interest, she brushed her hands off as she stood and glanced at the Were. "Well?"

"Well what?" He watched her, seeing her frustration at his not answering her question, then chuckled. "I know thou hath made a date with thy human friends, but I wished to join thee. When I arrived at the club, thou hast begun thy chase and I followed, thinking thou might need my help. But apparently thou did not, not with thy young hero coming to thy rescue."

Glancing down the hall, a few stragglers starting to shuffle out of their hidey-holes. Not wanting more attention Morgan lowered her voice and touched his arm.

"We need to get out of here. My night with the girls is ruined sooo...you need to get me some dinner. We can talk and maybe..."

She stared at a skinny black woman who leaned against a doorframe, scabs on her arms and bruises on her face from years of drugs and neglect. Something about these people, this place, knotted her stomach. Everyone looked so lost, so desperate. A flash of the young Were's face appeared in her mind. *What was he doing here?* Hating the feelings that tugged at her, she turned back to Malachi, wanting to escape this hell of hopelessness.

"Let's get out of here."

Nodding toward the stairwell she ran up only a few moments before, Morgan headed down the hall and regretted the loss of her newly-acquired heels. Damn, she had just bought them that afternoon and now here she was, trying to ignore the stickiness of the carpeted hall with who knew what the hell lay in the stained brown weave. From the smell of things, urine, vomit, and…she wrinkled her nose, reminding herself to get a pedicure first thing tomorrow morning.

Malachi followed the woman down the stairs, stepping over garbage, and out of the building. When they arrived on the streets, they found it mostly deserted, surprising since this was the worst section of town and as early in the night as it was. A few hookers stood huddled near street lamps, watching the couple as they waited for a date from johns far and few. As the two of them walked in silence, Morgan glanced at her lover every so often, questions filling her head only to be interrupted by thoughts of wanting to feel his hands on her body. Even in the stench of the street, she could smell his scent, warm, masculine, and inviting.

Retracing her steps, they emerged back to the center of the city, bright lights in the dark and the rush of cars as people headed to their favorite clubs, bars, or restaurants in search of fun and companionship. A few blocks down Morgan spied a restaurant with outdoor tables, and headed to it, motioning to the wait staff before they claimed the table. Sliding into their seats, she shrugged off her coat and set it beside her as a waitress brought over two menus.

~~~

Malachi watched thoughts dance across Morgan's face and knew she struggled internally with everything that had been happening these past few weeks. Though independent, he could sense her longing for him, her growing dependence on his presence. When her friend Terri had called, it took a while for her to be convinced for a night out. After finally agreeing, she had asked him to come but he balked at the idea, instead convincing her to spend some time with her friends. It would be good to see how she reacted without him, to test the strength of the potion the Queen had given him to keep her interested and compliant. He knew the cologne he got from the alchemist worked for she could barely keep her hands off of him, and so far everything went as planned but it was best to double check just to make sure. Last thing he needed was for her anger to flare and perhaps cause her to pull away and ask why he was really there. Of course, he followed her to keep an eye on the Morrigu, as per his Queen's instructions and the excuse he gave for his sudden appearance was plausible enough.

Biting the inside of his cheek, he scanned the menu as he thought. Even now he could feel her innate power rolling off her in waves, a power she normally kept in check. For the last two days, it had been like that, the leaking of power as if she was having trouble keeping it concealed.

Glancing up, Malachi watched her face, her eyes moving over the menu as she debated on what seemed enticing to her that moment. After dismissing one item then another before sighing Morgan set the menu down on the table. A thought occurred to him, a brief flash of insight, before he swiftly lowered his gaze. *Could it have happened? Already?* Being discreet, he inhaled, searching for her scent. Separating out and ignoring the smells of the city, the exhaust from cars, smoke of cigarettes, and meals being served, he found the delicate aroma of roses, jasmine, and spice that was all hers and let the enticing perfume wrap around his senses. That was when he detected it. Sure enough, a small off-balance in her fragrance, a slighter higher rise of musk and pheromones, appealing in its own way and bringing out the claiming nature of his kind. *She breeds…*

Pleasure and anxiety warred within him. He should be pleased, for he fulfilled his Queen's directive and sired a child on the Morrigu, yet watching her he couldn't help but wonder…what if? A child, one of his own. This would be the only time he could sire an offspring, and here he sat—instead of feeling happy and excited—filled with guilt and anger. The Queen had plans for the child, plans that had nothing to do with its welfare. Closing his eyes, he leaned his head forward and pinched the bridge of his nose. His time with Morriganna was near the end.

"Welcome to North's. Have you enough time to look over the menu or would you like some more?"

"I'm good," Morgan spoke up, her voice invading Malachi's thoughts and causing his eyes to open and focus once more on the menu. "I'll have the crispy chicken salad with sesame dressing and a Chardonnay."

"And you sir?" the waitress spoke again as she turned her attention to him.

Shaking his head to clear his thoughts, Malachi rumbled deep in his throat as his words came out in a soft growl. "Porterhouse, rare. A beer, stout."

"Would you like…?"

Looking up at the waitress, Malachi's eyes glowed in warning. "I do not care what else comes with it. Just get me the fucking steak."

Her head bobbing up and down like a bobble-head doll, the girl swallowed and took their menus, scurrying away from them to enter the open door of the restaurant and back to some form of sanctuary. As Malachi let out a weary breath, he spied Morgan watching him, her eyes dark and questioning. With a shake of his head, he blocked her inquisitive look and glanced out over the street.

For several minutes they sat in silence, listening to the sounds of the city and other diners speaking softly to each other before Morgan cleared her throat. She looked down, pondering, before looking back up at him. "Is everything alright?"

"Yes." Malachi glanced up at her, a slight smile on his lips. "Just thinking about the Bollags. Maybe I can visit the Ssri'tel'quessir Court and see if I can discover more information about their sudden influx of appearance."

Frowning, she tapped her fingers on the scarred wooden tabletop and nodded, as if sensing something had changed between them, but not knowing the why or how of it. Making a face, she reached up to tuck a lock of hair behind her ear. "So when are you leaving?"

"Tomorrow or the day after." He took a long drink from his water glass, halfway draining it before he set it back down on the table. Moving his hand to hers, he brushed her fingers with his, the touch enflaming her senses. "I think thou art with child."

Morgan blinked. "Exqueese me?"

"Thy scent is…different, it reminds me of the breeding females in the lairs." Watching her face for a reaction, he laid a solid hand on hers, curling his fingers around hers in comfort and security…and possessiveness. "Art thou pleased?"

~~~

Oh, yeah, something had changed, but not what she thought. *Pregnant? But how?* It took years in a relationship for a Sidhe to get pregnant and even then children were rare. Confusion set in and unrest. *A child…but a half-breed?*

She had a child once, a daughter, and one she rarely saw, though not by choice. Tessa was fully grown, a woman on her own living somewhere in Florida since she inherited her mother's exclusion from all the Courts and her father's annoying personality.

Morgan studied his face, searching for some sign about what he thought about the predicament, but all she saw was a stony outer shell and eyes that gave nothing away about his thoughts and feelings. Other than the warm grip he had on her hand and the slight way he squeezed it, she would have thought him talking about the weather. *He wants this child*, she thought, *but do I?* She already showed her failure as a mother with Tessa, could she ruin another life? Deep inside her, a warm spot grew, hope for a new beginning and something else. *My life has been nothing but tragedy and failure. Do I truly want to do this?*

Taking a deep breath, she held it for several long moments until she could regain control of her chaotic thoughts, and then slowly released it. Keeping his gaze, Morgan wet her lips as her throat suddenly went dry. He's the High Queen's pet, her personal assassin. This was but a fling, something to amuse her until she found who was behind her beloved King's death. Malachi's gaze wavered at her silence, revealing hope and anxiety. Damn, her heart about leapt out of her chest at the look of want he gave her.

"Yes, I'm…I'm pleased." Turning her hand in his, she squeezed it back in return as a smile split his lips. "A baby…wow. Was not expecting this."

"Neither was I. I had always wanted a child, but in my position," he breathed in, his eyes growing intense, "I never thought that was plausible. What thou gives me…"

～～～

The waitress reappeared, bringing a tray laden with their meal. Releasing her hand, Malachi sat back observing Morgan's stunned reaction, feeling a slight guilty in his treachery. *Mayhap Queen Moirethe will give me the child to raise, especially if it is a male.* If he persuaded her the child would be useful alive and under his care, there might be a reward in this plan after all but Morgan would be left heartbroken and disgraced by breeding with an animal. Pushing aside the guilt that niggled at the pit of his stomach, Malachi focused on the thought of raising a child of his own instead.

They ate in silence, Morgan avoiding his eyes and each in their own thoughts until they finished. Standing up afterward, she tossed three twenties on the table then headed to the opening in the small fence that surrounded the outlying tables, Malachi close on her heels. A chill forced its way down his spine, causing him to slow in his step and he turned, lifting his face to sniff the air, searching for what caught his attention. Nostril's flaring, he found the scent as the small hairs on the back of his neck rose and let out a low growl.

Across the street, standing below a street lamp, a man hunched, the hood of his old military jacket pulled up over his head, watching them. The young Were from the building, the one scented as a Wolf. The younger Were lifted his head, his face in shadows, and bared his teeth, snarling. The air around them became electrically charged, causing people on the street and back at the tables to shift in unease, unsure yet unaware as to what was taking place. Malachi felt a challenge begin to issue forth from deep inside his chest. Taking a step forward, he watched as the man straightened and tensed.

Studying the other Were, Malachi felt his muscles bunch and shift under his jacket, then noticed the way the stranger's eyes shifted from him to behind him at the same time he felt a warm hand touch his shoulder. A soft fragrance reached his nose, making him edgy. *Not here, not tonight.* He watched the Wolf's gaze switch between Morgan and him and cursed internally, having a premonition that the kid was possibly going to be a problem for him later. Gritting his teeth in anger, Malachi jerked to a stop as Morgan's soft voice reached his ear, her breath warm against the back of his neck.

"Reign it in, big boy. We don't need to draw attention here." Her hand relaxed its grip and left his shoulder.

With a last look and snarl at the other Were, Malachi gave a brief nod in acknowledgement and followed the Morrigu down the street.

17

"Fuck."

Staring at the slender white stick pinched between her fingers, Morgan cursed again before throwing the annoying thing into the trashcan with the eleven others. *Positive, all positive, but how?* Even though she used no birth control, it was well known how hard it was for a Sidhe woman to get pregnant. After all, it had taken her and her ex-husband over sixty years to get pregnant with their only child, but for her to get pregnant after only a few weeks of sex…Morgan ran her hand through her hair and paced the length of her bathroom.

It was rumored Weres were very prolific; after all, in the wild they had children abound. Yet the Weres in the Courts were prohibited to reproduce unless commanded to, kept neutered by chemicals in their food. Could that be the case? Since Malachi had been here, he hadn't been kept under lock and key and now she was pregnant.

Closing her eyes, Morgan sat down on the toilet and held her head in her hands. *Sweet Danu, what do I do now?* Her mind swirled around in a chaotic frenzy, moving from one thought to another. A baby appealed to her, but under these circumstances was it the smartest move? Surely Malachi would be punished if the Queen found out, and knowing that sadistic bitch she would have him castrated, keeping the proof in a jar on her nightstand.

Soft fur rubbed against her ankles, drawing her attention down. Sonji peered up at her with round yellow eyes, blinking in the slow ways felines tended to do when time meant nothing to them. *Where have you been hiding at?* She reached down to scratch behind the kitten's ears. Sonji answered by standing on her back paws, stretching up to touch her mistress's knee while making a soft *thrupt* sound. With a heavy sigh, the woman glanced back at the garbage can and shook her head. Argh.

With a growl, Morgan pushed off from her seat and resumed her pacing. What to do, what to do? Well, there was no question she would keep the child. To hell with what anyone thought. Halfbreed or not, the baby would be loved and cared for, but now she definitely needed to become involved with getting Moirethe off the throne, otherwise Arduin or others like her would keep coming.

Prince Ansil or Prince Khelvan? The third brother was too much of a simpleton to even consider in the race for the throne. But which of the two brothers should she throw her lot with? The elder resembled his mother and was a sight to behold, but looks alone did not mean he was worthy of the throne, no matter that some Sidhe believed beauty meant perfection. If such things were true, the Queen would have been the perfect choice to rule, but deep inside her was a rottenness that no amount of cleansing would purge.

What she remembered of Prince Ansil was a cool and aloof young man, not one prone to impulse, but calculating and intelligent. The boredom he eternally displayed was a façade he used to hide his interest in all things political and intrigue but a cruelness lurked in the depths of his eyes and rumors of his twisted bed games had reached even her ears. Even so, he never seemed to lack for female companionship.

Now Prince Khelvan on the other hand was snooty and angry, given to outbursts of fury that usually ended with destruction of some form or another. Ever one to remind others of his rank, he used his position to get what he desired, regardless of consequence. He despised his mother which was a plus to his side, though not a whole lot more about him Morgan felt was worth her time.

I need to go get advice. She rubbed her eyes, suddenly tired and drained emotionally. Thinking, she went through a list of possible people to talk to, dismissing one after another until she remembered the Cauldron Witch. King Silvas was headed her way when he died. Perhaps she would know more, more than she was willing to reveal to those that remained loyal to the Mor'sin'dar Court and its current ruler.

Making up her mind, Morgan opened the bathroom door and headed to her closet, pulling out a pair of boots and several daggers, weapons just in case her situation required them. Then she returned to the bathroom and stood before the full-length mirror. Scooting the curious kitten back with her foot, she breathed in, listening for any sound that Malachi might have returned, for he would try to stop her. Hearing nothing except the soft thrum of her fish tank and the steady tick of a wall clock, Morgan pressed her fingers to the cool surface of the mirror as she whispered several words in the ancient language of her people. Under her touch, the silvery surface rippled like water, calling her to enter. Taking a step forward, she entered the portal, leaving her kitten behind.

~~~

She appeared on the other side in a small storage room cluttered with broken items, golden candle sticks, and dark silks draped over furnishing.

Taking a deep breath, Morgan took in the scents from a world she had not been in for several hundred years. Nostalgia filled her soul, memories of friends and lovers dancing through her mind. Closing her eyes, she tried blocking out the sights, forcing her mind to calm, and then opened them again, straight-faced. That was all in the past, now was all that mattered. After walking over to the closed door, she set her palm on the wall beside it, concentrating. Sending her senses outward, she scouted the immediate area until she was sure the halls beyond were clear, then cracked open the door.

Sliding out, she silently closed the door behind her with a soft click before gradually heading down the stone hall, careful to stay attentive to any sights or sounds that would alert her to anyone that might discover her presence. Passing through several corridors, Morgan found the passage heading down toward the Underarch, the old Courts long closed from years of neglect and disuse.

For several hours, Morgan moved through the darkness, her night vision the only thing keeping her from running into walls or stumbling over broken columns, breathing through her mouth to avoid sneezing from all the years of dust built up. Not too long ago her King walked these halls, walked in secret to avoid detection himself, but from who and why? Not sure she would ever truly know, Morgan chased those thoughts away, thoughts that tried to drag her down into mourning, and continued her vigilant course through the past.

The hall ended, opening up into a wondrous chamber that even giants would have been dwarfed in. Tir nag Goll. Morgan paused for a moment, taking in the ancient splendor before her, and stared in awe before coming back to her senses. This had been the Courts of the Ancient Ones, the first of the Sidhe before they branched off into various factions.

My father is one of them. The small hairs on her arms stood on end as goose bumps raised along her skin. Her father, a man she tried to forget and one she rarely saw. The first time she saw him she and her sisters were children and he appeared from nowhere. She was no more than five, sitting on the floor with her sisters, when she looked up to find a man standing in the doorway. Remembering her mother's voice in the background, arguing with her husband, Morgan never understood the words yhey spoke, for they were whispering angrily. Later she came to understand that the one who sired her was not the man her mother had married.

The stranger studied her, ignoring her sisters, though they appeared the same in every physical way but color. He knew whose daughter she was, for her blood called to him, his power sang through her veins and announced to all she was different.

The next time she saw him was after her rise in the ranks of High King

Silvas's guard, her savagery and bloodlust bringing her to the sovereign's attention. She was brought before the King and charged with creating the Battle Crows, Silvas's personal assassins who would follow none but the High King himself. Her father appeared in the Great Hall after she received the name Morrigu, surprising all within by his proclamation of parentage. More than a few gasps and whispers could be heard in the following minutes and he disappeared once more after pausing to speak to her.

"Thou art my daughter, blood of mine. Make me proud and I shall give thee all I own. Thy soul will sing with each drop of blood thou shed and soon thee will come upon thy own. Know I will be watching thee."

His words were cryptic and still after all these years she had never figured them out. Not long after that, King Silvas wed Moirethe and the petty jealousies began in full. The last time she spoke to her father was after her banishment from the Courts. Harsh words spoken and heated tempers got the best of them. Since then they had not seen one another, not that she really cared. Other than giving her life there was not much he had ever done for her.

Continuing through the cavernous chamber, Morgan scanned the area. Great pillars stood in rows like silent sentries on guard for a kingdom long lost. Glancing up, she squinted, trying to find the ceiling, but blackness met her gaze instead. Out of nowhere, Morgan had the urge to scream just to see if her voice would echo. With a chuckle, she looked away, trying to decide which exit to take. From her view, there were twelve halls leaving this room, including the one she had entered through, three on each wall. All were as dark as the original hall she used, leaving her pondering how to find the Cauldron Witch.

How the hell does anyone find her? She glanced around. Perhaps by request only. Very few people had ever seen the Witch and none she knew of herself. It was rumored the Witch was older than even the Ancients themselves, as ancient as the world and its creation itself. If that were true, she would have more power radiating from her than any Sidhe of the realm.

Closing her eyes, Morgan spread her awareness out, seeking the spark of power that belonged to the Cauldron Witch. Slowly she turned in a circle and in her mind's eye saw the glow of eldrick power, shifting and flowing of energy through all the walls and pillars of the great chamber, swirling through the air like smoke to disappear in a great mass overhead. From each of the passages flowed the gauzy sifting haze, flowing like a lazy stream, each taking its own sweet time before continuing onto the life above.

It was to the passage down on the far right that caught Morgan's attention. The haze thickened to a fog, glowing brighter than the others and tumbled around like a river full of rapids, twisting and turning only to fall back upon itself.

"So, I'm guessing this is the way," Morgan muttered to herself, her voice sounding small in the vastness of the chamber. Opening her eyes, she released the spell that raised her inner eye and moved in the direction the flow of magick went. Once in the opening of the passage, she slowed her step, caution rising to the surface of her mind as she moved along. What was it the old stories had said? Visiting the Cauldron Witch had a price, for she always demanded a gift in exchange for her auguries. Oh well, she'd figure it out when she got there.

For several more hours she walked, hearing nothing in the dark of the tunnel except for the sound of her own breathing. Then in the distance a soft whispering reached her ears, words too low she could not understand them. Pausing, Morgan debated if she should continue, but instead letting out a deep breath, she put one foot forward and continued on. Soon light appeared in the distance, dim at first but growing brighter each step she took as the whispering became more distinguished. It was not voices Morgan heard but the sound of water washing against rock.

Water? Down this far underground? It was more than just a trickle or even a small stream; it had the sound of a large lake in a fierce wind or a small sea. Morgan hurried toward the light, pausing once she reached the end of the hall and stared at the sight that greeted her.

A cavern lit by light unknown was set deep into the underground. The ceiling curved upward with spires of twisted stone like pillars reaching toward it from the rocky ground. In the center of the gigantic chamber, filling the floor, was a great sea. Its waves lapped at the rugged shoreline, looking inviting yet ominous at the same time but something was off with the water.

Moving forward, Morgan stopped at the shoreline and kneeled down, skimming the tip of her middle finger over the liquid in case some danger lay within it, then she brought her finger up to her face for inspection. The color of scarlet met her eyes, warm and coppery scented. Blood. The sea was made up of blood, as if just poured from a vein.

Looking back up, Morgan scanned the room, the sea as far as her eyes could see, and noticed toward the center of that liquid what appeared to be an island, one made of stone. From the center of that, a pale glow rose as well as a soft cloud of smoke. Glancing around, there was nothing else to view and she decided that must be where the Cauldron Witch lived. Determined to proceed forward, Morgan stood, removing her weapons and clothes, placing them in an orderly pile, then gingerly dipped her toes in the blood water.

At least it's not cold. She waded in until the liquid reached her waist. Then leaning forward, she submerged herself, swimming with strong even strokes. It seemed she swam forever, her legs kicking with strength, pushing her body onward until finally, fighting exhaustion, she reached the rugged shore of the island.

Standing, Morgan brushed her hair back from her face, feeling warm droplets roll down her back, and stepped up onto a boulder. Reaching up, she found a handhold and began to climb, fingers and toes grasping for purchase as she pulled herself up until she reached the top. Standing up, she faced the center, ignoring the stings from small cuts on her hands and feet from the jagged rocks, and breathed in deeply as her eyes raked the immediate area.

A lone figure draped in gossamer rags sat on a small wooden chair facing Morgan, quiet and observant of the woman as the assassin stared back in return.

"Are you the Cauldron Witch?" Morgan asked, taking a step forward. As she did, a sharp pain attacked the sole of her foot, followed by a dry snapping sound. Glancing down, she noticed bones, delicate and slender, littered the floor she now stood on. Small animal and bird bones lay strewn about, mixed with something else. What that else was became quickly apparent when the dark-haired woman spied the small skulls lining the base of the cauldron—human skulls. Children, Morgan realized. The Cauldron Witch had a taste for infants.

Keeping her revulsion hidden from her face, Morgan looked once more at the Witch, studying the silent woman. Dressed in long flowing robes, face hidden behind veils, the Seer was all but indistinguishable. How tall she was, her shape, age, and appearance were hidden from Morgan's eyes; instead all that met the assassin was eerie silence. Heart thumping hard in her chest, she tried again.

"Cauldron Witch, I come seeking answers, answers only you can give."

"What will thou give?"

"Give?" Remembering the Cauldron Witch always requested a gift for service, Morgan's mind raced to find something suitable. *What to give, what to give?* She had brought nothing, not even her dagger. Resisting an urge to shield her flat belly and what grew beneath with her hand, she walked slowly around the cauldron as thoughts tumbled through her mind. The only thing she had of value with her was her life and her unborn child, neither of which she was willing to give away.

The Witch sat silent and unmoving as Morgan stopped no more than a few feet away. Up close, the tall assassin could see embroidery detail decorating the raggedy veils and robes covering the ancient Sidhe, ancient flowers and petals from a time long forgotten and felt the Witch watching her.

"I have nothing of importance to give, Witch. What you see is it."

Silence stretched between them, broken only by the soft lapping of the waves against rock until the Witch beckoned, raising a youthful hand from under the rags she wore to motion toward her. With a hesitation she rarely felt, Morgan inched forward slowly before stopping inches from the Witch's cloth-covered knees, looking down on bent head to wonder what lay beneath the gauzy fabric. Why did she keep herself hidden beneath layers of cloth when she lived alone in isolation? Was disfigurement something that cursed the Hag?

The Cauldron Witch's hand snapped out like a viper, snaring her wrist in a surprisingly strong vise grip which pulled her down toward the covered figure. Startled out of her thoughts, Morgan tried to react and jump back. The scent of wrongness reached her nostrils, hauntingly hidden between the stench of blood and death. Swallowing, she licked her lips, feeling herself pulled by force toward the Witch's head, unable to release her wrist from the steel-like fingers enclosed around it, fingers as young and graceful as her own.

"Daughter of the Thulath, I sense within thee children twice over. Twins—a male and a female. I demand payment for my augury and payment is thy girl child."

Morgan's eyes widened in surprise at the Witch's words, then she struggled harder to be free when she felt cold fingers brush against the flatness of her belly. Feeling her skin crawl in fear and disgust, Morgan's upper lip curled into a snarl.

"Release me, Witch, or a payment will be the least of your demands."

As soft laughter reached her ears and feeling fingers still traced odd symbols over her stomach, Morgan's temper rose, pushing aside any traces of fear she felt. Around them the air cooled significantly, dropping several degrees in temperature as frost coated the surfaces of the rocky landscape. The faint echoing of caws teased the ears, shadowy wings flittering just out of view, as the hissing of ice crystals forming along the cauldron warred with the magickal flames that licked up the sides of the metal bowl.

The laughter continued, though the grip around her wrist released suddenly, causing Morgan to stumble back slightly before she caught her footing.

"Thou art much like thy sire."

Rubbing the red marks around her wrist, Morgan flexed her hand a few times, working to get the circulation back as she narrowed her eyes at the covered woman. Biting back an angry retort, she instead asked, "You know him?"

"The price is settled and the child marked. When the prophecy is fulfilled, bring the girl to me and thy debt will have been paid." The Witch shifted toward the cauldron, rubbing her fingers together over what boiled inside, and the hiss of something hitting the bubbling liquid reached Morgan's ears. "Is that thy question?"

"Huh?" Startled, Morgan blinked, raising a hand over her belly and feeling her heart beat a thunderous storm within. What had she just done? Marked her baby? Dread threatened to choke her at the thought of what might happen to her unborn child just because she had the need for advice…from what? A Hag that probably has never seen the light of day, a creature so vile she's kept isolated from those of her kind. What did she just do?

"Thy question. Ask it."

"What was so important for King Silvas to come seeking you? He died on his way here. Who killed him, and does this have anything to do with me?"

Reaching her hand out toward Morgan, the Witch once more beckoned to the assassin. Morgan raised an eyebrow, not wanting to fall for that trick again, when the Witch pulled a curved dagger out from under her robes with her other hand.

"Thy blood is required for thy augury. Come so I may prick thee."

Shaking her head, Morgan snorted and then raised her hand to her mouth. Biting her palm, she tore skin, feeling the well of rich coppery blood fill her mouth, and side-stepped the Witch to hold her hand over the cauldron. As the crimson droplets rolled off her hand, dripping from fingers to the boiling liquid below, the sound of hissing filled the air.

"Is that enough?" Morgan asked, glancing over to the Witch. After receiving a nod, she stepped back out of reach and cradled her hand, willing her wound to heal.

Tucking her blade back under her clothing, the Cauldron Witch reached for the handle of the wooden paddle and slowly began to stir the mixture. "The augury is for thee, not thy King. His answers lie shrouded and if thou wish to know those answers, thou should seek thy Sire's realm and thy King himself."

The stirring continued, the rasping of the wooden paddle against metal almost grating on Morgan's nerves until the Witch spoke again. "A new ruler shall sit upon the Shadowed Throne and thou will be the one to place them there. Thy banishment will be lifted, but first thou must defeat an enemy from thy past. Much sorrow and tragedy surrounds thee and thou wilt have many trials. But thou must face thy past, fix the wrongs set in motion from years ago, and begin again anew. Until such things are done, thou shalt find no peace. To fail will have bigger consequence than what will tear apart more than a kingdom."

For several long moments, Morgan stood quiet, letting the Witch's words sink in. Her mind tumbled around, trying to grasp the significance of what the Witch told her. The kingdom rested on her? Was this why Queen Moirethe was trying to get rid of her? An enemy from her past? She had very few worthwhile of her time, most being in politics, an arena she seldom played in. Realizing the Witch was silent and watching her, Morgan nodded, her face set in a dark scowl. Turning on her heel, she headed back to the ridge to begin the descent downward toward the sea of blood only to be stopped by the Cauldron Witch's voice.

"Forget not the babe. When she is born, bring her to me."

With a growl, Morgan glared and began climbing back down the cliff to the rocky shore below.

18

Wringing water out of her hair, Morgan glanced around the old bathing chamber and watched the globe light bouncing off the water to reflect off the stone walls and ceiling. It had been ages since she sat in this room, ages since she laughed and joked with her sisters while cleaning the grime and gore of battle from her skin. Hidden down below the Court floors, deep in the tunnels of the Underarch, but nowhere near the hollowed grand chambers of the Ancients, it was a room discovered by the sisters during their mischievous youth and made into a place of solitude and sanctuary. Glancing around, she wondered what had happened to everyonewho had once occupied Tir nag Goll. Her fingers absentmindedly tracing the figures played out in the tiles underneath her legs and imagined the lives that once lived here. Mosaics of war, of a great battle, littered the floor. In it, warriors swung their swords in their King's defense, golden and powerful in their armor, while clashing with the dark raven clad females of the Battle Crows, women born to fight and kill. Those were her predecessors, those that served the Kings before Silvas.

Nemain had disappeared and it was unknown if she lived or not. Macha had left to join the Silent Sisters and still remained while Badb was dead, killed not long after the Morrigu was banished, dragged down in a battle lust that even she couldn't escape from. Killed by enemies who believed she was her sister Morriganna. The mistake was not revealed until after Badb's feathery helm was removed and her long honey blonde hair tumbled free. *Oh, my sisters, what have I done to you?* Skimming her fingers lightly over her stomach, Morgan remembered Nemain's smile as she splashed water at her, laughing at her latest conquest...

"He worships me, Sister," Nemain gave a coy smile, looking over her

shoulder at Morriganna while batting her eyelashes. *"I just do this and my man comes running."*

"Runs away, most likely." Badb tossed a bubble-laden sponge at her and laughed as the woman ducked, spinning in the water to face them. *"Thou knows that sneaky fox beds thee just to get closer to the Morrigu. Lord Thayne hast a fascination with our sister, lass."*

"Well, as long as he continues taking me to realms of pleasure and does that little thing with his tongue, I care not. As soon as he slacks in his attention, I shall release him from between my thighs and set him on the trail for the Hunt. We could always use some entertainment this next full moon." Nemain's white teeth flashed before she glanced at Morriganna. Seeing the expression on her sister's face, she drew her brows together in concern. *"Sister, why the stormy look? Ifin thee wish Lord Thayne, I twould gladly give thee time to dally."*

Sinking into the steaming water up to her shoulders, Morriganna let out a heavy sigh and watched the clear liquid take on a faint crimson tinge as the dried blood from her victories bled away. *"Tis nothing,"* she muttered under her breath, blowing at the bubbles that floated close.

"She caught Lady Gilthantrious giving a favor to her husband, Nemain." Turning to Morriganna, Macha tilted her head, eyeing the troubled storm brewing in her sister's dark eyes. *"Sister, I know that look, something more than a flirt troubles thee."*

Lowering her eyes to hide her thoughts, Morriganna contemplated the swirling red in the water. *Blood thins so much when diluted but does it ever truly flow away, ever become non-existent? If I slit my throat would my blood disappear in this water to never be known to have existed? To be washed away, forgotten?* Closing her eyes, she felt the soft lapping of the water against her skin, stirred by the triplets movements, and wished to float away like the bubbles, to be here one moment, gone the next. Even now Sorrien was...

"Morriganna." A hand softly touched her shoulder, drawing her from her troubled thoughts. "Speak, Sister. Thy words will not go beyond these walls."

Raising her eyes, Morriganna took in the concern on her siblings' faces, three people in all the realms she trusted and loved more than any other. Other than her King, that was, but still highly regarded. After all, blood was thicker than water. With a snort, her thoughts traveled toward the youngest of her mother's daughters. Young Medb. Spoiled little bitch. No love lost there. Never one of them, even in their youth.

Nemain's face came into view, delicate and beautiful, with dangerous green eyes and honeyed hair. The triplets favored their older sister in every way except for color, as if they were a twisted reflection that turned golden instead of the raven's wing of the Morrigu's hair. She was the shadow among sunshine, but it did not matter for the siblings. Ever since their childhood they followed their older sister unwaveringly, loyal until death. The Morrigu, goddess of war to the pagan humans that worshipped her people in the mortal realm. Daughter of one of the Firsts...the Ancients, the Doaine. They were her loyal Battle Crows.

"Sister, thou art troubled. Tell us who causes thee such anger and we shall join our swords to thine. Let us share thy pain and together we shall wreck vengeance and remind those that the Crows fight together in everything."

"Nemain, this is mine to claim, my honor damaged. I must be the one to dispense my justice." Morriganna watched her sister's face, seeing confusion, then understanding fill her green eyes. "But I ask you, Macha and Badb to find my husband unharmed and bring him back to our chambers for a talk. Canst thou do such for me?"

"Yes," the women said in unison, growing serious. It was rumored the Morrigu's husband had a wandering eye and that she ignored it but rather than keeping their rendezvous private, Lady Gilthantrious's flirtatious glances grew more brazen. Added to the mix that the Bone Hag, a mistress in the dark arts,

was true and strong friends with the Queen, it made it even worse, for the Queen's hatred of the Morrigu was well known.

Shrugging off the past, Morgan stood, grabbing the towel lying beside her, and quickly dried off. After dressing, she replaced her weapons and muttered a few words, once more leaving the ancient chamber in darkness, and headed out to search instead for something in the present. Contact needed to be made and decisions solidified, for no longer could she sit on the sidelines. Prince Ansil or Prince Khelvan? Queen Moirethe could no longer sit the throne. It was time for the Morrigu to make preparations to return.

19

The day outside was dreary, overcast with rain and a softly howling wind. Lying stretched out on a rug in front of the stone fireplace, Malachi and Morgan enjoyed the roaring fire and each other's company, basking in the warmth and the feeling of flesh upon flesh. Sparks popped every so often as the pitch in the logs sizzled, exuding the smooth smoky scent of pine. Lying in front of Morgan, Malachi's dark head nuzzled her lap as she stroked her slender fingers through his hair, the two of them talking soft tones about what had been going on in the Court since her departure.

As with all Fae in the Lands behind the Veil, life pretty much stayed the same. Other than High Lord Requiem's retreat back to his realm of the dead and the intensifying bickering between High Lord Arawn and High Lord Bran, everything else was pretty much as Morgan remembered it…boring with a mild case of pretentiousness. Keeping silent about her visit to the Cauldron Witch and her thoughts, she listened with interest to what Malachi told her.

"Later Lady Ernmas twas removed from the Courts. No one has seen her since. Tis as if she never existed."

Morgan stiffened as the name passed her lover's lips, closing her eyes to the memory of the beautiful youthful face framed with honey gold hair. It had been so long since she thought of any of her kin that it surprised her at how hard just hearing the name of her mother affected her. Malachi seemed unaware of her internal struggle to keep from getting up and pacing as he continued in their conversation.

"And the High Queen had disbanded what was left of the King's Crows and her own guards arrest anyone that shows the slightest form of treason, real or imagined. Her bid for the throne means war is near and everyone at Court knows there is a split in the Lands since the High King died."

"Of course there is. Moirethe is a fool if she thinks she can rule the Mor'sin'dar herself. She's a fool to think the Sidhe would allow such a thing. The law of rulership was set by Danu herself. The High Court is ruled by a King—period." Morgan kept herself distracted by watching Malachi's dark hair curl around her finger before continuing with her stroking. A gentle purring issued forth from his chest as her hand moved. "But Queen Moirethe never had much sense in her head anyway, for she always strove for more than she should. What do her sons think of such an act of defiance? Aren't they vying for a way to kick her ass off the seat?"

The Werepanther grunted in agreement, closing his eyes. "Yes, they squabble among themselves, seeking allies even as we speak. Even the Sin'din'dar Court is feeling the effect. King Tibault's new Queen shows support for Queen Moirethe."

"King Tibault's Queens have never had much sense as it is, for his taste in women tends to run to the pretty and empty-headed. So who is this new bride of his?"

"Aife, a pretty blonde from the House of Mac Cecht."

"I don't recognize her name." Reaching up, Morgan tucked a wayward strand of dark hair behind her ear.

"Thou wouldst not. She was born after thou had left the Courts."

With a roll of her eyes, she shook her head. "His bride is younger than his daughter, Princess Vivienne. With the way the Light King acts, he might have well wed his human lover." It was no secret among the Courts that King Tibault had a thing for the exotic and that his only daughter's mother was a human hearth witch from the Emerald Isle itself. She had been given the gift of long life by her Sidhe lover as a way of showing his love. When the King had taken their child to his Court yet never publicly announced her as legitimate the witch left Tiabult and never looked back.

Malachi chuckled at her comment, shifting his shoulders as if to make himself more comfortable. Morgan studied his handsome face as he rested and the faint expressions that crossed it. He's Queen Moirethe's assassin, she reminded herself. Assassin and pet. Goddess, she was a fool to let him so near, cursing herself for her lack of judgment, but still…she actually felt good with him around. Relaxed, more at ease. She knew what was going on inside of her, had seen it too many times before in the faces and actions of others. Love, how strange the word seemed, especially coming from her. Though it had been almost a century since her divorce from her husband, it still felt too soon for something like this.

Her ex-husband, Sorrien, had done a number on her and in return she tried to kill him. Tried, almost succeeded, but didn't go through with the actual action. For eight hundred years they had been together, eight hundred years putting up with his cheating and lying. Eight hundred years too long.

Looking down at Malachi's face, she hoped she wasn't making a mistake. Running her index finger across his brow and down along his aquiline nose, she closed her eyes and prayed to Danu for help but as before, she received no answer. *I've fallen to far out of grace.* The Cauldron Witch's words were vague enough to keep her senses on edge and Eryn's and Lorne's warnings rose to the surface of her mind. Be wary of all you meet and let no one near.

Feeling the Were stiffen in her lap, Morgan opened her eyes and watched him. "What's wrong?" she asked.

Malachi ignored her question, frowning in concentration as his dark brows drew together. Then like a cat disturbed from its rest, he jumped up and began pacing the floor in front of her while he rammed his fingers through the front of his hair, pulling it away from his face. With a strained look, he stopped and faced her.

"What?" Her eyes narrowed, waiting for some sign of what was disturbing him. A heavy frown pulled his lips down, the intensity in his golden eyes making it almost hard to keep his gaze but Morgan was never one to back down from a challenge. "Malachi, what's wrong?"

He walked to her, standing over where she lay with his legs spread wide, staring down into her beautiful face as if studying her before squatting down. With both hands bracing on either side of her, Malachi hovered above the Sidhe.

"I have a question for thee." His voice was husky. He lowered his eyes from hers, as if not sure how to ask his question or afraid of what her answer would be. "Morriganna, dost thou trust me?"

"Huh?" She blinked at him, surprised at what he asked and wondering what that had to do with their conversation.

"I must know. Queen Moirethe summons me and I must go, but before I do I must know if thou trust me."

Leaning her head back with a sudden jerk, Morgan sucked in a harsh breath as her eyes widened in surprise. Feeling her stomach drop and her heart reach up to choke her, she struggled to keep her feelings out of her face and voice. Squaring her shoulders, she watched him. *Malachi was summoned back? Did this mean he was leaving her? For how long?* Reaching out her hands, she set them against his chest, and then pushed him back out of her space. His presence seemed to suck the air out of the room around her, making things unclear and unfocused.

"Why are you asking?"

He glanced sideways at her, his face draining of all emotion until it was flat, and moved toward her again. She watched his eyes when sudden dawning came over her. All her senses sharpened as Malachi held her attention. A small vein in his neck pulsed with his heartbeat as he waited for her answer.

"Queen Moirethe calls and I must answer. To not do so forfeits my life and I have no wish to not see my children being born. I know not what she wants but I need to know before I leave…dost thou trust me?"

Kneeling down in front of Morgan, he lifted her shirt to expose her flat, perfect stomach. Bending his head, he brushed the softest of kisses to her stomach, right above where their children grew within her, then he closed his eyes while leaning his forehead against her belly as if listening to the life within. "Yes, I know we art having twins for I can hear their heartbeats as I lay my head upon thee. Art thou pleased?"

With a tight smile, Morgan struggled to answer. Did she trust him? She was falling in love with him, that much she figured out, but trust? Did he know about there being two babies earlier? If so, how come he didn't mention it before? *But he's telling you now.* Reaching up to hold the back of his head, she could feel the tenseness filling him and nodded. Time to take a chance. The only way to find peace was to fix the past.

"Yes, Malachi. I trust you." Fateful words. "But we both know you belong to Queen Moirethe. I'm not an idiot, sweets. When she snaps her fingers, you must obey." Pursing her lips, she looked down, catching a lock of hair in her fingers, and brushed the end with a nail. "I wish you'd leave her."

"I cannot. We have talked about that before. She owns me."

"I know. I just…" Morgan's words died off as her hand moved down to her abdomen, her thumb brushing back and forth over the taunt flesh.

Watching the movement, Malachi shifted uncomfortably and took her free hand in his as he moved the other to cover the one on her stomach and looked up into her face.

"I worry about thee and the children, Morriganna. The babes are the one part of me that I know are free. They are special...very special."

Looking up at his face, at the handsome planes of it, the sensual lips surrounded by the moustache and goatee, the high cheekbones, strong nose and heated eyes, Morgan felt her heart skip a beat. *Damn. How could one man, a Were at it, make me feel this way?*

Pushing herself up on her elbows, she pressed her lips to his, feeling them open as his tongue swept in to claim hers, and kissed him with the passion he seemed to always inspire deep within her. Around Malachi, there was no thought and reason, only emotion and the need to please.

Abruptly he stood up, releasing her hand and slipping away to make her feel alone. "I need to go now, but first, let me get thee something to eat. Just rest before the fire and enjoy the night."

Morgan watched him head to the kitchen, too tired to argue, and nodded. A few moments later, he returned with a plate of sliced meats, cheeses, and fruits in one hand and a small glass of juice in the other. Setting the plate down on the floor beside her, he handed her the glass. "Here, drink this."

Reaching up for it, Morgan took the offered glass, draining it dry, and then set it on the floor before picking up a slice of apple and taking a bite. "Two days?"

"I promise, no later than two. Then I shall be back."

With a sullen nod, she lay back down on the rug and closed her eyes, feeling the heat of the fire teasing the skin of her face, already missing him. She knew she was being silly, acting like one of those frilly girls she so despised, but she couldn't help it. Danu, she loved him. Without him near, she felt as if she were missing some vital organ in her body. Mainly, her heart. "Well, I'm not going anywhere. I'll see you when you get back."

~~~

Sitting on a chair, Malachi quickly dressed, pulled his boots on before standing, and buckled his sword belt around his waist, checking each of his blades once before slamming them back in their sheaths. With one last look at the tired woman on the rug before the fireplace, he flared his nose, breathing in deeply their mingled scents from mating and Morgan's own exotic scent of rose, jasmine, and honeyed spice. Time was almost up, he knew that. Pulling his lips in a tight line, Malachi rubbed the back of his knuckles across his bearded chin, then turned to leave, unsure where the future was heading. He had the feeling this was the last time there would be any form of peace for him.

20

Watching the embers of the dying fire crackle and pop, Morgan blinked and stretched her arms overhead as a million thoughts rambled around inside her head. Things were moving too fast. Everything in her life seemed to be going at full throttle, reminding her of an old picture movie she had seen almost a century before, an old black-and-white before "talkies" were invented.

Rubbing the palm of her hand over her belly, she imagined the children within, growing and thriving on their mother's life energy. With a slight smile curling up the edge of her lips, she stretched like a cat and sighed before a light ringing disturbed her rest. Reaching up on the small table at the end of the couch, Morgan's fingers felt around until they found the small cell phone, then grabbed it, lowering it down to her head as she pushed the speak button.

"Morgan speaking."

"I do hope you're not too indisposed, for the Prince has deemed to speak with you tonight." A rich male voice came from the earpiece. She could hear the lazy drawl he used when he hoped to be disturbing an intimate moment. Ignoring the lecherous tone, Morgan sat up, resting her back against the front of the couch, and shifted the phone to her other ear.

"Lord Aeron, I'm surprised you responded so fast. I didn't think you would deem to send my request to His Highness with such speed. To what is the honor of such a prompt act?" Morgan yawned, wiggling her jaw back and forth until it popped, then cleared her throat with a small cough.

He chuckled. "Lady Morriganna, you have not changed over the years. I find myself fascinated by such blatant disrespect. Tell me, are you this aggressive in bed or do you actually allow the male to take the lead?"

A slight smile curled the edges of Morgan's lips. "A man must have balls to take the lead, Aeron. I know it's hard for you to understand being the pussy you are but maybe one day you'll find someone a little more passive than you."

Aeron snorted at the insult. "The Morrigu has lost her gift of gab. Stick with weapons, sweetheart, for fighting with words is beyond your ability." After a pause, he continued, the sound of paper shuffling coming through the phone's earpiece. "Prince Ansil said he would meet you in the Hall of Records at midnight. The Court will be convening in the Garden for Songfall so there should not be any concern about you being discovered."

"Does he know why I wish to see him?" Morgan asked as she watched one of the logs in the fireplace shift, sparks popping at the movement.

"I didn't mention it, but I'm sure he has an idea why. He actually seemed eager to speak with you. Obviously he had never spent much time in your company."

Letting out an irritated breath the assassin closed her eyes for a brief moment as she pinched the bridge of her nose, then opened them to stare into the fire. "Okay, well, thanks for your help, Lord Aeron. I'm sure you'll be contacting me soon for a favor. Until then…" She hung up, snapping the phone closed before setting it back on the end table. Midnight. Just a few hours, so Morgan stood and stretched out the kinks in her muscles before heading up to her bedroom to shower and dress.

~~~

The Hall of Records was dimly lit when Morgan stepped a foot within. The deep cavernous room, lined with rows of shelves filled with neatly bound books and rolled scrolls, echoed her footsteps as she walked boldly down the aisle, waiting for the eldest Prince to reveal himself. Even though she didn't sneak, her senses were alive, highly aware of all around her. She knew this meeting, if he so wanted, could be a trap to betray her, to capture her and drag her off to the dungeons in the Underarch and the tender mercies of the Queen.

Sensing movement up ahead, Morgan slowed her approach and waited for the Prince to acknowledge her presence. It didn't take long for the man to slide from the shadows of the room. With a confident smile on his handsome face, Prince Ansil crossed his arms over his chest and leaned against one of the shelves as he waited for Morgan to reach him.

"On time, as expected. Well met, Morrigu. Tis been a very long time since I hath seen thee. Thou seems well."

"Well enough considering your mother has been messing with my life." Her eyes raked over him, taking in the richness of his clothing and the smug gleam in his eyes as he looked her over in return. When their gazes met, each with their own thoughts, Morgan thought she caught a glimpse of suspicion in the dark depths of his eyes, but it was quickly replaced by mocking self-indulgence. *Not as self-absorbed as I thought. He's as wary of me as I am of him.*

"I'm not on a social visit, I'm here for business."

"Just by returning to the Courts, thy life is forfeit, thou dost realize? As Prince of the Royal Court of the Mor'sin'dar, I could have thee bound and held for punishment." He watched her face, searching for a reaction to his threat, but not finding any, he continued. "Why hast thou sought my presence?"

"I was resigned to living my life among the humans, then your mother decided to add me to her plans, so since she included me, I'm gonna jump in with both feet. Given the choice between you and Khelvan, why should you sit the throne?"

Prince Ansil blinked at the bluntness of her question. He stared at her in silence for several moments and she could see his thoughts tumbling around in his eyes until, coming to a decision, he relaxed his posture and turned his body to lean back against the shelving. Presenting her with his profile, he stared off into space.

She studied him, seeing the reason why he was so popular with females, for he was a perfect specimen of a handsome male. Tall, well-built, strong-jawed, he was passionate about whatever he put his mind to. Not as self-serving as she had thought, but a man of intelligence and determination. Though having his mother's golden looks, he was his father's son. One day he would be a good leader for their people.

Drawing in a deep breath through his nostrils, Prince Ansil face set as he looked down for a moment, and then turned his head toward her. "Khelvan tis a strong man, one who would fight for what he believed in and would give everything he had to make sure it came to fruition. At this time, his heart…his mind is elsewhere. He would take the throne just to get it away from Mother, but until he resolves his issues, he isn't the right one to lead our people."

"And you? Do you think you are?"

"I was raised to rule, taught that the welfare of our people comes first and foremost. Father showed me the secrets of the Underarch, secrets passed from ruler to heir and no other, but he died too soon." Ansil's jaw clenched, the only show of emotion he had about his father.

"At one time thou had loved my father," he continued. "If what thou say is true, then honor that memory and help me remove that woman from the throne. Our Court is one of Darkness and Shadows, but she has caused more deaths through her treachery in the last century of life."

This time it was Morgan's turn to turn away. With a deep drawl of breath, she nodded. "Then we're in agreement, but we need to do this as soon as possible because I'll be indisposed in a few months. I…"

"And keep thee as a secret, a very dangerous one." A slight smile tugged at the corners of Prince Ansil's lips. "Lady Morriganna, for this thou shall be reinstated back into the Court. I shall lift thy banishment and pardon any wrongdoings on thy behalf."

A brief surge of hope filled her chest, making Morgan almost feel giddy and lightheaded with the thought of raising her children in her homeland. Too long she had been gone, too long from the sights and sounds that had haunted her dreams. "Thank you, Prince Ansil," she responded, using his title as a sign of respect, something she was rare to do. "If you are anything like your father you will hold my loyalty. But if you…"

Morgan never finished her threat, for Prince Ansil suddenly lurched forward, eyes wide in surprise. He blinked once, twice, moved his mouth as if speaking, then looked down at his chest as a small bead of crimson appeared on the front of the rich clothing. In a swift move, Morgan crouched, helping the wounded man as he fell to his knees. He stared at her in disbelief, touching his chest and the smear that grew there, and then lifted his hand to look at the scarlet gleam that covered his fingertips.

"Why…?"

"It wasn't me, Your Highness." She whispered softly before she spoke a word of warding to raise a shield of protection over them. A soft golden glimmer appeared, starting from the floor around them, and rose until meeting a half circular dome above. Once that was done Morgan reached down to his chest, drawing her magick to her to heal Ansil, while she pulled her gun out from under her jacket. With narrowed eyes she scanned the surrounding darkness for the the Prince's killer.

"Burning…" the Prince whispered harshly, a bubbling sound emanating from his chest as dark spittle flecked his lips and chin. His cough was rough as he hunched forward, spraying blood from his mouth to splatter the side of her face and neck. Morgan focused her attention fully on healing, concentrating her strength to heal Ansil as she searched internally for the wound that was killing him. She could sense the destruction rapidly taking place within the Prince's chest, a spread of poison that blackened his internal organs and turned them to sludge. Before she could take away his pain and begin the healing he expelled a soft groan, his eyes rolled back in their sockets. Suddenly he slumped forward.

Too quick, within seconds, he was dead. With a grunt at the dead weight, Morgan slowly lowered the Prince to the floor and stared at his corpse, watching her last chance at redemption rapidly slipped through her fingers. The sound of boots echoed around the chamber as guards appeared from out of the aisle. Turning toward the newcomers, she raised her gun when a light suddenly flared in the dark room, momentarily blinding her. Lifting her free hand to shield her eyes, she braced for attack when a sharp voice spoke out.

"Thou art under arrest, Lady Morriganna, for the death of Prince Ansil and King Silvas as ordered by Her Majesty, the Queen of the Mor'sin'dar."

Glancing around at the stony faces of the guards surrounding her, Morgan mentally planning her escape as she stood. Carefully stepping over the body of Prince Ansil, she faced the group of Sidhe, gathering power around her in an electric bundle of energy. "You can try."

The crowd of guards parted like the Red Sea as a tall, dark-haired Sidhe moved forward between them. Breathing heavily, Prince Khelvan glared at the blood-spatter on her shirt before he dropped his gaze to his brother.

"Ansil."

Rage burning in his eyes, Prince Khelvan looked back up at Morgan and snarled. Grief etched across his face, the Prince took a step forward, raised a hand, and sent a ball of eldrick fire at her, unmindful of the valuable books lining the shelves around them. Dodging to the left, Morgan rolled out of the way and behind a row of bookcases as the area she had recently vacated lit up in flames. The guards scrambled around, hoping to cut off the escaped prisoner, while Prince Khelvan threw fireball after fireball in the direction Morgan had disappeared in. As the guards moved around the rows, he hurried over to his brother and pulled the larger man out of the way of the flames to gather him in his arms.

After several minutes of searching, the guards returned to their Prince and reported their findings. The Morrigu had escaped, disappearing into a dark corner of the room, but they had managed to stop the spread of fire from destroying the rest of their written histories.

"I care not about the histories! Find that bitch and kill her!"

Several of the guards scattered again, setting off in search of their prey as more footsteps softly invaded the room. Prince Khelvan looked up, ready to verbally thrash any who dared disturb him, only to find the Queen of the Mor'sin'dar standing above him, surrounded by her favorite courtiers. A delicate brow raised in question and when he closed his eyes and nodded, the only answer he received was the swish of fabric as his mother and her allies left.

21

Breathing heavily, Morgan wiped Prince Ansil's blood from her face as she stared into the mirror above the counter. What the hell happened? Obviously it was a setup, but by who and why? Not Prince Khelvan, for he honestly looked upset at his brother's death but then whom? And why did Prince Ansil die? As a way to get rid of him or a way to discredit her? Did Queen Moirethe hate her so much that she would be willing to sacrifice her eldest son?

Placing her hands flat on the counter, she stiff-armed against it and lowered her head in contemplation, eyes closed. This was ridiculous; first King Silvas and now Ansil? Was the draw for the throne that powerful? What depths would Moirethe go to keep herself seated securely on the throne of command? When they were young, the two had never gotten along, and when Moriethe had become Queen and Morgan the Morrigu, it had become worse.

Always it was a competition for Moirethe, to be more beautiful, more powerful, and more deadly. Didn't the Queen realize by now that she wanted nothing to do with the throne? Opening her eyes, Morgan stared at the crimson-stained water and felt her muscles tighten in anxiousness. All in one fell swoop, her wish to be rid of the problem plaguing her vanished—any hope of being allowed a return to the life she once had, the banishment lifted, and mayhap protection for her unborn children, gone.

With a harsh laugh at her circumstance, Morgan pushed away from the sink and turned around. How did they know about the meeting? Lord Aeron would be a fool to betray her that way, knowing she would hunt him down and kill him and Aeron was no fool. Not Lord Berith because he held honor above all else. No, it was someone else. Growing steely-eyed, she ran through a list of names of informants that might have knowledge of the ambush before settling on Lord Thayne, the Queen's own spymaster. The man was loyal to no one but himself and the only guarantee that he wouldn't turn her in at the drop of a hat was what he thought the price of his silence would be worth to him. A true mercenary, he was.

Walking across the room, one of many reserved for dignitaries, Morgan pressed a hand against the closed door and shut her eyes. Concentrating, she expanded her awareness to the surrounding area and drew in a breath. She relaxed her body, trying to shove the angst of the past few hours out of her mind, for now was not the time to for it. She needed to keep her mind clear seeing she was still within Moirethe's stronghold. Last thing she needed was to let her guard down and be caught unaware.

As soon as she sensed the area around to be clear, Morgan slipped from the room, staying close to the shadows before reaching her destination, a secret opening to one of the hidden passages that littered the Court. Glancing at the mural that decorated the stone wall, she lifted her hand, pressing her fingers against the smooth surface, and added enough pressure to indent the placement slightly. At a low hiss of stone sliding against stone, she moved inside, sliding the door back, and continued down the dark corridor.

For several moments Morgan walked in silence, remembering the direction to her goal before she stopped at a slight turn in the passage and opened the door to emerge behind a curtained area. After gliding down the few steps to Lord Thayne's room, she sent out a mental probe to test any magick that might have been protecting the door and found a ward set in place. Bending it enough to sneak past, she entered the sealed room without setting the silent alarm off.

Glancing around, Morgan took in the lavishness of the chamber. Lord Thayne was always the dandy extravagant in his décor and the rich fabrics that covered his furniture and walls proved it to even the blind. Listening for any signs of life as she moved within Morgan smiled at the wealth he displayed so blatant. Never one to withhold from himself the finer things in life. Though a wicked debaucher, Lord Thayne was an excellent information-gatherer.

After checking his bedroom and bathing chamber, Morgan settled down in a plush chair draped in rich burgundy wine velvet to wait for the spymaster's return. To her surprise it didn't take long, leaving her very little time to come up with a plan to question him with. The sound of a doorknob turning caught her attention and she leaned back, drawing the shadows around that side of the room, and watched as the door opened.

Lord Thayne strolled in, followed by another who paused to stand within the doorway. Morgan's eyes narrowed at the sight of the other man, tall and broad-shouldered, body thicker than the lean spymaster. He was definitely not Sidhe but one of the Weres that served the Court. Holding her breath, hoping the man's animal senses didn't detect her, she watched and waited, urging him to leave. As if hearing her thoughts, the handsome Mor'sin'dar dismissed his servant after reminding the Were to keep his eyes open, and then firmly closed the door behind him.

Shaking his head as if frustrated, Lord Thayne brushed his fingers through the front of his snowy white hair then moved over to a large teak wood desk. He picked up a few papers that laid on top, shuffling through them before pausing and suddenly grew tense. Morgan watched as his eyes flickered first one way then another as he scanned the room and his lips pulled down in a frown when he didn't spot what was bothering him. *At least his senses are still keen.* With a dark smile the Morrigu released the shadows surrounding and chuckled at the surprise that etched across the handsome Sidhe's face when she was revealed to his sight. Papers fluttered to the ground, forgotten as the Spy Master gathered eldrick power into his grasp as if he prepared for a fight.

"Interesting greetings, Lord Thayne. Nice to see you haven't changed any." Morgan's voice dripped with sarcasm.

Hesitant, the tall man stepped forward, his brows gathering together. A slight glimmer of fear flashed through his blue eyes before quickly becoming replaced with typical Sidhe arrogance. With a confident raise of his chin, nostrils flared, Lord Thayne stared down at the woman seated before him.

"Lady Morriganna, it appears the rumors are true, for tis thy name is circulating around the Court this very hour. It seems thou hast been busy in thy spare time." He circled the Morrigu warily until he came to a chair not far from her, but far enough away that he would be able to defend himself if need be. Morgan took note, an amused smile on her face and watched the Spy Master take a seat. He leaned back nonchalantly, as if trying to dispel any notion that she worried him then with a dashing smile, he continued. "It seems that banishment has dealt sweetly with thee. Thou seems fit and"—his eyes roved over her breasts—"healthy."

A smile flittered over Morgan's lips at the comment. The years had not changed the Sidhe; he still lusted after her. Perhaps that could work to her advantage. "You seem quite…healthy yourself, my Lord."

For several quiet moments they watched each other, as if measuring each other up in search for any newly revealed weaknesses. When Lord Thayne's heated gaze finally met her own indifferent one he finally broke the silence. "Thou art here for a reason, Morrigu. What brings thee to my humble abode?"

"Answers. Answers I'm sure you already know the questions to."

"Ah, so thou seeks a favor from me but offers nothing in return. What, my dear Lady Morriganna, wilt thou offer as compensation for such information? And why doth thou believe I should not open my door and send for the guard. After all, thou hast just been discovered to have killed the High Prince. Prince Khelvan himself was witness to the event."

"I did not kill Ansil and well you know that. And calling for the guard? You know if I believed the thought even entered your mind seriously, you would be dead right now." Raising an eyebrow, Morgan ran the tip of her tongue between her lips, wetting them. "And as for price, what do you want?" When he opened his mouth to answer, she lifted a finger to cut him off. "Except sex, of course."

The smile that had grown suddenly faded. Thayne's eyes narrowed as he studied the woman, and then nodded. "A favor then, one I can call in and thou must answer without protest and immediately. Agreed?"

Morgan pondered the open-ended price, and then reluctantly nodded. "Except for anything that causes my imprisonment or death, and then yes, I agree."

Once again Thayne smiled, giving Morgan the impression she just stepped into something she would regret later. Feeling the gathered power that Thayne had called fading, she rubbed her mouth as she thought of her first questions.

"Who set me up? Prince Ansil's death…he could have died at any time and any place. Why with me?"

"Seems obvious to me, it was to place blame on thee, Lady Morriganna. Thou still hast friends within the Mor'sin'dar and with Prince Ansil's death and the fact that he died at thy feet, it guaranteed that those who saw favorably at thee now see thee as a traitor. There are those who now wonder if the rumors were true and if thou really had killed King Silvas. Those that before never gave credence to the rumors are beginning to doubt. And with Prince Khelvan being the one to see thee with his brother, it added weight to the rumor."

"I didn't kill Prince Ansil nor did I kill Silvas."

A soft smile curled up the ends of Thayne's lips, bringing a roguish look to his already handsome features. "I know. Thou loved the King and even in thy banishment would never harm him. But the Queen has had many years to plan this, many years to twist ears and influence others not normally influenced by her. Thou must admit Queen Moirethe is a beautiful woman and when she so chooses can be quite charismatic."

"So Moirethe had her son killed?"

"And risk the wrath of her Court?" He laughed. "Of course not. Thou hast killed her son."

Morgan closed her eyes, irritated at the way Thayne twisted his answers. Cracking them back open at the sound of him shifting in his chair, she glared at him. "I was told I had an enemy in the Court. One newly returned."

"Is the Queen not enough?" At Morgan's hard stare, he chuckled and continued. "There is one that has recently arrived." Looking down at his hand, he curled his fingers and pretended to study his nails. "I would have never figured thou to be an animal lover."

Morgan's brow furrowed at his comment. "What do you mean?"

Glancing back up at her, a sly look replaced the heated one he had as he watched her. "Moirethe's little assassin. The one thou art enamored of. Though it seems the enamoring only goes one way. That was the reason thou hath ruled sex out of payment, correct?"

Ignoring the storm cloud brewing on Morgan's face, he continued. "Look toward the one holding thy boy toy's leash, Lady Morriganna."

"The Queen."

Thayne pursed his lips and shook his head slowly.

"Moirethe gave charge of Malachi to another?"

A smile was her only answer.

"So Malachi has been following the orders of another, this…newcomer?"

Still no answer came, just the smile on Thayne's face, which grew bolder.

Morgan's face grew stony. "So everything he said…" She bit back the last part as her eyes narrowed with a dangerous glint. "Moriethe and this newcomer plot against me."

"Nothing ever just happens, Lady Morriganna, especially not when related to the Mor'sin'dar. If anyone knows that, thou should. Thou hath been the loyal servant of King Silvas for how long? Even through the banishment. Thou hated that command yet still, thee obeyed. What made thee think that thou were different? Who knows what the Queen promised as a reward." Raising a finger to his temple, Thayne tapped on it. "Think about it. Thou art a smart one."

"Is he here?"

With a smirk, Thayne shrugged.

Receiving her answer, Morgan stood up with a quiet fury building within her. With a warning glance back at him, she pierced him with her gaze. "Remember your payment, Thayne. If you betray me and I find out, you will regret it."

"Oh, don't worry, dear one. I plan to collect that payment and if thou art dead, I cannot." His grin widened, exposing even white teeth. "One question before thou dost leave, if I may? King Silvas...what was he to thee? Obviously more than sovereign. Was he...thy lover too?"

Morgan shot the Spy Master a seething glare before moving to the door. "Not everyone thinks with what is between their legs, Lord Thayne. Some people actually have the ability to earn respect and loyalty. Silvas was one of them. He was a good man and King. And he was my friend."

Opening the door, the Morrigu slipped out into the hall and disappeared.

22

Lying back on his bed in his chambers, Malachi gnashed his teeth and seethed at the ceiling from his Mistress's new demand. He wasn't a toy, some animal for these Sidhes' amusement. It was demeaning. He was an assassin, but here he lay sprawled over his bed waiting for his new Mistress, a temporary diversion for his Queen's ally to keep her entertained. His body felt coiled tight, his mind anxious and furious at the memory from the evening before. Morriganna was here or had been here, meeting with that spoiled Prince Ansil, and now she was blamed for his death. Fuck.

Killing the Prince was no problem for him; slipping the poison into his wine was easy enough. The Prince's wine-taster was female and easily seduced. Knowing the poison was a two-parter, she had no problem swallowing the deep purple liquid, for the wine itself would not kill the Prince, but added to the poison that lined the lip of one side of his goblet, the toxins combined and reacted fairly fast. He did not know the Prince was meeting with Morriganna that night and the fact that he died in her presence was, to him, pure fortuitous. That the guards arrived when they did, followed by Prince Khelvan, meant Viraska knew about the meeting, which meant that the death had been planned solely for the Morrigu's benefit.

At this moment, he hated everyone but none so much as himself. He needed something to get his mind off Morriganna, his mistakes and regrets; mistakes for following his Queen's orders, regrets for taking business too far. Sooner or later Queen Moirethe would discover Morriganna's pregnancy and then it would be too late. Remembering the look in her green eyes when he asked if she trusted him, he felt his stomach twist in knots. He gained her trust, one of the things he was working for, and here he was, feeling like an ass for betraying her to a Queen he hated. Swallowing back the lump growing in his throat, he growled.

He was a fool to hold tight to the illusion. Who did he think he was? He could never gain his freedom nor could he think of ever having his children. If Morriganna ever learned about his betrayal...

He closed his eyes to the thought. The woman was deadly, not someone to be treated with a careless hand, and here he was, playing the game the Queen demanded from him. He hated his Queen, hated the Sidhe, hated them all.

A sudden noise brought Malachi to a sitting position, his feet on the hard stone ground. Resting his muscled forearms on his knees, he tilted his head, straining to hear the noise that caught his attention in the first place. Perhaps it was one of Queen Moirethe's little spies coming to see if he was behaving. Snorting, Malachi ran his hand over his bearded chin. He didn't know the meaning of *behave*.

From out of the corner of his eye, Malachi noticed something white flutter by and shot out a hand. His fingers wrapped around a slender wrist with an iron grip as he hauled the owner down in front of him and stood, slamming the person backward into the wall opposite his bed. Stilling at the sight before him, his grip loosened around her throat. As before, when he first laid eyes on her, Malachi felt speechless. She was incredible. His throat dried as his cock sprung to life. As much as he hated this woman, her beauty was overwhelming and her sexual appetite was voracious.

"Oh!" Viraska blinked her blue eyes as her lush mouth circled in an outraged O. Taking a deep breath, she pressed her breasts out as she whispered, "What art thou doing?"

Once again it was time to play, the role of beast to his new mistress's beauty. Dropping his eyes from her face to the pink nipples that thrust out so invitingly behind the sheer material of her gossamer gown, Malachi let a low rumbling growl deep within his chest. His new mistress enjoyed inflaming his Were senses with her teasing. Sex was something she used as a weapon. She enjoyed the control she had over the opposite sex, and he knew she wielded it well against him. As much as the thought of Morriganna gave him excitement and family, this creature against him gave him a thrill of the erotic and forbidden. Sex was something he enjoyed and with Viraska he knew she wanted him not because of a drug he slipped her, but because she got off on fucking a dangerous animal. Setting her back on her feet, he kept a firm grip around her throat, knowing she enjoyed the thrill of violence, and stepped closer to her body to feel the softness of her breasts press against his chest.

"Is there something thou dost needs?"

"I am fairly certain that thou knows why I am here," Viraska purred as she looked up at him from under her dark lashes, the shoulder strap of her gown sliding down her satiny shoulder.

The vibration in her purr caused Malachi's erection to strain against the leather of his pants. All thoughts of Morriganna ran fleeing from his head, chased out by this vixen before him as he stared down at her succulent form. He knew the scent that emulated from her was created to entice and arouse, but he didn't care that he was being manipulated. The animal within him was being called forth and the beast wanted out, wanted to claim and be satisfied, wanted to throw her to his bed and ravish her soft lush body.

"I know," he whispered, his voice growing husky as he loosened his grasp, lowering his hand to caress the creamy flesh just above her breasts. Rubbing his thumbs above the swell, he dipped it in between those perfect mounds and felt his mouth water from wanting to take one of her nipples into his mouth and suckle like a babe. Was this what Morriganna felt like around him?

Viraska's eyelids drooped as she slipped the tip of her tongue between her lips to wet them. She tossed her head back a little, a deep red lock of hair curling enticingly around one of the nipples. With a rough grip on her arm, he pulled her from the wall and tossed her towards his huge bed, remembering what her skin felt like pressed underneath him against the black satin of his bed covering.

Skittering on her stilettos, Viraska fell forward on the bed. Glancing over her shoulder, her eyes flashed in indignant anger.

"What is the matter with thee?" she snapped as her temper flared, then just as quick it seemed to vanish. Turning over on the bed, she laid back, her legs more than a little spread as she gave him a seductive smile that invited his attention.

With a smirk on his face, Malachi's eyes roved over her barely-clad body, taking in the abundance she offered him in a wanton fashion every night since he had returned. Nothing was hidden from his gaze; full pert breasts, flat stomach, and the little thatch of red hair at the apex of her thighs. The dress she wore was little more than icing on the cake, more of a bow to be pulled off a gift than a covering meant to hide what was beneath, and he itched to run his hands over her soft satiny skin. Where Morriganna was darkness and strength which hid her vulnerability, Viraska was feminine and softness wrapped around a core of steel.

Flipping her hair back in defiance, Viraska gazed up at him with a sly look in her eyes, spreading her legs and exposing the treasure they hid. "I find I am in need of something strong between my thighs."

Glancing at the offered sight, Malachi felt a slight twinge of conscious as Morriganna's face appeared before him, but the beast in him raged forward, wanting to claim this morsel that lay so invitingly on his bed. Lust won out as his lover was shoved from of his thoughts. "So I am nothing more than a tool to fill thy needs then?"

"Why, of course," the woman replied in a casual manner as if it were no big deal.

Malachi's eyes once again lowered to her thighs and the secrets hidden just out of his view as his nostril's flared. Her arousal was high, the light musk emitting from her growing headier. He glanced up, caught in fixation while she moved her hand to her face, taking a finger, and then drawing it into her mouth before closing her red lips around it. His own mouth grew parched at the sight of her sucking on it playfully and his cock jumped at the thought of her lush lips wrapped around him.

Then her words sunk in. Shaking his head to clear it, Malachi growled. "I may be on loan to thee, but thou dost not own me. Understand I fuck thee because I choose to." Letting out an angry breath, he muttered, "Why did Queen Moirethe allow thee my use?"

"Our Queen asked me to rid her of the Morrigu." With a venomous smile, Viraska lowered her hand to her breast, letting a tapered finger circle a tight nipple, knowing Malachi's eyes watched her every move with hunger. "I told her I would…for admittance back into the Courts, a position, and some time with thee."

Malachi stilled at her admission. "The Morrigu?"

Looking up at him with a coy smile glossed over her lips. "Yes." Sliding her hand down over her stomach, the redhead moved it between her legs, hiding her pink parts from the Were's heated gaze. "The same Morrigu thou art currently playing with." Spreading her legs wider, she slowly moved her fingers back and forth, rubbing the sensitive area as her body reacted and grew damp.

He could smell her arousal miles away and up close it was intoxicating. Lowering his head, he snarled, "What dost thou have against the Morrigu? Thou art recent to the Courts." His tongue flicked out to wet his lips and inhaled, taking in the scent of her lust as he tried to contain his baser instincts.

"I understand thou hath made this Morrigan thy lover, yes?" Spreading her legs wider, she rubbed herself in small circles, dipping her finger inside her core before moving it back to rub again. "Is she prettier than I am? Is her body…sweeter?"

"She is very beautiful."

"More beautiful than me?" Raising her hand to her mouth, she slid her finger between her lips and closed her eyes in bliss, making soft *mmm* sounds as she sucked it.

With a growl, he lowered his body down on the redhead, pushing her back even more while he braced a hand on either side of her head. She squirmed beneath him, lifting her hips against his as she brushed her naked mound into his leather-clad erection.

"Thou art beautiful, too." Malachi whispered huskily as he lowered his head, slipped his tongue into her mouth to silence her questions. He moaned as he kissed her, tasting her arousal and the excitement she brought with it.

"No." She turned her head away from him, pouting. "I am Viraska. I do not come in second place. I am more beautiful."

Grasping her chin between callused fingers, Malachi roughly forced her head back then grazed her bottom lip with his. She bit back. Growling, he forced her mouth open for a rough, punishing kiss, forcing his tongue between her lips and captured hers with his own. He sucked on it, tasting and teasing, as she gasped and squealed, using her hands to push and pull at him. She enjoyed it rough, Malachi knew, making no move as she struggled, but using his sheer size to overpower her. Her struggles only served to make him harder as he continued the bruising kiss. When she bucked up against him, pulling at his shirt, his hair, her mouth matched his in passion as she swept her tongue over the roof and along his teeth, her lust rising each passing moment. He reached down between them, and unlaced his too tight pants, freeing his demanding shaft from its restraint.

"Thou belongs to me now, Malachi. Morriganna is an old crow, too dry to satisfy a man such as thee. Continue to please me and I shall reward thee in ways thou could never imagine."

Malachi rubbed himself against the apex between her legs, his ridged shaft becoming coated in her all too enticing wetness. She shuddered underneath him and he had not even entered her yet.

"Reward?" His interest perked immediately. "What kind of reward?"

Shaking her head, she smiled a secret little smile. "Thou could have thy…freedom, yes? The ability to have a family, children…a life outside the Courts beyond the whelm of the Queen." Her breathing quickening from his movements.

Reaching up, Malachi tore the sheer fabric off her gown to expose her breasts to his sight. He needed something to make him forget what was going to happen soon and she was just that thing. "What?"

"Freedom, my dear kitty. I offer thee the one thing beyond thy control." Arching her back, Viraska offered him her breast and gasped as he drew her nipple into his waiting mouth.

At Viraska's movements and groans, Malachi obliged her by opening his mouth wider to devour as much of the soft skin of her breast as he could. Moving his hips forward, he thrust into her, the sensation ripping a low growl from the very center of his being. She was so tight, wrapping around the length of him like a hot, moist glove.

"Is thy Morriganna as good as me?" She thrust up against him, wrapping her shapely legs tight around his waist as her hands moved their way down his sides to grasp his ass. She thrust again, taking him in deeper as she waited for his answer.

"None of thy business, Viraska," he snarled, angry at Queen Moirethe and this beautiful creature beneath him for their petty games of revenge. He moved within her, setting a rhythm with his hips, as his demanding thrusts pinned her smaller body to his bed. Damn them for making him do this, for involving him with Morriganna and the chaos about to take place. Thinking of his unborn children, children he probably will never know, he thrust into Viraska with a vengeance, bruising her tender flesh with his pounding. Gritting his teeth, he focused his eyes on the backboard, trying not to enjoy the action, but failing miserably.

As if reading his thoughts, Viraska laughed, and then slapped his face to catch his attention. Using that moment to take him off guard, she shifted beneath his bulk before maneuvering him over onto his back and straddling him. Grabbing his wrists in both her hands, she raised them over his head and pinned them to the bed.

"No, I changed my mind. Her taint is all over thy body. Perhaps it would be better for thee to return to thy Queen and her plans for thee." Viraska made to get off of him, only to have Malachi grab her hips and slam her fully upon his shaft, not stopping until he was buried deep inside. He grabbed her wrists this time and pinned them together behind her back as he rammed himself harder into her.

Between gritted teeth, he growled out his words, "How can thou gain me my freedom?"

With her eyes flashing from bright blue to a sickening yellow, Viraska looked down at Malachi, her voice condescending. "No, I changed my mind. Thou art too wrapped around the Morrigu's ankles. Even now thou hides something about the woman. Whose loyalty dost thou belong to?"

Watching her breasts bounce up and down with each thrust, Malachi thought over her question. He cared for Morriganna, but did he love her? Was he willing to betray a woman who long ago showed him a kindness when others didn't and even now carried the one thing besides freedom which he wanted?

Freedom…something he had always dreamt of but thought beyond his grasp. If it was true she could grant him that, perhaps he could have the children too.

"It belongs to my Queen and thyself. What do I need to do?"

23

The creature that appeared six months ago and had come to the Courts asking for revenge on the Morrigu stood in the corridor facing the open room. Lord Requiem narrowed his eyes as he watched the Bone Hag pause in the doorway, and smile at someone hidden from his view. He flexed his jaw, knowing from the sly smirk on her face and the cruel twinkle in her eyes that there could be only one thing that would make her that happy. Her plan to harm the Morrigu was underway.

The person within the room stepped forward, coming into view and revealed a handsome Were with dark hair and a goatee. Lord Requiem moved back into the shadows where he stood, certain that the assassin missed him as his golden eyes glanced down the hallway. Very few creatures could sense the Lord of the Dead when he didn't wish to be revealed, and waiting in silence he watched as the Were was secure enough in their solitude to pull Viraska against his chest with a passionate kiss.

Studying the couple, Lord Requiem shook his head, wondering if the Werepanther would be so quick to betray his lusts with this creature if he could see what he did when gazing upon the countenance of that "woman".

To others Viraska appeared as a beautiful, seductive female and, to some, the epitome of desire; petite, voluptuous, with long, thick red hair and pale creamy skin. Rich, full red lips, high-ripe breasts, her scent was described as enticement and erotic dreams. To the Death Lord and any who truly understood the aspect of this creature, they saw through the illusion. Instead of a desirous woman, in its place was a wretched corpse of walking putrid flesh. Where her body was voluptuous, with breasts women would envy, he saw weeks-old rotting flesh, with bits of skin hanging from stringy muscle and white bones showing through different areas of her frame. Her breasts were pendulous and hollow, nipples hanging from them as they swung in rhythm of her movements. Clumps of hair were missing from her skull, hanging limp over her scrawny shoulders like seaweed. At one time the woman had been one of the true great beauties, but that was years ago, before hatred and dark magick twisted her into a creature of vengeance. Now the woman was a member of the Ssri'tel'quessir Court.

Malachi's hand lowered down the creature's back to grope her ass before he stepped back into the room and closed the door. With a satisfied smile, Viraska turned and leisurely sauntered down the hall, away from where Lord Requiem stood deep within the shadows.

The Morrigu was here. A subtle fragrance suddenly wrapped around him; soft and warm, dangerous and dark. Breathing in deeply, Lord Requiem straightened his shoulders and turned his gaze to the woman appearing next to him. She was obviously unaware of his presence, her attention fully on the door further down the hall and her normally cold green eyes shimmered with unshed tears. Studying the Lady Morriganna's profile, for he had never had the opportunity to be this close in her presence unobserved, he took in her beauty; the strength and vulnerability that warred within her being. He watched her jaw clench as she swallowed hard, her lips drawing into a tight line of anger and determination. For a moment he was tempted to reach out to give comfort, to stroke her long ebon hair, hair that blended with the darkness around them, draping along her slender body like a cloak made of shadowy feathers.

Feeling his chest tighten, Lord Requiem's hands closed into tight fists. She always had this affect on him when she stood near, though she never seemed aware of his presence except when forced to acknowledge him. Taking a step back from her, he flexed his fingers and slid them into his robe, calming his reaction to her nearness before clearing his throat. The Morrigu's eyes flickered toward him, startle quickly turning to annoyance.

"Forgive me, Lady Morriganna, I did not mean to intrude." His words faded away as he studied her lovely face. "Thou seems to be troubled. Is there any way I may be of service to thee?"

The Morrigu ignore his question as she drew in a deep breath, visibly trying to control her inner turmoil. An icy beauty, she had always seemed untouchable, yet here she was, watching the scene before them and was actually upset. What happened to the confident woman who reacted to anything that disturbed her with violence and bloodshed? Instead she seemed as a woman in distress and hurt, but why? Could it be...? His eyes wandered to the closed door for a brief moment before returning back to the woman facing him and felt his chest tighten. Did she not listen to his servant? Had not Lorne warned her of Queen Morithe's slave? Did the Morrigu know the man she slept with dallied with enemies?

Keeping his tone neutral, Lord Requiem's spoke softly. "Tis been a long time, my Lady. Tis good to see that thou art well." Noticing her eyes straying back toward the door, he sighed, imagining the chaos she must be going through. He still remembered the last time she had been betrayed by a lover. Chaos and bloodshed reigned upon the Court. Something Viraska would do well to remember. "Thou hast come to Mor'sin'dar for a visit?"

"No," she was blunt in her statement. "I apologize if I bothered you. I'll be on my way." She turned to leave only to find her way blocked as Lord Requiem stepped forward.

"Tis no bother."

Morriganna's eyes narrowed at the impasse and she raised her head to give him a hard glance but the Death Lord remained in her way. Keeping his face hidden deep within the shadows of his cowl, Requiem watch anger etch across her icy eyes and the slight way her dark eyebrow rose in warning but still he did not move. "Morrigu, didst thou not receive my warning?"

"Ah, Lord Requiem, yes, I did. Thanks for sending Lorne. He was a nice diversion." Her voice dripped with sarcasm. Morriganna stepped back, hostility radiating from her body in waves. "So, tell me the truth, for I'll know if you lie, why are *you* here?"

"Apparently the same reason thou art." He clasped his hands behind his back. He could almost hear her teeth grinding as her eyes narrowed in thought.

"Who was that woman?" she asked, her voice icily cold.

Glancing around the corner, Lord Requiem noticed the corridor was now empty and touched Morriganna's elbow, motioning down the hall. Leading her to a vacant room he waited until she, with some reluctance, entered and then closed the door behind them. He moved to stand in the center of the room, giving the prickly woman some space so she wouldn't feel trapped. It was better to make her feel she had the freedom to leave when she chose.

"The woman is known as Viraska, a Bone Hag." He noticed a small furrow between her eyebrows. "Thou did not come for her though. Thou wished to see the Were."

With a deep breath, Morriganna closed her eyes and slowly let her breath out. The tension emanating from her was so thick Requiem felt he could take a knife from his belt and cut it. Keeping his expression indifferent, he watched her move away and pace around the room, clenching and unclenching her hands into fists when suddenly, she stopped and froze, her shoulders straightened as if a thought had suddenly come to her that needed answered.

"Lord Requiem, Lorne said you were trying to help me? Why? We have never had conversation before beyond a few words, so what interest do you have in whether I live or die, return to Court or not? It's not that my love life or even any part of my life should mean anything to you."

"My reasons are not thy concern, Lady Death, but it is fair to say I hath always respected thee and when I heard rumors concerning thee I thought to...involve myself." Drawing his robes closer to himself, Requiem pondered his thoughts and how to proceed. He understood the concerns and fears she must have, finding out those she chose to put her trust into betrayed her. He understood her loneliness and about unresolved love, but it was not something he wished to speak about, especially not with her. Instead he drew in a deep breath before continuing.

"I mean not to be abrupt with thee and I shall keep thy secret of being here to myself, little one. Thou may go and know that thou art safe with me, but I warn thee, do not return and once thou art home cast out the Queen's creature thy bed. I fear that what game the Queen started has gone beyond even her plans. Moriethe is not known for her forgiving heart, but Viraska has something more than mere vengeance on her mind."

Morriganna's hand went to her belly and her face stilled. For a brief second she glanced at the closed door as if expecting someone to burst in then her eyes hardened once more. Lord Requiem watched the movement, intrigue filling his thoughts as it dawned on him what the motion meant. The woman was playing with fire. Did she not understand what her actions did? Did she not even care? Shaking his head in disappointment, he stepped forward. She looked lost, afraid, and very alone. No longer did she have an amused King to keep her safe nor could she depend on her reputation built around fear, for if she successfully bred with the Queen's Were, whatever respect she might have had left in the Court would be gone. The fear would still be there, for the Morrigu had a deadly temper, but the respect would be no more.

With a sigh, Requiem touched her shoulder, feeling the tremor building under the outer steel she showed. She knew what would happen if word got out. "Thou must go now, Morrigu, before someone wanders upon this place and discovers thee. I would hate to have to kill just because thou felt the need to quench thy curiosity."

Slowly Morriganna nodded her head then turned away, her dark hair falling to hide her expression. Quickly she slipped out of the room, hurrying down the hall to disappear in the shadows without looking back.

Most interesting, the Death Lord contemplated the small revelations he had just discovered. Not only did the Were sleep with Viraska, but with the Morrigu as well, not to mention the fact that the later was pregnant. *Oh, what wicked webs we weave.*

24

It was early afternoon when Malachi stomped into Morgan's warehouse and flopped down on the black leather chair, glancing around the room for any sign of his lover. Tired and wary, body and soul, he groaned, wiping a hand down his face as he closed his eyes, and leaned his head back. The scent of jasmine, rose, and exotic spices breezed by his nostrils, filling his senses and making him exhale heavily. He missed this small familiar comfort, didn't realize how much he missed it until he came back. Cracking open his eyes, he glanced up to see Morgan leaning against the far wall, the one decorated by the mural of the ShadowedLands. Arms crossed over her chest, she watched him, her lovely face reminding him of one of the statues that decorated the great Halls.

"It's been more than two days. It's been almost a week. What did Moirethe want?" Her voice held a touch of frost to it.

"Things of no importance. She wanted a recount of what thou hath been up to throughout this time. I had to give her what information I could in order to come into her good graces again. The Queen is no fool, no matter thy opinion, and in order to keep my head and my position, I had to mention the Bollags and thy thoughts about where they arrived from. She is amused that thou believes she sent them to cause a distraction to her activities and perhaps will send more just to irritate thee. Her interest lies mostly in thy intent on returning to the Court. I informed her that thou still honored thy word to the King."

His eyes wandered over her body, searching for some sign of her pregnancy and found none. She was still as slender as the day he met her. With a sigh, he looked up at her face, finally meeting her icy gaze. It was not the reaction he expected to his homecoming. Frowning, he wondered at her hostility. "How art thou feeling?"

She shrugged in silence, the anger coming off her in waves. Keeping his face clear of any reaction, Malachi motioned her to him, wondering if she would comply. *What was up with her?* He searched and questioned others if she had remained in the Hollow, but no sign of her had been discovered. Not even Thayne, the Queen's spymaster, had word about her appearance, except for the fact that she had been discovered with Prince Ansil's body.

Putting an inviting smile on his face, he held a hand out to her, beckoning her forward. He watched her push off from the wall, walking over to him, her hips swaying lightly as a soft smile blossomed across her face; though, glancing up, he noticed her eyes remained chilly. When she was close enough to take her hand, he turned her around and led her to his lap.

Settling her on him, Malachi rubbed a hand over her stomach and lowered his gaze from hers. Her stare was intense and direct and he didn't like the feelings that arose in him from it. Swallowing, he tried to wet his suddenly parched throat. "I just worry about thee. It has been a while and I missed thy warmth."

"I've missed you too, *love*," her tone was icy cold as she drew out the last word.

Growing wary of Morgan's mood, he decided to try another route. Cupping the back of her head, he pulled her face down for a long, drawn out kiss, his tongue sweeping through her mouth, tasting her with soft strokes.

He heard Morgan sigh about the same moment he felt her melt in his hold. Feeling her arms slide around his neck, he drew her close and kissed her with the hunger he had been carrying for a while. He had missed her touch, her kiss, and the way she made love, but the memory of the time spent with Viraska flashed before his eyes. Feeling guilty he held her tight against him, one arm wrapped around her back as his fingers entwined in the dark mass of her hair, forcing her head to him. Focusing on pushing his secrets aside and to just enjoy his time with her, Malachi readjusted her position on his lap, pressing his growing erection against her ass. He needed to be within her. Moving a hand down her side, he caressed the side of her full breast, before moving it to the hem of her shirt, intent on removing it. At that point he felt her stiffen and pull away from him, her lips retreating to leave coolness where once there was heat.

The ice he heard earlier in Morgan voice was present in her jade eyes and her nostrils flared as her jaw clenched tight enough he could hear her molars grind.. *What was happening?*

"What?" Running the palm of his hand over his face Malachi closed his eyes.

"What?" Morgan repeated back at him, her voice filled with venom.

Shocked by the amount of force present in that one word Malachi opened his eyes and studied her face for some sign of where her thoughts led, trying to keep his own body from reacting and growing tense. It was when she turned her gaze back on him that his real training set in. Already the room was feeling cooler and as she looked at him he was reminded who sat on his lap. Not a play toy, not someone to be used lightly but King Silvas' personal assassin, the Morrigu herself. Somewhere along the line he had forgotten that, thinking of her as only a woman who could be seduced. Watching as the pupils of her eyes expanded, leaking inky darkness into the soft green color of her irises Malachi shifted under her, careful to keep his stance causal and unconcerned.

"What exactly were you doing in the Court, Malachi?" She asked, her voice changing to something softer, something dangerous.

It raised the small hairs on the back of his neck as warning bells went off. Every sense within him came to life, advising him to leave now, but he knew if he did he would have failed and both Queen Moriethe and Viraska would see him pay for that mistake in both blood and pain. Instead he kept his tone relaxed.

"Thou knows." Watching her, Malachi was cautious of his words and movements. She was wound tight. Something made her wary, something set her off. She knew he had to visit, to report back to Queen Moirethe. Though she hadn't liked it, she agreed it wouldn't be smart for him to ignore the summons, and he knew she understood any further summons would be answered likewise. He was grateful for that since it would be easier to stretch the truth about what happened there than to straight out lie to Morgan, for she seemed to have an unerring way of knowing when he outright lied. Stretching the truth or omitting became easier, but now…what was happening? There was no way she knew…

"Yes, I know." She whispered as if she had just read his mind. "Anything else you did other than report to Queen Moirethe?"

Keeping his voice even, Malachi watched her with care, unsure what she was hinting at. He needed to be careful in his answering because Morgan was obviously hunting for something. Did she know it was he who killed Prince Ansil or did she know about the deal he just struck with Viraska?

"What's wrong?" Leaning forward, Malachi nuzzled her neck, trying to elicit some form of relaxation in her. Instead she stiffened more and he could then sense the pent up violence in her rise. She was too quick to distrust, not that he blamed her. After this past week…Why he was here with her might be a lie, but he was honest about one thing—his feelings for her were true, he did care.

"There's a scent all over you, Malachi, and it's not Queen Moirethe's." She lifted her eyes to capture his, and then glanced at his lips in meaning. Leaning toward his face, she breathed in deep, her mouth near his. "You've been kissing someone else and you've touched her…intimately." Letting go of his hands, she slid off his lap to look down at him, hostility clearly written over her face. "I should slit your throat right now."

Surprised by her words and actions, Malachi berated himself for his stupidity of not realizing as good as he was with hiding things, she was just as good at finding them. Torn between guilt and anger at his predicament, he fell back on the one thing he could rely on…anger.

"I did not betray thee, Morriganna, my heart is thine. But…" Turning his eyes from hers, he closed them again as he felt his own anger rise to the surface. "I lied earlier, that I admit tis true. The High Queen dismissed me from her service."

Turning, Morgan opened her mouth to comment, but he cut her off. "She gave me away, tis my new Mistress thou smells, but understand, I had no choice."

Opening his eyes again, he held the Sidhe's gaze with his own heated ones.

"I may be an assassin, once the High Queen's assassin, but I am still a slave. I have no choice in what she does to me, whether a beating or, in this case, giving me away." His shoulders slumped, as if all the weight of the world settled on them. "Do not ask me why, Morriganna. I know not why, but when I got there I found I had been gifted to another. Dost thou understand how humiliating such a thing is? I was the Queen's personal assassin, but now I am nothing but a pet for some spoiled follower that her Majesty has designed to favor for this week."

Malachi waited for a sign that Morgan believed his words. He watched her give a short nod, saw the anger still burning in the depths of her eyes and her mouth tighten into a straight line. He could see the wheels churning, as thoughts and questions passed through her head but gradually she calmed, her breathing growing even, though she kept her eyes glued to his face. She nodded her head again as if tired. Morgan raised a hand to her head and rubbed a temple with the tips of her fingers.

"Malachi, I don't know who to trust anymore. Who do you belong to?" She turned her head to look at him. "I know Weres. You aren't weak; you're strong and more than able to ward off an amorous female. And if a beating would have been the result, you should have taken it."

"Beating?" he snarled back at her. "Thou said that thou trusted me, yet thou calls me liar. I risk much being with thee. I lie to my Queen, give up my honor all for thee and our babes. Thou needs to hold to thy own word and honor it, if thou says thou trusts me, then trust me. Anyway," he added, his eyes narrowed, "I am not the only one with secrets. Seems thou hath made a trip thyself to the ShadowedLands. And Prince Ansil, how is he doing these days?"

Morgan's eyes snapped to his, anger flooding back into the dark orbs. "What the fuck do you mean by that? It was business; I was trying to get help for getting the Queen off my back. Fuck, Malachi, give me more respect than that. I want to trust you, but you're making it damn hard. If it was the other way around, how would you feel?"

Malachi pushed himself off the couch and stood to his full height, towering over her. Leaning toward her, he put his face near hers and whispered in a quiet, deadly voice, "Do not treat me like I am stupid, Morriganna, I do not take kindly to it. I am not a Sidhe, I am not free, and I am not in control of what I am forced to do at my mistress's bidding. If we are to be together, thou must get used to that knowledge."

"Then leave the Court. Run away from them. I told you already I'd protect you. If you loved me like you claim to, you'd have no problem leaving," she retorted back, standing toe to toe with him. "I'm carrying your fucking kids, Malachi. Were kids. For that, worse than banishment could happen. But you don't see me quaking in fear. Grow a backbone and leave the Court. Fuck Queen Moirethe's wishes, fuck your new Mistress."

Malachi took a menacing step toward her, backing her into a wall. Pressing his hard frame against hers, he leaned his face forward, his lips a scant inch above her own.

"Canst thou protect me? Tell me, Morrigu. Dost thou really think that thou can protect me or our babes? Thou who must go to a now dead Prince for help? Not only were thee banished from the Court by King Silvas, but now thou art blamed for his death and the death of Prince Ansil. Every step thou take brings thee and our children closer to destruction. What I do, I do for us. Dost thou think I enjoy this? That I want to stay? She wants thee dead and if I can keep thee alive, I will do it, even if it means fucking my new mistress."

He watched as Morgan turned her face from his onslaught and closed her eyes. She took a deep breath, her body rigid and he could feel the fury deep within her staining muscles. Gradually she grew still. As her breathing changed tempos, becoming even and steady, she spoke in a quiet voice though the words came through clenched teeth.

"You want me to trust you, but I need you to trust me. I can take care of myself. I've done so for thousands of years, through wars and battles, politics and intrigue. I don't need you to protect me, I need you to honor me. If you want to be with me, you can't have sex with others, even if it's your new owner. Leave Court forever. If you're not willing to, then stay away, go back to your Queen and mistress and *leave...me...alone*."

Malachi could feel her body shift against the wall as he pressed his hard form against hers. He could feel the pounding of her heart beat and hear the catch in her breath as she leaned her head back against the wall. Staring down at her, his nostrils flared and he inhaled, lowering his head to breathe in her scent at the bend of her neck. Her breathing quickened at the movement and with a smile of triumphant he pressed his lips over the fluttering pulse in the sensitive area on her throat. Pressing his hips into hers, Malachi braced both his hands on either side of her head and brought his face so close to hers they were almost touching noses.

"Understand me now, Morriganna, if thou thinks to make me leave and keep me from my children, then thou art seriously mistaken." Knowing the potion he had been slipping into her food and drink kept her controllable he sank his teeth deep into her shoulder in a display of animalistic dominance.

A cry of pain erupted from Morgan as he tore into her flesh. He felt her knees buckle and knew the only thing keeping her from collapsing to the floor was his body pressed against hers, pinning her to the hard wall. He could feel her struggle in his hold, reaching up to grab a handhold of his hair and tug as she tried to pull his head away, but his mouth remained latched onto her shoulder, his head immobile by the strong muscles in his neck. The sound of her cry echoed in his ears as he sank his teeth further into her sweet flesh and the sound sent a warm pleasure throughout him. The jolt of it made his bite loosen and he groaned, growing hard again.

As his tongue probed the puncture marks he left in her delicate flesh, Malachi heard a soft gasp followed by a low moan of pleasure. With a smile he pressed his erection against her, feeling her respond and grind back. She groaned again and his pulse jumped as the heat within him rose to scorching.

Moving his mouth from the bite, Malachi brushed his lips along the smooth length of her neck. She shifted against him, her body reacting eagerly to his touch and taking the opportunity, he lifted the hem of her shirt higher until his fingers caressed the underside of her breast. Cupping the weight in his palm, he moved his thumb to circle the hardening bud of her nipple and felt a sense of satisfaction at the groans he enlisted from her. His mouth worked around her throat, nibbling at her earlobe before trailing along her jaw while his hand worked her breast, kneading and squeezing as an almost painful ache of need filled him.

His hunger deepened as Morgan's arms pulled him closer. Her voice rose in pleasure as his lips worked, and then cried out as his fingers rolled a tight nub. Lowering an arm, Malachi ran a hand along her thigh, cursing the fabric there and grasped it tight. As she pushed her hips against his, he lifted her leg to slide it around his waist and ground harder against her, letting the throbbing bulge in his pants reveal his intentions. Her lips pressed against his hair and he felt fingers move over the back of his head, cupping it as she held him close.

"Dost thou want me?" His voice came out hoarse and tight.

"Yes," Morgan hissed back and as if to prove the point one of her hands moved down his neck, along his shoulder to his chest. Malachi groaned as her fingers skimmed across his T-shirt-covered chest, tweaking a nipple once before continuing on its downward trail. When her fingers came to rest along the band of his blue jeans, he pulled his head back from her neck and stared down at her with pupils slit like the predatory cat he was.

"Touch me." He demanded and she did, lowering her hand to skim fingernails along the rough denim until she reached the prominent bulge and then she cupped him firmly.

Malachi let escape a feral growl against her soft skin at the touch, feeling his control slipping even further away. Viraska, freedom; the Morrigu, the children. It all came rushing to the forefront of his mind. As much as he hated the Bone Witch, he would do what was necessary to gain his freedom from the Courts but did that future include the woman before him?

"Thou art mine, Battle Crow," he repeated, wiping a trickle of her blood from his mouth with the back of his hand. "Do not forget it again."

When Morgan looked up at him, her eyes were hazy with passion. She ran her tongue over her bottom lip and nodded. Satisfied with the way things were turning out Malachi lowered his head to the bared breast in his hands, running the flat of his tongue over the taunt nub before sucking. He smiled to himself as he felt her other hand run down his chest, skim over his abdomen to work at releasing the leather belt around his waist. It jerked open, followed by the buttons that held the fly shut and soon the silky touch of her hand slipped in.

As her fingers wrapped around his warmth, and a low growl of pleasure erupted from deep in his throat followed by a low rumbling purr. He was almost lost in the feel of her stroking him when suddenly her hand disappeared and he was thrown backward by a terrible force. Flying across the room, he hit the far wall with enough impact to crack the plaster from ceiling to floor. Dazed, Malachi managed to keep from falling down and looked up, shaking his head, to find Morgan staring at him with icy fury on her face. Eldrick magick crackled around her hands, fingers curled into claws as she flexed them dangerously.

"Enough. I'm not going to let you make a fool out of me. I'm giving you a chance to live. Leave…right now and I promise no repercussions."

Growling low in his chest, Malachi stood, readjusting his pants over his erection and turned his face away, too shaken to look at her. "Fuck," he swore under his breath. He needed to fix this situation and fast. Rubbing his sweaty palms over his face, he worked on calming his nerves, realizing how close he had come to being blown out of existence, and took a few steps away to put some distance between them, leaving the outline of his body on the wall. "Morriganna…"

"You heard me. I will not allow you or anyone else to use me for whatever plans you have. I don't give a damn about Queens or mistresses, so don't give me any excuses. You did what you did because you chose to, not because of any threats. Whatever they have planned against me I will meet head on, and be aware I'll not be besotted by a bit dangling from the Queen's fingertips."

Malachi's face hardened at her words. His lips tightened in a straight line, as he watched her with a dangerous glint in his eyes. She was angry and hormonal and nothing he said or did would make a difference. The rage he felt brewing inside him, pushed away the fear and threatened to break any moment. He needed to leave before he lost it and did something he regretted more than he did now. At least he had Viraska's promise for freedom. Freedom to one day choose for himself.

"I did not wish to hurt thee," he growled, his voice deep and harsh before he turned around and stalked out of her home to head back to the Court and report the outcome. *Gods, this had better be worth it..* He focused on Morgan and the possible what ifs. The look in hers eyes was proof enough that it would take more than some flowers and a few pretty words to make things right. She hated him and no matter what excuses he could come up with he knew she had the right to.

~~~

After Malachi headed around the corner of the warehouse, he paused, leaned back against the brick building, and closed his eyes to the daylight. Too much, too soon, quickly things spiraled out of control and there was nothing he could do to keep from sinking himself. His children entered his mind, unknown blobs in the Morrigu's womb at this moment, but soon they would be born and he would have no part of them. Even if she did live, did survive whatever plans his Queen had planned, there was no way she would let him near them. He could see it in her eyes. Stay away and live, come back and die. Stupid woman. If she thought to keep him away from them she would have a fight on her hands. Perhaps with Viraska's help he could…

The hair on the back of his neck stood to attention while a now familiar presence filled his senses. A soft feminine voice caressed his ears.

"Malachi…thou hath not been truthful to thy Queen."

At the sound of Viraska's soft voice, Malachi remained still. He recognized the sadistic pleasure that purred in it, knowing the power she held over him. In truth, there was not much difference between the Morrigu and the Bone Witch. Both offered life or death to him, but now only Viraska was in the position to fulfill it. A slight tick in the corner of his eye showed the irritation and anger he felt as he turned to face the beautiful redhead his Queen gave him to, and he swallowed back a sharp retort. Now was not the time for his anger.

Once again he found himself surrounded by her erotic scent of sexual promise and enticement, wrapping around his body like a soft warm cocoon. Breathing in her exotic perfume, Malachi felt his body react, his shaft growing ridged as it strained against the buttery softness of his leather pants.

"So, thy mating was successful after all." Her accented voice held a touch of malevolence beneath it. "I am sure thy Queen will be pleased with that, but why hath thou not told her yet?" Viraska stepped out of the shadows to reveal a lush figure clad in a vague gauzy gown that draped her body from her slender shoulder to her shapely ankle. Though to the eye she seemed nothing more than an exclusively sexual creature and oblivious to anything not pertaining to the erotic arts, Malachi could feel the darkness radiating from her. "But though thou hast succeeded in one mission, it seems now thou hast failed in the other. The Morrigu has removed thee from her abode."

"It matters not. What was to be done has and tonight I will report to the Queen the success of our…time together," he snarled, fighting the attraction he felt growing, along with a raging hard on. He could smell the pheromone wafting from her, the same type he had used on Morgan to keep her interested, and gritted his teeth.

With a subtle smile, Viraska sashayed to the tall Were and ran a small hand along the small of his back, causing his abdomen to clench and tremble with want beneath the woman's skillful caress.

"Well then, hurry along, my pet. I shall inform our Queen of thy announcement tonight."

She flashed Malachi a breathtaking smile, moving her small hand to cup his covered erection. With a gentle squeeze, she disappeared, but not before he saw the smoldering promises in her eyes, leaving the Were alone again. With a heavy sigh of longing and frustration, Malachi reached into his pants and adjusted his swollen cock to a less painful position before pushing off from the building.

Pacing the pavement, Malachi's brain swirled with chaos as every once in a while he glanced at the building, thinking of the woman within. *What the hell am I going to do now?* It was too late to deny the pregnancy, for Queen Moirethe would know tonight and Morgan had kicked him out anyway. The bitch Queen was sure to be displeased by his performance.

Shaking his head, he rammed his fingers through his hair, brushing it away from his forehead. He hadn't been lying when he told Morgan he loved her, but it was not enough of a love to defy his Queen or new Mistress and besides Viraska promised him his freedom. Maybe one day he'd be a slave no more. When that happened, he would find her again and beg for her forgiveness. Perhaps then, enough time would pass that she would grant him that. Stopping his pacing, Malachi pressed his hand against the sun-heated bricks.

"I am sorry, Morrigu. It was fun while it lasted." Stepping back from the warehouse, Queen Moirethe's assassin left.

25

There's nothing like drowning your sorrows in a good bottle of whiskey when times get you down. Problem is, pregnant women weren't supposed to drink, but did she care? With a shrug, Morgan looked down at the glass of Pepsi in her hand, wishing it was filled with the smoothly burning taste she so craved, and watched the ice shift to clink against one another. Her whole attitude on the situation surprised her for normally she'd be cruising for a fight, looking to hurt and destroy, but instead…she sat at a bar wishing she could get drunk. *What happened to me?*

Setting the now empty glass on the counter, Morgan let out a soft belch, ignoring the look of disgust on the face of the woman two seats away from her, and ordered another from the bartender. Rubbing the bridge of her nose between her thumb and forefinger, she lowered her head. *What a fucking predicament I got myself into.*

"Enjoy yourself, Morgan. I know it's been awhile since you last heard from him, but cheer up. He'll be back soon and then partying will be out." Terri slid her friend another drink, a diet Pepsi with a lemon wedge. "Pretend it's tequila."

Moving her eyes from the glass, Morgan glared at the annoying, cheerful brunette next to her. "Leave me alone. Why don't you go bug that guy over there? He keeps looking at you."

Turning in her seat to look before looking back at the dark-haired woman seated next to her, Terri rolled her eyes in annoyance. "Too stupid looking. I'd rather bug you." She lifted her shot glass and downed her tequila, then sucked on a lemon and smiled. "Fucking A! Let's go find someone to dance with."

The crowd on the wooden dance floor moved with an easy flow as a ballad sounded while couples pulled each other close for an intimate embrace. The lights dimmed as the voice of Bryan Adams filled the air, singing about what he would do for his lady love, to live or die for her. Shaking her glossy mane, Terri spun back around, the look on her face one of disgust.

"Crap, a love song. Thanks for bringing me down, Morgan."

Looking around at the faces littering the club, the human faces that filled her day and never gave her a time of respite, Morgan raised the bendy straw to her lips and sucked in a deep swallow of liquid brown, wishing for the millionth time for something stronger. *What I would do for a scotch right now.* She put a hand on her belly. Though her abdomen was still flat, she was becoming more attuned to what was within. The children always seemed to become agitated when she was upset, flittering around inside her womb and making her on edge. It seemed that it was happening more and more frequently and nothing she did seemed to lessen it.

Shh, little ones. Morgan tried to calm their flittering. She could feel their anxiousness as her own rose in tandem.

Poking her in the ribs, Terri grinned crookedly. "Liven up, woman. You frown anymore and they'll tell us to leave."

"Shut up, Ter, before I hurt you."

Terri's grin widened, then froze as a rich masculine voice spoke in Morgan's ear.

"Thou hast been betrayed, Morrigu. Run."

Feeling the tickle of warm breath against the delicate curve of her lobe, Morgan turned her head slowly toward the voice beside her. There, she met the pain-filled violet eyes of her informant and former business associate, Eryn Sye, one of the few Sidhe from the Mor'sin'dar Court she had spent more than a couple of fleeting moments with from time to time. He leaned toward her in a conspiratorial way, his shoulders hunched over with one arm wrapped around his abdomen in a self hug as he rested his side against the polished wood curve of the bar. A wince of pain crossed his handsome face and his lips tightened in a white line, sucking in a deep, harsh breath while his eyes kept moving towards the door in an urgent manner.

The scent of blood filled Morgan's nose, causing her to swallow back a sudden hunger before a dark crimson smear spreading quickly over his shirt caught her attention. A gut wound, very painful but not deadly to one of her people. Yet from his pallor and the slight tinge of blue around his lips, she knew he had been poisoned as well as stabbed. Only one poison was fatal to the immortal Sidhe, cold iron. The fact that he was here now, warning her, spoke volumes to his inner strength and his friendship with the Morrigu.

"I shall endeavor to hold them off as long as I can," he gave a harsh whisper under his breath before running the tip of his tongue between his lips to wet them. Urgency sharpened his gaze and he stared at her intently, but his eyes flicked back toward the door of the club, only to narrow and harden at the sight that greeted him. "All debts owed are fully paid now."

With a sharp nod at his statement, Morgan followed his line of sight, turning her head in time to watch as several tall men enter the bar before pausing, their bodies darkening the doorway as they scanned the room. Each wore the royal uniform of the High Court of the Mor'sin'dar and each carried a cold iron long sword with a wickedly curved blade in their hand. In the hand of the guard in the front was wrapped a thick, leather leash that held a huge monstrous dog-like creature with bunching muscles under a dull green coat. It strained against the controller that held it bound, growling with menace to all as glistening ropes of saliva hung from its meaty jaws and shark like, yellowed teeth.

The beast was a Cusith; hounds that were relentless hunters feared for their veracity and viciousness when it came to their prey. They never gave up the hunt nor could those they chased escape them. Great, just what she needed to brighten up a normally medial night. The few people in the club began screaming in terror as the guards spotted her, letting go of the beast's tether to release him to tear through the tables, heedless of anyone in its way.

Without a second thought, Morgan drew a dagger from an arm sheath hidden beneath her sleeve and let it fly, watching with a mild form of satisfaction as it sunk deep within the creature's muscular shoulder with a meaty sound. Smoke rose from the wound as dark blood seeped out, the droplets hitting the floor with an acidly drip. The splattering burned the wood, hissing and bubbling only to leave dark pocks on the otherwise perfect floor.

The hound stopped for a second, confusion and surprise showing on its face at the audacity that the woman had wounded it, then narrowing its eyes in rage, leapt toward her once more. Drawing another dagger, Morgan braced herself for the attack she knew was coming.

Staring in shock, Terri scrambled around the bar as Morgan pushed her out of the way. Crouching low with her feet spread to keep her balance, she studied the Cusith as it sprang at her. Snarling, with great globs of saliva dripping from its powerful jaws, it snapped, causing the Morrigu to jerk her body back out of its reach to avoid getting bitten. Then, she reacted, slashing with her knife across the front of its chest. The metal sizzled as it cut through the creature's flesh before getting splattered by its acidic blood.

Morgan hissed in pain as the droplets struck her, feeling as if her flesh were being eaten away. Gritting her teeth against the sting, she slashed again and side-stepped as it swung its massive paw toward her in an arch, its deadly claws barely missing her shoulder.

The Cusith hissed and growled, bending its torso at an impossible angle to swipe at Morgan again. This time its sharp claws caught her head, slicing the left side of her face open from cheekbone to ear. Dazed, tears of pain almost blinded her as the impact knocked Morgan back on her ass. She could feel the warmth of the blood pouring from the wound as the poisons from its claws quickly spread, making her face feel as if it were on fire.

Blinking back tears, Morgan shook her head to clear away the pain, and then scrambled around behind a table before knocking it over to shield herself from the beast's next attack. The creature growled again, swiping at the table to leave long jagged marks down its polished surface. Crouching behind her shield, a dagger in each hand while blood dripped down her neck, Morgan readied herself, feeling the wound the beast inflicted start to swell. The gashes began closing as her natural healing took over, sealing to leave a dull throb, and her body fought the invading toxins from her system. The creature jumped again, bounding over the table and in mid-leap turned its body to face her before it landed in a crouch on the floor, growling deep in its throat as it prepared to vault at her, but luck had its hand on Morgan's shoulder that night.

As the Cusith leapt into the air, claws extended for the killing blow, Morgan struck. With a lightning-swift move, she plunged her daggers into the soft underbelly of the bounding creature, slicing the weapons in opposite directions while splitting its belly in half. Flesh and muscles parted while blood and intestines poured out to splatter the ground around her in a wave of smoldering gore. Scattering back in a hurry to avoid the mess, she slipped on something warm and squishy, hitting the table behind her that had been her shield, only to find herself pinned between it and the beast's corpse.

Breathing heavily, Morgan narrowed her eyes at her sudden predicament, and then pushed the dead beast off her with a grunt before scrambling to her feet. Moving away from the table, she stepped over the corpse and looked around while backing away a few feet onto the now emptied dance floor. With a deep breath, she filled her lungs with cleansing air, slowly let it out then readied herself for the fight to come. Slipping another knife from its place in her boot, she crouched low in a fighter's stance and eyed the assassins who were there to kill her.

"Ready when you are, boys."

One of the Queen's assassins smiled as he moved away from the pack, spinning his weapon in his hand in a silvery arc beside him. With almost blinding speed he struck, moving within five feet of Morgan as his sword arched toward her neck. She jumped back, the blade a whisper's width of missing her throat, and ducked as another blow followed in tandem, each movement a graceful and lethal dance. Damn he was good. It seemed Moirthe the spared no expense for her death.

Narrowing her eyes, feeling the world around her slow down and sharpen, the Morrigu studied her opponent's movements, searching for his weaknesses and an opening to strike. His sword weaved around, blurring the air in front of her with a silvery arc, as it nicked at the claw marks on her face. She winced when it starting to bleed again and swore under her breath. She was so not in the mood for this.

With a quick feint, Morgan dodged to the right, ducking and twisting on the balls of her feet as the blade struck the center of the spot she had just vacated seconds before. She followed the move by ramming her knife deep into the back of the assassin's unprotected knee before pulling it out sideways, hamstringing the bastard. She finished the move with a low backward spin, smashing the heel of her boot into his other knee as—to her satisfaction—a crack filled the air. Then she spun out of the way of his falling body.

With a grunt of surprise, the assassin dropped to the floor and turned his face toward Morgan. When he did, she plunged her knife deep into his right eye, using the full weight of her body to impale it through his brain. While his body shuddered in death throws, she turned her attention back to the others that had come with him, ignoring the sound of his sword clattering on the floor and the soft exhale of breath that announced his demise.

Standing back up, Morgan pulled her gun from the holster she kept under her jacket and narrowed her eyes to stare down the site, firing it at the Sidhe who had held the leash of the Cusith. The muzzle flashed as the roar of the shots filled the room. With an explosion of bloody gore, his left eye popped like a grape, his head snapping back from the impact before he hit the back wall and slid to the ground on his knees, leaving a trail of crimson streaks in his wake.

With a scream, the Sidhe clawed at his eye while the other four guards moved forward, each gripping tightly their own lethal blades. Choosing another target, Morgan fired again, this time in a starburst pattern over his heart. The Sidhe stumbled to a halt, blinking his eyes with each bullet entering his flesh then fell backwards as blood quickly seeped through his tunic and poured steadily to the floor beneath him in an ever spreading pool of red. She hoped to slow them down but with the weapon she was using she knew it would do very little good. At least it was causing some pain.

At that moment, Eryn stepped forward, drawing a curved long sword from its sheath at his side while gripping his belly wound with his other hand. Thin blood dripped though his fingers as he grimaced again, but he moved forward to intercept a blow meant for Morgan. With expertise, he raised his weapon to parry while the guard's blade struck down. Metal clashed, sending blue sparks flying in different directions. Morgan heard him grunt at the strain, but he held his blade steady before he pushed his attacker back.

"Sie d'os ethein, Eryn," his attacker growled, moving forward again as his blade circled the other's and slashed at the guard's chest.

From the corner of her eye, Morgan watched Eryn's grip wavered on the sword, weakening from blood loss. Turning her gun in that direction she fired, the bullet parting the air beside her friend's head before entering between the eyes of the Sidhe he fought. Blood splattered Eryn's face as the guard's head snapped back from the impact and at the same time Morgan wrapped an arm around his waist to pull him back out of danger.

"Not today, Eryn," she hissed in his ear, unwilling to let a friend fight her battle. "Die on someone else's time."

Pushing him behind her, Morgan moved and aimed her gun at another before pulling the trigger. She noted a dark-haired Sidhe standing by himself at the back of the room gesturing with his hands. His eyes were locked onto her face and a cruel smirk curled the corners of his lips. The small hairs on the back of Morgan's neck rose as an intense electrical current of magick filled the room. Within seconds, the mage's head jerked back as a bullet entered his skull, knocking him down and stopping the drawl of power to leave in its place the feeling of void.

At the same time the Sidhe Morgan had shot earlier stood back up, his eye now nothing more than a dark, bloody hole. Shaking his head to clear his vision, the guard glared at her with his remaining eye as he pulled a wicked-looking short sword from its sheath, and charged, baring his teeth in fury. She fired at him again, the bullets hitting him square in the chest, but instead of falling he grunted with the impact and swung his weapon at the woman with enough precision to cause her to either jump back or be sliced. She chose to keep her guts inside and moved out of his way.

Unfortunately Morgan forgot Eryn was behind her. He stepped back too, trying to avoid her and managed to stumble against the bar, catching his foot in the rungs on one of the barstools. It tumbled over with a loud clatter and bumped into the back of Morgan's legs. By twisting her torso, she just missed getting disemboweled by the razor sharp edge of the sword being swung at her.

"Lle holma ve' eda, biean shiham du thulo benshlou, Morrigu." The Sidhe's grin turned sinister, white teeth showing through his blood-streaked face while the socket where his right eye once sat quickly filled with thick coagulated ruby mess.

"You can try, Irvel, but I don't think you'll like the results." Ducking under his blade again, Morgan skimmed to his right and kept in mind the last two assassins heading toward her. Liquid pain ripped over her back when Irvel's blade came away bloody.

Breathing hard, she lifted the gun to fire again, only to find the magazine empty. *Damn.* With the weapon now useless, Morgan threw it at her attacker, hearing the satisfying clang of metal on metal then from her periphery, she watched as Eryn raise his sword to block the descending blade of one of the other Sidhe. His legs gave way, blood loss finally taking its toll, and he crashed down hard on his knees. One of the assassins saw his chance and swung his sword through the air to cut at a sharp downward angle, neatly removing her friend's head from his shoulders.

"No!" she cried.

Turning toward him, Morgan ignored the immediate danger to her as blood gushed upward, splattering his killer's face and hers. *Not Eryn! Not Eryn!* her mind screamed when his body slump to the ground, a circle of crimson quickly spreading around his corpse. Numb, she turned back to the three remaining Sidhe circling her with an air of triumph. With a flick of his blade, the Sidhe that killed Eryn removed the dark liquid that coated its shiny metal before speaking in a deep voice.

"Our Queen hoped to have thee brought back alive, bitch, but thy death will please her too."

Morgan blinked once, twice, and stared deep into the eyes of the leader in challenge while the color of her irises quickly bled away to a bone-chilling darkness. *If they want the Morrigu, then let them have her.* She was tired of playing nice. Shifting out of her glamour, small tremors of excitement raced throughout her body. An icy wind whipped around the room as the temperature dropped several degrees, enough for them to see their own breaths. Across the mirror behind the bar and the glasses throughout the room, frost formed, spreading along their smooth surfaces in a crystalline effect.

With a tilt of her head, the Morrigu gave a crooked smile and raised a hand to point a single finger at the man who killed Eryn before curling it back toward her, beckoning. His eyes narrowed in confused irritation before widening in panic, then lastly bugged while his face turned first red, then purple. Gasping for breath, he dropped his sword to the floor as he clawed frantically at his upper body. The other two Sidhe watched in silent disbelief when their leader's chest heaved, his body stiffening in pain.

As his back began to buckle, loud cracks overflowing the room. Horror filled the eyes of the others as the cracking sound increased. Suddenly his shirt ripped from the center and his chest suddenly burst open like a ripe melon. Meat and bone exploded outward in a shower of bloody rain while Morgan curled her fingers into a tight ball before jerking her arm back toward her as if pulling on some invisible rope. Summoned forth, the dying Sidhe's heart burst from his ribcage, showering gore on those unlucky enough to be near the scene. The still beating muscle pulsated as it flew toward the Morrigu's waiting hand and she smiled, her gaze traveling over the shocked expressions around the room with the judging eyes of an avenging goddess.

Terri gapped at the morbid scenery, horror quickly transforming her expression. Around her everything seemed to move in slow motion before time caught up in a rapid flash of light. It was then that one of the Sidhe decided to strike, while everyone else stood transfixed by the sight.

"Morgan! No!" she screamed.

At Terri's warning, Morgan turned only to find herself face to face with the one-eyed Sidhe and a moment later a sharp pain filled her chest. With a gasp, she glanced down, watching as his blade entering her sternum. Looking back up to meet his gaze, she stared at him dumbfounded, and then snarled. *You can't kill me that easily.* Grabbing his shoulder with her free hand, she pulled herself up the blade until they stood face to face, their noses almost meeting. Dropping the heart to the floor, the Morrigu reached up to grab the back of the guard's neck, pulling his head down to hers in a morbid lover's embrace. Wetting her lips, she smiled up at him, seeing the hate in his eyes as he jerked his sword out and her knees buckled. Slowly her body slid down his as she released him to land in a kneeling position at his feet.

Feeling her blood pour free from the wound, Morgan watched it pooled around her, and gradually raised a hand to her belly, to the life hidden inside her. Here she was, a long-ago banished assassin from the Courts of the Mor'sin'dar, a month pregnant, kneeling before the representative of the Queen who hated her guts. Ironic, wasn't it? As the guard shifted above her, Morgan bowed her head and she closed her eyes as she felt her unborn children's terror.

"Shh, little ones. It will be alright. Momma's not done yet."

"Thou should not have come back, Morrigu. Thou wert banished for thy crimes. The Queen would not have sent us if thou would have left well enough alone. But to murder our King and Prince, there is only one answer for that crime." The one-eyed Sidhe whispered while he tightened his grip on the pommel of his sword. "I once respected thee...thy skill." He paused for a moment before he glanced back at his fallen leader and the steaming mass of flesh that was once his chest. "Tis such a waste."

With a heavy sigh, he raised his sword overhead, readying it to give the final blow.

"I never betrayed Silvas and the Prince, Irvel. It's the Queen you should have been wary of."

With a flick of her wrist, Morgan pulled a dagger that was sheathed in his boot. Not smart to have a weapon so handy in the near vicinity of a trapped assassin. In one quick and graceful move, she pushed herself up, straightening her legs under her and rammed the blade into his gut. Using the strength of the lift as she forced herself to stand, she pulled the dagger up to split him from naval to neck, feeling a resistance before the blade's magicks helped it slice through muscle and bone like butter. Once again standing, Morgan faced Irvel before smiling.

"I don't die that easily."

With a sharp tug, she pulled the blade free to release his body. As he crumpled to the floor in a boneless heap, Morgan spun around to face the last guard who moved forward. His face twisted in surprise and agony before he shuddered. Eyes rolling up in their sockets, the Sidhe slid to the floor to reveal Terri, looking angry and scared at the same time, with a bloody, curved dagger clenched tightly in her grasp. For a second she stared at Morgan before dropping the weapon. It clanked on the floor as she took a step toward her friend then stumbled, slipping on blood. Catching her balance, Terri straightened, visibly trying to calm herself.

"Damn, Morgan, when I talked about partying, I didn't know you had this in mind." With a strained smiled, Terri looked down at herself and the blood on her shirt before turning back to the taller woman. "Well hell, ruined a perfectly good shirt." With those final words, she passed out.

Catching her friend before she hit the floor, Morgan gathered the smaller woman in her arms and gave her a quick once over, spotting a wound along the side of her neck. It probably happened during the fight, most likely from flying shrapnel as a table broke. Sensing a burst of magick go off outside, Morgan lifted her friend over her shoulder in a fireman's carry then stood back up. Slipping slightly on the blood that slicked the floor, she caught herself on the edge of an overturned table and straightened her shoulders.

Calming her breathing, Morgan glanced around again, her eyes skimming over the wreckage and poor Eryn. *Shit.* Stopping next to a fallen guard, she squatted to grab a sword from the floor before swiftly heading through the carnage back toward the kitchens to look for an escape route. With times like this she'd just teleport out to appear miles away, but with another mage nearby, he'd be able to locate her in no time if he hadn't already put a shield up around the building to keep her from doing just so.

Once in the kitchens, finding the exit was easy enough. The door was still propped open where the cook could have a quick pop out for a smoke if he so chose. Said cook, of course, was nowhere to be found, probably took off out of the building as soon as the first guard hit the floor.

Morgan headed outside into the back alley, closing the door behind her. After carefully setting her friend down, she spied a dumpster and pulled it over to block the back exit. It screeched and protested its new placement, but turned quiet once firmly in place, giving Morgan a moment to catch her breath and look down at the wound below her breasts. She lifted her T-shirt, wiping the blood away from her skin with her fingers, before noting the wound was slowly closing. Good. She breathed a sigh of relief before noticing shiny red droplets on the ground and cursed at the blood trail she was leaving behind.

Tightening her lips in irritation, Morgan wadded the bottom of her T-shirt up in her fist and pressed it to the wound, hoping to staunch the flow, then after making sure the exit was blocked, she picked Terri back up before heading down the alley opposite the front of the club. She glanced around the corner to see if the coast was clear, but ducked back into the alley when a police car drove by. It slowed down as it headed around toward the entrance of the building, its blue and white strobe lights flashing while its sirens blared. Great, just great. Human involvement. Let them deal with the other guards; she didn't give a flying fart as long as she was far away.

Sucking in a harsh breath, Morgan ignored the burning pain from the sword wound and adjusted Terri's limp form on her shoulder. The blood made it hard to keep a steady hold on her friend by soaking their clothes, but she secured the unconscious form and looked around. Nostrils flaring at the coppery scent, Morgan felt her mouth water and swallowed, tasting the imagined salty tang in her mouth. Leaning her head back against the alley's brick wall and closing her eyes for a second, she willed the hunger to pass and listened to the unconscious woman's shallow breathing. Just a little drink would accelerate her healing but now was not the time. Instead Morgan turning her attention inside, concentrating on placing a small protective shield over her unborn children and willed them to calm down. Her mood affected the babies and right now she was agitated.

After waiting a few seconds to catch her breath, Morgan continued forward, sticking to side streets and shadows. After weaving her way through alleys for almost half an hour, the sounds of sirens fading, she stopped and looked around, noting that she was in the warehouse district near the wharf. The smell of brine and fish stink reached her nose as she searched for anything that could be use for shelter until she was positive the coast was clear and the hunt was off.

Picking a warehouse facing the water, Morgan kept to the shadows and leaned a shoulder against the wall then listened for sounds of pursuit. When nothing reached her ears, she studied the brick building, finding a small window high on the wall and a metal door to the left of a huge trunk entrance. Still hesitant to use her magick to bypass any locks, Morgan hurried to the entrance. She tried the handle and, shock upon shocks, it was unlocked. Maybe one of the gods took pity on her or decided she amused them enough. Not willing to let this gift go by, she hurried in, closing the door behind her before sliding Terri off her shoulder. Bracing her friend against the door, she bolted the locks shut then glanced around the interior of the warehouse.

The open bay was dark; the street lights from outside gave the area a gloomy illumination that could put any horror movie to shame, making her wonder where the chainsaw-wielding killer was going to leap from. To the immediate right of her was the sealed truck entrance; on the opposite wall was a single door that led to a back area. Beside that was a metal staircase that led up to an office with a large glass front that showed a shadowy interior. A few crates were scattered around the room and she could hear the rustle of little feet and squeaks, revealing that they were not alone in here.

26

The few rats that were brave enough to stand their ground when Morgan first entered quickly scuttled out of her way to their hidey-holes as she hurried across the open expanse of the warehouse floor to the lower door. When she reached it, she tested the handle to find the door locked shut. Carefully laying Terri's limp body down along with the dead Sidhe's sword, she squatted and reached into her boot to pull out a lock pick set, ignoring the burn in her back from where the sword had sliced her earlier and the ache in her abdomen. For a moment the room spun and Morgan swayed for a bit, before leaning against the wall to regain her balance. She held still until her vision cleared, taking several slow, deep breaths then realized that blood loss was starting to catch up with her.

Wetting her lips, Morgan lifted her shirt to check her wound again, surprised at what she saw. Instead of a closed wound, it gaped wide, revealing a wet red center that bled freely. She could only imagine what the exit wound on her back looked like and gritted her teeth at the sharp pain when she probed it with the tips of her fingers. It wasn't healing like it should, but she didn't have time to figure out why. As soon as she didn't have assassins on her ass she'd see a healer, but now...

Lowering her shirt, she turned her attention back to the lock. At least one thing was going her way; the lock itself was a simple key and tumble one. Pulling out two thin metal picks, she slid one in and pressed down on a lever as she jimmied the other around until it caught. *Click.* With a smile, she turned the handle then she stood back up and began shoving her picks into her back pocket.

The explosion caught Morgan by surprise, propelling her body forward into the door while shrapnel studded her back with tiny pieces of metal. With a grunt, she dropped to the floor and pulled herself into a small ball, protecting her neck and the back of her head with her hands. When the bright light from the explosion died down, she turned her face toward where it had gone off and blinked, trying to clear the dizziness that threatened to overcome her. Her ears rang from the loud noise, deafening her to any sounds her attackers might be making and from the corner of her eyes, she could see Terri stir.

"Whaaa…" the small woman mumbled, cracking her eyes open as she tried to focus on what was going on around her. Reaching up, she weakly touched her wounded shoulder, and then dropped her hand back down.

Feeling vibrations emanate from the cement floor, Morgan glanced back toward the entrance and squinting her eyes just barely make out three sets of feet not far before her. *Fuck, my night just keeps getting better.*

"No use hiding anymore, Morrigu. We have found thee. Just come with us quietly."

The rich voice barely penetrated Morgan's brain as she concentrated on the figures, the words sounding as if spoken far away through water. Swallowing a few times to try and relieve the pressure in her ears, she sat in silence before stumbling forward to stand. Blinking again to clear her vision, Morgan straightened her shoulders, feeling the burn in her back from the metal shards and the aching throb in her gut. While licking her lips to relieve the sudden dryness, she tilted her head and listened to the movements of the men as they moved around the open floor. After a moment of studying their positions the she swallowed to relieve the pressure in her ears and coughed, regretting the movement as soon as she did.

"So she sent nine men after me? Where's Ghost?" Danu, her voice sounded pathetic even to her.

"Behind thee," a masculine voice whispered so soft against her ear she almost missed it. His breath warmed the back of her neck as he shifted closer to her, brushing his body against hers before chuckling at the winced at the pain she gave.

Closing her eyes, Morgan gritted her teeth to keep from screaming. He knew what he was doing with each small touch, every slight movement…pushing the metal shards deeper into her skin. The prick was as sadistic as she remembered him. Inside her, her children were terrified, reacting to their mother's unease. She tried calming her babes, but to no avail. Instead they shifted in the womb.

Daddy.

Closing her eyes to that simple word, Morgan felt anger surge through her. That bastard would never be a part of her life, of their lives again. *He's not here, I'll protect you.*

The babies shifted again in angst as if disturbed by the news, so she checked the shield she'd placed over them earlier, finding it still strong before moving her attention back to the assassin pressed against her. Cracking her eyes open, Morgan watched Ghost out of her periphery while keeping track of those assassins half a warehouse floor away. Once more his breath tickled her ear, moving the delicate hair along the nape of her neck as he leaned in to brush his lips against her skin.

"I have missed thee, Morrigu."

Morgan stiffened at the light kiss for it was well known in their circles that Ghost's kisses brought death to mortals and immortals alike. That was his gift, his killing specialty. Perhaps that was why he seemed to favor her when she was still at Court, for she was immune to his touch, considered immortal even among the immortal Sidhe. Rather than respond to his taunt, Morgan opened her eyes and stared at the other three Sidhe standing before her, daring them to make a move. She was wounded, but not helpless. *Come fight me at your own risk.*

"No," came a weak cry from the floor.

Glancing down, Morgan watched as Terri reached out a hand to grab Ghost's ankle. The pale Sidhe looked down and tilted his head to view the human who dared to touch him. Taking a step back, he shook off her grip with disgust, then with a lightning swift move, pulled his short sword from its sheath and thrust it through her chest. A gasp escaped from Terri as little bloody bubbles appeared from her wound. One slow breath in, then all the air left her before her head leaned back against the concrete floor, her eyes vacant as they stared up at the ceiling.

Terri! Morgan's eyes widened in disbelief at the sight of her friend's lifeless body. Drawing in a harsh breath, she stared unblinking, feeling numb. It was her fault Terri was dead. She should have left, should have moved on, should have…

Ghost shifted from Morgan, circling around her body until he stood in front, face to face. Their gaze met as her eyes drained of emotion, leaving only a deep empty void in its place while the numbness turned cold. Unnerved by the sight, the assassin backed away and drew his sword again, giving the Morrigu a slow nod to acknowledge the unspoken promise that her eyes held. Looking him over slowly, Morgan returned the nod and knelt down to retrieve the sword she had abandoned earlier. After straightening back up, she hefted the blade, testing its balance before moving to start their little dance.

Ghost dodged out of the way, spinning in a small circle until once more he faced Morgan's back, but when he moved to strike, she whirled around and lifted her blade to counter his. The sound of metal sliding across metal vibrated through the air to fill their ears and grate the nerves in their teeth. Morgan pressed her attack, stepping into his space as her sword moved in dazzling speed while Ghost backed off a pace, narrowing his eyes in concentration to keep her from slicing him into ribbons.

Over and over, Morgan swung her blade in an arc, each time connecting to catch either metal or flesh. Her lips twitched into a crooked smirk as he grunted in pain when her sword sank into his bicep, slicing open muscle before continuing along its path. He backed off a step, switching his weapon to his other hand before he continued to defend, all the while keeping his eyes on the Morrigu's beautiful face.

Inside Morgan felt herself go into her familiar routine of death, voiding herself of emotion, intent only on the kill. She savored the dark zone, the peace it brought, the total freedom to know she would triumph in the outcome. Not that she was vain, though in truth she was a bit as all Sidhe are, but because she no longer cared. *Cut me, burn me, do whatever. In the end I will come back and hunt you down.* He must have seen that, for his already pale Sidhe skin lightened even more. After all, there was a reason she had earned her title. Lady Death, the Morrigu, the King's Justice.

Spinning around, Morgan crouched as she sliced at his legs, the edge of her blade sinking deep into the front of his thighs. Ghost jumped back, running a hand over the wound to check the damage while keeping their gaze locked tight. She watched him wince and stumble at the pain and damage, but he straightened, determination etched across his handsome face.

Morgan knew the pain he suffered. After all, she was riddled with wounds that were wearing her down too. Keeping outwardly calm, she moved with a deadly ease, but inside she cursed, feeling her body weakening from blood loss and exhaustion. Morgan knew her aim wasn't as steady as it should have been and her gut burned from the stress of the open wound that wouldn't heal. Running the tip of her tongue between her lips to wet them, she felt her breathing grow harsher as sweat stung her eyes.

Ghost smiled. Morgan's eyes sharpened at that small inflection, knowing she needed to end this quick, for she was losing stamina. Anything longer and he would wear her down enough for him to get a lucky blow. Stepping back,

Morgan prepared to strike, but at that moment a wave of dizziness overwhelmed her, causing her to stumble to the floor and land hard on her knees.

Blinking to clear her vision, she watched him move toward her. A soft menacing chuckle reached her ears and Morgan felt more than saw him shift his sword in his hand as he spun to strike. On the downward stroke, she forced her body into action, thrusting her sword upward with all her strength to impale him upon its sharp blade. He stilled for a second, his face twisting in a mixture of shock and disbelief.

"No," he whispered as Morgan slid the weapon in deeper before jerking it free to watch his body crumble to the floor. Following the blow with a downward stroke of her own, she neatly severed Ghost's head from his shoulders before turning to face the three remaining Sidhe.

Lungs burning from harsh breathing, shoulders rising and falling with each intake and exhale of air, Morgan rose to her feet. Slowly she raised her sword before her, prepared to fight to the death. Instead of the battle she envisioned, she felt something slam into her chest, lifting up off her feet to crash against a wall with a mind-numbing force. The cement cracked under the sudden impact of the blow. Stunned, Morgan stared aghast at what met her eyes while excruciating pain ripped through her chest like a fiery inferno.

Feet no longer able to hold her, Morgan slid down the wall, leaving a trail of scarlet and cloth behind. From out of her chest appeared a long wooden spear, its shaft twisted and carved in an intricate pattern of vines and roses with runes of a magick long forgotten among her people. She reached a hand over to pull it out, but on first touch a sharp pain of lightning ripped through her, the movement tearing a scream from her lips louder than a banshee's wail. Nausea overwhelmed her in a vortex of grayness while her consciousness threatened to flee to spare her the intensity.

Gasping for air, Morgan let go of the spear shaft, her breathing coming in short, shallow breaths. Blood filled her mouth and leaked from between her lips. Spitting it out she grimaced at the pain that simple act caused. As a soft echoing of footsteps reached her ears, she looked up to find a small seductive woman with thick coppery hair walking toward her in a leisurely stride.

27

When Viraska reached the Morrigu, she knelt down, moving the skirt of her rich gown away from pooling blood and leaned in. For several long seconds they stared at each other, the redhead in what appeared to be morbid curiosity, and Morgan in complete loathing before the Bone Hag raised a delicate bejeweled hand to wipe a trail of blood from the corner of the assassin's mouth. Lifting it toward her face, Viraska eyes flickered to the dark crimson color that streaked her pale finger and raised it to her lips. Touching the tip of her tongue to the liquid, she closed her eyes as if savoring some small delicacy and smiled.

"Thy blood is sweet," she murmured, flicking her gaze back to the wounded woman's face as her eyes grew sly. "Dost thou remember me?" she asked, and then laughed as Morgan tossed her a venomous look. "Thou had killed my sister, Morrigu. Long, long ago thou killed my family for some imagined insult. Thou had taken everything from me and now I have come to take everything from thee."

For several long moments, Morgan stared at the woman, wondering why she seemed so familiar, then it hit her. The woman in the hall. The perfume that clung to her reached the Morrigu's nostrils and clenched her jaw at the scent, the scent that Malachi had claimed to be his new mistress. But there was something else, some memory that was teasing her; red hair, the sly smile, knowing look...Bone Hag. She was supposed to have killed them all. Obviously she didn't. Now it made sense.

"I remember you, Viraska. How could I ever forget? I thought I killed all the Bone Hags."

Morgan coughed, bringing up blood into her mouth again, then decided what the hell and spat it at her. It landed in a crimson glob on Viraska's perfect pale cheek to run down in a stream to her jaw before dripping down to the silken gown wrapped around her legs.

The Bone Hag's face twisted in disgust as she looked at Morgan before a cloth appeared in her hand. Wiping at the offending mess without looking, Viraska cast a brief glance over her shoulder to see if anyone noticed, revealing a faint smear left across her high cheekbone, before turning back to the assassin with a cold, shark-like smile.

"I was not home when thou slaughtered Gilthantrious and our family, but I hath never forgotten. I wanted thy head for this, but King Silvas banished thee instead. Imagine my surprise hearing thou had come back to the Court. Even returning without permission thou were still not punished. Instead he gave thee leave to join the Sin'din'dar Court." A snarl twisted her beautiful face. "Still thou escaped punishment. But our beloved King left a loophole. His death. And now he has died and Queen Moirethe has not forgotten. With her calling for thy head, it seemed perfect timing. No longer will I have to be concerned with thee."

"You'll always have to be concerned with me, Viraska. I don't get rid of easily." Morgan laughed, narrowing her eyes as she made the comment, then coughed again, bringing up more blood. Her vision began to swim. Leaning her head back against the wall, Morgan blinked a few times to clear her vision when a hazy figure appeared to the right of the Bone Hag. Focusing her eyes, she drew in a sharp lungful of air in shock at who she saw standing there before looking away in disbelieving grief.

Soft feminine laughter surrounded Morgan as she swallowed back the blood, feeling a sudden urge to scream. A deep sense of sorrow grew within her, quickly building into frustrated anger when she finally cried out in fury. Viraska laughed again and reached out a hand to turn Morgan's face toward her and Malachi.

"Dost thou now see? Nothing twas as thee believed." With those words, Viraska let go of Morgan's jaw to reach down and twist the spear shaft. A scream ripped out of Morgan's throat from her action, enough pain coursing through her senses to cause her to almost blackout. As it was, her vision grew dim and swam again.

"He has done as I bid since the beginning, following my instructions to the fullest. He convinced thee of his feelings for thee and thou believed his lies. Now, my dear Morrigu, thou art alone and humiliated, soon to be dead. Betrayed by the very one thou hath swore thee loved above all. But fear not about thy babes. I have plans for the little ones. I will take thy children and make them mine to do with as I wish. Just think of it—thy children in my service…forever. Apt payment, I think, for the lives thee took."

Viraska moved a graceful hand down toward Morgan's belly and smiled warmly, deep in vindictive thought, though the chill in her eyes never left. When the Bone Hag's palm skimmed over Morgan's abdomen, the assassin jerked away from her touch. Glancing over her shoulder, Viraska called to the remaining Sidhe, commanding them as she took a step back to stand beside Malachi. Running a small hand seductively along his arm, she commanded over her shoulder, "Transfer the children into the surrogate, and then kill this creature."

Turning her eyes from Viraska to Malachi's, Morgan felt the pain of his betrayal. *Why?* He stared back at her with golden eyes, dark and void of any of the warmth she had seen in them throughout their relationship. *I'm such a fool to have believed anything he told me, a fool to fall in love with him.*

Malachi's nostrils flared as he looked down at her beaten and bloodied form, a ghost of a smile on his lips then lowered a hand down to her, but not close enough so that she could reach out and take it.

"Thou could always come with me." The smooth voice that always brought a tingle of warmth over Morgan's body washed over her emotions. He was teasing her, she knew. Viraska already made her declaration—the Morrigu's death and the removal of her children. He stood there without complaint, the bastard.

"Never," Morgan gritted out between clenched teeth and turned her face away to stare at the far wall. Malachi *tssked* as he knelt down in front of her, brushing a soft kiss across her cheek with a smile. Then exhaling a soft breath, he whispered, "Too bad. I am already missing you."

Closing her eyes at his taunt, Morgan drew herself inward, feeling nothing inside but pain, loss, sorrow, and the acceptance of more to come. She listened to the sounds of Malachi standing up and moving away as distant footsteps grew near.

28

Lord Donn Requiem took a deep breath and straightened his broad shoulders when he headed inside castleTech nDuinn. Moving as quiet as a summer's breeze, he walked down the black-stoned hallway, coming up short when he spied two of his guards talking in muted tones farther down the hall. The blonde guard looked up at his Lord, pausing mid-sentence, then moved to intersect him.

"Is business taken care of?" Connor asked, looking impatient.

Requiem narrowed his ebon eyes at the man's impudence and pushed past him. "Why art thou here and not watching the woman I assigned thee to?"

As the Death Lord walked past, the second guard, this one dark haired, pushed off the wall and followed close behind.

"Peace, Milord, for the Bone Hag is under guard. The last report was that she was relaxing in a bathing chamber, surrounded by bubbles. I doubt she can get in much trouble there," said the guard, Darius, answered as they made their way toward the gardens.

Continuing on his course, the guards footsteps echoing around him, Lord Requiem, felt the current around him shift as tension filled the stony corridor. Something was wrong. His guards watched him warily and after a quick glance at Conner, a scowl crossed the Dark Lord's face. Something strange was going on here. Conner never spoke out of line.

Abruptly, Requiem paused and slowly looked around, sensing something out of place. His sudden halt caused the two large men behind him to veer off or run into his back. Holding up a hand for silence at Conner's protest, his eyes moved over his guards' faces. "Has anyone else been here since I was gone?"

"No, Milord, only us," said Darius. "Why? What dost thou sense?"

Requiem's nostrils flared as he turned back to the gardens. Tilting his head, he listened, intent on figuring out what caught his attention, but the only sound that reached his ears was the breathing of his guards and the flittering of the strange night creatures that inhabited this world.

What is it that I detect?

All his alarms were going off, though he could sense nothing wrong in the immediate area. Heading down the stone path toward the center of his night gardens, Requiem spotted a slender blonde woman sitting quietly under the moonlight, her hands folded on her lap. She wore a sheer white gown draped over delicate shoulders that cascaded over her body more as an accent than a covering. A slight smile lifted the corners of her ruby lips, giving the impression of a Cheshire cat.

"How did Queen Moirethe get here?" He asked calmly. "Who allowed her entrance?" Darius seemed genuinely puzzled and though Connor remained silent, he shifted his weight from his left foot to his right as if uncomfortable.

Requiem silently turned to face his guards then focused his full attention on the first. Watching the blonde Sidhe blanch under his scrutiny, the Dark Lord narrowed his eyes. There it was, admition. Betrayal. From one of his own. An icy wind flowed around them, rustling Requiem's robes as he reached for Conner.

Startled, the guard moved to step back then froze, his liege lord's hand scant inches from his face. For a moment nothing happened then Conner's eyes bulged, the veins in his neck strained. Suddenly the Sidhe exhaled a breath and burst into a bright flame that quickly extinguished, leaving ash to blow away in the cold wind. Lowering his hand, Lord Requiem glanced at his remaining guard before turning back to the seated woman. Queen Moirethe turned her head at his approach and with a wide smile, exposed even white teeth as she laughed. Requiem stopped, narrowing his brows together as comprehension slowly sunk in behind the meaning of her visit. Glancing around he extended his awareness farther. Still nothing. Everything here was peaceful except for…*No.*

Concentrating on opening the small connection Lord Thulath had created for him to keep tabs on his troublesome daughter long ago, he breached their bond and stumbled backward as intense pain shot through his body. Darius quickly moved forward, grabbing his shoulders to keep him from falling and the Dark Lord straightened his back. Requiem could receive no thoughts from Morriganna's mind, but two tiny voices crying out in unison rocked him. Almost choking on their terror, he pushed it aside, trying to concentrate on their mother. *What in the nine hells was happening to the Morrigu?*

Requiem swore under his breath as he shook off Darius's hand with a look that caused the Sidhe backed off in fear.

"What tis wrong, Lord Requiem?" The guard stepped away.

Another flash of intense pain filled his body and Requiem cried out in rage. Without another thought, he flashed himself to its source, appearing in a darkened section of an abandoned warehouse. The scent of smoke and fresh blood filled his nose as a scene of destruction met his sight.

~~~

"Transfer the brats then kill her," a woman's soft voice ordered.

Turning, Lord Requiem watched as three males and a veiled woman walked across the open chamber toward the far wall as a petite red-haired female and a tall dark-haired man moved off to the left. The woman stood smiling in satisfaction, her hands clasped together before her in glee. As if sensing him, she turned her face toward Requiem and sent him a bright smile.

Recognizing the Bone Hag, his eyes hardened as he moved forward, his dark robes whipping about him in an invisible storm.

"Viraska."

Blowing him a kiss, she gave a short wave and glanced up at the man next to her. The Were Malachi, the Queen's assassin and the father of Morriganna's unborn children. His gaze followed the Bone Hag's as it slid passed the dark haired man, noting the prone form of a human female lying in a pool of cooling blood when he caught sight of the Morrigu herself.

Heading toward her, Lord Requiem drew a dagger from his robes and threw it hard at one of the guards, hearing the satisfying *thunk* as the blade found its target to sink deep into the middle of a broad back. The Sidhe grunted and faltered, spinning around with the other two following suit. Surprise registered on their faces as they recognized the High Lord of Tech nDuinn and faltered before Viraska ordered them to combat. With a fluid motion, Requiem called forth his dark sword to his right hand, the blade of which gathered any remaining light in the room to create a shadow that wove around him. He spun the weapon in a quick circle before moving to meet them across the warehouse floor.

A lethal dance began as sword met sword. Two of the guards met Requiem, their weapons flashing as they arched their blades down to cut him, only to be reflected by his own weapon as he spun to slice at their abdomens. One skipped back, avoiding the blow, but the second guard's shirt opened, revealing a thin cut, blood beading along the length as a faint ribbon of smoke rose from the wound. The Sidhe stared at him, eyes wide with shock, and cried out in agony as the icy darkness of the sword moved through his body.

A wave of menace rolled off Requiem when he swung again. With the grace of a dancer, he moved his sword to block a blow from the first Sidhe before slashing down in a sharp angle, slicing his opponent's neck clean through. Hot blood sprayed the air as Requiem stepped back, calling on his magick to become incorporeal. The second guard swung his sword at the High Lord's. While his blade passed through Requiem's chest as though he were made of smoke a throwing star made a sudden appearance from an attack from behind. Flying through the Death Lord, it hit the guard he fought in the torso, sinking in with a meaty thud. An almost comical look of surprise crossed the guard's face as he looked down with wide eyes. Tossing an Arctic glare over his shoulder at the star-thrower, Requiem pointed a sword at the next to last Sidhe.

"I have not forgotten thee."

Returning his attention back to the man in front of him the Dark Lord neatly removed the guard's head, depositing it with a bounce near the Bone Hag. Before his opponent's body hit the floor, he spun, heading toward the remaining Sidhe.

Lifting a hand, dark sparks arching between his finger tips, Requiem grabbed the Sidhe's throat and lifted him off the ground. The guard struggled but the Death Lord held his neck in an iron grasp, squeezing his throat tightly. The guard gagged, desperate for air as he struggled for release but nothing broke the hold. Soon the sound of cartilage popping and cracking filled the air and slowly the Sidhe quit struggling. Arms hanging loose by his sides, the guard began to prayed aloud for mercy.

With a tightening of his jaw, Requiem reined in his self-control. He captured the guard's eyes and began drawing forth his opponent's life force. The Sidhe screamed in agony as his soul was gradually ripped from his body, leaving the once strong warrior nothing but a hollowed husk. Dropping the corpse to the floor in a crumpled heap, Requiem looked back to where the Bone Hag had stood but found the spot empty except for Malachi.

"Tell my mate I shall be back later." A dark smile turned up the Were's lips as he moved his eyes from where Morgan sat impaled against the cement wall to the Lord of the Dead. "It twas not all bad, thou knows."

Requiem took a step in his direction, his expression promising something far worse than death for the arrogant Were. when Malachi chuckled and pulled something out of his pocket to toss it toward him.

"Here, this should keep her calm when thou breaks the news to her. It worked well to keep her docile while I fucked her."

As Requiem caught the object Malachi threw, the Were disappeared, leaving him alone in the warehouse with Morgan, the trembling veiled woman and five corpses. With a quick glance down at his hand, he saw a small vial half-filled with a pale azure liquid. Certain that neither the Bone Hag nor the High Queen's assassin would return, he pocketed the vial and quickly moved to the shadows surrounding the wounded woman. The Morrigu lay against the wall, head leaning forward with her long dark hair matted in tangles and blood hiding her face from his view. From her chest a large spear protruded, the weight of it cradled on her knees as blood pooled around her still form. Deep regret and despair filled Requiem's heart at the scene. *I have failed her. Failed her father.* Moving to her side, Requiem knelt down, brushing her the limp strands of hair from her face.

"My Lady. Morriganna," he whispered, but she did not respond. Leaning over her he pressed his lips to her forehead, feeling warmth in it, and sat back on the heels of his feet to look her over. A multitude of wounds covered her slender form in various places and her breathing was shallow. Placing his fingers on the side of her neck he felt for her heartbeat, finding it faint yet steady then reached down to put a large hand over her abdomen. Her children were safe.

Glancing back up at the scared surrogate, Requiem felt his temper flare. "Run," he commanded her then returned his attention to Morgan while the soft patter of running feet reached his ears. A metal door opened and closed in the dimness, slamming shut and once satisfied they were now alone he reached out to grasp the shaft of the spear. Carefully wrapping his fingers around the wood, he readied himself to remove it when she suddenly screamed, leaning forward into his arms. Catching the glint of metal behind her, he looked to see four prongs poking out of her back and swore. Knowing what he had to do, Requiem shifted his weight to his knees and leaned Morgan against him, holding her tightly with one hand as he grabbed a barb with the other.

"Sorry," he whispered against her cheek. "This will hurt."

With a twist he snapped the end off barb, ignoring her cry of pain, before moving to the next one. A metallic *twang* sounded as the barbs hit the concrete floor, bouncing once before settling against the wall. Once there was no danger of the barbs retracting around her heart to rip it out, he grabbed onto the spear shaft and steadied his hand. She screamed again at the touch, her body shuddering in agony while sweating profusely.

"Malachi…" she whispered, her voice faint.

"Shh, do not worry about him, little one. I shall take care of everything, but first I need to get this thing out of thee. There is going to be more pain but I shall try to help thee." Pushing her head against his neck, Requiem brushed her hair aside to get a better view at what he was doing.

"Lord Requiem," Morgan nodded weakly, her lips moving softly against the flesh on his neck. "Do it."

Leaning her back against an upraised knee, he held her secure with his arm braced around her shoulders and his hand gripping the side of her neck. Looking down at her face, he noted how pale it was with two red blotches stained her cheeks from the pain and her hair matted to the side of her face. She raised her green eyes to look at him and gave him a self-mocking smile. "The Lord of the Dead has come for me."

"Trouble seems to follow thee, little one." He smiled down at her, leaning in to capture her lips with his own. At the moment they touched, he jerked the shaft out, stifling her scream with his mouth. She stiffened for a moment, then her head fell back limply. Tossing the spear aside he worked to staunch the flow of blood now flowing freely from the wound. It bubbled with each strained breath she took, followed by a hollow wheezing sound as she exhaled.

Requiem's lips tightened in a straight line as cold anger blazed through him but at her moan of pain he forced his thoughts from revenge. Her injuries were grievous and not healing as they should. Running a finger along the side of his neck, he split his flesh, allowing beads of crimson liquid to well forth along the cut before they trailed down to disappear beneath the dark material of his collar. Pulling Morgan's head up toward the gash, he pressed her lips to his neck and urged her to drink. Blood magicks were used to repair grievous injuries and knowing that a High Lord's blood was more powerful than any mere Sidhe's, he ordered her to use it as a healing elixir.

"Drink, my Lady. Drink and heal thyself."

When she didn't respond, he pulled her back, looking at her face. Morgan's eyes were closed, lashes sooty against skin as pale as snow from blood loss, and her breathing almost nonexistent.

"Morriganna!" Requiem slapped her cheeks lightly while cradling her in the crook of his arm. "Wake up. I know thou can hear me."

He slapped her harder, knowing the pain would bring awareness, until her eyelashes fluttered. When she cracked her eyes opened, he caught her gaze and held on to it fiercely.

"Thou wilt do what I tell thee and drink. I cannot heal thee. Thou needs to do that now. Drink from me. The blood of a High Lord would be an elixir to the blood magicks thou has within thee."

Pushing her head back up to his neck, Requiem held her there until he could feel her mouth press against the small wound he made, sending an erotic tingle to course through his body. Shifting to hide his attraction, he cleared his throat, focusing his mind on something else other than the feel of her mouth on his flesh. Soon the soft butterfly touch of her lips was replaced by a sharp pain as she sank her teeth into his neck to begin drinking. With a sigh, he sat back, stretching out his legs and pulled her into his lap to hold as she drank.

Absentmindedly stroking Morgan's hair as she fed, Requiem's eyes wandered the room, stopping when they reached the human female's corpse. Frowning, his thoughts pulled inward as he wondered how Lord Thulath would react to news that his only child was injured, until a soft wind blowing through the warehouse caught his attention. The light breeze teased the High Lord's ash blonde hair, raising it around his head in a chaotic dance to tangle in his lashes and he reached up to tuck the strands behind an ear. At that moment a small glow appeared, drifting downward from the ceiling to stop in front of him before gradually growing brighter and larger. When the light grew to man-size, a tall slender form shimmered inside it into the shape of a single female.

Taking a step outside the light, a woman of immense beauty gradually emerged. Once her feet touched the cold concrete of the ground, a serene smile radiated from her face as the scent of springtime and rain filled the area. The light breeze lifted her moonlit glow hair, sending it rippling around her as if floating in waves of a summer lake. Though feelings of peace surrounded her, Requiem felt a small tremor of fear and humbling respect pass through his core.

"My Lady Danu," he whispered, bowing his head in reverence. Then he asked louder, "Why hast thou come?"

The goddess gave him a kind smile, her face glowing like a gentle summer day. "It is for the one thou holds, my son." The Earth Mother spoke as she gracefully walked toward Requiem until she stood within touching distance. She watched as the woman fed off of him, shaking her head in sorrow. "Why dost thou persist in thy fascination with the Morrigu? Her sire spoke and charged thee not with her heart but with her life. She has a destiny to tend to, Dark Lord. The Thulath saw to that the day she was conceived."

"I care not. I ..." He looked away, unable to keep his anger restrained.

"Do not be hard on thyself, Donn. Thy purpose is to bring death, not to protect." Danu glanced back at him, her beautiful face softening with sympathy. "Put thy heart away, for it will cause thee nothing but grief. After all, look at the fate of those who have experienced it." She looked at Morgan, and then reached up into the wreath of flowers that decorated her flowing hair and plucked out a small orange buttercup. "Blood magicks will not help her now for her children drain her strength. Have her drink this. It will revive strength, but only this one time."

Requiem took the offered flower filled with a glowing iridescent dew and watched as the Sidhe's Mother Goddess turned elegantly back to the center of the glowing sphere before pausing. Looking back at him, a sad smile shadowed her lips. "Do not interfere with her destiny, Donn for she must travel this path alone and make right that which was torn asunder. She is not for thee."

Turning back to the glowing sphere, Danu paused for a moment and turned slightly to look over her slender shoulder at him with compassion filled eyes. "My son, the time for us is almost finished and from there thou must make an important decision. It will be very hard decision for thee, but thy choice, depending on what it is, will affect the Lady Morriganna vastly. Not everything we do is always to our own best interest."

Lifting her hands up to the sky, the sound of thunder clapped, rattling the metal brackets which framed the building as lightning streaked through the upper regions. Suddenly a bright flash of light filled the room and she was gone. As the dimness of the warehouse returned, Requiem blinked several times for he adjusted his eyes to the sudden darkness.

Puzzled at the goddess cryptic statement the Dark Lord pulled Morgan back from him to look down at the woman in his arms, then at the small flower in his hand. Raising the petals to her mouth, he poured the rich amber liquid down her throat and coaxed her to swallow before pocketing the blossom. Warmth swiftly spread throughout her body, filling her with renewed strength and healing her wounds.

Carefully sliding the unconscious woman off his lap, Lord Requiem settled her as comfortable as possible on the cement floor then stood up, wiping his hands on his dark robes before he strode over to the bodies of the Sidhe guards. Squatting down beside one, he tugged at an ensign on one of the man's sleeves, ripping the rich material then he shoved the fabric in his pocket as he straightened. Glancing around dismissively at the remains, he muttered an archaic phrase under his breath and turned away to head back over to Morgan as the bodies disintegrated into ash, crumbling in the slight breeze of his movement.

Reaching the unconscious woman, Requiem squatted and gathered her limp body into his arms then stood back up. Cradling her to his chest he stepped into the shadows, leaving the corpse of the human for the human authorities to deal with and took the Morrigu to her home.

29

Quiet.

Morgan listened to the sound of her breathing, feeling the gentle rise and fall of her chest before she opened her eyes. The first sight they lit upon was the faint green glow of numbers on the face of the alarm clock. Six-fourteen am. Morning.

Feeling lethargic, she lay silent, listening to the emptiness of her warehouse, feeling a dull pain deep in her chest, over the place her heart would be. Taking a deep breath, Morgan grimaced as the pain sharpened, moving her hand between her breasts and skimmed her fingers lightly over skin she knew bore no scars. The wound was no more; only the lingering effect of the damage haunted her now. How many times had this happened before? How many wounds had she suffered? How many deaths? Too many to count, but each time with the same effect; she healed, quick and efficiently.

I hurt.

She lay for several hours, watched as the numbers slowly clicked by and feeling the hollowness, the emptiness of her home fill her. Blinking, she rolled over on her back and squeezed her eyes shut against the brief flash of pain that shot through her torso. Too much given, too much lost. It had been too good to be true, she knew it, knew it deep inside, but she had refused to see the truth. How pathetic she had become, how weak and useless. Feeling the bed shake, she cracked open her eyes and peeked to find her little gray kitten walking over the covers to her. Sonji mewed in question, blinking her wide yellow eyes, and then moved closer to sniff at her mistress's side. After a brief lick, she moved farther up until she sat next to Morgan's head and curled her tiny fluffy body around her. With a pitiful mew, she leaned over and licked her mistress's cheek before a gentle purr emanated from her.

Morgan returned her gaze to the ceiling and warily watched the shadows being chased away by the morning light, feeling her body tremble as muscles tightened from apprehension. The house felt empty, very empty. Dullness washed over her senses, leaving her filled with nothing but a numbness to fill the void. All was gone. She could feel that. Everything she had, gone. Just like that, in a blink of an eye.

Lowering a hand, Morgan brushed her fingers across her belly, though no signs showed of her pregnancy. The twins rested within her peacefully, as if they were blissfully unaware of things that had transpired within the past twenty-four hours. She sucked in a shaky breath, holding back the tears that threatened to spill, then let it out, trying to relax though her body refused to unknot. The unshed tears collected behind her lids stung at her eyes, causing her to blink before she turned her head to the side to bury her face in a pillow. A silent sob escaped her throat as the silky fabric rubbed against her face. Even the sheets no longer carried his scent, not even the slightest trace of his fragrance, his body's warmth. So empty she felt. So empty and alone.

Lying on the bed, Morgan choked back the pain she felt, gritting her teeth as she waited for her grief to end, but there was no end, nothing vaguely like it within sight. Time ticked by as if lethargic, leaving her accompanied by the purring of a little gray kitten and her misery.

After several hours passed, the twins within her grumbled, their fluttering restless within her womb. Morgan ignored them and sat up, catching her reflection in a large mirror that stood opposite her large bed. She stared at the nude figure in it, willing it to go away, but the stubborn visage refused. Sitting still, she listlessly watched the woman within the silvered glass. Her long, tangled black hair hung across her shoulders and back, framing a pale face and body. Her jade eyes looked glassy and dull, her lips pale, void of all color. Her skin looked dry and frail, cheeks flushed as if she were feverish. How far the mighty had fallen. Malachi's words.

Morgan slid herself forward across the bed until her feet touched the carpeted floor, curling her toes in the softness, and walked across the floor until she stood in front of the mirror. The eyes that stared back at her looked haunted, empty. Reaching out a hand, she touched the mirrored face, and then turned away, heading into the black-tiled bathroom.

After flicking on the light, she blinked several times and shielded her eyes from the glare of the overhead, while holding onto the doorjamb to gather her balance. Once the wave of dizziness vanished, she walked over to the glass-encased showers and opened the door to turn on the water, watching it heat up. Feeling the steam rise in the air, fogging the glass doors and the mirrors on the walls, she closed her eyes. Leaning her head back, her dark hair cascaded down her shoulders.

I hurt.

Closing her eyes to the pain that lanced its way through her chest, Morgan stepped into the shower, closing the door behind her. Needles of hot water pounded on her skin, burning where it landed, bringing dead nerves back to life. A gasp escaped from her lips as she moved deeper into the scalding water, mumbling words with no meaning, memories slowly swirling down into a vortex. Forcing herself to stand under the burning water, feeling the heat and pain, Morgan relived the past few months, making herself remember and study past actions. She reached out a hand to steady herself on the shower wall as a wave of dizziness enveloped her once more. Lowering her head, she closed her eyes and leaned her forehead against the glass as water poured over her head. A sob wracked her body, yet she still refused to release her tears. Instead she gritted her teeth in a fierce smile and moved her other hand up to the area between her breasts and rubbed hard as if trying to relieve the pain that kept building inside her.

No, she cried, praying to Danu to lend an ear to a killer like herself. *This is payback for everything I've ever done, everyone I've ever hurt, every life I've ever destroyed.*

Dropping to her knees, she slid her forehead down the glass wall, feeling her body shake hard. In her mind, she saw dark eyes stare up at her, lifeless. Another sob hit her, this time harder, causing Morgan's body to quake in sorrow. *Poor Terri. She wasn't even supposed to be involved. She should never have been there and it was all my fault. Eryn, why did you come? To warn me...but you died for your trouble.*

Her knees hit the dark-tiled floor as she rubbed the spot between her breasts harder, leaving a red mark as her nails began digging into the delicate skin. Eryn gone, Terri gone, Malachi...gone.

Morgan's lips moved in a silent prayer as water dripped from her down-turned face. She moved, sitting on the tile and gathered her knees to her chest, pressing her back against the glass wall and lowering her face to her knees. She hugged her legs tight, wanting so desperately for comfort but finding none.

I hurt.

She began to rock, hugging onto herself, seeking any kind of comfort, even if it was illusionary. Tears that had been held back now rushed forth to mingle with the shower water as she lifted her face to scream. Long, loud, and ragged. It poured from her until her throat tightened and her voice cracked. Then her sobs broke, leaving her feeling like a broken mess.

Shoulders shaking hard, Morgan once more lowered her head and cried tears she had not shed for hundreds of years as she felt her heart break. She cried till nothing more could come, till she was spent and exhausted.

Rousing herself from her misery, Morgan stood, turning off the water, and opened the shower door. As she walked out, she grabbed a towel and slowly dried herself off before heading back into her bedroom. There, she opened the closet and stared at her clothes.

Numbly, she reached in and pulled out something to wear and dressed before heading down the stairs toward the living room. Moving through the dark, quiet warehouse, Morgan went over to her couch and sat down to pull her boots on. As she moved, she felt her heart harden and narrowed her eyes.

She couldn't remain here. Too many of her enemies knew of her sanctuary now, especially since the man she had been beginning to fall in love with betrayed her. *What a fool I am.* Morgan rubbed a hand over her stomach, feeling the light fluttering of life within. *I'm such a fool. Ignored all the warnings. I knew…I knew, yet I ignored it.*

Packing a small bag of clothing and weapons, she vanished it to be held until she needed it and called out for her little kitten. After the bundle of fur ran up to her, Morgan scooped up the small purring body and headed out the door, placing a ward over the structure to prevent entry until she later returned.

Right now she needed to find an ally, someone who would be willing to give sanctuary and protect the children still within her. The only question was who?

To be continued...

Maggie Berkley

Turn the page for a sneak peek of

Behind The Throne:

Book Two

of the

Morgan Crowe Trilogy

by

Maggie Berkley

1

Seattle, Washington (now):

With a start, Morgan Crowe bolted upright in the bucket seat of her Mustang and drew in a sharp breath. Releasing it, she sagged forward as the memory of extreme pain and warm lips quickly fade into the background and slowly became more aware of her surroundings. Draping an arm over the steering wheel, she rested her forehead against the cool metal links, listening to the soft complaints of her kitten, Sonji, from the backseat, and swallowed several times as she worked to calm her frantic heartbeat. Rubbing a hand between her breasts, she gritted her teeth at the phantom pain, pushing aside the nightmare that woke her as she situated herself in the here and now, not the once was. Never troubled before from actions in the past, this memory refused to free her from its hold, keeping tight reign of her thoughts and actions.

Not safe.

As her heartbeat slowed and her breathing calmed down, Morgan rubbed her face with her palms before brushing her fingers through the front of her hair, pushing the dark mass back as she breathed a sigh of relief.

Oh, sweet Danu, I'm so tired. Leaning her head back against the dark leather headrest, she closed her eyes and sunk her body into the curve of the seat, feeling dejected and worn.

It had been almost four months since she left Portland and her past, four long months since she had contact with anyone she knew—not that many still lived. A memory flash of a shadowed interior inside an abandoned warehouse, a human woman staring blindly at the ceiling—*Terri*—and intense pain. Morgan pressed her hand to her chest and gritted her teeth. Visions of a seductive redhead sashaying across the blood-strewn floor, kneeling to smile and whisper sweet promises of revenge. *Malachi*. This time a different pain streaked through Morgan's chest. The handsome Were she called lover standing over her with indifference and the High Lord Requiem cradling her in his arms with an intensity in his eyes she had never seen before then…nothing. Try as she might, Morgan could not remember.

Death's Daughter.

A self-depreciating laugh issued forth from between lips that were pulled tight in disgust. Cracking her eyes open, she turned her dark head to gaze at the large gray brick house with creeping ivy along the walls before taking a moment to rub the heavy mound of her belly. The twins within were ready to come and they pushed against her back, kicking her bladder every chance they had. Thankfully, now, they were quiet, giving her some respite from their constant torment.

It was too near her time, she knew. The children were coming and Viraska wanted them. It was getting harder to protect them, to stay ahead of those sent by the Bone Hag, and with each day that passed, Morgan felt her strength weakened by the babes within her womb. Finally, she relented and now here she was, parked out front of a house, one that belonged to the daughter of an enemy—but one who had the power to keep her and the little ones safe.

With a weary sigh, Morgan exited the Mustang, ignoring the pitiful mews of her kitten begging for release from her cage in the backseat, and headed up the walk to the large oak door that decorated the front of the house. Behind the gauzy curtains on the windows, shadowy figures moved, revealing someone was home, so she grasped the bronze knocker and rapped sharply three times before stepping back. *Danu, I hope I'm not making a mistake.* Nervousness was not a feeling she enjoyed.

Seconds passed, feeling like hours, before the door opened to reveal a tall, breathtakingly handsome man with rich, woodland brown hair that only a Sidhe could have. It was pulled over his shoulder, wrapped tightly in a braid, and reached all the way to his waist. With a look of disdain, his equally rich brown eyes roved over her form, pausing briefly at her pregnant belly, before narrowing. He frowned.

"Ye might want tae go tae the hospital." Though his voice was warm and velvety thick, his upper lip curled as if he smelled something he could have stepped in.

Great. Last thing she wanted to see was Court Sidhe, and even though he was Sin'din'dar, one of the Light Court, it didn't make having those bitchy wannabe's around any better. At least he didn't seem to recognize her; instead his nasty expression was from ingrain snobbery and not hostility. *Buckle up and ignore it, Morgan. You need to be here.*

Steeling herself for rejection and her eventual rise in temper, Morgan raised an eyebrow and met his gaze. "I came to see Vivienne. Is she here?"

The Sidhe continued to stare, and then after a long stretch of silence, he finally answered. "Aye, but she is nae available right now. Ye can come back later."

He started to shut the door when Morgan stuck out a hand, stopping it from closing with a thump, and pushed it back open as she stepped forward.

"I'd prefer to wait, thank you." She met his eyes, keeping the contact in a battle of wills, until he stepped aside, making room for her to enter.

As she passed by the Sidhe, his nostrils flared as if scenting something familiar. A hand grasped her shoulder to halt her and then turned her back toward him.

Morgan's eyes grew icy as they bored into his. Her jaw squared, molars grinding, while mentally preparing for a fight. Pregnant or not, she'd beat his ass and apparently the thought dawned on him too, for his dark brows gathered together as he searched her face. When not finding what he was looking for, he released her, pulling his hand away as if burned.

"Who are ye?" he asked.

"A friend." Morgan gritted through her teeth, daring him to challenge her answer. "I met Vivienne years ago and she asked me to visit. I've decided now was that time."

He took up the gauntlet, questioning her further, as his frown deepened. "Ye seem familiar. Have we met before?"

"I really need to sit." Morgan flashed him her sweetest smile while patting her belly to emphasize the point. "We can talk about it then." *Shit, just what I needed, a prissy, nosy Sin'din'dar Court Sidhe.* She wasn't looking forward to this.

Dismissing any further conversation with the brown-haired male, Morgan turned to where she thought the living room would be and stopped dead in her tracks. Surprise barely flittered through her mind before she fettered her expression, draining it of any revealing emotions as she faced the new threat. Reclining in seats about the room were two more Sidhe and she cursed herself about shitty luck when she recognized one of them.

A long, lanky male rested spread-legged in a wingback chair, dark wrap-around sunglasses covering his eyes, with hair the color of midnight draped over his shoulders. However, it was the man to his left that held Morgan's attention. Sitting cross-armed in the middle of a couch was a giant of a Sidhe. With a bull-like neck, broad shoulders, and thick arms, he reminded her of a small mountain. Coarse, steel-gray hair was pulled back from a square face and the expression on it screamed asshole.

"Why are ye here, assassin?" Markaso, SwordsMaster of the Sin'din'dar King, leaned forward as his pale jewel-colored eyes narrowed in recognition. The bear-like Sidhe's voice cut through the silence, grating and rough with a touch of iron, his tone enough to stiffen Morgan's spine. "I am a sportin' man. I will give ye three seconds tae run, then I'm hunting ye."

Alerted, the other Sidhe stood cautiously up, his expression solidifying as he repositioned himself in case he was needed. A slim dagger suddenly appeared in his hand. The male behind Morgan moved close enough so she could feel the heat from his body.

"Assassin?" he asked, his voice warm with a hint of danger.

Taking a step to the side, Morgan readied herself to hightail it out of there, since she was in no condition to fight, when a sharp pain streaked through her abdomen. With a grunt, she leaned against the wall, holding her stomach, and gritted her teeth to bite back a cry. *Not now! Not now!*

"No one's hunting anyone in my house!" an irritated feminine voice cut through the room with enough authority to stop everyone in their tracks. Vivienne nic Tibault, all five foot three inch of Sin'din'dar spitfire, stood with hands on hips as she glared at the men in the room. "Lucky for you I got hungry. Lady Morriganna's my friend, so back the hell off, Markaso."

Walking over to Morgan, she looked at the taller woman with concern-filled eyes. "Are you all right? Is it time for the birth?"

Working on controlling her breathing, Morgan gave a weak smile, her lips pulled tight against the pain. "No, I still have time yet." She straightened with a low grunt, glancing at the woman. "Hey, Viv, long time, no see. Not visiting at a bad time, am I?"

The grin that curved the lips of the petite redhead was amused as she bent to check out Morgan's extended abdomen, placing small, delicate hands on the woman's belly to feel the babies kick. *Always a healer.*

Morgan knew Vivienne had been living in America for the last several years, apparently having escaped the Courts and her overbearing father. It surprised her that the healer had looked up her phone number and left a message, inviting Morgan to visit. Of course, she ignored the message, not wanting to get involved with anyone of the Courts, but now she was not so choosy. The time for her babies' birth was drawing near and she needed someone who had enough clout to seek sanctuary from. Though Vivienne was only a Changeling, she was also the daughter and favored child of the High King of the Sin'din'dar. Stifling back a grunt of pain, she wondered why the young woman really left the safety of the Courts in the first place.

Life was never easy in the Courts, especially for a half-breed, but Vivienne's father had given her his name and, therefore, his protection. In return, she had her father wrapped around her little finger. The only problem in that relationship was the King could not give her the royal title, for too many of his "loyal" subjects would have protested. Instead, he granted her a Ladyship, which would have to make due. The last time Morgan had seen the girl was several hundred years ago, when she had convinced her beloved King Silvas to let her work for King Tibault, and that had been too brief a moment in the long lives of the immortal Sidhe.

Movement to her left drew Morgan out of her reverie as a tall, dark-haired man with a sensual, generous mouth appeared behind Vivienne. Wearing dark brown slacks and a button-up tan shirt with the sleeves rolled up over his strong forearms, she couldn't help but admire his broad-shouldered, lean form. Raising her eyebrows in surprise at seeing a Were in Sidhe dwelling, Morgan opened her mouth to question the small woman when another brief jolt of pain coursed through her belly. Biting back a grunt, she turned her eyes to Vivienne and watched the small woman.

"Right now I want to get Morriganna seated. You"—Vivienne motioned with her head to the steely-haired man seated on the couch—"move."

Moving an arm around the small of Morgan's back, Vivienne helped her sit down before pulling over a low stool and placing her feet on it.

"I'm fine, Viv, really. Just a little…tired." Morgan glanced at the different men in the room before turning back to the redhead. "So, are you having a convention going on or did you recently acquire a harem?"

With a snort, Vivienne shook her head. "A harem would be easier, believe me. It's a long story. I'll tell you later." She frowned, her eyes narrowing in concern. "You look like hell warmed over, Lady Morriganna. Worse shape than I'd ever seen you in."

Morgan lifted an eyebrow and replied dryly, "Really? Thanks so much for pointing that out."

"You're most welcome." Turning her head back to the Were, Vivienne motioned toward the kitchen. "Grant, would you contact Dr. Houseman and ask him to drop by tonight on his way home from work, and while you're at it, please get the lady a cup of tea."

"Wait," Morgan breathed in between clenched teeth, willing the labor pains she felt to pass. "No humans. I don't want a human touching…" She grimaced as an arch of pain shot under the swell of her belly. "…me. It'll pass. The babies are just…moody right now. I'm fine."

She eyed Vivienne expectantly, waiting for some sign she understood. Finally, the healer nodded. "Fine, no human doctors, but you must listen to everything I say, agreed?"

"Agreed."

Vivienne glanced up at the Were and shook her head. With a shrug, he headed for the kitchen, ignoring the comment from one of the Sidhe about being a lap dog. Anything following was quickly cut short by a sharp look from Vivienne. Apparently, they had orders by her father to obey anything she commanded, for her guards had the decency to look abashed, shifting in their positions before turning away.

"Reymar?" she continued, turning to the brown-haired Sidhe. "Be a dear and go clear out the room across from the nursery for our guest."

Turning to the remaining men, Vivienne looked each one in the face. "Whoever is bunking in there needs to double up with somebody else. Pregnant women get private rooms."

Before the small Sidhe woman could continue, a voice from the kitchen rang out, "Which tea?"

"Green tin." Rolling her eyes, Vivienne turned her attention back to the others and was about to continue when Grant called out again.

"Bloody hell! Which one do you want me to make? You've got six different green tins."

Sighing, Vivienne muttered under her breath, "Moron," before replying louder, "Green tin on the left."

A few seconds later, Grant stepped back out of the kitchen, carrying a tray with a plain ceramic teapot and a single cup. He studied Morgan as he set the tray down before handing her a cup filled with steaming, pale liquid.

Setting a hand on Morgan's knee, Vivienne continued. "Now before I yell at you for wandering around this close to your due time, let's get the unpleasantness over with." Turning to the main staircase, she let out an ear-splitting whistle and hollered, "Oy! Khelvan! Come down here for a sec."

Morgan closed her eyes at the name called and tensed as the sound of heavy footsteps clumped down the carpeted stairs. Last time she had seen this man she had been standing over his brother's corpse and now was not the time or place to try to explain to the Prince what her involvement was with his death. What the hell was a member of the Royal Mor'sin'dar Court doing here? Morgan felt dread build in her as knots formed in the pit of her stomach.

"Vivienne, thy dwelling is atrocious."

Stepping down onto the landing, Prince Khelvan swept the thick length of ebon hair over his shoulder, letting it fall down his back in waves as he turned to face the small redhead. Light from the ceiling lamp caught silver strands that streaked through rich mass, giving the illusion of molten metal in a sea of black glass. As his gaze swept over the room, they landed on Morgan and widened in recognition before narrowing in fury.

"What tis that creature doing here?!" His voice boomed throughout the enclosed space, the power in it rattling the windows and causing a small crack to appear in the ceiling above them. Light plaster wafted down, drifting on his broad shoulders and hair in white dust. "Thou wert banished from the Sidhe."

Vivienne's back straightened as she looked around the room, placing her hands on her hips in indignation. "I don't see any creatures in this room. I do see a couple of morons, an asshole, and a jackass, though." The last was directed at the man who pointed a finger at Morgan, his lips pulled back in a snarl to reveal even, white teeth. "But I don't see any creatures."

"Make no jest about this, Lady Vivienne, for she is a killer, long banished from any of the Courts. After the death of my father and brother, the Queen gave edict that no Sidhe was to give her shelter." Picking bits of plaster off his shoulder, Khelvan's glare stayed set on the pregnant woman, who in turn let out a loud yawn.

Vivienne was having none of it. "She has not been found guilty in any court of law, Khelvan, so knock it off. Lady Morriganna is no better or worse than you or me and since she sought me out, I deem to give her what she came for, sanctuary. Now if you're finished, I'd like to make an announcement." The Prince opened his mouth as if to protest, but Vivienne continued on. "I, Vivienne nicTibault, daughter of King Tibault of the Sin'din'dar Court and healer to all, hereby grant Lady Morriganna, known as the Morrigu, the protection of my house and of my person until such time as she no longer needs it. In other words, for those of you in the room with testosterone poisoning, if any one of you morons so much as breathes on her wrong, I'll kick your ass out of my house."

The steely-haired Sidhe choked, his face turning a dark shade of red, as Prince Khelvan spoke up in protest.

"By Danu, Vivienne, hast thee lost all sense of mind? She is an outlaw!" he bellowed, stepping quickly toward the small redhead. "I demand thee retract that!"

"Oh? And you, my Prince, what are you?" she asked, soft green eyes turning icy as they landed on the Mor'sin'dar Prince. In return, Khelvan growled at her. "For someone who has such a problem with animals, you're acting remarkably like one right now. Don't throw stones, old friend, unless you're ready to take a few blows yourself."

Watching the scene before her, Morgan smiled, amused. At least the children within her let up and she could enjoy the spectacle the Prince was making of himself. Glancing toward Khelvan, she blew him a saucy kiss behind Vivienne's back, knowing how it would throw the proud man into a tizzy.

"Nice seeing you, too." Then she dismissed the mighty Mor'sin'dar Prince by turning her head away from him while watching his reflection in a large mirror across from her. He smoldered in fury, the veins at his temples throbbed, and his face turned two shades of red. When he noticed her watching, she smiled sweetly. "Try something stupid and you'll find out real quick why I was nicknamed the Lady Death."

Sputtering in anger, Khelvan turned to Vivienne, as if for support, then snarled when the small redhead looked away.

"Enough of this." Catching Morgan's attention, Vivienne nodded to her extended belly. "Now what are you doing up and about in this condition? Shouldn't you be home with the father of your child, preparing for the birth?"

Lifting the steaming teacup to her lips, Morgan sipped at the hot liquid inside before making a face. Setting the cup down, she remained silent, not wanting to reveal anything considered a weakness before the Sidhe presence. Avoiding the healer's eyes, she answered.

"He left and I've had to keep moving, courtesy of the Dark Prince's mother and her puppets." Morgan leaned back, her belly quite pronounced, and frowned for a second as she rubbed it. "They killed my friends."

"As if thou had friends." Khelvan sneered.

Morgan ignored the comment, keeping her gaze on her stomach. Vivienne tossed the Prince a dirty look and then nodded, her delicate brows drawn together in thought as Grant moved to stand behind her. He rested a hand on her shoulder as his fingers gently massaged at the knots building in the muscle. "So you've been traveling ever since? Why didn't you seek out your father or your ex-husband? Why did you come to me?"

Shrugging, Morgan looked at her nails, hating having to answer questions in front of so many, but knowing she had to in order to elicit Vivienne's help. "My Sire and I don't speak and Sorrien and I have been divorced for a long time. It's not his problem I'm in this mess. I came to you because you're the only Sidhe I know with healing powers outside the Courts who I trust to deliver my babies and has enough clout to keep my enemies off my ass for the time I need to give birth."

Morgan glanced around the room, taking in the hard set of faces and the angry looks settled there. "I shouldn't have come here. Your house is too crowded as it is." Grabbing the arm of the couch, she moved to hoist her weight up. "After all, it's filled with morons, assholes, and jackasses."

Putting a hand on Morgan's shoulder, Vivienne gently pushed her back on the couch as she took a seat on her coffee table. "Nice try, sugar, but you're staying. I have plenty of room and if anyone"—she glanced around the room, her eyes threatening—"and I mean anyone does anything to threaten or coerces you to leave, I will send them packing on the first train out. Understood?"

Then, with a smile, she returned her gaze back to Morgan. "Anyway, it's nice to have female company for a change. I'm tired of all the cock fights and preening."

Nodding, Morgan could feel the anger and distrust rolling toward her like waves from the men in the room. *Say what you want, Viv, but I doubt they're listening.* Pushing the feelings coming from the men and her own anger back, she looked up at Grant and then back at the redhead.

"So, when did you keep a Were? I thought you were against such stuff?"

The Were's dark eyebrows drew close. His face flushed as he opened his mouth, but any retort he might have given was cut off as Vivienne answered first.

"He's neither slave nor pet. Grant is my husband." She reached up, placing her small hand over his larger one as he gently squeezed her shoulder. They exchanged glances as a smile crossed the healer's face, her eyes glowing with affection.

Khelvan stepped forward, his face red in anger. "No, he is not. Nor will he ever be. Animals have no place in the bed of a Sidhe."

"You call me a Sidhe now? How many times did you throw Changeling at my face?" Vivienne retorted back. "Cram it, Khelvan. We've already had this conversation. I would sooner slit my own throat than to welcome you back in my bed. Don't even presume to think because I'm allowing you to remain here that you have such a chance."

The Were moved forward to block the approach of the Prince and the two men glared at each other, locked in a silent war of which there could be no real winner where, perhaps, the healer was concerned. Grant flexed his jaw at the challenge, his strong hand tightening enough on Vivienne's shoulder to bring forth a slight hiss of pain from her.

"Rein it back in, cowboys. I'm not for sale. I chose who I wanted, so grow up and live with it." Standing up, Vivienne placed her fists on her hips and tapped her foot on the hard wooden floor of her living room. "You seem to forget, I'm a grown woman living on my own and I do what I want to do, no questions asked."

Reclining back on the couch, Morgan listened to the exchange and watched as the Prince stepped forward.

"Tis enough! The conversation is not about thy sex life but thy safety at having a killer stay in thy home. She slaughtered a whole household in a fit of rage," Khelvan thundered, pointing at Morgan as he glared at the petite redhead. "Vivienne, why dost thee welcome with open arms one of the most dangerous assassins in both the Light and Dark Courts? Art thou insane? She just killed Ansil and who knows who her next victim will be."

"Look at her, your Highness. She needs my help. I'm not going to turn Morriganna away just because of an incident that happened over five hundred years ago. She's my friend."

"What I speak of, my Lady, happened less than a year ago! She murdered my brother! I witnessed it myself." Khelvan strode toward the pregnant Sidhe, their eyes locked in a contest of wills. "She is a killer who has no qualms about slitting one's throat that gets in her way, woman. Toss her out on her ass and be done with it." Morgan snarled at his comment, but was cut off before she could make a reply. Raising a hand, he pulled forth eldrick magick, the current sparking dangerously around his fingers. "Better yet, I shall deal with her myself."

Vivienne moved to block the Prince's movement and looked up into his face, holding her ground. "Later, Khelvan, you can deal with it later. Right now, she's heavily pregnant, ready to pop any day now, and not up to be put on trial. She's under my protection and until she leaves of her own free will or I remove her myself, she will stay. Understood? Even you cannot break sanctuary once given."

Stepping around Vivienne, Khelvan turned back to face Morgan before pulling the heavily pregnant woman up by her arm. His hard grip was bruising, the electricity coursing through his fingers singeing her flesh and she could feel the force of his anger so strongly it nearly bowed her over, but Morgan's own anger boiled to the top like a turbulent volcano. Glowering at him, she gritted her teeth.

"Release. Me."

Pulling her up close enough that their noses almost touched, Khelvan stared at her, his eyes blazing, while he whispered softly so only they could hear his words. "Thou should be killed."

At that, Morgan smiled tightly before giving him a small peck on the lips. "Sorry to let you down."

In disgust, Khelvan tossed her back on the couch, then spun around to Vivienne. Pointing back at the pregnant assassin, he demanded, "Get that thing out of here! The next time I see her, I shall kill her myself!" As he stormed out of the room, a loud thunderclap echoed within, rattling the glass hard enough in the windows to crack.

All eyes followed the Mor'sin'dar Prince as a quiet invaded the room. "Dumbass," Morgan muttered under her breath and then looked up sheepishly at Vivienne, shrugging her shoulders again, as if to say she was sorry.

The Sidhe with the sunglasses stood up and walked past Vivienne, tossing his dark hair over his shoulders as he went. "She is trouble, my Lady. Best send her away before it touches thee." He headed toward the kitchen, following in his Prince's wake.

At that moment, Reymar walked down the stairs, carrying a toddler with bouncy blond curls. Clearing his throat, he spoke, "The room is ready, me Lady. Do ye want me tae take her bags up?"

Suddenly looking tired, Vivienne nodded as she ran a hand over her eyes, and then she took the child from his arms. Reymar looked toward Morgan, then glanced over by the door.

"I have one bag and a grey kitten in the car." Reaching into her jeans pocket, Morgan pulled out a small ring of keys and tossed them to the guard. He caught it in one hand before heading outside. Turning her attention back to her host, Morgan rubbed the underside of her belly. "I'll behave. I promise."

"Don't worry about it, Morriganna. It's my house. What I say goes."

"It's Morgan now; I haven't used Morriganna since the Courts."

Vivienne nodded and smiled. "No problem, Morgan." Leaning back into Grant as he wrapped a comforting arm around her shoulder, she hugged the little girl and then looked up at him, a tight smile on her lovely face. "Is anyone hungry? I feel like pizza tonight."

"Peezzza? Mommy, peezzza!"

"Great, I don't feel like cooking tonight."

Stepping away from his wife, Grant took the little girl in his arms and sat her on his hip as Vivienne headed toward the kitchen. "Make yourself at home, Morgan, and don't worry. You and your children will be safe here."

The kitchen door swung back to a close after they entered, the soft mingling of voices reaching Morgan's ears. She heard Khelvan continuing his tirade before the sound of the back door suddenly swinging open rattled the walls. With a sigh, she closed her eyes, running a hand over her face, until the burning gaze on her back caused her to stiffen. Turning her head, she found Markaso standing by the chair the dark-haired Sidhe had occupied earlier, his eyes cold and face stony.

Maggie Berkley

ABOUT THE AUTHOR

A long time fan of dark fantasy with a touch of romance, Maggie Berkley grew up in a world all her own. During long times of parental lock down as a teenager due to a rebellious nature, she wrote short stories and plays and as time went by drew upon her love of fantasy and horror to write fan fiction. Due to the encouragement of friends and family she decided rather than keep her stories for herself she would publish. This is the result.

Maggie lives in Portland, Oregon with her husband of many, many years, an extremely tall teen-age son, one rowdy puppy and two cats that rule their lives with an iron claw.

Maggie currently has three novels published. Enter The Night, Behind The Throne, and Out Of The ShadowedLands from the Morgan Crowe Trilogy, as well as a short novelette, Diary Of A Vampire. She also co-scripted a short film called The Ban-Sidhe.

Feel free to contact her at maggieberkley@yahoo.com

She can also be found on:

http://twitter.com/maggieberkley

http://facebook.com/maggieberkley

and her homepage http://maggieberkley.jigsy.com

www.ingramcontent.com/pod-product-compliance
Lightning Source LLC
Chambersburg PA
CBHW070809180626
46818CB00001B/186